Also by the author

Ravennetus

being the second book of
The Twelve Pearls

The Fire of Han-Thol

J. David Dean

Pandea Publications
1998

Published by

Pandea Publications
P.O. Box 680635
Marietta, GA 30068-0011

The Fire of Han-Thol is a work of fiction. The characters in it have been invented by the author and any resemblance to actual persons, living or dead, is purely coincidental.

Dean, J. David
      The fire of Han-Thol / by J. David Dean -- 1st ed.
      p. cm. -- (Twelve pearls; bk 1)
      ISBN 0-9646604-5-8

      1. Dor (Imaginary place)--Fiction. 2. Ravens--Fiction.
    3. Ravennetus (Fictional character)   I. Title

PS3554.E168F57 1998   813'.54
                                      QBI98-293

Library of Congress Catalog Card Number 97-92641

Dedication

To my wife, Audrey,
who has, with great love and patience,
taught me the lessons of
The Pearls

Preface and Acknowledgements

This book, *The Fire of Hanthol*, is the first of a series which I have come to refer to as *The Twelve Pearls*. The first book conceived and written was *Ravennetus*, the second in the series. The central character in *Ravennetus* is a boy, Nelsyn, making the journey into manhood. Ravennetus, an ancient ancestor and leader of a long forgotten religious order, appears to Nelsyn and his father, Daenan, as a spirit guide. Ravennetus is the guardian of a powerful secret, the key to world domination. The world is dominated (Ravennetus would say served) by he who controls the unfolding of the World Dream. Ravennetus has a rival for this power, the evil Barthol, who seeks to control the World Dream to his own perverse ends. Nelsyn and his father are caught in the conflict between these two demigods.

The reason for the involvement of Nelsyn and his father in these momentous events is that, before Ravennetus was forced to leave the Now, he hid The Twelve Pearls, the essence of the secret, in the future. The hiding place for one of those turned out to be the unconscious mind of the boy, Nelsyn. Thus the action which takes place in *Ravennetus* is linked to an older story. That older story is the material of this book.

The writing of this book was inspired by a desire to know for myself what happened in that earlier time. It was also inspired by the example of C. S. Lewis who wrote, in novelized form, stories that would teach lessons about life. While this is a purely fictional story, which due to its setting necessarily contains elements of paganism, I hope it will not be lost upon the reader that the underlying principals are those of a theology that espouses a benevolent patriarchal God whose chief desire is to lead his children back to the Garden.

The foundation for the story was laid when I read a book by Erich Neumann entitled *The Origins and History of Consciousness*. This classical treatise of Jungian thought provides insights into the development of the conscious mind of man, drawing on myths from around the world from the very beginnings of recorded time. Once I read this book, I knew that I not only wanted to construct a story to tell the early history of Ravennetus, Barthol, and Allisyn, the princess of Aestri who stood at the very core of their rivalry, but also to novelize the mysterious and intriguing process of the development of human consciousness.

The story began to coalesce around the scene in *Ravennetus* where the spirit of the Old Priest and Daenan meet for the first time in the Otherworld. Ravennetus tells him, "The secret of the world dream does not lie within you, it lies within your son. That is where I hid it when I reached out into the future and let it fall, like a pearl, into the ocean of time."

That image of the pearl and its function as a symbol of something of great and lasting value, seemed to be the right connection to the earlier story. I then began to conceptualize the characters I would use to build it. Ravennetus had to learn all that he knew from someone, so a character who would be *his* mentor was needed. That character took the form of a god and the name of Brahan; the name coming from the root word 'han' (in the language of the fictional land of Aestri), meaning light (or fire), *Bra*han being the bringer of fire or light. The bringer of fire would also be the bringer of consciousness; the bringer of light would be the bringer of wisdom.

It was sometime later that I first was introduced to and read, as part of my research for the book, *The Celtic Shaman* by John Matthews. In it there is a chapter in which he describes the Celtic gods. One of them is Bran (alternate spelling Brahn). Brahn is a "titanic lord of the gods, ...a god of inspiration, ...he may be imagined as a great and noble figure striding across the land or as a *raven*... He is patron of *storytellers*, and may be invoked as a *protector of travelers*, and is also a *giver of primal and ancestral wisdom*." The similarities between Ravennetus, the Brahan I had envisioned, and the Brahn of Celtic myth were too great to be ignored!

But that was not the most striking coincidence. More eerie was the discovery made when reading a chapter of Hugh Miller's *Scenes and Legends of the North of Scotland*, which I had picked up sometime later in Cromarty, Scotland. On pages 156 and 157 of the 1994 B&W edition, Miller writes of --

"Kenneth Ore (or Coinneach Odhar, the *Brahan Seer*), a Highlander of Ross-shire, who lived in the seventeenth century, ...that when serving as a field laborer with a wealthy clansman, who resided somewhere near Brahan Castle, he made himself so formidable to the clansman's wife by his shrewd sarcastic humour, that she resolved in destroying him by poison. With this design, she mixed a preparation of noxious herbs with his food, when he was one day employed in digging turf in a solitary morass, and brought it to him in a pitcher. She found him lying asleep... He awoke shortly after, and, seeing the food, would have begun his repast, but feeling something press coldly against his heart, he opened his waistcoat, and found a beautiful smooth stone, resembling a *pearl*, which had apparently been dropped into his breast while he slept. He gazed at it in admiration, and *became conscious* as he gazed that a strange faculty of *seeing the future* as distinctly as the present, and *men's real designs and motives* as clearly as their actions, was miraculously imparted to him. (All italics are mine.)

Reading this, I must admit, made the hair on the back of my neck stand straight out and confirmed once and for all my belief in Jung's notion of the *Collective Unconscious*! It was this discovery that propelled me in earnest into the story.

Later another curious connection concerning the pearls came to light. As I pondered their origin, they became, to my way of thinking, *seeds* that had dropped from the mind of Deus, the Father-god, into his mouth, there to become coated with the Divine Milk (as a grain of sand becomes coated with the secretions of the oyster to become a pearl) with which he was nursed by Han-nys, his sister-mother. He then planted these *seeds* or placed these pearls into the Now. This idea bears a striking resemblance to the words of Father Zosima in Dostoevsky's *The Brothers Karamazov* in which he explains man's "mysterious, sacred sense of a living bond with another world, with a lofty and superior world" by stating his belief that, "God took the seeds of other worlds and sowed them on this earth and they sprouted in His garden".

Another concept which rather mysteriously weaved its way into the story was that of the blighting of the ravens. In the first chapter of *Ravennetus*, Daenan tells his son that ravens were beautiful, sweet singing birds until they were cursed by Barthol. He turned their multicolored feathers black, changed their sweet song to a rasping croak, and caused them forevermore to eat the flesh of carrion for their subsistence. This bears resemblance to the mythical tale of Aesculapius, whose mother was Coronis, a woman loved by the Greek god Apollo. When a raven came to him bearing the message that Coronis had been unfaithful, Apollo, in a fit of anger, changed the raven's plumage from white to black.

The story, as all stories do, grew in the telling, and thus *The Fire of Han-thol*, came to be. Please enjoy it and its sequel, *Ravennetus*, and anticipate the next book of the series, in which the scattered puzzle of the Pearls will once again come together and the world will be forever, and for better, changed.

I would like to especially thank my family for their reviews, suggestions and patience as I wrote and rewrote the many drafts.

Thanks also to Robert Howard for his art and for his helpful suggestions.

JDD, 16 February, 1998
Woodstock, Georgia

Key to Pronunciation of Names and Places

In the language of Aestri, all the single vowels are short. Thus the 'a' in the first part of the name 'Ravennetus' is not pronounced like the 'a' in 'raven', rather like the 'a' in 'raw'.

Vowels have a long sound if followed by an 'e'. For instance the name Daena is pronounced 'Day-na'.

A double consonant ending like 'dd' or 'nn' on a word gives emphasis to the syllable in which it appears.

The letter 'c' when used at the beginning of a word, always has the soft 'c' sound, like in 'cease', unless it is followed by an 'r', when it has the hard 'c' sound. Thus Craeghedd is pronounced 'Craig-head'.

The 'ch' sound is always hard, like a 'k'.

The letter 'y' when used as a vowel has a short 'e' sound. For instance, the river 'Cyryn' is pronounced 'Ser-en'. 'Allisyn' is pronounced 'Ali-sen'.

Where there are two vowels together and the second vowel is not an 'e', they are pronounced like two separate soft vowels. Thus 'Nyad' is pronounced 'Ne-ad'.

The consonant group 'th' always has a 't' sound. Thus 'Barthol' is pronounced 'Bartol'.

beautiful than ever. He came up out of the waters in the east, a ball of flame, ever consuming and ever regenerating himself. Han-Thol, Osyn called his new fire, that which conquered the darkness, or that light which came out of the darkness. Then Osyn took a handful of the flame and set it on his brow; the rest of the flame he gave to Hanthol, the sun. And Osyn was transformed and elevated above else and gave himself a new name, Deus; he that rules over all.

"When Hanthol rose out of the sea, he was exhausted from his struggling and so it was not long before he rested. When he rested he went down into the waters again, because he had found something enduring there. And thus it is that the fires of Hanthol draw their strength from the waters of Nyso. The next morning Hanthol rose from the waters again.

"Always he rises up in the morning, looking for his sister-mother, Han-nys. But ever he is doomed to run after her, to catch only glimpses of her from afar; ever he is frustrated to be united with her again. For the power of Thol-nys was not completely broken in the great battle and still she has the power to keep them apart. Even Deus cannot heal the wound that separates them until the last day, when they will become as one again, and all will be reconciled.

"Now Hanthol, the sun, sprung from Osyn, just as Han-nys, the moon, sprung from Nyso.

"Deus set Hanthol in the sky to rule the day, just as he set Han-Thol on his brow, just as he put Han-Thol in our minds, to rule over our interior kingdom. Han-Thol is the light within us that burns with the fire of Deus. So Deus is within us and without. His light makes bright our path, both within and without.

"Han-nys rules the night with the reflected light of the fires of Hanthol. Thus she takes those fires, cools them, transforms them and makes them beautiful, makes them into a thing which can be looked upon; a thing of wonder. Yes, Thol-nys cast Han-nys into the sky, but The Terrible One unknowingly cast her into the interior kingdom as well.

"There, within us, Han-nys accomplishes the same purpose; there she cools the fires of Han-Thol; there she transforms them and reflects them, and makes them a thing of beauty and wonder. But if she is not nurtured and brought to her proper place within the kingdom, then the fires of Han-Thol can rage out of control and consume all who come near. That is her

3

purpose until the last day, when Han-nys and Han-Thol will again become as one.

"After his victory, Deus thought great thoughts, contemplating who he was and his purpose for Being. And as he pondered these questions, twelve seeds dropped out of his mind and into his mouth. As he rolled them about with his tongue, they became coated with the Divine Milk remaining there from his nursing at the breast of Han-nys. Layer upon layer of the Divine Secretion built up around the seeds and when he spat them out, he saw that they were Twelve Pearls. And he knew that they were very precious, that they were his Essence, and the answer to all the great questions; that together, they constituted his reason for Being.

"And he also knew, in that moment, if Thol-nys discovered them, she would know him completely and be able to overcome him. Still he was glad he had made them, for although their very existence made him vulnerable, they gave meaning to his Being. So, to prevent Thol-nys from finding the Pearls, he passed them from the Otherworld into the Now. And he decreed that woman should find them and give them to man just as Han-nys had given life to him and nurtured him with the Divine Milk. Thus woman and man should stand side by side in the final victory over Darkness."

Part I

Chapter 1
The Twins

It had already been a long night. A few torches had sputtered and gone out and had been replaced with fresh ones. Even so, the light was barely strong enough to illuminate the low bed on which the woman lay. The stillness of the night was punctuated by her cries as the pains of labor rose, then receded. Carthyn was grieved to find her so long in labor. She had begun her pains early in the afternoon and still did not seem to be much further along now, with the moon about to set. He looked at the woman, her skin glistening with perspiration, her belly distended. Her eyes, when they were open, looked glazed, as if she had a fever or was roaming the landscapes of the Otherworld. She was lying on her side now, oblivious to what was going on around her, absorbed in her own agony. Another woman sat at the foot of the bed, chanting rhythmically in a barely audible voice, her eyes closed. Still other women were arrayed around the bed. One of them bathed the brow and face of the laboring woman.

Carthyn walked out of the room as the next wave of pain seized the woman and the cries awoke in her throat. He could not bear to hear them again. He walked quickly, but her wailing followed him down the long low hallway, overtaking him before he could escape through the entry of his dwelling. In the semi-darkness he fumbled with the bolt and slipped out into the moonlight, shutting the doors at last on the haunting, pursuing sounds. The night was still and damp and the smoke from the peat fires burning within lay thick and close to the ground. Now the woman's cries were distant and muffled, like an echo, but

7

still they found his ears. He walked around the perimeter of the wooden stockade that enclosed the village to insure that the guards were at their posts, to busy himself against the thoughts of the woman striving to permeate his brain. At the back of the house he paused in a shadow and leaned against the fence. Peace was his for a moment. Now he heard only the gurgle of the Iechryn as it flowed just beyond the village wall. He heard the sounds from within the house no more. Had they ceased or had the voice of the river drowned them?

He saw again in his mind's eye the face of the woman who lay in his house in childbirth. What a strange story had followed her here! She had been found wandering in the forest near the river at dusk by women of his household as they drew water for the evening, alone and wearing only a thin white robe with a scarlet scarf tied about her neck. No one had ever seen her before. No one knew from whence she had come. She had seemed possessed by a spirit. A light emanated from her, causing her to glow faintly as she moved. Indeed, one of Carthyn's women thought she was seeing a spirit as she watched the image weaving aimlessly among the trees. The strange woman could not speak, could not tell them her name or how she had come to be there.

Carthyn remembered seeing her for the first time. He had been arrested by her beauty, captured as surely as if he had stumbled into a deep pit, like those the hunters dig to catch wild beasts in the forest. He recalled once seeing a young male lion caught in such a trap. He remembered the look on the face of the lion as he peered down; oddly expressive, he had thought. Looking into his eyes, the spirit of the lion had leaped out and entered into him. Carthyn felt in that moment the feelings of the lion, restive, frightened, in awe of the dark vertical stifling walls of the pit, of strange odors and noises, of things he did not understand. That was the way Carthyn felt when he saw the woman for the first time, confused, frightened, awed. And yet he felt something more, a sense of his destiny unfolding. Never before had he felt this.

His thoughts were brought swiftly back to the present when a scream, just on the edge of his hearing, erupted from within the house. All his senses trained themselves there, intent, alert. *He felt again what the lion that had fallen into a pit might have felt hearing the noises above him and beyond the earthen walls of his prison, confused, longing to run free and wondering*

8

about his fate. Hearing nothing more, Carthyn relaxed again. The voice of the river lulled him back once more into deeper waters.

Carthyn's mother, Meyde, had urged him to take the woman in and care for her. She argued that a god must have put her there to be discovered by his women and that to turn her away would bring a curse upon the household. He had listened to his mother, needing little encouragement to do as she advised.

In time it became evident that the strange woman was with child. Yet no one, to Carthyn's knowledge, had lain with her; he himself had not. The rest of his women swore this to be true. Meyde had an explanation for this as well. She reckoned that the child had been inside the woman when she came to them, and counted the days until she suspected the young woman would deliver. She had whispered that perhaps the nameless woman bore the child of a god. Carthyn had listened with unsettled ears. *The lion within him paced back and forth expectantly on the floor of the humid hole, his eyes dilated in the darkness, his ears erect.*

Now it was her time, Carthyn thought. Now they would see that which the woman would bring forth, male or female, gŏd or mortal. Now they would see if his mother had been right.

On the low bed, the woman, between pains she thought would tear her body apart, lay in a swoon. The vision she had seen in the forest on that day replayed itself over and over in her mind. A strange light had illuminated a clearing ahead of her, the like of which she had never seen. It was not the light of the sun or the moon; more like a rainbow it was in its variation of hue and intensity. She could not remember how she had come to be in the forest. But that suddenly had ceased to matter. She had felt an overpowering compulsion to walk toward the light, to enter the clearing. She did so, making her way through the variegated streaks of purple, green and red light. In the center of the clearing she had become drowsy and laid down. Her flesh tingled as if the very atmosphere sizzled with little lightning discharges. She looked up and saw a great bird in a pine tree. It was of marvelous size and color like the light that shone all around her. Its back and wings were of a deep purple, its throat was crimson and its breast and feet were an emerald green. Its

9

song was enchanting. Then a light brighter than the sun filled the glen, and all other colors and shapes fled from its intensity. She fell asleep.

In her sleep she dreamed that the splendid bird had come down from the tree and landed on the ground beside her. But when she opened her eyes there was no bird, but a man; a beautiful man with a fire that seemed to burn on his brow. All the light in the place seemed to come from that spot. He wore an emerald green tunic and a mantle of purple. Around his neck was a crimson scarf. He drew his mantle off and laid it over the two of them. A nimbus enveloped the glade and nothing seemed to exist outside it. She perceived that they rose off the ground, becalmed on a cloud-like pillow while violent storms ravaged the earth below. The fire was inside her now, burning with an intensity that she could scarcely bear. Time seemed not to exist.

A voice spoke to her saying, "Vessel of the Fire of Han-Thol, blessed be the seed of Brahan within you." She had not comprehended the words. The intensity of the light waned and when the woman awoke there was neither light nor bird nor man. But she had been changed. She could not speak. She felt a warm glow deep within her like embers of a fire. The clothes she had worn were gone, replaced by a robe of the purest white, soft and warm to the touch as though it had been hung on a hearth. The crimson scarf the man had worn was tied about her own neck.

Now the vision faded as the pains returned, tearing at her belly like wild dogs on a carcass. She felt the fire erupting within her once again, yearning to leap from her groin. She cried out but the pain was too intense for her. The cry died on her lips as she slipped into unconsciousness.

Carthyn walked down the hallway toward the bedchamber, all strangely quiet now. As he approached the low bed, he saw that the sheepskin covering had been pulled up over the woman's face. Her hand escaped from under one edge. It was waxy blue in color, like the tongue of a deer that had bled to death, lolling inertly from immobile jaws. The cry of a child broke the silence just as the sun emerged from behind the eastern hills and threw its first light through the open window. This first boisterous cry was followed by another. The chanting

10

woman seated at the end of the bed rose to meet Carthyn. She was dressed in a quilted robe, adorned with small silver medallions in the shape of sea shells about the shoulders and chest. They jingled as she approached Carthyn. In her hand she carried a bundle of long feathers bound together with a leather thong.

"The nameless woman is dead, Carthyn. But she has given birth to two sons. One is fair-skinned with eyes that shine like the morning star. The other has skin of a darker tone and his eyes are black. They both have a curious birthmark on the back of their neck." And she left the room. Carthyn walked over to the low wooden cradle in which the newborns had been laid. He watched them for a moment. His eyes drifted back to the bed where the topography of the animal skins vaguely suggested the body of the boys' dead mother beneath. *The lion clawed at the walls of the pit and leaped toward the light above him but to no avail. He fell back, hungry, thirsty, panting, exhausted.* Carthyn's heart pounded and his temples throbbed. In an anxious rush, he left the room.

Throughout the day Carthyn's thoughts were consumed with the boys and their mother. Toward noon he walked back into the room where they had been born. The body of the woman had been removed and taken to the Place of the Dead. Two of the women of his *anyll* had taken the boys and were nursing them. His thoughts were drawn back to the dawn of the morning. He asked the woman nursing the fair-skinned boy if he could see the birthmark on the back of his neck. She raised the boy up with her hands under his arms and showed the mark to Carthyn. It was a curious shape, a bird in flight. Carthyn was both surprised and filled with awe to see this sign, for his own totem animal was the Brahn, the raven. He looked at the birthmark on the neck of the other boy. It was similar.

The lion screamed in desperation from the confines of the pit. He called out to his mates, called for help, called to be rescued from the otherworldly confines of the deep dark hole, called for light and air and freedom. Carthyn felt his heart jump again. The boys appeared to be strong and healthy, the kind of boys that any man would be proud to call his own; the kind of boys that might grow to be men of renown in the clan. But he knew that the law called for the male offspring of a mother who died in childbirth to be killed. It was the law of Nyso, the Great Mother, to keep the weak ones purged from the bloodline.

11

But his mother had said that these boys might be the sons of a god. Would the clan still have them killed? He did not know. And what of the birthmark on the necks of these boys? Was it not a sign that they should be under his protection? He was awed by the fact that their mother had come to him; to *him*, to Carthyn. It seemed now that all these strange events were coming together, swirling, coalescing in his thoughts. The birth of these two boys seemed to give them meaning at last.

At dusk, he went out to the Place of the Dead with the priests of Nyso because the nameless woman had been of his *anyll*, the women of his household. They performed the ritual intended to pierce the veil for the passage of the dead woman to the Otherworld and then lit the pyre upon which she lay. Carthyn watched, transfixed by the flames as they consumed her body. She had been beautiful and Carthyn had enjoyed her companionship, even though she could not speak. She had seemed happy to be accepted by him and had made him smile. She was different from the other women of the *anyll* although he could not say why or how. Perhaps it was because he had felt close to the Otherworld in her presence.

But now he would see her no more. As he watched the flames, her hand, the same that had fallen from beneath the skins of the bed, fell toward him out of the fire. It blackened and curled upwards as if beckoning to him, as though it were asking him a question. *From within the pit, the young lion looked on, cocking its bewildered head. Then it lay down with its head upon its paws, still staring at the flames. From above, the cries of other lions reached his ears. They were lamenting, bewailing the loss of their brother, who would come no more, who no longer would wrestle with them in the dust and tall dry grasses, who would never again join them in the hunt.*

That night Carthyn was summoned to the Council of Meyde. She was the matriarch of their clan, the Ieche, and whenever there was an important decision to be made concerning the people, Meyde would call the elders together. Tonight, as always, she was seated in a chair on a low dais at the far end of a long, low-ceilinged room, already lined with elders of the clan. Other older women of the clan's ranking families sat beside her to the left and right. A stone altar was situated in the center of the room. Smoky fires burned in each of several insignificant and inefficient hearths that lined its length. Much of the smoke from these fires had curled up into the rafters, adding yet another layer of soot to the blackened timbers. Carthyn coughed slightly as he entered and took his place of honor among the men.

The council started chaotically. Some of the men began to drum. Chanting rose here and there from among the women. Bit by bit, the chant was picked up by the men and soon its low hum filled the room, slowly blending together into one rapturous song, permeating the senses of all who were gathered there. After a long while the chanting stopped, dying off as clumsily as it had begun, and the room fell silent. The council members swayed slightly like the tops of trees in a low wind. Although their eyes were open, they seemed to be asleep. But their collective spirit was alert.

Meyde stood. "Tonight," she announced in a gravelly voice, after clearing her throat, "we meet to decide the fate of the two boys born of the nameless woman. The facts are few. She came to us unknown and remained so because she could not speak. We believe she was with child when she came to us, perhaps by a *god*," here she stopped and paused to let the effect of this last word sink in. She searched the group with reddened eyes from deep within her wrinkled face. "So we took her in. She was with us until this morning when she gave birth to two sons and died. We do not know more. Our clan law is clear on such matters. The male offspring of one too weak to survive her labor must die. There is no place in the clan for such weaklings." She stopped, watching warily for any reaction from the assembly. Seeing none, she continued on.

"However, we took this woman in because we thought she might have mated with a god. So I believe we should consult the oracle, to see if this woman was indeed divinely mated, rather than to simply execute the law. If the boys are sons of a god, then it would bring his wrath upon us to kill them. Do you agree?"

The room hummed an affirmation.

"Bring the sacrifice forward," she demanded.

From the back of the long room where Carthyn had entered came a young woman leading a ram, newly born that very day. He bleated and balked and she pulled vigorously on the tether to bring him along. Meyde lit a fire on the altar and the young woman lifted the ram onto the stone. It jerked to free itself and

13

bleated passionately. Meyde took a leather thong and tied its spindly legs together. The lamb struggled a moment longer then lay still. Another dark-haired young woman handed Meyde a knife and she raised it heavenward, invoking the blessing of Nyso, then plunged it into the heart of the young animal. The lamb bleated once again, quivered spastically, then lay still. Meyde cut its stomach open, removed its entrails, and threw them into the fire. As the smoke of the sacrifice ascended she studied its color and the way in which it curled and rose and fell on the currents of air in the room.

A moment later she made her pronouncement.

"The sacrifice has opened our eyes to the wisdom of Nyso. Nyso tells us that the boys must die. Are there any here who would object?"

The embryo of a thought took shape deep in Carthyn's mind and he struggled to speak it as it ascended. His eyes fluttered.

"These boys... are marked... with a mark... a bird... flying... a bird in flight. It is... at the back of the neck," he stammered, and as he spoke he raised his finger to the side of his own neck.

"I have seen this mark," Meyde answered. She dipped her fingers in the blood of the ram and sprinkled it with authority into the fire. The blood sizzled and a gray smoke rose anew.

There was a long pause as she studied the smoke pattern.

"Nyso has not changed her pronouncement. They must die. Are there any who further object?"

There was no response.

"Carthyn, you will execute the law," she stated finally. *In the pit, the lion was suddenly aware of someone approaching. It curled back its lips, barred its fangs, growled low and crouched.*

With that the elders rose slowly and filed out of the room. Carthyn led the men out. He knew now what he must do. Nyso had spoken and the boys must be drowned in the river at dawn; returned to the waters of the goddess from whence they had come. He went to his bedchamber, passing through the room where the women of his household awaited him. Still dreamy from the council, he hardly noticed them. As soon as he had passed by, they blew out the candles and went to their beds. Carthyn did the same.

14

Try as he might Carthyn could not sleep. After a time, he got up, moving silently past the sleeping women, and stepped out into the open night. He walked mindlessly to the main gates of the stockade and motioned for them to be opened. The surprised gatekeeper did his bidding and Carthyn entered the woods.

The moon had set. In the depths of the forest before him, Carthyn thought he saw a dim light. Led onward by curiosity, he approached it. There, in an insignificant clearing, he saw the figure of a man. The man held out a hand, palm upwards in greeting. As Carthyn walked to the edge of the clearing the man rotated his palm up and outward toward him, signaling him to stop. Carthyn stood bemused, awaiting instruction. The man spoke.

"The boy must live. See to it," he said softly but clearly. Before Carthyn had the chance to ask for an explanation the apparition turned its back and stretched out its arms. It leaped up from the ground as it did, transforming itself into an immense raven. It circled the glade three times in the delicate light of the stars above Carthyn's head and flew away into the blackness.

Carthyn walked back to the village carrying this image. He hailed the gatekeeper and returned to his house and his chamber. He climbed onto his bed and there remained seated for a long time contemplating this message from the Otherworld. Was the raven-man talking about the newborn boys of the nameless woman? Then why did he not say *boys*, instead of boy? The raven-man must have been talking about some other boy. The oracle had said the boys must die. How then could this raven-man be saying that the boy should live? Whose word was stronger, the word of the raven-man or the word of Nyso? It must be some other boy. Carthyn was very confused. What other boy could the raven-man have meant? Finally he lay back down, exhausted from this internal debate. But now he was certain again. The oracle had said the boys must die and so they must die at dawn. It was the decree of Nyso. He went to sleep without further thought.

An hour before dawn Carthyn awoke to a loud and irritating sound. He pulled on his clothes, short leather pants, stiff from too many crossings of the river, and a thicker leather jerkin. He walked across the room to the post where his short copper sword hung and strapped it about his waist. He took a quiver of arrows and flung them over his shoulder, then placed his arm

15

through his bow and left the room. He walked to the adjoining room where the two infants were crying in anguished fits. Since their sentence of death had been passed no one had fed or even touched them, as was the custom of the clan.

Another man was in the room, a priest of Nyso dressed in an ankle length sarong, who would go to the river to witness Carthyn carry out the sentence. The priest placed the two distressed infants in a rough sack and slung it over his shoulder. *The lion sat up, alert.* The two men left the house and passed through the main gate of the stockade. Soon they were walking by the Iechryn. They stopped at the shallow ford where Carthyn would walk into the river to drown the boys and sat down to await the first light of day.

The eastern sky began to gray only moments later. The muffled cries of the babes still came from the sack. The priest handed it to Carthyn. Carthyn took the bundle and stood up. He stood there for a long time, as if, the priest thought to himself, his feet had sunk into the mud. The sky was growing lighter minute by minute and the priest was getting nervous and impatient.

"Go on," he insisted, "carry out the sentence!"

Still Carthyn did not move. The message of the dream had returned and the painful internal debate was taking place within his unwilling brain once more.

"Go, now!" the priest said, giving him a nudge.

Carthyn only stared at him.

"The boy must live!" Carthyn finally blurted out.

The priest was taken aback, unsure what he had just heard. Had Carthyn defied the decree of Nyso? It could not be.

"No," the priest replied pointing toward the water, "these boys must die."

"Wait," Carthyn said, handing the sack to the priest. The priest took it, completely at a loss as to what to say or do with Carthyn. *Carthyn remembered watching as Huryn, one of the clan hunters, drew his sword and foolishly jumped into the pit with the lion to prove his bravery.* Carthyn pulled his sword from its sheath while the priest watched him in suspense. *Carthyn saw Huryn stumble as he hit the ground. The lion was upon him in an instant, with his great teeth at the man's throat, rending, tearing.* Carthyn looked at the sword, then at the priest. As their eyes met in the dim light, Carthyn ran his sword through the priest's stomach. The man crumpled to the ground

16

in a shocked silence, still clutching the sack. The crying of the babies broke out anew as they hit the ground. Carthyn untied the bundle and opened it. He took the two infants out, holding them each in one rough hand.

His eyes first fell upon the dark one and he studied him for a moment. Then his eyes wandered to the fair one and the words came back. "This boy must live!" So he put the dark one on the ground next to the dying priest. He wrapped the sack around the fair one, put the bundle under his arm, and waded into the river.

The cool gray-green waters of the goddess swirled around his ankles, his thighs, then his loins. They tugged gently but firmly, pulling him toward the thoughtless depths, yearning for the heat of the baby. Carthyn suddenly felt himself faltering in the sucking mud of the bottom where it had been firm a heartbeat earlier. The sack dipped into the current and the goddess reached for it with eager, lascivious hands, whirlpools forming on her fingertips. Then another force seemed to take hold of Carthyn, buoying him up. He regained his footing and the sack emerged dripping from the water.

Carthyn crossed at last to the south bank. The dawn wind sighed in the trees by the river's edge and the water droned the goddess' lamentation over her loss. Looking back through the forest shadows, Carthyn could barely make out the unmoving form of the priest lying on the bank, the other boy wailing at his side. *The lion took a last mighty desperate leap, using the body of the crumpling Huryn to springboard himself from the pit; then dashed by Carthyn to freedom.*

Carthyn turned and walked briskly away.

Chapter 2
Gods' Play

Carthyn walked for hours, climbing successive ridges which led him further up and out of the Vale of the Iechryn to the south, further and further away from his home. He stopped for a while to fashion a sling from the sack so he would not have to carry the boy under his arm; they would both be more comfortable that way. The baby seemed to be quiet now much of the time. Perhaps it was because they had left the village where his young spirit had sensed danger, Carthyn thought. Perhaps it was because they were being led on by the spirit of the raven and he was comforting the boy, now under his protection.

Carthyn walked on. The boy was very quiet now; too quiet Carthyn thought. He removed him from the sling. The infant seemed hot. Carthyn poked him with a finger to rouse him, but the boy would not wake up. It occurred to Carthyn that the boy had not eaten in a long while. Perhaps he was dying. The voice had said "This boy must live!" Carthyn became frightened. What was he to do? If he let the boy die the wrath of Brahan would fall upon him. But how would he feed him, what would he feed him? Carthyn was confused. All this thinking had exhausted him. He wanted to lie down and sleep but he knew if he did the boy would certainly die.

He found a stream springing down from the highlands to the Iechryn in a series of short falls and foaming little pools. He plunged the boy into the water and quickly removed him. The infant began to scream. Carthyn took his finger and let the few drops of water drip off the end into the boy's mouth. The little

18

jaws worked feverishly to find more. Yes, he was hungry and Carthyn knew he must find something for the boy to eat. But he was bewildered. He had never done anything like this before. Why was he doing it now? He had never been away from his clan, away from the mothers to whom he could go for advice. Perhaps he should go back. No, if he went back they would kill the boy. And he himself had slain a priest of Nyso. Why had he done that? What possibly could have possessed him to do such a thing? He was alone now, with the boy. They were outcasts. They could not go back.

In the midst of his indecision, Carthyn did the only thing he knew to do; ask his totem. He reached for his crane pouch and removed the sacred stones. Finding a level spot in a little clearing he placed them around in a circle. He faced toward the four principle directions in succession, asking the blessings of the spirits of each, then took his place in the middle of the circle, facing to the east, with the boy in his lap. He chanted to invoke the spirit of the raven and it was not long until he was rewarded. A large raven came and landed in a tree above him. Next the bird dropped down just outside the circle immediately before him. As the bird strutted into the circle it was transformed before Carthyn's eyes into a man; a man with a golden light on his brow, a tunic of emerald green, a mantle of purple, and a crimson scarf about his neck. The man spoke to him.

"Greetings to you, Carthyn of Ieche! You have done well. You have saved the boy."

"I have followed the instructions of the raven-man but now I am lost and I do not know where to go. The boy needs food or he will die. I do not know what to do."

"I will care for the boy," said the man with the shining brow.

"Who are you?" asked the perplexed Carthyn.

"I am Brahan, son of Deus. The light of Han-Thol is upon my brow. This boy is my son by the woman you cared for."

Carthyn began to tremble. He was in the presence of a god, the god of his totem, the Raven-god, Brahan.

"Do not be afraid, Carthyn. I have plans for the boy and for you. Go now and leave the boy in my care. Walk up the mountain. There you will find a doe nursing her fawn. Take my mantle with you. When you see the doe, throw the mantle over her back and she will not run away. Milk her and bring the milk back here to the boy. Go now."

19

Brahan reached out and handed the purple cloak to Carthyn who left the circle and walked up the mountain. As he walked he wondered how he would get close enough to the doe to throw the cloak over her back. He looked down at his body. He studied the way he placed his foot upon the ground. He tried to emulate a deer, to walk as a deer would walk. But it was not his animal and he could not imitate it well. He concentrated upon walking like a deer, thinking like a deer, becoming a deer. Soon he had become a deer, placing his hooves carefully, making little noise as he went. He stopped and craned his neck forward. He grunted, the sound of it leaped up the mountainside above him. He went on, stopped to listen, then stood. He scraped his antlers against a nearby sapling peeling off the tender bark in thin spirals.

Further on, just as Brahan had said, he found the doe. She did not seem to notice him. He approached her slowly and cast the purple cloak over her back. The doe stood enchanted while he milked her into the turtle shell cup that always hung at his side. When he retrieved the cloak from her back and laughed the doe bolted with her fawn. Carthyn walked back down the mountainside with the foaming milk in his palm, feeling its heat through the turtle shell. He reentered the circle and fed the boy, a few drops at a time from the ends of his fingers, dipping them in the warm milk and passing them to the waiting lips. When the boy had eaten, Carthyn looked up at Brahan.

"Now what would you have me do?" Carthyn questioned.

"Follow me," Brahan replied.

With that Brahan leaped up from the ground, becoming the multi-colored raven once again and flew into the tree top. Carthyn picked up his stones, put them back into his crane bag, then placed the boy in the sling and set off after the raven-god.

They walked for many days in this way towards the south and the east. Whenever the boy was hungry, they would stop and Carthyn would find a nursing animal. Then he would throw the purple mantle over her, milk her, and return with milk for the boy. Carthyn was surprised to find that although they had walked for many days, he himself had not been hungry. He wondered at this, but not for long.

"Soon you will have no need of food," said the Brahan, as if he were reading Carthyn's thoughts. "I intend to take you with me once we have delivered the boy," the raven-god continued. Carthyn listened without question or response. "You will cross over into the Otherworld with me. For no one may look upon the face of Brahan and live."

Carthyn was not frightened by these words. On the contrary, he felt a great relief to know his fate. He had been in the Otherworld many times before, led there by the raven. He had sat at the council fires with the spirits of the raven clan. But always before he had returned to the Now.

Three days later, man and god stood looking up at a tall mountain. Brahan pointed toward the summit. The tree line ended about three-quarters of the way up. The top was rocky and barren and enfolded in cloud.

"This is my home, Brahan-mara, the holy mountain."

They began to climb. At first the going was easy as they walked along a well-used trail. But soon the trail began to steepen and the path became rocky and less well marked. The trees grew thinner and shorter as they approached the top. Carthyn had never seen the like of these trees; trees that looked so gnarled and so old yet had the stature of mere seedlings.

Brahan suddenly stopped their ascent short. He pointed to the slightest of paths which led off to the right and slightly downward toward a tumble of boulders screened by a thicket.

"Now take the boy and deliver him. In the thicket there is a cave. In the cave you will find the den of a lioness. She is gone now but her cubs are there. Take the boy and lay him among the sleeping cubs, then return. Go now, quickly, before she returns."

Carthyn did as he was told. He approached the lion's den with trepidation, listening intently for the slightest sound, a padded footfall or the brushing of a twig which would betray the lioness' presence. But he heard nothing. He took the sling from his shoulder and pulled out the sleeping boy. Carthyn looked at the infant as he lay there, the head cupped in his large calloused hand, the slight body resting on his forearm. Carthyn felt a twinge of remorse about leaving him behind. He was the only father the boy might ever know. This might be the last day he might live, for what would the lioness do when she found the infant among her cubs? He crawled into the cave on his knees. The light grew dimmer as he went deeper. Now he had to drop down to his free hand as well. His eyes began to adjust to the

21

darkness. He smelled the pungent, musty odor of the cat mixed with the urine of the cubs. Soon he saw the purring knot of sleeping cubs and the small pad of grass upon which they lay. They were no older than the boy, but well-fed and content. He placed the boy among them and retreated toward the light. As he emerged from the cave, the lioness screamed from a rock ledge above him. Carthyn's heart leaped into his throat. He searched the rocks quickly. Seeing her he stepped slowly away. His steps came quicker as he made his way up the path toward the place where he had left Brahan and the main trail.

"Well done," the raven-god said when Carthyn stood once again before him. "Now come and sup with me." Carthyn watched as the raven leaped up from the rock and beat the air with his wings. Carthyn followed on foot, his eyes lifted upward, fixed on the soaring bird. He watched enviously as the raven flapped his wings, circling overhead. He stretched out his own arms, rippling his fingers, emulating the flutter of wing feathers and walked along a barren shelf until he came to a cliff. Before him a wide valley was spread. Brahan soared into the void.

Carthyn felt a longing to follow stronger than any urge he had ever known. He closed his eyes tightly and threw himself off the cliff. He heard the wind whistling in his ears as he fell, tumbling, plummeting toward the earth then sweet singing and a voice encouraging him to fly. He opened his eyes. He stretched out an arm, now covered in feathers of deepest purple. He stretched out his other arm and turned over in the air, righting himself. He looked at his chest, a swath of shimmering emerald. Above him and to his left he saw Brahan, the raven-god, his head tucked beneath his right wing, calling to Carthyn and urging him onward. Without further hesitation Carthyn flapped his wings, ascending close behind the great bird, and was seen by man no more.

In the village by the Iechryn, the sun was well above the low hills to the east when Meyde inquired as to the whereabouts of Carthyn and the priest who had accompanied him to the river. No one had seen them. Another of the priests was sent there returning with the dark child in his arms and the report of the dead brother. Meyde was outraged. How could her own son break the law of the clan? It had never happened before. She retired to her alcove until noon. At that time she emerged, ordered the preparations for the funeral of the priest, and called another council to be held that evening. Then she retired once again to her chamber, demanding that the boy be brought to her.

When he was brought she laid him in her lap, regarding him carefully. The boy was clearly weak from lack of nourishment, yet he cried lustily. As she watched the child she was suddenly caught up in a vision. She fell backward, pinned to the ground. A voice cried out to her. "Here lies Nyad, the begotten of Thol-nys, the scourge of Osyn. Raise him as your own. When he is ready, I will call him. Then he will be Bar-Thol, the son of darkness. Others must die in his place."

When the voice had stopped Meyde rose trembling from the floor, cradling Nyad in her hands, and ordered him taken to the *anyll* of Carthyn.

That night the council of Meyde was convened again. When all were seated the drumming and the chanting began as on the previous night. She laid the infant Nyad upon the altar and invoked the spirit of Nyso, the Great Mother, as she always had, but the Great Mother did not appear. In her stead another came, Thol-nys, the Terrible One.

Meyde opened her mouth to speak but it was not her voice that came forth. "Nyso is fallen," she cried, in an utterance that shook the walls of the room and caused the very earth beneath them to shudder. The people covered their ears. "Nyso is vanquished, and Osyn will fall at the hand of Thol-nys. The rivers will run red with his blood and the sky will be blackened with his bile." As she spoke a dark vapor began to seep under the walls of the Council Chamber and creep along the floor. It swirled around the altar, fingers emerging and slithering upward like serpents toward the child. The tentacles wove themselves together and formed a light-devouring wreath around the baby, protecting him from what was about to transpire.

Suddenly, possessed by the evil spirit of Thol-nys, Meyde grabbed the sacrificial knife and ran toward the place of the men. She grabbed the eldest of them by the hair and plunged the knife into him. As the blood of the old man flowed, the other women, themselves ecstatically possessed by the spirit of Thol-nys, crawled forward and dipped their hands in it, tentatively at first, then greedily. They smeared it on their faces and arms until their skin was red, their hair matted with it. Besotted with blood, they writhed upon the floor, tearing at their clothes and hair in a depraved frenzy. The other men, seeing and smelling the blood, froze, too frightened to move. A few of them rocked back and forth, singing their death songs.

When the possessed women had taken the lives of all the men in the Council Chamber, they ran into the village, pulling men from their couches and male infants from their cradles, purging the clan of them. The blood-orgy lasted far into the night and when its power was spent, all the men of the clan lay dead.

Meyde left the chamber, still under the powerful influence of the spell of Thol-nys, and took Nyad back to the women of Carthyn. They were shocked when they saw her, her eyes leaden, her robes spattered with blood, her arms reddened to her elbows. The fear of her overcame them and they prostrated themselves upon the floor before her.

"From this day forth, you are the women of Nyad," Meyde said solemnly, holding the infant before them. "See to it that he has what he needs and give him everything he desires. This is your duty now." The boy was awake and screaming to be fed. Meyde handed him to one of the women and she fearfully cradled him to her breast.

Chapter 3
The Lion Boy

The nameless boy of the nameless mother emerged from the *ghral* with his lion brothers and sisters. He was naked but his skin was toughened from years of living in close proximity to rock and branch. The young lions scampered down the hillside and the boy followed them as fast as he might. What he lacked in speed he made up in cunning. He knew where his siblings were headed and he took a shortcut which led him, leaping and sliding, down steep ravines and through a long dark tunnel in the rock. He arrived at the drinking hole before them and cried out to let them know he had beaten them once again. As he crouched down for a drink, the others came up, stood panting beside him, and lapped up the clear water.

After refreshing themselves at the pool the lions climbed just above it to a grassy, sun-drenched knoll to doze. As he lay there for the third day running, the boy contemplated the differences he had recently, and to his profound amazement, begun to discover between himself and the others. He stood on two feet and they walked on four. Their bodies were covered with fur and his was for the most part devoid of it, except for the shaggy mane that crowned his head in a tangled mat, a significant disadvantage that kept him inside on colder days. At the end of their feet were terrible claws which enabled them to tear their prey and that sometimes cut him deeply when they were only playing. His own claws were always worn down to blunted stubs and not much good for hunting. Their large mouths contained strong jaws and sharp teeth, convenient for smothering and devouring prey. His own mouth, by

25

comparison, was small and weak and his teeth were more like the smooth stones of a river bed.

He held his hand up and gazed at it. It was funny how his fingers could be bent to grasp things, something that his brothers and sisters could not do. He pulled a handful of grass and tickled his sister Tasha's ear with it. She rolled over, showing her annoyance even in her sleep, and rubbed the ear with her paw. He laughed. That was another thing. The only sounds his family could make were roaring or purring. How he loved to lay against his mother Gorsina's side when she was purring loud and long, when she had gorged herself on a kill and was resting, her magnificent flanks rising and falling with her contented breathing! But he could make many sounds. He could make the laughing sound like water trickling over stones.

More than these, he seemed able to do something even more incomprehensible. He seemed to be able to ...to *reason*. While his family's *instincts* were highly developed, they were at a loss when he tried to *explain* something to them. They could not *understand* his signs for water or grass or deer. It was so frustrating at times! But they could *smell* a herd from a mile away. How wonderful it must be to have a nose like that! They were so different, so very different!

His brother Garsch rolled over and lay on his back now, his hind legs spread to the sky. He looked at the powerful cat for a while, his eyes roving from his massive chest to his sleek belly and finally coming to rest on his groin. He looked between his own legs. Here was yet another difference.

He had seen his mother give birth to ten litters of cubs, yet none of the cubs ever came out looking like him. They always came out looking exactly like his brothers and sisters. And they grew up so fast! In a year they would scamper off, never to return. He missed them when they were gone, but he always liked the new ones that came too. But why ...why never any more like him?

Suddenly Garsch sat up and sniffed the air discerningly. He rolled over, got to his feet, and trotted silently to a ledge overlooking their watering hole. He came back quickly and turned about with that certain twist of his head, indicating that they all should be very still while he watched. The boy, curious himself to see what was transpiring, crawled slowly and quietly to his brother's side. What he saw made him gasp. Garsch gave him a sharp, menacing look.

26

There, a hundred yards away at the watering hole, were some creatures who looked very much like *him*. At least, they stood on two feet. One of them was squatting down, running his finger lightly over the impressions the feet of the lions had made in the wet sand.

The skins of these creatures were very strange indeed. They were smooth like his but they were of various colors. In their hands they held objects. One held an object that looked like a slender tree with no branches. At the top it had a shiny tip, sharp like a big thick claw. A few of them held even more slender young trees that looked as if the wind were bending them in a storm, but the wind was not blowing. Everything was still. On the back of one was a pouch that held many thin reeds like those that grew by the upper end of the watering hole where the stream meandered into it through a small sunny meadow. Sometimes, the boy remembered, he would pull those reeds up and wave them in the air. He liked to hear the *whooshing* sound they made. He wondered if these creatures liked that too.

The creatures were rather quiet and still until the one who was squatting leaped up and ran a few feet away, pointing with great excitement at the ground. With his finger he traced a track that was very different from the others. Suddenly the boy feared that they were looking for him, tracking his own particular footprint, the one so different from all the rest. The men looked around then fanned out as if they were searching. The funny feeling that always came into his stomach when he and his family were about to attack arose inside.

Now one of the two-legged creatures approached very close to where the lions lay. The boy watched as Garsch's eyes enlarged and his tawny head flattened out against the ground. He felt the muscles of Garsch's legs and ribs grow taut beside him and he felt his fierce brother pull his hind legs up underneath. In a split-second Garsch had leaped from the plateau above the creature with a scream and was upon him, biting at his neck and tearing at his chest. The creature cried out, a haunting cry, the like of which the boy had never heard, but which he would never forget. The boy felt something new within him he had never felt before, not at all the feeling of exhilaration that normally accompanied a kill; the excitement of it was blunted by remorse.

While his other brothers and sisters pinned themselves to the ground, the inquisitive boy raised his eyes to a level from which he could watch events unfold. He first heard, then saw, the other creatures running toward the pair fighting below him. Two of the men pulled the reeds from the little pouches on their backs and held them in the air with the bent trees. Then an amazing thing happened. There was a singing sound and one of the reeds was sticking from Garsch's side. Garsch screamed and let go of the creature he was rending. Another reed suddenly appeared in his thigh. The ends of the reed looked like the tails of birds. Garsch screamed again. The man with the long tree ran at him and poked at him with the sharp claw-tip. Garsch slapped at it with his paw. Then another reed appeared in Garsch's throat. When that happened, Garsch fell over roaring and slashing at the ground with his paws. Then the creature who had squatted came and plunged the slender tree into Garsch's chest and the young lion moved no more.

The creature whom his brother had attacked was bleeding profusely and the smell of the blood was agitating the boy's other brothers and sisters. Suddenly, Gorsina appeared and the boy and his siblings ran away with her as fast as they could run. When the boy finally climbed back into the *ghral*, the others had already been there for a long time. He was exhausted and terrified and drifted off into a troubled sleep.

The next day when the family went to the watering hole, the boy wandered off and went to the place where the fight had taken place between his brother and the other creatures-like-him. He bent down low to the ground and scratched the soil. The smell of blood met his nose; the blood of his brother. He saw another stain and scratched at it. This too was blood but it had a different smell. Suddenly he had the urge to draw his own blood and to compare the two smells. He took a loose stone and cut his finger and sniffed at the blood. Then he sniffed the soil again that had been soaked with the creature's blood. The smells were the same! The blood of each deer smelled like the blood of all deer, the blood of each auroch smelled like the blood of all aurochs, and the blood of each rat like the blood of all other rats. And his own blood smelled like the blood of this two-legged creature!

He sat down for a moment. Were these creatures he had seen really the same as him? If so, what a marvelous discovery!

But how unsettling! He wanted no part of creatures who went about hunting lions for sport or for any other reason. He wondered again about their strange skin and about the bent trees they held that could kill and about the reeds that they could make appear inside you. He mourned the loss of Garsch for a time. Then he and his brothers and sisters went back to the knoll and lay down in the sun.

That afternoon, the family pulled down an auroch. After they had feasted the boy approached the carcass of the animal, still warm. He pulled at the skin, at first speculatively. Then he grabbed it and spent the next hour or so pulling it away from the remaining sinew and muscle of the carcass. When he had finished he wrapped it around himself and walked to where the family was dozing. Tasha woke and stared at him, blinking, not believing what she saw. Her brother had tied the front feet of the skin around his neck, trying to emulate the skin he had seen on the other creatures-like-him. The skin dragged on the ground behind him. He was covered with the animal's blood which greatly aroused the curiosity of the others when they saw him.

That night, the boy noticed how much warmer he was sleeping in the skin of the auroch. It made the rocks a little more comfortable to lie on as well. He liked it, so he kept it. After a few days, however, the skin began to stink, and the others would not tolerate his being in the *ghral* with it. So he had to choose between lying with them on the rocks and sleeping by himself outside.

As days passed he came to be more and more cognizant of the many differences between him and the other lions. He wanted to see the creatures-like-him again but he was afraid of them. He wanted to stay with his family too, but he was growing more and more detached from them.

The next night he slept outside again. As he lay upon his back, he gazed up at the stars. He had noticed them before, these little lights in the sky. He had always fancied they were the eyes of animals crouching in the heavens, reflecting the light of the White Face. But somehow they looked different now. He imagined he saw various shapes there. He became frightened when he thought he saw the shape of one of the creatures-like-him carrying a bent tree that shot the deadly reeds. He rolled away, frightened, but when he turned to look again he could not find it. Now and again a light would streak across the sky. There was nothing in his experience to compare it to, and he was filled with wonder. He pulled the putrid skin tightly about him. It might stink, he thought to himself, but it was warm. Besides, *they* had fur which covered them. How could they deny him a hide of his own?

The next day he tried to talk to Tasha about the lights in the sky but all he got in response was a vacant stare. She turned up her nose at the stench which accompanied him now everywhere he went. He was disappointed and frustrated and growing restless. He wondered if he could talk about the lights in the sky to the creatures-like-him.

The next day he approached his mother to tell her that he was going away. He made the signs he had seen his brothers make when they had gone away and she understood. It was time, Gorsina replied. She wished him well. He said goodbye to his other brothers and sisters and walked down the mountain.

As he went, he saw a young fir sapling that had died prematurely. He pulled it out of the ground and stripped off the branches close to the trunk, thinking it looked very much like the slender tree with the claw tip the creature-like-him had carried. He stood with his feet apart and poked at an imaginary beast with it. He laughed out loud. Then he walked on, his robe trailing behind him in the dirt.

He thought he might walk near the stream and look for footprints of animals as he had seen the other creatures-like-him do. He stopped at a sandy ford to examine the tracks there. He saw fox and raccoon and kine and deer, but there were no footprints like his own. So he walked on.

Eventually, the winding path beside the stream became less steep and the stream broadened into a small tarn, still high up on the shoulders of the mountain. At the upper end were reeds and grasses standing in the water. As the boy watched the wind began to play among them, tossing them to and fro and causing their reflections on the surface of the water to dance. He bent down to see his own reflection. At first the surface of the water was too rough and he could see nothing. But gradually, as the wind died, the sky and clouds came into focus, then the tops of the trees and finally, his face appeared. It was not the face of a lion but the face of the creatures-like-him he had seen on the mountain. He smiled and saw his teeth. He laughed and saw the sparkle in his eyes reflected from the depths. Then the wind tossed the reeds again and the picture contorted and faded from his view. He heard voices. Wary of being seen, he hid himself

30

among the dank reeds on the spongy ground, crouching low and silently, the way he had been taught as a young cat.

A group of creatures-like-him came into view up a broad path that followed the opposite shore of the lake. These creatures were different yet again from those he had seen on the mountain. They were fairer, smaller, more delicate and more graceful. They carried no sticks of death. He was reminded of the contrast between his brothers and sisters. Perhaps these were the females of the creatures-like-him. The hair on their heads was longer and their skins were brightly colored and seemed to flow around them like water. In the midst of this group was one who was the most fair yet, and the others seemed to show deference toward her, even though she did not appear to be the biggest or the strongest or the oldest. He was perplexed by that. They were laughing as they walked along and the music of it filled his ears. He thought it the most beautiful sound he had ever heard and his eyes filled with water.

The group of women came to a halt about fifty yards away. There they spread cloths on the ground and placed baskets on top of the cloths. The fairest one unfastened a clasp that held her gown on her shoulder and stepped out of it. The lion boy watched with increasing interest as she shed her bright skin like a snake. Beneath it was another body with skin much like his own. She waded into the water to bathe while the others took clothes from the baskets and washed them in the water near the bank. The fair one began to swim, like an otter, sliding effortlessly through the water. She called out in a merry voice to those behind on the bank and made a waving gesture with her hand. She swam toward the lion boy then abruptly stopped and stood up in the water. Now that she was closer he could observe her features in greater detail.

The hair of her head was black, like the wing of a blackbird, and her eyes were a golden-green, not the yellow-gold of the eyes of his brothers and sisters. Her mouth was red, quite in contrast to the color of her skin, which tended to be white like snow or clouds rather than a tawny brown like his own. She held her arms out on top of the water as she walked and let the little waves wash over the tips of her fingers. The skin of her chest was smooth and white. She turned her back to him now and parted the waters with her hands. Then her feet flipped up toward the sky and she disappeared below the surface of the water. This startled the lion boy and he waited anxiously for her to reappear. When she did she was a long way off, heading back toward the other creatures-like-him. He watched her climb cat-like out of the water, which pleased him greatly. One of the others ran and placed a bright-skin around the fair one who sat down. The rest took smaller bits of bright-skin, dried her hair and combed it with small flat sticks. The lion boy watched until all this grooming activity was complete and the group stood and walked back along the margin of the lake from whence they had come. The music of their laughter faded from his ears and he was alone once again.

The sight of the women had completely captivated him. He thought to follow them but feared to do so, for they might lead him unawares to the men with the death-sticks. But he hungered for their companionship. That night the black-haired one appeared in his dreams.

On the next day he came again to the lakeside and crouched once more among the reeds. The performance of the previous day was repeated. On the third day, the same thing happened. He watched every movement and observed every action of these young women with heightened fascination. He wondered how he might get their attention without startling them, for he did not want them to run away. He wanted to see the fair one up close. He wanted to smell her and touch her and see if he could make her understand his thoughts.

The lion boy had been away from his family for four days and he was beginning to get hungry. He realized now how much he had depended upon them and the kills they made for food. His stomach growled. He tried to catch a small rodent among the reeds but was unsuccessful. Finally, his hunger and excitement about the creatures-like-him overcame his fears. He determined to show himself to the women the next day and see what would happen.

At the time when the Yellow Face had just passed the zenith, he placed himself among the reeds. It was not long until he heard the musical voices of the women as they came into view. Once again the fair one dropped her bright-skin and entered the water. Once again she swam out into the lake. This time, when she was at the point closest to him, he stood up.

When the girl saw him she gave a little cry and swam quickly away. Then, as if she changed her mind about fleeing, she stopped at a safer distance and turned around to face him. She was in the middle of the lake, her head just above the water.

He walked into the water up to his knees, among the swaying reeds. She watched him, blushing, as he waded in.

Suddenly a cry went up from the opposite shore. The others had seen the boy and were pointing. One in particular seemed quite alarmed and called to the fair one to swim back. But most of the others were simply amused at the sight of the dirty, naked boy with the matted mane of brown hair. One ran to get help and returned accompanied by men with the death-sticks. A group of them walked around the lake, coming up behind the boy. At first they seemed hostile, but when they saw that he was only a boy, the one who seemed to be their leader beckoned him to come. Without apparent fear now, the boy walked toward them, the skin draped over his shoulders and trailing behind him on the ground. He stood proudly, the rough staff in his hand.

The men were amazed at the sight of the boy, his hair littered with bits of dried grass and leaf, his skin tawny and rough.

"He smells like the den of a bear," one of them said. The others laughed. The boy laughed too. When it became clear that the boy did not know their language, they were yet more perplexed. Where had he come from? They motioned for him to follow. At first he did not understand, but by degrees he took the meaning of their gestures. One of the men held out his hand gesturing for the boy to give up his staff. The wild boy complied. The man turned and began to walk. As the boy followed the one who had spoken to him, the others closed in behind. That made him uncomfortable. Seeming to sense this, they maintained their distance and soon he felt more at ease. They led him to a village, which seemed to the boy like his *rhasch*, the home territory of his people. The village had many broad, straight paths amid low wooden structures which reminded him of the *ghral*, the cave in which his own family lived. The people of the village stopped and stared at the naked savage walking down the street escorted by their own men.

Soon they came to a sizable *ghral*, in fact, the largest in the *rhasch*, and the man who had spoken first to the boy motioned for him to sit down. The other men sat down around him but the one who had spoken disappeared into the strange wooden *ghral*, the like of which the boy had never seen. He looked around in nervous wonder then lowered his eyes to the ground. There was a strange smell in this *rhasch*, like the smell when the fire comes down from the sky and burns the forest.

33

In a moment people emerged from the wooden *ghral*. The first was a tall man and the first thing the lion boy noticed were his bright-skins. They were of many colors, rich, dark and thick. He carried a staff in his hand and upon his head he wore a circlet of metal which caused his brow to shine, as though a star had come down from the sky and had settled there. His hair, like the hair of the fair one the boy had seen, was black and was pulled back into the likeness of a tail. The tail coming from the man's head perplexed the lion boy greatly. The only tails he had ever seen came from the backside. He peered curiously around at the man's backside but he could see no tail there.

Following the man was a woman. She was also dressed in bright-skins, lighter in hue than the man's. But that was not the thing that interested him most. If the young girl he had first seen had been fair, then this woman was surpassingly beautiful. Her eyes were blue like the sky had been this very morning when he awoke. Her skin was fairer than the girl's. It had a translucent quality like the whiteness of milk upon the pink nose of a nursing cub. Her hair was auburn, the color of the maple leaf after it had passed the height of its color, just before its fall. Upon her head also sat a shiny circlet in which was set a red stone. It glittered whenever she moved her head. She looked into his eyes with a penetrating but gentle stare. For a moment the boy could not look away.

Then yet another man came and stood by the woman's side. He was not as tall as the first man, nor were his bright-skins so fine. His hair was the same color as the woman's although his skin was mottled, as if dirt had been spattered on it and dried there. The boy thought this man must not be very clean. His eyes held no lamp of compassion as did the eyes of the woman. They were rimmed with a redness, the redness of blood and their color was dark, like the cold, dead blood of the slain. He at once struck the lion boy as possessing a terrible tension. He had the aspect of one haughty and proud, yet behind this veneer was a whipped, fawning, servile creature, with a hot head but a cold heart. For his part, the man immediately felt something in the presence of the savage young boy he did not like.

Following this second man emerged another creature, bent low to the ground with age and leaning heavily upon a staff. The lion boy did not know what to make of this creature. Unlike the others, it was completely beyond his reckoning. He tried first with his eyes, and when they failed him, with his nose, to judge if it was a creature-like-him, and whether it was male or female. But the fullness and mustiness of the creature's clothes disguised any shapes or odors that might have told the wild boy anything further of its nature.

The tall man with the tail-on-his-head and the twinkling brow spoke.

"You say you found him in the reeds by the lake, Ulf?"

"Yes, Khol, one of Thena's handmaidens came running and told us that a wild man was standing in the lake. We ran there with weapons drawn but we found it was only this boy. He was just this way when we found him, naked and dirty, with this rotten robe upon his back and nothing else. He held the pole I have here in my hands." The boy liked the man they called Ulf. He was a small man, not much taller than the boy, with a thick black mane of hair and laughing gray eyes.

"Where are you from, boy?" Tail-on-his-head asked.

"He appears not to understand our speech, Khol," said Ulf.

"What do you make of him?" asked the tall man at length, addressing himself this time to the Old One.

The bent old woman shuffled over toward the boy for a closer look, sniffing as she approached him. She bent down and looked deeply into his eyes for a long time. Then she turned on uncertain feet back toward the tall man.

"He has the smell of a wild animal, like a lion. But he seems docile enough. I should like to consult the oracle before I pass judgment."

With that, Eengla, the Old One, sat down heavily and produced a small bag from inside her shirt. She opened it and pulled out a handful of sticks, casting them to the ground in front of her. She rocked back and forth for a moment with half-closed eyes. Gradually, the eyes became animated and round as she studied the resulting configuration of the sticks. She turned her head toward the tall man and spoke.

"This boy has been sent to us for a purpose. It would be wise to take him in and give him a home."

"Bah!" The sound erupted from the lips of the man with the mottled skin and blood-rimmed eyes. "This boy is nothing, only a dirty little savage, and he stinks! He is ignorant. He has no potential. There is no depth to him. Look at his eyes! They bespeak of no intelligence. This boy can be of no use to us. Send him back to the hills!" he sneered.

"Calm yourself, Gorn" said Tail-on-the-head. "There is no

35

need for anger. What about you, Moira?" he asked, addressing himself to the woman. "What are your feelings about this boy?"

Now the woman spoke. There was a tenderness in her voice, in contrast to the sharpness of Blood-eye's tones. It put the lion boy at ease and made him feel secure. Her words covered him like the warm moist tongue of his mother, cleaning and caressing him.

"I believe the words of the Old One," she said. "This boy has come to us for a purpose. I cannot see that purpose, but my heart says that we should take him in."

The second man, the one called Gorn, who was Moira's brother, turned abruptly, contemptuously, and left the others staring at the little animal. The lion boy sat in the shade of the trees, trying to read the eyes and expressions and movements of those who had deliberated his fate, not understanding the words they spoke.

Chapter 4
Wine of the Harvest

"No, no Dayn, that is not the right symbol for it," Thena insisted.

"Why?" Dayn inquired, "it sounds the same."

"But it is not. If you use that symbol for 'woman', people will think you are vulgar," the girl shot back.

"I cannot learn this," Dayn replied.

"Yes you can... you can! It is not so difficult." Thena's voice softened and she stroked his hair, then tenderly pressed her hand against the side of the boy's face. In recent weeks she had developed a fondness for her foster brother that threatened to wander naively beyond the bounds of mere sibling affection. As of yet, Dayn seemed not to recognize it.

The curtain was pulled back and Thena's mother, Moira, stepped inside. She had heard the rise in Thena's voice and had come to investigate their progress.

"How is he doing?" she inquired.

"Not well," the boy answered for himself. "I cannot seem to understand this thing called writing. I cannot understand why the symbol for mother is not the same as the symbol for cow. They are both mothers, are they not?"

The woman laughed and her eyes flashed.

"If you call a woman a cow she will scratch out your eyes, like a lioness." She raised her hands with fingers spread and curved toward Dayn showing her teeth and snarling playfully to demonstrate her meaning. Dayn laughed carelessly.

Thena crossed her arms and exhaled, a little jealous of her Mother's playful advances and Dayn's unthoughtful response.

37

"If you are to be raised in the house of Khol as his son, then you must learn to write," she reprimanded. "And that is the end of it." She cupped his chin in her hand and slowly, too slowly thought the girl, pulled it away. "Thena, show him again," Moira demanded. The girl tried again.

"Look, the symbol for the mother is *like* the one for cow, but it is *not* the *same*. See here, it has this mark which crosses through the circle a different way," the young girl repeated. Dayn picked up the stylus and dipped it into the little bowl containing a dark blue ink. With some difficulty he made the symbol for mother.

"Is that better?" he inquired.

"Yes, much better," Thena remarked. "Now do it again... practice."

Dayn put the stylus to the leather writing surface and made the mark several more times.

"Now then," Moira said taking the stylus and hide from Dayn, "this is the symbol of Faen, the goddess of the harvest, the principal goddess of our village. You see, it is like the symbol for mother only it has this *curat* on top. And this is the symbol for Nyso, the Great Mother, its has a double *curat* at the top. Do you understand? The *curat* placed on any symbol causes it to be elevated in importance. By placing the *curat* on the symbol for man you get king or ruler, and by placing the double *curat* on the symbol for man you get the base symbol of the lesser male deities. This is the sign for Brahan, the fire bringer." She watched Dayn's eyes as she spoke the name.

Dayn's attention was riveted to the hide as she made this symbol and he etched it into his mind.

"Yes, I see now. It begins to make sense. There is a pattern."

"Good," Moira replied. Saying this she got up and walked through the curtain into the next room leaving the boy and girl alone once again.

"You have learned much since you came to us," Thena said at length. "I shall never forget the first time I saw you, standing in the reeds by the lake," she giggled. "You know, I was never afraid of you. I liked you from the very beginning."

"And I shall never forget the first time I saw you." Dayn lay back now on the sheepskins which covered the floor. "Though now you seem different to me, more real. On that first day, I remember seeing you as I remember seeing clouds. But you

38

were the loveliest cloud I had ever seen."

Thena blushed slightly, bringing her face close to his and looking into the depths of his eyes.

"Tell me again about living among the lions," Thena pleaded.

"No," returned Dayn, "I want to hear more about the stars."

Harvest time was approaching and the people turned all their attention to the fields. Wheat for the making of bread was beginning to form the grain. Ripening grapes painted the vineyards with the first blush of purple. Then, inexplicably, the weather turned hot and there was no rain for the entire cycle of the Heron Moon. Nightly vigils were held and sacrifices made to Faen, but still the rain did not come and the heat did not waver. The tender stalks of wheat turned brown in the fields, the grapes withered on the vine.

There was a notable change in the attitude of the villagers. They became irritable and quick to anger. Fights broke out over nothing among the boys. Everywhere the people looked for the cause of their troubles. Some looked suspiciously at Dayn. Rumors about him were whispered by the fireside after the children had been put to bed, and Moira's brother Gorn was at the root of them.

Then without warning the weather turned cool and the sky opened. The rains poured relentlessly from the heavens and torrents formed in the fields. Dead crops were washed away in the floods. The men turned to the forest to hunt so there would be food for the winter. Dayn went among them. The grunting of the bucks seemed to awaken something primal within him. His instincts proved unerring and he led the hunters with great success to the herds.

In the house of Khol the air itself seemed different to Dayn, somehow heavier and closer. The household was less prone to mirth, at times even sullen. He wanted to talk to someone about it but did not know how to express himself. One day he pulled the Old One aside and spoke to her.

"Everyone is sad that the harvest has failed. That sadness seems to have fallen heavily in particular on this house," he told her.

She looked at him with ancient eyes.

39

"Seasons come and seasons pass. From time to time the earth must be renewed. Sacrifice must be made to Faen when the crops fail. The sacrifice she requires is the wine of the harvest and that is Khol. Khol must die and the earth must drink his blood when the sun dies on the shortest day. This is the only way we know."

Dayn was stunned. He could not believe the words of the old woman. For the rest of the afternoon he stayed to himself. Sometime later he spoke with Thena about her father and the fate that had been revealed by the Old One.

"No, Khol is not my father," she explained. My mother, Moira, is the mother of our people. She is of a line directly descended from the goddess Faen, as I am. Khol is her companion so long as the harvest is blessed by their union. When the harvest is no longer blessed, then her companion must be sacrificed. After that she will choose another. It is in this way that the fertility of the earth, the surety of our crops, the fullness of our lives, is guaranteed. Khol must be united with Faen, just as my father was. It is his sacred duty, his privilege, the greatest deed he can do for his people. It is our way, it is the only way."

Dayn went furtively to Khol, seeing in his mind's eye flashing pictures of men slaughtering his lion brother, Garsch. It seemed long ago now, but suddenly vivid in his recollection.

"Khol, I must speak to you," Dayn entreated. "But it is not easy... not easy for me to speak. Since I came to this village you have been as a father to me. Now they tell me that you must die, for the crops have failed. But it seems unfair to me. Do you control the winds and the rain and the sun in the sky that they can hold you responsible for the life of a seed? And if you cannot be held responsible for the life of a seed, how much more so can you be held responsible for the lives of the people? Explain it to me and save yourself from this fate, my father."

Khol smiled and looked sympathetically into the boy's eyes.

"You have learned much since you came to us, Dayn. Of reading and writing and speech. But these things are hollow without the knowledge of the spirit which casts the light of wisdom upon them. Of planting and harvesting we have not instructed you. In these things we have been negligent. And in doing so we have wronged you.

"In the ancient times, people lived much as you lived when you lived with the lions. They roamed the plains, stalking their prey, eating when they were successful and starving when they were not, freezing in caves when the weather was cold and parching on the plains when the summer was at its peak. In this time before the gods, man was utterly without knowledge and hope. He was a blind, homeless savage.

"Then came the day when Faen revealed herself to the mothers. She revealed to them the mystery of the seed; how it must be placed into her womb, the earth, there to sleep until it is awakened. The seed is awakened by the blood of the father. The blood of the father enters the ground and causes the seed to grow. If the blood of the father is weak or is used up, then it must be replenished. This is the teaching of Faen.

"Faen chose humankind, above all the other animals, as the vessel of her wisdom. The knowledge of planting and harvesting, the blessing of Faen, are what separate man from the beasts of the earth. This blessing is much. It is that which has led us to stay by the crop, rather than roam the earth in search of prey, to build houses and villages of wood, rather than to lay our heads upon the rock, to drink the wine of the harvest rather than the blood of the slain.

"So now you can see why I must suffer this fate. The Great Mother, Nyso, is everything. Faen calls me to unite with her. And I know that union will be glorious, surpassing any joy I could ever know in this life. Our progeny will be the lifeblood of these people, my blood will nourish the seed, my death will become life. These are the teachings of Faen, without whom we have nothing. This is the fate to which I willingly submit for the good of the people."

Dayn lay awake for a long time that night, unable to sleep, the words of Khol swimming in the waters of his thought. It seemed a terrible fate which Khol must suffer. How could he submit willingly to this? Yes, he had heard Khol's words, but they made no sense to him. What a strange people he lived among! He thought about his other family, the lions. Among them the father was only supplanted when he was too weak to defend the herd or too old to lead them in the hunt. And then only when a stronger male came along. He fought for himself, for his place at the head of the family. There was pride there and a joy in life. Yet Khol's joy was in death. There was none

41

stronger or more capable here than Khol. Of that he was certain. It seemed an awful waste. Could Khol not be of better use to the people alive than dead? He fell asleep in a quandary.

That night he had a dream. He had begun to dream more and more since the beginning of his life in the village, but he had never had a dream like this one. In this dream he saw Moira, the mother of the clan, draw two symbols on an animal skin using a stylus. On the left hand side she drew the symbol of Faen, the goddess of fertility, the goddess of the harvest. On the right she drew the symbol for Brahan, the bringer of fire. The symbol of the goddess became the image of Moira and the symbol of Brahan became the figure of a young lion. The young lion stalked across the page and consumed the image of Moira. Then the young lion lay down to sleep. When the lion awoke, he was no longer a lion, but a man, and a light was on his brow; not the burning light of the sun, but the soft light of the moon.

For the next few days, Dayn pondered the dream. There was something vaguely familiar about the connection between the symbol of Brahan and the lion, but he could get no closer to its meaning than that. The connection between Moira and the goddess was clear but why had she been eaten by the lion? The raven was the totem for Brahan, not the lion; he could not interpret the dream's meaning.

In frustration he went again to the Old One and told her his dream. For a long time she sat in silence, breathing heavily. Then she spoke in a voice that crackled like lightning in the heavy air of the room.

"Since the first day I saw you I have known that your coming was the advent of suffering, and not of joy, for our people. I have known that your coming would utterly destroy us and our ways. No one can be the same once she brings a lion into her house, once she lets him roam the streets of the village. Then no one is safe. Then everyone must pay. But I have known something more. That this change *must* come, this *destruction* must come, this *suffering* must come. And you are the bringer of it. For you Dayn... you *are* the son of a god! You *are* the lion, you *are* the son of Brahan! You must take the wisdom which Brahan bestows and you must consume the wisdom of the goddess, yes... you must eat the goddess. Then you will give birth to a *new* wisdom, you will show us the *new* way. The new way will be illuminated by the light of Han-Thol... Han-Thol, the light that comes out of the darkness. But

42

nothing so bright can burn forever. The fire must be tempered in the waters and reappear as the light of Han-nys. The middle way will be revealed."

"I find no comfort in your words, Mother, and little that is clear. Yet that which I understand frightens me. What am I to do?" asked Dayn.

"Tomorrow you must leave the village before daylight. Follow the stream that leads to the sea. There you will find a horse. This horse must be tamed, he must be ridden. Tame him and ride him back here before seven days have passed. For in seven days will come the shortest day and Khol will live no more."

"What is this *horse that must be ridden*, Old One?" asked Dayn.

She looked at him with uncertainty.

"This *horse* is a four legged creature, tall and swift, that dwells by the sea. You must climb upon his back, you must make him understand your words and do your bidding. From that vantage, you will see things that none other have seen. You will see the new way!"

For the remainder of that day and night, Dayn pondered the words of the Old One. What she had said was surpassingly strange. It went against every precept of the goddess' teaching that a man should wander off alone, outside the protection of the mothers. Why would she advise such a thing? Was she not a guardian of the Rites of the Goddess? Would she not pay for such heresy? While this part of himself was hesitant, another part was filled with excitement and a sense of adventure, much like the feeling he had the morning he left his lion family to seek his own way in the world. He quivered with it and looked forward to it with a mischievous anticipation. Turning the village upside down might be fun! And perhaps he could make Khol see the mistake of his complicity with the ancient and barbaric ritual that would lead to his death. He made up his mind to go.

As he lay in his bed with his eyes half-closed he heard a rustle. The curtain that covered the entrance to his room was pulled back and his sister, Thena, walked in. He wondered why she had come.

"I could not sleep, Dayn. All day long I have watched you. You seem far away. When I have been close to you, you have hardly noticed me. Have I done something to offend you?"

"No my dear," Dayn answered. Then he hesitated.

"Then what is wrong? You can tell me."

Dayn thought long before he answered. Ever since the Old One had interpreted his dream, he had felt different, separate from the others, as if the doom she pronounced for him had visibly marked him. He felt the stares of the others more keenly. He longed to share his secret with someone. Besides, he felt a special regard for this girl, his sister. What would she think if he suddenly disappeared without telling her? Thena's eyes were shining in the moonlight and in that moment, he felt he could trust her. He must tell her.

"Thena, tomorrow I am leaving the village. I will not be gone for long, but I must go away. There is something I must do. I am going alone."

"You cannot do that, Dayn!" she whispered excitedly. "It is not permitted. It is madness. To leave the village without the permission of the mothers is to break the law, but to go alone is madness. You will die! You mustn't!"

"I have to, Thena. It was revealed to me in a dream. It is my fate. Please, don't cry. I will be fine. You will see. I will return safely. But I must go and return before the shortest day. It is all for Khol. I have to do it for him."

Thena brought her face close to his and her warm tears fell on his cheek.

"Will you think of me, while you are gone, Dayn? I couldn't bear to part with you, even for a little while, if you didn't promise me that," she pleaded tremulously.

"I will promise you, Thena."

She inclined her head and placed a fretful, child's kiss on his lips, then lay down beside him, resting her head innocently upon his chest.

Gorn had awakened in the night to go outside and relieve himself. As he walked by Dayn's room he heard whispers and stopped to eavesdrop, thinking he might hear something useful, for he was always searching out ways to disadvantage the young man. When he recognized the voice of his niece he leaned forward, listening intently.

Chapter 5
The Son of Brahan

On the morrow Dayn was up before dawn. He left the village secretly, as the Old One had advised. When the villagers discovered he was gone, some, most vocally Gorn, said it was a good thing. Gorn had believed him to be the cause of the failure of the harvest and had spoken openly of it in the Council of Elders. Some, like Ulf, were disappointed to see him go, for they had been hunting with Dayn and had witnessed his prowess. Most of the villagers thought little about it and waited for the day when all would be put in order by the sacrifice of Khol. Moira felt a keen sense of loss and frustration, as though a part of her had been wrenched away. Thena was afraid for her brother but kept his secret. Several parties of hunters were sent to look for him, but they did not range far from the village. All returned empty-handed.

Dayn made his way nimbly down the path by the stream which flowed out of the small lake above the village. The waters of the stream became louder as he went, joining with those of other streams that fell in with them. They seemed to be laughing, as was his heart. Eventually, the voice of the swelling waters drowned out all else. When the sun went down, Dayn slept on the outstretched limb of a great water oak which stood fast by the bank, dipping its roots into the cool waters to replace those that had been offered to the sky. When the sun rose, he was up again and on his way. All the while he kept his eye out for the horse that must be ridden. But he saw nothing.

At the end of the second day he began to wonder if the Old One had sent him chasing after the wind. Perhaps there was no

45

horse. What was a horse anyway? Would he be able to recognize it when he saw it? Perhaps the Old One had simply tricked him into leaving. So be it. If it was so he would be on his way. He would not go back.

All along he had pondered her words. Could he truly be the son of Brahan, the son of a god? It seemed unlikely. He knew no mother besides the lioness and had never seen or heard from Brahan. Surely no father, especially a divine one, would abandon his son to the world as he had been abandoned, to be brought up in a cave by wild beasts. He had received no direction, no assistance. But something deep within him resounded with the name and the symbol of the god. Perhaps... perhaps it was just possible that he was his son.

But to eat the goddess, to consume the wisdom of the goddess, what could this mean? How would this be accomplished? And why would it entail the suffering of the village and the destruction of their way of life? He had no such tendencies. If anything, he wanted only good for them. Khol had been good to him. And he would like to save Khol from his fate. But how could he do this? The horse... first to tame and ride the horse. The Old One had said if he did, he would see things no one had yet seen. Perhaps he would see a way to save Khol.

That night a gleaming white creature appeared to him in a dream. He had never seen a horse before, but he knew instinctively this was what he sought. He approached it but the horse took fright and ran away. He tried to catch the horse again but it bolted. It was some time before he caught up with him again. Suddenly in his dream, Dayn realized that he was a lion. So that was why the horse had run! If he could only change his shape. So he changed himself into a mare and trotted up easily beside the beautiful white stallion.

Daylight broke on the third day of his journey. Dayn's instincts led him onward. He found himself for the better part of the morning in the thick of the forest near the river. Where was the white horse? How might he find him? It occurred to him to climb a tall tree and look about. From the top of the tree he saw no horses but he did see a taller hill not too far away. He climbed down from the tree and made his way to the hill. When he reached its summit, it was midday. He looked in every direction but saw nothing. To the north lay a little folded valley into which he could not see. He decided to try his luck there.

By the time he reached the valley it was nearly dark. He thought again of the sacrifice of Khol which would occur at sunset on the shortest day and pressed on. In the moonlight he came to the sea. Although he had heard tales of the ocean around the fires in the house of Khol, no description had truly prepared him for the sight of it. It was vast, dark, heaving, and frightening beyond his imaginings. He thought he heard thunder and looked up at the sky. But the sky was clear. He heard thunder again. The thunder came from the sea. He watched the writhing waters for a long time but did not go near the shore.

In the spray he saw vague shapes and heard wild neighing. Suddenly, as he watched, from out of the waters came a herd of horses, running, led by a magnificent white stallion. They ran down the beach to the edge of his sight in the dim light and stopped. He ran after them. As he approached they became aware of him and ran away. Each time he got near them, the wary beasts were off again. It seemed an impossible task to get near the white stallion, much less to tame and ride him back to the village. But he had found him! He had seen him! The Old One had spoken true!

That night he slept on the beach and dreamed again the dream of chasing the horses in the form of a lion, then changing to the form of a mare and getting close. But there was more this time. As he stood by the horse wondering how he would mount him and ride him, there appeared a bright man wearing a purple cloak over an emerald green tunic with a red scarf at his neck. The man spoke Dayn's name and pushed back the hood, revealing his face and his brow, brilliant with a light that shone like the sun. He touched the clasp of the cloak and it fell open at the neck. He unwrapped it from about his shoulders and held it out to the boy.

"When you are near him, take this cloak and throw it on his back. Then you may do with him what you will. I will leave it in a tree by the river." And he was gone.

When Dayn awoke the dream was vivid in his mind, as if it had actually occurred. He ran to a place where the sands of the shore were littered with the fallen leaves of great gnarled oaks. The leaves prickled the bottoms of his feet. In the meager light he tripped over a root and fell on his face. When he looked up, there was the cloak of his dream, hanging from the end of a broken limb. It seemed to reflect the dim light of the new day

47

with a thin sheen. Grabbing it and tossing it over his shoulder, he ran back to the place he had last seen the herd.

The horses were not there but there were tracks. He followed them. He was frustrated by their incoherence; they shot off in many directions, it seemed, only to return to the same spot. Finally, like one untying a knotted rope, he found a path that led him away from the water's edge and into a series of rolling dunes, dotted with vegetation, just beyond the beach. When he finally tracked the herd down it was noon. As soon as the white stallion perceived him, they were off again. How would the cloak do him any good if he could not get near enough to place it on the stallion's back?

Running after the herd would never work, he thought. His instincts, the instincts of the lion, the instincts of the chase, were all wrong, and he must conquer them. He sat in the warm sand among the dunes until nightfall, thinking, trying to reason how he could get near the stallion. Twilight fell and the moon rose full and round above the mountains to the east. He was exhausted and took comfort in her light. He lay back and let his mind drift, let his thoughts wander among dunes, their pale heights, their shadowy clefts. His attention was drawn to the surface of the orb above him; the lights, the shadows. He imagined the white stallion running among the shadows. The shadows. The shadows. A cold breeze rose off the ocean and he drew the purple cloak, which lay beside him on the ground, about his shoulders. Again he looked at the shadows of the dunes. He looked at his own shadow. His own shadow! Where was his shadow? He cast no shadow! He looked all around him. He had no shadow. He took the cloak off and threw it aside and his shadow fell before him. He pulled the cloak around him again and his shadow disappeared!

Elated with this newfound knowledge he ran off, following the tracks of the herd, the cloak wrapped about him. It was nearly dawn when he found them but the moon still held court in the heavens. He neared the resting horses, flitting from shadow to shadow among the oaks. The herd was in a clearing just beyond the edge of the trees, the white stallion standing in their midst, unaware as yet of his presence. A dark mare stood beside him. Dayn eased forward, undetected. Now he moved among the horses themselves, the cloak pulled tightly about him. He stepped carefully, keeping out of sight of the white stallion behind this horse, now that one, now the next. Slowly he made

48

his way toward the center of the herd. Now he stood next to the dark mare. Beside her on the other side was the white stallion. He sank down and crawled beneath her belly, emerging silently in between the two horses. This would be his only chance.

Swift as a lion pouncing he threw the cloak on the stallion's back. The herd panicked and galloped off in all directions. The dust and thunder and confusion of their flight blinded Dayn for a moment. But when the dust had cleared and the rumbling commotion had subsided, there was the white stallion, standing alone and proud, waiting for his master.

Standing on his toes, Dayn was able to grab the spotless mane near the withers of the great horse. He lunged upwards onto his back, his legs dangling above the ground, then spun about on his stomach, finally drawing his head toward the handful of mane he tightly gripped. The stallion stood perfectly still all the while. Dayn straddled the broad back. Never before had Dayn, in truth never had man, sat on the back of a horse until this moment. The stallion shifted his weight beneath the boy. He grabbed the white mane with his other hand.

"Do my bidding now, Mataforas, for so I name you, *He Who Comes Out of the Sea*, and take me to the village of Khol."

As he spoke the sun rose above the hills, bringing the clear dawn of the seventh day, the shortest of the year. But behind him clouds were closing in. Mataforas gathered his legs beneath him and sprang forward, running like the wind up the Vale of the Cyryn. At first Dayn was frightened and kept his eyes shut tightly. But as he rode he came to trust the pumping muscles of the broad back beneath him, the deep even breathing of the great lungs, the drumming surge of the tireless legs, and his confidence grew. He opened his eyes and saw the world flowing by. And Mataforas glided along, his gallop as smooth as a calm sea at morning.

Toward the middle of the day, the temperature dropped and snow flakes began to swirl around them. Little by little the sun was extinguished as the skies shut. A frigid fog rose up from the river. A white rime of frost appeared along the banks and a thin glaze of ice formed in the slackwater bends. The trees stood impassively along the road, their dark trunks like silent watchmen, while the finer branches accumulated a hoary coat of ice which seemed to shine from within. Horse and rider left a thin trail of frozen breath hanging in the air as they passed.

It was difficult for Dayn to tell the exact time of day, but he

49

knew there was no time to lose. What would he say to Khol when he arrived, to Moira, to the villagers? How could he prevent the death of one fixated on death? How could he cool the fires of sacrifice? How could he change the way things had been done for centuries? And what about Faen? Would she not intervene? Who was he to challenge the wisdom of the goddess, the lore of the long ages?

The rhythm of the horse beneath him and the drumming of its hooves upon the road had a hypnotic effect upon Dayn. The fog became thicker now. Soon it was hard to tell where he was, or where he was going, even if he were going still. Suddenly in a vision, Dayn saw Khol upon the altar, a huge stone in the middle of a barren field, blackened with the blood of many sacrifices. A wooden pole was wedged into the stone, piercing the heart of the altar. From this pole Khol hung by his feet. A flint knife was in his hand. His eyes were closed as though he were asleep. All around him were dark shapes. The drumming of the horse's hooves became the drumming of the ritual of sacrifice. It was a driving, unstoppable beat, the rhythm of moon and tides, the heartbeat of the earth. Khol placed the knife against his throat and gave it an easy shove. Dayn's vision disappeared.

When he arrived at the village night had fallen. The blood of Khol had already been spread upon the snowy mantle of the fields. Dayn saw the light of many torches and rode toward it. He heard a single enchanted, chanting voice, the voice of Moira. As Dayn rode into the firelight the voice stopped. The glistening coat of the white horse caught the light of the torches and threw it back at the gathered villagers. The animal itself seemed to burn. Smoke boiled from his skin and pumped from his nostrils. The people drew uncertainly back, in awe of the spectral horse and its rider.

Moira was not intimidated. She had come to the part of the ritual in which her new consort, that one who would bring prosperity to the tribe and assure the fertility of the earth womb for the next generation, was to be chosen. Looking through the eyes of Faen herself, she fixed her gaze on the image of the boy seated upon the tall, sinewy stallion and called out in a loud voice. Behind her, the body of Khol hung lifeless, his feet secured to the top of the pole by a loop of rope, his blood upon the snow.

"You, Dayn, ...you are the chosen of Faen, you will be my

50

husband, ...you, the lion of the hills, you will be the wine of the harvest."

Dayn was dumbstruck. He could not raise his voice to speak, neither did he seem to possess a will to move. Moira stepped down from the stone toward him. She ordered him removed from the back of the animal and placed standing on the ground before her. Someone grabbed the purple mantle from the back of the horse. Immediately Mataforas tossed his snorting head and galloped away from the restless crowd into the night. Moira leaned forward and placed a kiss upon Dayn's unresponsive lips.

Gorn leaped to Moira's side. Grabbing her arm he twisted her away from the boy to face him.

"You cannot mean this!" he shouted, his face close to hers. "This is sacrilege! This boy is not of the blood of our village. Look, he runs away, not telling anyone where he has gone, then comes back mounted on a beast! This boy is possessed by evil spirits! This boy is the reason the harvest failed! If he had not come among us Khol would still live! This boy is the cause of Khol's death, and yet you want to take him as your consort? It cannot be! Devastation will come of this!"

Moira stared with an unflappable sense of purpose straight into the eyes of her distraught brother. "Bring him to me," Moira demanded of those who held the boy, in a whispered command.

"You don't know what you're doing!" Gorn whispered urgently. "I know something."

Moira turned to him with a piercing look. Gorn swallowed.

"Your daughter, Thena, and this boy... I heard them together, in his room, the night before he left. They were..."

She did not let him finish.

"What are you saying Gorn?"

"I am saying you cannot take him... if he... and your daughter..." Gorn's voice trailed off and he purposefully never finished his sentence.

"No! It cannot be. I will prove that it is not so if need be," Moira said with determination.

Chapter 6
The New Wine

Dayn was not seen by the villagers during the Eagle Moon for there were many initiations through which he had to pass. Most were of a private nature. Many secrets were passed from the woman to the boy, and with each passing day her influence on him grew. He no longer resisted her teaching as he had at first. Each day he was steeped more deeply in the mysterious waters of the goddess and gradually he seemed to accept, to welcome, his role as husband of her priestess, the guarantor of the life and prosperity of the village.

Thena was questioned by her mother concerning Gorn's allegation of a tryst between her and Dayn and Thena told her the truth of what had transpired. While Moira was upset that her daughter had kept a secret that could have proven to be more than an embarrassment, she was relieved that Thena's affections for Dayn had not crossed the boundaries of propriety. Still, there was a tension that developed between the two of them. Her daughter's affection for her new consort became an embarrassment for Moira. Thena felt the first hint of enmity for her mother at having wrenched her dear brother away. But the strained relationship between mother and daughter was not the worst effect of the incident, for whenever Gorn had the opportunity, he spread the rumor that Dayn was more than a brother to Thena and that only sorrow would come of Moira's choice. His jealousy for the boy festered.

When Dayn finally saw Thena once again things had changed dramatically. Moira had forbidden her to speak to him until a year had passed, until the shortest day had once again come and gone. Thena slipped past him in the hallway with her eyes cast down. Dayn had a fleeting memory of time spent sitting with her, learning, questioning, laughing, but it left as quickly as it came.

The Old One was anxious for Dayn and she looked for any opportunity to speak with him. She knew what was happening. She knew that Moira was erasing all that had been and was imprinting him with what would be. Moira seldom left Dayn alone during the early days of his initiation and it was nearly impossible to see him, even in the company of others. But Eengla knew she must get to him before it was too late.

One afternoon when Moira was attending to an errand of some importance at the other end of the village, the Old One sought Dayn out. He was sitting on a pillow in Moira's rooms, practicing an inner ritual in which she had instructed him, his eyes closed, his breathing measured and slow. Eengla knew she hadn't much time.

Stumbling in on thick, crooked legs she sat down with a grunt before him, patiently to wait. Momentarily, he opened his eyes. He was dreamy and it was some time before the Old One could get his focused attention.

"Dayn, son of Brahan, it is I, Eengla, the Old One who speaks. Awake to your thoughts." Dayn perceived her as through a thick veil.

"Dayn, son of Brahan, listen well. Arise young lion and stride forth." She made the symbol of Brahan on his forehead with her bony finger. Feeling her touch, he jerked his head instinctively backward. She repeated her words and made the sign of the god on his forehead over and over until he seemed to recognize her and what she was saying.

"Dayn, do you remember... do you remember the talk we made before you went away?"

"I... I think so," Dayn stuttered.

From her lap she picked up a skin stretched over a frame, the one upon which Moira had drawn the symbols of Faen and Brahan.

"Look," she said growing impatient.

"You are the son of Brahan. The son of Brahan is the lion. The lion must rise up and eat the goddess. Do you remember, Dayn? Do you remember the talk that we made?"

Dayn rubbed his eyes and pressed his fingers against his temples.

"Yes, I remember."

"Do you remember the horse, the white stallion? Do you remember, Dayn?"

"Yes, I remember the horse. I rode him here, where is he?"

"Do not be troubled. He is nearby. He will come if you need him. Dayn, look at me. Do you remember this?" As she spoke she opened her outergarment slightly to reveal a rich purple cloak hidden beneath.

Dayn's eyes registered his recognition of the mantle.

"Yes, that is the mantle I threw upon the stallion's back to tame him. He gave it to me."

"That's right Dayn, *he* gave it to you. Do you know who *he* was?"

"No I did not know him. All I remember is that upon his brow was a light. It shone like the sun."

"It was Brahan, Dayn, your father. You saw him in a vision. He told you how to tame the horse and he gave you his cloak to help you accomplish it. And a great feat it was Dayn, a greater thing than anyone has ever done, a great thing to befit a great man, a great thing to befit the son of Brahan.

"Listen to me, Dayn. There is a seed in you. A seed of greatness and Moira is going to kill it if you are not careful. You must not let her kill it. You must nurture it and let it grow and blossom. And when the time is right you must rise up and strike down the goddess, Dayn. You must devour the goddess and transform her wisdom with the wisdom of Brahan, the bringer of fire. You must bring the new thought to us."

Dayn was alert now.

"Yes, Eengla, I remember all that you have said. I will do this thing that you ask. I will do it."

"It is good that you remember Dayn. Now, listen to me. Learn, learn all that Moira can teach you, but in learning do not become the slave of her thought. This is what you must do. When the temptation comes, the temptation to sink into the warm pool, remember the white stallion. Think of the white stallion and do not let him out of your mind. Remember Dayn, you tamed him and rode him. *You* Dayn, *you are* the son of Brahan. Remember!"

More moons passed and Dayn grew in stature and knowledge under the tutelage of Moira. Gradually she

54

reintroduced him to the company of the men of the village and he reformed his bond of kinship with them. He learned their ways and he shared his abilities with them. Whenever she could, Eengla would come secretly to Dayn, always with the same words, the same message. He must learn all that he could, but he must remember who he was, and what he must do. Always she reminded him of these things. Thena's feelings for the young man deepened but she was forced to keep them hidden. Always and openly, Gorn continued to treat him with contempt and secretly looked for ways to undo him.

As time went by, Dayn's relationship with Moira became more and more important to him. He shared a powerful spiritual Oneness with her and he felt that Oneness being drawn toward and enfolded by the spirit of the clan. The more deeply this Oneness was brought into the sphere of the clan spirit, the stronger was its pull, as though their Oneness sought unity with something at its very center. The attraction between these two energies became the center of his very existence, vital and compelling. But always the warnings of Eengla echoed in his mind and he took care lest he wade too near deep waters.

His relationship with Moira came to the center of his Otherself as well. The seed about which Eengla had told him had indeed been growing. It was nurtured by the soil of the Oneness with Moira and was energized in waters of her thought, but it yearned for the sun and took its direction from that sacred source; Han-Thol, Eengla called it when they would secretly meet, the light coming out of the darkness. The feelings for Moira and the thoughts about Moira that arose from the growing of this seed were very different from the swimming, enmeshing feelings which he felt in their Oneness. These were thoughts of his own, thoughts he did not share. These thoughts arose when she held him in her arms at night and he looked into the depths of her eyes, when she invited him to stroke her auburn hair and touch her soft white skin. When this happened he felt this sense of his Otherself more strongly than at any other time.

Thus two forces existed within him; the one that wanted to be hopelessly entangled with her, to become her, to fall into the waters of the Great Mother and dissolve into her infinity; the other that wanted to stand on a mountain top, to greet the sun at dawn saying to it, "I am I" and claim Moira as a part of itself.

So it was that the time came for the planting of the crops. Moira had instructed Dayn in the ritual that was to be performed at the spring equinox. She presented Dayn formally to the clan as her husband and the guarantor of the harvest that was to come. He had all but forgotten about Khol now.

Dayn was dressed in a robe of emerald green cloth and he walked into the fields followed by the women of the village who were of age. This group in turn was followed by the men who carried wooden staffs bearing images of the goddess, Faen, and symbols of fertility. In each field the women took a handful of earth and sat in a circle around Dayn. The men ringed the field with their standards. Dayn spoke.

"Mother Faen, goddess of the earth, goddess of fertility, goddess of the sky that brings the cool rain and warm sun. I bear witness of your people gathered here in your fields, rich with the blood of the harvest king. We have kept faith with you, we have done all that you have asked us to do, we have lived in accordance with your divine bidding, we have made good our promise to you. Take now this seed and fulfill the promise to your people."

One of the women began to chant. When they were enraptured by the music Faen came, walked among them and blessed the fields. Those who saw her were stricken, toppled over in insensible ecstasy until she had gone. When the women were revived, they would go on to the next field. When the day was done they had thus blessed all the fields.

That night Moira took the young man to lie with her for the first time since she had claimed him as her husband. Eengla had told Dayn this would happen and how, at that time, when he felt himself at the pinnacle of the mountain, he would be most in danger of falling into the deep waters. She told him when that moment came, to keep in his mind, above all else, the image of the white stallion, and he would be safe. And that he did.

Gorn sat in his rooms and stewed, his loathing for Dayn and his rival's growing position of influence eating away at him. Now this upstart, this foreigner, was in fact the husband of his sister, the matriarch of the clan. Now his malice for Dayn was complete. He pledged to find a way to end him and made a pact with Faen to accomplish it.

Chapter 7
The Otherself

Dayn spent the better part of the summer in the fields and the woods. He was not required to work or to hunt or tend the flocks. But while he found no pleasure in planting and cultivating crops, or in the tending of sheep, he took great pleasure from the hunt. Ulf and his companions taught him the art of hunting with the spear and the bow, and Dayn taught them in turn what he knew of the ways of the animals that roamed the forests and plains.

The men of the village were skilled hunters; their skills rooted in the dawn of time when man lived in nomadic herds, like the animals they hunted. First, they would prepare their weapons. Next they would take a mixture of cooked animal fat and wheat flour, mix it with pigments made from the juices of the stems or berries of plants, and paint themselves to look like the red deer or the bear.

When their weapons and bodies were readied, they prepared their spirits. Gathered around a fire in late afternoon, they would invoke the spirit of the animal they sought. When its spirit entered them, they would make the dance of that animal. With spirits and emotions charged, they went forth, led by the spirit of the animal to their prey. Many times Dayn accompanied them and often they returned successful, bearing the kill high upon their shoulders. But many was the time they returned empty-handed.

After one such unsuccessful hunt, Dayn sat by the evening fire of Ulf. Ulf was a good man and a good hunter but reticent, like most men of the village. Dayn felt secure in his presence and trusted him. Tonight, something unusual happened. Ulf spoke first.

"It is strange to me that sometimes we find the animal we seek and kill it," he mused, as if he had read Dayn's very thought, "and sometimes we do not. Yet before every hunt we do the same ritual. Why then do we sometimes please the spirit, and other times we do not? Why is this Dayn?"

It was the first time in Dayn's experience that any of the clan, in particular any of the men of the clan, had asked Dayn a question that began with the word 'why'. His pulse quickened and he thought for a moment.

"I think it is not because of anything that we do, or do not do, to appease the spirit of the animal," Dayn replied thoughtfully. "What if I told you that the success of the hunt has nothing to do with spirits at all, that it only has to do with how well we track the animal and how well we shoot, that it has only to do with our skill?"

Ulf's eyes became round. "This is not a good way to speak of these spirits, Dayn. If you speak like this, they will be offended," he said with great concern. "Besides, I am a good tracker and a good shot. I am always the same. My success has to do with whether the spirit of the animal is willing to let me find him and shoot him, and this depends upon whether or not we have pleased the spirit before we begin the hunt."

"When I lived among the lions, we performed no rituals. If we were hungry, we went hunting. Sometimes we killed and sometimes we did not. But there were no spirits involved, Ulf. The faster, the stronger, the more enduring the lion, the more successful was the hunt."

"But there *were* spirits involved, Dayn. You simply were not aware of them. When the lion kills an auroch it is because the spirit of the auroch allows the spirit of the lion to kill it. When the lion does not kill it is because the spirit of the auroch does not bow to the spirit of the lion. When we perform the ritual imploring the spirit of the animal to allow us to kill, it is so that our chance of success is better. Skill has little to do with it. Permission of the animal spirit has everything to do with it."

"Let us pretend for a moment, Ulf, that there are no animal spirits, that they do not come, that they do not enter into your mind and body before the hunt, and that they cannot lead you to their fellows in the woods," Dayn conjectured. Ulf's brow knitted with concern.

"How can you say this, when all these things *are* true, when they *do* happen?"

"Suppose you went on a hunt without the spirit of the beast within you, without asking its permission to kill it?"

"Then we should fail to kill."

"How do you know this?"

"Because," answered Ulf, "it is true. It is like this." He patted the ground with the palm of his hand. "It always has been."

"Suppose I took you hunting for deer tomorrow morning, without invoking the spirit of the deer, and we shot one. What would happen?" Dayn inquired.

"Then the spirit of the deer would be angry and the deer would go away and we would go hungry."

"But then you agree that we can find a deer and shoot it without the spirit being in us?"

"Perhaps, but the spirit would be offended."

"That may be, but you admit to having just killed a deer without the spirit of the deer being in you. And if you did it once, you could do it again. Have you ever shot a deer without invoking his spirit beforehand?"

"No."

"Then how do you know the spirit would be angry? How do you know the rest of the deer would go away?"

"Because, it is the way things *are*. It is the way things have always been. It is ancient wisdom that has been passed down through the generations. My father told me this, and his father told him. The hunter is only successful when the spirit of the animal comes and joins the spirit of the hunter, within the hunter. The spirit of the hunter is nothing. The spirit of the animal is everything. It is only when the hunter has the permission of the spirit that he can kill. Just as it is in our lives. If we want to do a thing, we must ask the permission of the mothers, and they must give their blessing. If not, and we do that thing anyway, they become angry."

Dayn sighed with frustration. How could he make Ulf see differently, or if not that, at least make him question what he believed? He decided to try another argument.

"Ulf, what makes us different from the animals we hunt?"

Ulf thought for a while before answering.

"We have weapons and they do not, for one."

"And why is that?"

59

"They do not need weapons."

"Why?"

"They have claws and fangs and horns. We have none of these. Therefore we must have weapons for attack and defense."

"Why else do we have these weapons?"

"Because the gods gave them to us."

"Because we had need of weapons then, the gods showed us how to make them?"

"This is true."

"So if we have a need, the gods decree that our need will be met?"

"Not necessarily. If we obey them and follow their ways, then we may trust that our needs will be met. But if we do not, they will abandon us. Then we will die. It is the same with the animal spirit. If we perform the ritual, we trust the animal will allow us to kill it. If not, they will be angry and go away."

"So if we have a need, and we ask the gods to fulfill it, then they may do it, but they may not?"

"It is so. For the gods do not have to do as we ask them."

"Why would they not?"

"Because it is their pleasure. If they always did what we ask of them, then they would not be gods but servants. Sometimes they do not fulfill our needs, so that we may know that they are gods."

"Why, then, do we need such spirits, such gods, such mothers? We must always submit to them, yet they may choose to fulfill our needs or not. If this is so, it seems to me that we need different gods, different mothers, those that will allow us to choose, or none at all!"

"No, no Dayn! Do not speak this way. If we anger them, they will bring havoc upon us. They will turn against us. Without the gods, without the mothers, we will die.

"You say, then, that a man may not defy the gods and live?"

"He may live, but his suffering will be great."

"Perhaps, but perhaps not. Perhaps there is another god, one who would allow us to choose. And perhaps he is stronger than those other gods and would protect us from them."

"Who is this god?"

"I do not know his name, Ulf. But I believe he exists. Will you believe me if I show you that what I say is true, Ulf?"

"I will try. But how can you prove there is another god?"

"I will find a way. It is why I have come here, to this village."

When Dayn returned to his dwelling the night had already swallowed the sun and Moira was upset. He had been gone a long time and she had not known his whereabouts.

"Where have you been, Dayn?" she demanded.

"I have been speaking with Ulf. We hunted today."

"Did you not remember that at sunset we eat and that thereafter each night we must make ritual to Faen? You know that you must be here for that. You know that you are required. Do you want to... to suffer the same fate as Khol?"

"Moira, I cannot explain my negligence except to say... I, ... I do not know what came over me. I know that what you say is true. I know my duties. It will not happen again."

The next morning Dayn was awake before sunrise, planning what he would do following his morning ritual with Moira. As the creeping light revealed the outline of her body beneath the blankets, her head lying upon the pillow next to him, her face, her eyes, the curve of her nose, and the tint of her lips, he reflected upon the events of last evening. Although he had not admitted it, he knew exactly what had happened, exactly why he had been negligent. It was his Otherself. It had completely taken over his mind during the conversation with Ulf and had driven out all else. But he could not say that to her. She would not understand. He hardly understood himself. He would have to be more careful.

After their morning prayers Dayn suggested that he should go hunting with the men. He reassured Moira that the events of the previous day would not be repeated so she gave her consent to his going.

But he did not go hunting with the other men. He went alone. He wanted to shoot a deer and bring it back to Ulf's fireside and tell him how he had done it. He knew very well how to find the animals and stalk them without the aid of these so-called animal spirits. And he wanted to prove to Ulf it could be done without ill effects. He wanted to awaken him. He wanted there to be one other man who could see the things he saw and think the things he thought. He wanted to shine the light, to light the fire of Han-Thol, in the dark recesses of another human brain. For if he could convince Ulf, he could convince others.

The afternoon was growing hot as Dayn stalked the stag and his harem down into a cool glade. Dayn was upwind of them now and the sun was behind him. With the stealth of a lion, he moved around the herd, facing into the wind and sun, fitting an arrow onto his bowstring as he went. He stopped, seeing the rack of the vigilant patriarch rise above the undergrowth where the herd stood. Dayn bent the bow and let his arrow fly. It struck the stag in the shoulder. The herd bolted and Dayn gave chase. The blood of the stag dotted the ground and was easy to follow. The scent of it grew stronger as he ran. There was a scrape where the stag had fallen and had got up to run again. Dayn leaped after him, throwing his whole being into the chase. Now he saw that the stag had separated himself from the herd, leading the hunter away in his last attempt to save them before he expired.

Dayn knew the end was close now. He saw the stag standing, panting and spent, his antlers tangled in the branches of a larch up a slight rise from where he himself stood. Dayn drew an arrow and let the fatal shaft fly. The stag kneeled to the ground, his head in the soft black humus, his back legs still erect. He rolled over with a grunt and was dead. Dayn ran toward him and removed a knife from his belt. He took the stag's head, hoisted it upon his shoulders, and set out for the village.

It was late afternoon when he arrived. He set the trophy behind the oak beside Ulf's door and knocked. Ulf's wife answered. Seeing Dayn, she called her husband, who promptly appeared.

"Come, Ulf, I have something to show you," Dayn said proudly. He led the man to the oak tree and pulled the stag's head from behind it.

Ulf grinned at the sight.

"It is much to have killed so great an animal."

Dayn motioned for Ulf to follow and they walked by the river. Dayn explained what he had done, that he had hunted the beast without the ritualistic invocation of the spirit of the deer. Could Ulf not see now how this was possible, that the spirit of the hunter was stronger than the spirit of the deer?

Ulf was worried and said he was afraid that the deer would leave now. Not only had Dayn killed without the blessing, he had killed one mighty one among the herd, one mighty in stature, mighty in spirit. He would have to talk to the others. He wished Dayn had not done this. Frustrated, Dayn walked back to his own dwelling.

The next day, Ulf came to Dayn, full of concern.

"I have spoken to the elder men of the village about this thing you have done. They are fearful. They say that you must purify yourself and make sacrifice to the Great Deer so that he will not be angry and take the herds away."

Dayn was crestfallen. Afterwards Ulf spoke privately to Moira concerning her bull-headed young husband. Gorn came to know of Dayn's impetuous act and spilled poisoned words into Moira's ears. Dayn noticed that she began to regard him differently. There was a watchfulness in her eyes, as though she were expecting at any moment some wild and aberrant behavior. Thena heard about it as well. Although she avowed concern over what Dayn had done, she secretly delighted in Moira's discomfiture.

The next week Dayn went through the purification rites and made sacrifice to the Great Deer. He did it, not because he believed that it would have any effect on the hunt, but because he did not want to alienate Ulf and the other men. He realized his action had placed an undue burden upon his friendship with Ulf. Ulf would be grieved to think that Dayn had endangered the whole village just to prove a point to him. Removing this burden from his friend was reason enough to go through the purification, but Dayn found another. The killing of the deer, he discovered, had been less a desire to help Ulf see the truth than an arrogant desire by the Otherself to prove itself. For a moment it had taken over. His desire to help his friend was only a veil over what had become his real motive. He had done the right thing, but for the wrong reason. When he went through the rites of purification he did it not to atone for affronting the Great Deer, but to put the Otherself back in its place.

Everyone felt relieved afterwards. Moira seemed calmer and not so curiously anxious. Ulf seemed less tense and Dayn felt he had done the right thing.

Still, deep inside him, his Otherself continued to grow. And the more it grew, the more it pained him to merely follow along, continuing to do things in the traditional way, playing a role as just another member, albeit an exalted one, of this group of submissive men. They were all good men of a sturdy people, but they lacked initiative. He could tell they lacked that sense of the Otherself that he had. He knew they would be content to move forever in the same circle, ever treading the same grain, never shedding the yoke of Faen.

But in Ulf he saw something different. In Ulf, Dayn thought he recognized the tinder that might be ignited by a spark, a spark of the fire of Han-Thol. Even though Ulf's power to reason was almost inert, he was at least willing to listen. And if he would listen, then he would eventually be taught. The others... they could do nothing alone. The clan was everything to them and without the clan they were nothing; no will, no thoughts. Dayn needed Ulf. He needed an outlet for his ideas. He needed someone who would listen, even if Ulf could not completely comprehend. He would surely go crazy if he were not able to communicate with Ulf. How Dayn longed to cultivate the seed of the Otherself he knew was lying dormant there within his friend! Then there would be *one* other. Together, they could share in the vision the others lacked.

Dayn's real problem, however, lay not with Ulf, but with Moira. She was matron of the tradition. She seemed to recognize the seeds of change in him and knew that she would be eager to stamp out the sparks of a new flame. She would maintain the old ways, but at what cost? At the cost of their relationship? Her love for Khol had not stopped him from cutting his own throat, from leaving the Now and uniting with Faen. He wondered what would happen in the event his tie with her was severed; castigation, expulsion from the clan, death?

And of course there was Gorn. Gorn had not liked him from the first day he had arrived. Gorn hated and feared him. Anytime Dayn made a mistake or did something that called attention to his differences from the rest of the clan, the indignant Gorn was there, sowing seeds of mistrust. One day perhaps Gorn would turn Moira and the others against him. What then?

Although he feared this, he feared more to have the fire of his Otherself extinguished. He feared to live a life of frustration. He feared to live a life in which he knew that change must come and find himself without the courage to do what must be done to bring it about. Had Eengla not said that he was the son of Brahan, the bringer of fire? Had she not said that he would bring change, even chaos, to the clan? Had she not said that it was necessary?

On a day near midsummer while Moira was gone from the house, Dayn sought out the Old One again. He found her in her small room, lying down. She appeared to be asleep. He approached her on silent feet and sat down beside her couch of sheepskins. She breathed heavily and unevenly. He sat patiently, not wishing to disturb her. In a few moments she rolled toward him and opened her eyes. A smile curved her ancient mouth, wrinkled up the side of her face, and narrowed her eyes to mere slivers. She reached up with her stiff and shaking hand, wiping some perspiration that had accumulated on her lip.

"Dayn, it is good to see you. It is good that you have come. I feel in my bones today that my time is almost gone. I have felt this before and it has passed. But today the feeling lingers. Soon I must go to the Otherworld. It is good that you have come."

She continued to lie upon her side.

"There are some things I must say to you, some things that you must know, before I am gone. First, you must take the purple cloak. It was I who took it from the white stallion's back so that no one else would get it. It is wrapped up in the black sheepskin at the foot of the bed. But let no one see it, especially Moira. When she sees it she will know that soon her time will be no more. Beyond that, I cannot say what she will do. When she sees it, beware of that which follows.

"You know that you are different Dayn, different from these others. I have heard of some of the things you have done. Ha, ha! They make my old belly shake with laughter! They sometimes seem strange to you, and you wonder why you do them. Strange as they seem to you, stranger still do they seem to those around you. The Otherself that awakens within you, Dayn, will not be denied. You will find that you will continue to challenge the old ways, you cannot help it, it is in your blood and your bones. You will not stop until you have accomplished your purpose. This is your destiny. Your destiny will influence your behavior and your behavior will cause you to stand out from the rest like a black sheep in the flock. Those who stand out from the rest are never safe. You must be watchful. You must protect yourself.

"And now comes the final revelation. You wonder how I know all these things. I wonder that I was chosen to know them, Dayn. I wonder why I was favored to live to see your coming. But it is of no consequence. I am but a messenger and a vessel. If it had not been me, it would have been another. Not so with you Dayn. I have told you that you are the son of Brahan, but I have not told you the rest.

"I am your grandmother. Yes, me, old Eengla! Your mother, Yvanna, was a woman of this village. She and Moira were born at about the same time. When Yvanna came of age, Gorn wanted her to be his woman, but Yvanna refused him. When the time of the matriarch of the village, Lana, had come to go to the Otherworld, she made it known that either Moira or Yvanna would succeed her, but she died before revealing her final decision. A council was held and Moira was chosen. To have his revenge on Yvanna for her rejection, Gorn convinced Moira to banish her from the village, saying there would only be trouble if she stayed. Moira was jealous of Yvanna and was only too glad to agree. She in turn convinced the Council. I was brokenhearted for my daughter and angered at Gorn. But the law says that whosoever takes the life of a woman of the tribe must provide for her family. So, when Yvanna was banished, the council ruled that Moira should be required to take me into her house and support me.

"After Yvanna was turned out of the village, I had many sleepless nights. Night after night I prayed to the gods to keep her safe. Then one night Brahan came to me in a vision. He told me not to be troubled. He told me what had happened and that he was going to set things right. He said that Yvanna would bear him a child. That this child would have a special purpose, a greater purpose than any who had yet been born. But the price for this would be the death of Yvanna, for no one could see his face and live. To lie with him was to be both her blessing and her curse. He said I should be proud that my daughter would be the mother of this child, that bearing this child was enough for anyone to do in a lifetime, and I should not be grieved that she should die because of it.

66

"Then he said he would bring the boy to me, that he would cause him to come to this village. He said that I should know when he came and not to worry. I did not worry, but I lived in high expectation, wondering when the time should come that you would arrive. I was happy when you came. I was happy that you were chosen to live in this house. I was happy that you were chosen to be exalted among all the men of the clan to be the husband of Moira.

"But I fear for you Dayn, I have always feared for you, because I fear Moira. She is too beautiful, too charming, too seductive, too steeped in the traditions of Faen. And because I know your purpose, that you should destroy the old ways of the goddess and bring forth the new wisdom, I fear that you will be brought into conflict with her and with the clan. She knows nothing of that which I have revealed to you, nothing of your parentage. I have not told her because she is dangerous. I cannot see the end of this, but I know that you must beware."

After Eengla had said all these things she was tired and she rested. She asked Dayn to bring her a cup of water and when she had sipped the cool drink, she said one thing more. She motioned for Dayn to bring his head close to hers.

"When the time comes, ride ...the white ...horse." Those were the last words she spoke. Then she slept, a sleep from which she could not be awakened. Dayn was at her side when she died later that afternoon and quietly grieved for her.

He knew that he must do something with the purple cloak before Moira returned. So he took it, still rolled up in his grandmother's black sheepskin and carried it to his room. There he looked about for place to hide it but found nowhere secure. So he went to the house of Ulf. When he spoke with his friend, Dayn told him that he should take this robe, a robe that belonged to his own grandmother, and keep it safe for him. Ulf did not ask any questions. And Dayn knew in his heart that Ulf would keep their secret.

There began a week of mourning for the passing of The Old One, the oldest female member of the clan, and therefore the keeper of many sacred objects. These were passed along to the next oldest mother among them.

Dayn was on the horns of a dilemma. He had come to love Moira, he had joined with her in body and in spirit. But now that the Old One had revealed to him the nature of the relationship between his own mother and Moira, his Otherself

67

spoke out on the matter. How can you, it asked, go on living with this woman? How can you do her bidding, how can you go on pleasing her and being the object of her pleasure, how can you live with *me* within you, and *her* beside you?

This bothered Dayn greatly. It now seemed that his Otherself was plainly set on making trouble. It was getting out of control, developing a will of its own. How was it that this Otherself had grown so strong within him? How was it that it could make him do its bidding? Would it really have the power to destroy his relationship with Moira if it so desired? Would it seek to bring about something so calamitous for him? What would he do? How could he master this other power within him? It seemed impossible that it was there to begin with. He was completely at a loss as to how it would be controlled, if it could be controlled.

On midsummer's day there was yet another ritual to insure the harvest. His Otherself rebelled at going through with it. Dayn could feel its power and the tension it produced within him. He made it through the ceremony but afterwards felt physically ill. He knew this illness was the doing of his Otherself. If it had the power to make him ill, to make him lose the contents of his stomach, what else might it make him do?

As soon as he felt he could walk again, he went to see Ulf.

"Ulf, I have come to ask a favor. I want you to come away with me for a few days. I need to talk to you. I need to talk to someone who can understand me. Now that the Old One has passed, I have this need. Can you do this for me?

Ulf looked at him with misgiving.

"Why do you want to go with me, alone? Anything that we can do together, we can do much better with the others along. If we go alone, then we shall be outside of the protection of the mothers. We might come to harm in that way."

Dayn knew that whenever any of the men went away from the village, they always did so in groups. They felt more comfortable that way. And always their going was sanctioned by the matriarch so they would be under her protection. Dayn also knew that his going away alone had been widely discussed and discredited. Had he not come come back once on the back of an enchanted beast, had he not once killed a deer without

68

making the Ritual of the Hunt, on these unauthorized forays? He knew he was asking much of his friend.

"I know this is an unusual request, Ulf. But I must have some time to think and someone to talk to for a while. The passing of the Old One has affected me in a way I cannot describe to you. I need still to mourn her. That is why I must go away."

Ulf considered his words.

"Let us go to Moira. Let us tell her that we want to build a shrine for the Old One, and that we ask her blessing for this undertaking. Ulf too, misses the Old One, and your idea to mourn for her in a special way is a good one."

"Yes, I agree with you, Ulf, but only if you make the request of Moira."

"It will be as you say," Ulf replied.

Chapter 8
Wild Horses

A week later found Dayn and Ulf prepared to leave the village. They had provisions for a few days and weapons for protection. Dayn asked Ulf to bring the black sheepskin along with him.

Moira was concerned about their going. She did not understand the need for it. She had noticed something different about Dayn recently. He seemed more distant since the Old One's passing. She remembered how ill he had been on midsummer's night. Perhaps he did need to mourn for her. But why could he not do it here, in the village? When she had asked him, he told her that he did not know; that Faen had said he should go away. She had wondered why Faen had not revealed this to her. But if he must go, at least he would be with Ulf. And there was no man in the village more trustworthy than Ulf. She had that comfort at least.

Gorn used this new, unheard of development to sow more discord. Here was yet another example of the wayward eccentricity of this foreigner. He had no place here. This journey would bring evil and sorrow to the clan. Inwardly he hoped that the trip would be fatal. Nothing good could come of two men wandering alone in the wild. Perhaps they would be killed by wild beasts or drowned or fall from a high place. He prayed that they would never return.

Thena, like her mother, did not understand her brother's request. But something within her admired him for it. Something within her always admired the strange, unprecedented, wild, untamed, beautiful things he did. And she loved to listen to him tell her about his adventures, what he was feeling and thinking when he broke tradition. There was a light in his eyes when he spoke of these things and his words fanned the fires of passion within her young heart. Every time he transgressed, she loved him the more for it, even as her uncle hated him the more.

Dayn and Ulf set off down the river. The clan turned out to see them to the limit of their tribal lands. At first the two of them walked along carelessly. They talked as they went and Ulf seemed at ease with their undertaking. But as soon as their conversation ceased, Ulf began to look around nervously.

"We are walking beside the river," he said, pointing out the obvious to Dayn. "How much longer will we walk in this direction?"

"I do not know Ulf. Are you uneasy?"

"This place we are going, where is it?"

"I don't know Ulf. We must follow our instincts."

"Would it not be better to ask a spirit?"

"Which one?"

"Can you talk to Faen? Can she tell you where to go to mourn for the Old One?"

"I do not know, Ulf," Dayn replied. "I do not know if Faen will talk to me."

"Then we should talk to another spirit," Ulf concluded.

"Very well Ulf. Let us leave the road and come to a place where we can talk to the spirits."

They turned to the left off the road and walked into the woods, away from the river. Ulf found a clearing were he felt secure and he sat down. Dayn sat down beside him. A mistle thrush sang overhead.

"Now Ulf, why don't you conjure up a spirit and find a direction for us."

Ulf took some stones out of his crane bag and set them in a circle around the two of them. He sat facing to the north, the direction open to wisdom. He took the drum from off his back and started drumming and chanting. Dayn watched him for a while then sought his own insights. He cleared his mind of every thought and waited patiently for an image. It was not long until the image appeared, quite clear and distinct. It was the image of the white stallion. He saw it running along the beach. He watched, in awe of its speed and strength. He watched it run for a long time, unwilling to let go of the beautiful vision. Then

71

as he watched, the horse stopped running and seemed to approach him, as if he were standing right there on the beach with the marvelous animal. He opened his eyes and there, standing just beyond the circle of Ulf's stones, was Mataforas.

While Ulf was still calling the spirits, Dayn arose. He carefully picked up the sheepskin and unrolled it. He lifted the purple mantle from the bundle and shook it gently out, noticing as he did the subtle play of colors. Hidden among the purple were fleeting shades of emerald and crimson and gold. He walked to where the spotless white animal was standing, shining with a brightness like morning light on new snow, like the glint of sunbeams on the rolling ocean. Dayn put his hand to the horse's muzzle. Mataforas whinnied softly.

Ulf stirred at the sound of the animal. Slowly he came out of his trance, turning to face his companion and the strange visitor. When he comprehended what stood before him he scooted himself to the edge of his circle of stones, as far away from the beast as he could get. His mouth felt dry and he swallowed thickly.

"Do not be afraid, Ulf. This is Mataforas, the horse that brought me back to the village on mid-winter night. He will not hurt you. This," he held out the purple garment toward Ulf, "was given to me by Brahan, my father. It is a magical robe. With it I tamed the stallion."

He took the mantle and threw it over the horse. He grabbed the mane and launched himself onto the broad back, then swung around and straightened up. Ulf's eyes grew wide as he watched. Dayn gently kicked the sides of the great animal and walked him around the circle to where Ulf was sitting.

"Come," said Dayn, and he stretched out his hand and arm to his friend. Ulf stood up, shouldered his pack and looked at the younger man doubtfully.

"Come," Dayn said again. "See how easy it is. Come, I will ask the spirit of the horse to let you ride with me," he said smiling.

Reassured by Dayn's words, Ulf gathered his stones and put them into his crane bag, then placed his hands of the back of the horse. He sprang upward as he had seen Dayn do. Dayn had to grab his leather pants to keep him from falling back. Then Ulf swung his right leg over the stallion's haunches and pulled himself up uncertainly behind Dayn.

"It is far from the ground," Ulf said with a nervous laugh.

72

Dayn laughed too and soon they were on the trail once again, riding downriver in the rustling shade of the water oaks.

"Did the spirits tell you where we should go, Ulf?" Dayn inquired half-mockingly.

"No, Dayn, they never came. I think they were frightened away by this big white horse."

"It is just as well. I think this horse can show us where we should go. Are you willing to let him take us where he will?"

"It is not a natural thing. When we go, we go with a purpose and we tell the mothers. I cannot see this purpose and there are no mothers to give their permission."

"The mothers gave us permission to go where we must go. They did not know where our path would lead. But they gave us their blessing to go."

"Yes, but they gave us permission to go to mourn the Old One, perhaps to build her a shrine. I think we are not going to do this anymore."

"And how can you be so sure of that? I say that we still go to mourn the Old One. I feel that. And I feel this horse will show us how to mourn her best. And if a shrine is to be built, he will show us the place for it."

"Your head is very full Dayn. Sometimes I am afraid it is so full it will burst like an over-ripe melon."

The men rode for another two days, letting the horse take them where he would. They continued down the river. Dayn recognized the subtle change in terrain as they left the hills behind and came to the rolling plain before the sea. Dunes appeared. Dayn could not wait to see Ulf's reaction when at last they came to the ocean.

Ulf was dozing behind him when they arrived, clinging tightly in his dream to Dayn's waist. From inside his head came a new sound, something out of his reckoning. Like a waterfall it was, only rhythmic, undulating, pulsating. Was it the heartbeat of the earth that he heard, or was it the beating of his own heart, the tide of his own lungs? Then, all of a sudden, there came from overhead the cry of a bird, then another. He slowly came to his physical senses, awake yet not awake, so fine was the line between waking and dreaming for Ulf and his kind. He saw gulls wheeling above his head. He saw the glint of light upon

73

the waters, the waves coming ashore. Beneath him and Dayn, Mataforas shifted his weight, jostling him, bringing him an increment closer to consciousness. The stallion grunted tremulously and pawed the sand.

Ulf slid off the back of the tall horse and walked toward the crashing waves. He walked to the edge of the water and felt the cold water wash over his feet. Reaching down with his hand, he made an imprint in the sand. He watched the waters come and fill the little indentation, then retreat and erase it. He waded into the chaotic surf and reached down again, taking a handful of water and bringing it to his lips. When he tasted the brine he spat and turned to face Dayn. He gazed for a time at the young man seated upon the white horse, then walked back up the beach toward him. Taking the horse's muzzle in his hands, he stroked it, feeling as if for the first time its softness, its warmth, its life. He raised his eyes and looked at Dayn, then eastward into the hills.

"Ulf cannot go back," he half-whispered. Dayn scarcely heard his words above the din of the grinding waves.

Dayn dismounted and pulled the purple mantle from the horse, throwing it around Ulf's shoulders, and led his friend further back up the beach. They climbed to the top of one of the dunes and sat surveying the broad expanse of the sea. There were tears in Ulf's eyes.

"What is out there, beyond the bitter waters?" Ulf asked finally.

"I do not know, Ulf. Perhaps there is much."

"How much do you know, Dayn? How much is revealed to you that is hidden from me?"

"Nothing is revealed to me that is not revealed to you, Ulf. To each the same is revealed. It is what is inside us that is different, our ability to see what is. There are things you can see, Ulf, that I cannot see. You can see into the misty realm of the spirit. In that world my vision is dim and weak. But there is another world, Ulf. This ocean is part of it, this horse is part of it. In this other world, in the Now of my Otherself, I can think thoughts that are a mystery to you. I can venture from the confines of the village without fear. I can take the initiative to do things on my own, a thing that seems so foreign to you. Yet I know that you possess the ability to think these thoughts, to do these things, to break tradition with the past and step with me into the future. I long for you to see the world the way I do, to see the Now through the eyes of the Otherself."

"Perhaps Ulf is ready to go with you."

They sat long gazing at the heaving ocean. The afternoon was advanced when Ulf realized the stallion had wandered off. He made remark of it to Dayn, who said he had noticed it earlier.

"Do not be concerned, my friend," he reassured Ulf. "Mataforas will return."

Later, Ulf hunted and brought back a large bird that walked upon the ground. They built a fire on the beach, cooked the bird, and ate their fill of it. Its flesh was delicious and the juice of it ran down their fingers past their wrists and dripped from their elbows. They laughed as they ate.

Although the day had been warm, a breeze arose to chill the night air. Dayn went to gather wood that lay everywhere scattered upon the beach, bringing it back and tossing it onto the glowing embers of the cooking fire. Soon the fire blazed again and they huddled next to it for warmth. Here, upon the western shore, the light of the long day lingered. They lay back to look up at the stars, pointing out to one another the shapes they saw. In a few moments they were both asleep, Ulf with the purple cloak still about his shoulders.

That night Ulf dreamed that a man, a man dressed in fine clothes and bearing the finest of weapons, came to the edge of the waters and found him lying there. The fine man carried a shield, broad and high. It was square at the top and came to a point at the bottom. The man led him to the water's edge and asked him if he would like to float upon the waters, to see what lay beyond. Ulf said that he would, so the man laid down the shield upon the waters and Ulf found that it floated. Ulf had never seen such a thing before; it curved upwards on the edges and was cupped in the middle. It separated the sky and the waters and looked like a large leaf that had fallen onto the surface of a lake. It amazed him. The man motioned for him to get in and he did, the boat rocking unsteadily upon the waves. The man gave the boat a push and soon Ulf floated alone upon the undulating surface of the moonlit waters.

He placed his hand into the sea and wondered what could be down there. He climbed out of the boat and slipped into the ocean. He found that he floated easily but nonetheless held on for a time to the side of his little craft. He put his head into the waters and peered downward. More curious now, but still confounded by the opaque sea, he allowed himself to sink.

75

Beneath him all was dark. Above him he saw the shining bottom of his little boat becoming smaller and more dim as the waters enveloped him.

As he sank he felt that he was not alone, that out in the waters shapes were swimming, watching. His feet hit the sandy bottom. The light was very dim. He saw the ominous shapes swimming just beyond his ability to discern them.

Suddenly a great fish approached, looming onto the little sandy strand where he stood, beaching its immense head. It was a fish like no other he had ever seen. It had a broad, flat head and a wide mouth. From its lips, flowing in the currents, were tentacles that resembled the whiskers of a cat. He spoke to the fish.

"Who are you."

"I am a fish, can you not see? I have fins and a tail, can you not see them?"

Ulf looked down the side of the great fish, whose sleek flank receded in to the blackness of the waters. Nearby, the fish's pectoral fin fluttered. Further back in the blackness, he could barely make out the fins at the tip of the powerful tail.

"What can you do for me?" Ulf asked.

"I can show you visions," the fish replied. "Come inside," it said, and opened its mouth wide. Ulf saw that the mouth was so large he could walk upright into it. He stepped forward, placing his foot upon the lower jaw, which was like a step, only rough, with small saw-like projections. He stepped again and entered the mouth, then walked down the passage of the gullet and entered the fish's belly, where he sat down. He looked up at the wall of the belly. It looked like the wall of an ancient cave, like the ones he had seen with animals painted on them not far from the village, relics from the days before Faen had come.

As he watched, pictures appeared. First, on the left hand side was a bean. The bean split in half and became a pair of human ears, above and to the right of where the bean had been. Lower down, close to the bottom of the wall and to the left, a chameleon appeared. Then on the upper right hand corner of the wall came the shining shape of his little boat. The bright image of the boat changed and became a weapon, a knife, or perhaps a plow, a cutting tool. Then there were no more pictures. He sat for a while, awaiting more. At length, when none came, he got up and walked toward the mouth of the fish. It opened and he stepped back onto the sandy bottom of the ocean.

"Well?" questioned the great mouth. "Did you find what you sought?"

"I saw pictures," Ulf replied.

"Then take them with you," the great fish replied. It closed its mouth and turned. Ulf watched the sleek body, amazed when the great tail flicked and propelled the fish, with the swiftness of a heartbeat, into the blackness. In that heartbeat it was gone. He looked up and saw a pinpoint of light above him. Thinking it to be the boat he swam upwards toward it, but as he approached and it became no bigger, he thought it might be a star instead. Other stars joined it in the heavens. He opened his eyes and realized that he lay upon the beach, still wrapped in the purple cloak. The fire had all but gone out. Above him the vastness of the heavens was brimming with stars. He had never imagined the sky to be so big, the ocean so vast, the world so wide. Then he drifted back into sleep.

He awoke as the sun paled the stars and suffused the eastern sky with an orange light. He rolled over and called to Dayn who rubbed his eyes and sat up. Dayn laughed when he saw the ocean. Ulf laughed with him. They laughed uncontrollably until they thought their sides would burst. They wept, then they laughed and wept together, finding emotions they could not explain erupting from deep within. When these strange emotions had passed they were hungry. Ulf unwrapped the remainder of last evening's supper from his deerskin wallet and they ate a cold breakfast. The sun rose bright and hot above the hills and warmed their backs. It was good to be here, together.

Mataforas came running down the beach. He pranced into the surf before them and whinnied. He stood on his hind legs and pawed the air then plunged into the waves and began to swim. The waters closed over him, all save his magnificent head, weaving him on a watery loom into the fabric of the deep. The foam washed the glassy, rolling surface of his back. His head disappeared momentarily, covered by a formidable wave. Then it reappeared, somewhat further out to sea. Very soon the two men on the beach could not see the white flag of his flying mane in the breaking of the surf. Ulf looked at Dayn, whose eyes were locked upon the place where he last saw the swimming animal.

77

For a long time they stood, Dayn unwilling to look away, Ulf growing restless at his side, when suddenly Dayn pointed oceanward.

"There he is!" he cried.

Sure enough, the pearly head of the horse was there again, this time swimming back toward the beach.

"Look!" Ulf cried, pointing toward the horse. "There is another, and another!"

From out of the deep there appeared the heads of many horses now, swimming strongly alongside Mataforas, coming ashore with him. To Dayn, straining his eyes to see what Ulf saw, there appeared to be only the head of the white stallion, surrounded by the plunging, rearing, tossing surf. But to Ulf, the heads of the rest of the herd were clearly visible. Presently the hooves of the stallion struck the beach and he emerged from the sea. Behind them came the others. Dayn could see them now as they rose, rank upon rank, from the charging flood. Mataforas turned and ran down the beach. The others followed. They disappeared around a rocky headland, a looming dark shape like an immense haystack, then came charging back towards Dayn and Ulf.

Mataforas led the herd toward the two men at a slow trot. The horses came on, surrounding them, enveloping them in their midst, milling about them playfully, unheeding or uncaring that the two were there at all.

"Ulf," Dayn said, his voice quivering with excitement, "Mataforas has brought us this herd. He is making a gift of these horses to us."

Ulf was too amazed to speak. Dayn took the cloak from around Ulf's shoulders and flung it upon the back of the stallion. He pulled himself up onto the whitewashed back. Ulf walked through the herd until he found a dusty gray horse to his liking. He grabbed its mane and swung up upon its back, then pirouetted around to find Dayn. He rode the gray through the unraveling knot of horses toward his companion, laughing once again. Dayn kicked the stallion and took off up the beach at a gallop. Ulf was on his heels, followed by the rest of the herd. They thundered among the dunes. Soft clods of damp sand thrown up by the hooves of the herd struck their faces, arms and legs. They rode for the pure pleasure of feeling the pumping muscles of the horses beneath them and the hammering joy of the herd around them. They rode with abandon, heedless of

78

direction or distance. They rode until they were exhausted, until the herd was spent.

Finally coming to a halt, Ulf fell ineptly from the gray, landing in an exploding spray of sand. He got to his knees a little stunned, a fine layer of sand pasted to his skin with perspiration, his jet black hair dusted with the white powder. He spit sand from his mouth then threw back his head and laughed, uninhibited. Dayn saw him fall and sit up and was caught once again in the contagion of his laughter. Never had the two men experienced such unmitigated joy. They were alone, to their delight, in the world; no goddesses, no mothers, no permission asked, no permission granted, no transgressions, no repercussions.

Ulf got up and wobbled toward the ocean. He waded in up to his knees and dove in. He tried to swim but the waves pushed him landward, grounded him, rolled him over several times, then deposited him unceremoniously onto the beach. He got up dizzily, fighting to maintain his feet in the retreating surf. Doused by a wave, he fell down comically on his backside . He got onto his hands and knees and crawled into the warm, dry sand where he collapsed, laughing, face down.

Dayn came down to join him.

"Do you think we have mourned the Old One long enough?" he asked.

Ulf howled with laughter. He shook so that he had trouble getting his breath.

Dayn smiled.

"It is... it is not... proper... to treat... the mothers... so lightly!" Ulf blurted out between desperate gulpings for air.

"I do not treat it lightly, Ulf. You only take it lightly. The Old One, before she died, she told me something. She told me she was my grandmother. She is the one who sent me off the first time, before Khol was sacrificed, before I came back to the village astride this stallion. She told me that I must go, that I would find the horse and tame him. She told me to come back before sunset on the day of sacrifice. But I did not arrive in time to save Khol.

"This thing we have done, to find the white horse again, to find this herd, to experience this thing we have experienced; this we have done to honor her. In this way we have mourned her, and have built our shrine to her; she, who foretold the vision of a new world."

79

Ulf stopped laughing and caught his breath.

"This thing that you have said, say it again, for the words have passed through me like a wind through the trees."

Dayn collected his thoughts and repeated to Ulf all that his grandmother had told him, the story of his life; about Yvanna, his mother, about Brahan prophesying to The Old One of his coming, about his life among the lions, about his dream of the young lion devouring the goddess and the Old One's interpretation of it, of the gift of the purple cloak from his father Brahan, and the taming of the white stallion. And finally he returned to the point at which he and Ulf left the village and found the white horse and tamed the herd. This then, this celebration, was their tribute to the Old One.

Ulf sat silently and listened. He did not understand it all, but he heard and learned and understood enough. This boy, Dayn, had been given a gift and a challenge, and he, Ulf, had been chosen to go with him. A new life awaited him, a new life awaited them both, filled with promise and danger, hope and fear. He knew that turning back was impossible. Dayn had planted a seed within him, he had cultivated and watered it. And now that they had tamed the herd and ridden the horses on the beach, a blossom had appeared upon the vine, the flower of Ulf's Otherself, the opening of his infant consciousness.

Chapter 9
The Dream

Dayn and Ulf rode the long miles back to the village, playfully, not knowing and not caring what consequences might have to be faced when they returned. With them they brought the herd, some thirty in number. Up beside the Cyryn they rode, leaving first the dunes, then the broken plain, before entering the familiar forest. Ulf saw these old surroundings with new eyes. His sight was clearer, less misty. He talked and laughed with Dayn as he rode. Upon the gray horse Laeticia Ulf rode, for thus he had named her; Laeticia, the bountiful heart of joy.

Around noon they stopped to eat. They dismounted and Dayn spoke to Mataforas and stroked his muzzle. Ulf opened the deerskin wallet and spread the last of the meat before them on the ground. Mataforas led the herd off to find grass to eat and dust to roll in.

Ulf was quiet and ate as if he were in deep thought. Dayn noticed the change and approved of it. Whereas Ulf might before have seemed dreamy and dull, he now appeared intense. But his intensity was directed somewhere far from where the two of them sat eating their meal.

Momentarily Dayn spoke.

"Ulf," he called to his friend. Ulf was frowning. This was new as well. Ulf never frowned. "Is something wrong?" Dayn continued.

A moment passed before Ulf spoke.

"I am remembering something that happened to me when we slept on the dunes. A very strange thing. Nothing like it has ever happened to me before. It was like a trance, like being possessed by the spirit of an animal, but not like that either. I have no word for it. It was... like... like being awake but still being asleep."

"What happened?" Dayn asked with intense interest.

"A man came to me while I lay on the beach; a man with fine clothes and the finest weapons. He carried a shield, but unlike any shield I have ever seen. It was not made of hides but of metal like a sword. It was very large, square at the top and pointed at the bottom. I followed him to the ocean where he turned the shield over and laid it on the water. He asked me if I wanted to know what was out there. I said yes and he sat me down on the metal shield and pushed me out onto the water. I felt something I had never felt before, I don't know how to describe it. It was like being surprised by a boar in the woods with no weapon. But not just that. It was also a feeling like when you ask me why. Then I want to know. So this feeling is like wanting to know, but being afraid of knowing."

"Yes," Dayn exclaimed, "I know what you are saying. I have had that same feeling before too! Go on."

"I climbed off the shield and got into the water and sank right down to the bottom. At first I was afraid I would drown but found that I could breathe underwater! I stood on the bottom with the water all around me. Then the head of a gigantic fish appeared. It told me it could show me visions if I came inside. So I walked into its mouth and sat down in its belly. Inside the fish's belly was a wall and on the wall I saw pictures."

"What did the pictures tell you?" Dayn asked, his curiosity growing.

"The pictures were very strange. They appeared and disappeared, like a herd of deer moving through a thicket. They danced and changed.

"First there was a seed. Then it split in two and became like ears, but there was no head between the ears. Then there was a chameleon, then my boat, ...or the shield of the fine man. The shield became a short sword or a knife. I could make no sense of the pictures whatsoever. I left the belly of the fish and swam back to the surface. I thought I saw the shield riding there but it turned out to be a star, then more stars appeared and I found myself lying back on the beach. But I hadn't been anywhere! I was not wet! I did not smell like a fish! I am certain I never left your side!"

When he had finished, Ulf sank back into the depths of his thought. But Dayn did not let him rest for long.

"This vision you had. I think it is like... like what I tried to explain before to you. Do you remember when I told you that once while I slept I saw the symbol of Faen and the symbol of Brahan. And the symbol of Faen turned into Moira and the symbol for Brahan turned into a young lion? And the young lion strode across the page and devoured Moira?"

"Yes, I remember. You said it was a vision from inside your head."

"Yes, Ulf, and the Old One told me what it meant. Your vision means something as well. But who will tell us what it means? The Old One is dead."

The two men had gone as far as their immature logic could take them and they ate the rest of their meal in silence. When they had finished, Dayn gave a long, low whistle and Mataforas reappeared, bringing the herd along. Dayn and Ulf mounted, turning their faces once again to the village and away from the westing sun. They rode, more subdued than in the morning, with thoughts hanging like weights inside their heads.

That night they slept in the trees. It was chilly and Dayn drew the purple cloak of Brahan about him. He lay like a big cat, his torso and head on a great horizontal limb, his arms and legs dangling off either side. Before he slept he turned the vision of Ulf over and over in his mind; a seed, ears, a chameleon, a shield and knife. None of it seemed to fit together. He turned his head and lay his other cheek against the itchy bark. Finally, when his thoughts had come and gone, and come and gone again, Dayn drifted into sleep.

In the night Dayn thought he heard something shuffling about under the tree. He opened his eyes and peered down but nothing was there. He returned to his sleep. Later he heard the noise again and again he awoke. Once more he looked but nothing was there. He was determined not to let the night noise arouse him a third time.

And indeed he did not. The next time he heard the noise, he heard it not with his ears. He heard it, shuffling footsteps, grunting breaths, inside his head. The Old One came stooping along and sat beside him on the limb where he lay. He looked at her and she laughed. Dayn laughed too. Then she took the sticks from the pouch at her waist, as Dayn had often seen her do, and cast them down in her lap.

83

"The seed is the infant Otherself within Ulf." She picked up the sticks and threw them again, examining their pattern intently, her face close to them. Raising her head, she spoke again. "The ears... the ears are the cultivators of the seed, of the new self. They will hear, and they will interpret in new ways, and send images to the new self."

She picked up the sticks and cast them a third time, bending over them inquisitively, and looked at them long before raising up again. "The chameleon is a hider, a changer of color, a secret. In the village the chameleon may look like any ordinary man. But the new thoughts are still there, hidden, waiting." Satisfied with her pronouncements, Eengla pushed herself up and began to walk away. Dayn jumped up and followed her, catching her by the arm and turning her, with difficulty, to face him.

"What about the shield, the shield that becomes a sword? You have not revealed the meaning of the final part of the vision," Dayn said anxiously.

The old woman's face twitched and she looked at Dayn from beneath bristling eyebrows and the sagging folds of skin that formed her eyelids. "Are you so dull, Dayn? The shield is that which protects, the sword that which kills. That which protects may turn against you. The chameleon will be cut open and the seed inside dragged out and killed, unless, unless..." And she disappeared.

Dayn awoke to the scream of a lion in the distance. From below, Mataforas whinnied restively. Laeticia and the rest of the herd milled about. A thin dawn crept into the eastern sky. Dayn sat up and pulled the cloak around his arms and legs, chilled in the last hour of the night. He jumped from the tree and landed on the ground beneath it, crunching the dry leaves and last year's brittle acorns. He called Ulf. Together they walked to the river and splashed water on their faces to remove the sleep and oils of the oak bark. The herd moved down for a drink, following their new masters.

Light filtered through the tops of the trees. Dayn and Ulf swung up on their horses and led the herd along the path beside the river. The vision of the Old One returned to Dayn as he rode. He pondered it but did not yet mention it to Ulf. There was still a missing piece, something he did not yet understand. About midmorning they got hungry. Ulf spoke of it first. They brought the herd to a halt and slid from their mounts. Dayn

Dayn's eyes narrowed. "What then of these horses, Ulf? What of this herd? Are they a lie, are they a vision? No, I tell you they are not!"

"They came out of the sea," Ulf rejoined.

"They are flesh and blood, Ulf. We call and they come, we mount them and ride, we feel the muscles of their backs here in our groin. My father gave me this cloak," he said, holding the rich purple mantle in the face of his companion. "Is this, too, a lie? He showed me how to use it to tame the stallion. Is the white horse a vision? Watch and listen."

Dayn whistled. From far away the stallion whinnied and in a few moments trotted up, pressing his muzzle against Ulf's chest as if he understood the point Dayn wanted to make.

"*I* tamed this horse, this flesh and blood horse, Ulf! *I am* the son of Brahan, the bringer of fire!

Ulf lowered his chin to his chest. "It is as you say, Dayn," he muttered in resignation. "But what will we do?"

"Let us go our own way. We will find others to join us. We will find our own path. We will take what the earth has to give us. What need have we of villages full of mothers, of mysteries that cause us to cut our throats for the good of the tribe? Let the mothers cut their own throats if that is what they wish! We have no need of them!"

"You can give up Moira so easily, Dayn? You can give up her companionship and her times of willingness? It all comes together, Dayn, in one body. You can have her, but with her comes the obligation. It is all one package. Without the obligation, without obeying, there is nothing else. Without the one, you can not have the other."

"Perhaps, and perhaps not. Could I not take her away from the village? Would she not be dependent on me then? Could I not bend her to my will?"

"Perhaps, but you might as well have a slave. And who could be content for long with only a slave at his side?"

Dayn turned away from Ulf. Why should he continue to argue? It was futile. Ulf would not come with him. He could go away with Ulf, but he did not think he could go alone, not yet, perhaps not ever. He recalled with disquieting clarity how lonely he had been before Ulf had been awakened. He thought now about what Ulf's friendship meant to him. They were two islands that had emerged alone from deep ocean. All around, in every direction, was only the crashing roll of bitter waves.

87

Ulf had shouldered the deer and was headed back toward the river. Dayn ran to him, grasping his wrist, and stopped him.

"I will return with you to the village, Ulf. But you must promise me this. That whatever happens, you are my friend and I am yours. I will be at your side in any trouble, and I will stand with you, no matter if it means my life. Will you promise me the same?"

Ulf looked into Dayn's searching eyes.

"I do promise this thing to you." A smile forced Dayn's lips apart and he followed Ulf down the hill.

Chapter 10
Brahan Speaks

It was late afternoon of the following day when Dayn and Ulf came to the outskirts of the village. The sun, burning brightly, threw their shadows far up the road before them. The first thing they saw was Dag, a sheep herder of the village, driving his flock to new pasture. What Dag saw on the other hand, was a vision, a vision of a great wind. The wind raised a mighty dust before it and in its midst was a hundred-headed beast. Mounted on the beast were two blackened men. He threw down his herding stick in terror and ran wildly into the village, shouting as he went.

The two riders came slowly on, too tired to care what might come of Dag's flight. Drawing closer they heard more shouting and were met by the hunters of the village, led by Gorn, who challenged them in the road.

"Stop!" shouted Gorn. Looking into the sunlight and dust he could not himself determine who, or what, was coming. He leveled his bow at one of the figures he made out to be a man.

"Gorn," shouted Ulf above the melee, "put down your weapon. It is Ulf and Dayn. We have returned."

Gorn angled his bow downward at the sound of Ulf's voice, then raised it once again. He aimed it now at Dayn. His fingertips trembled at the thought of letting the arrow fly and ending the life of his hated rival then and there. Another voice called his name. It was Moira's.

"Gorn, what is it?"

Still trembling with the bowstring pulled to his cheek, he answered her. "It is Ulf, and Dayn," he said hesitantly, the last

89

name tasting bitter as he spat it from his lips.

Moira came to his side, quickly sizing up the situation. "Put it away, Gorn!" she demanded and reached with her outstretched arm, pushing Gorn's bow off its mark, but never taking her eye off Dayn.

"What is the meaning of this, Dayn?" she demanded yet again. "Why have you returned thus?"

"I found the white stallion, though I was not seeking him when I departed. It was not my intent to find him. But so it happened. He had with him this herd of steeds. Ulf learned to ride. We brought them home, thinking they might be useful to the village," the young man replied.

"Useful? What possible use could these beasts be to us? They will do naught but consume our stores of grain and trample our livestock and children. Away with them!" Gorn shouted.

Dayn, challenged by the insults of Gorn, kicked Mataforas' flanks and walked him forward to tower above the man. Intimidated, Gorn shrank back.

Dayn dismounted, pulling the purple cloak about his shoulders, and stepped, face to face, chest to chest, in front of Gorn, taunting him. He set his jaw and was about to say something when Moira wedged herself between them.

"Gorn, take the hunters and go, now!" she said through clenched teeth, staring Dayn in the eye and never looking away.

"Dayn, go inside," she added, her teeth still set, but with a rounder voice.

When Dayn had gone Moira looked at Ulf, questioning his loyalty without words. Ulf returned her gaze, feeling suddenly impotent and uncertain. Moira had that effect on them all. Haltingly, he slid from the back of Laeticia.

"Do something with these," she said to him at last, indicating the herd with a sweep of her arm, and strode off to her lodging, following Dayn.

That night Moira knew she must speak to her young husband. She knew the time had come to take action, but she did not know what that action would be. Part of her wanted to plead with him to change, but that would be improper. Another part was irate that his continual disregard for custom was undermining her judgment in choosing him as her consort in the eyes of the people; there had been an element from the beginning that had doubted the wisdom of it. Another part of her was simply in awe of him, how different he was, how utterly unlike

90

the others, how utterly impossible to control. No other men in the village were interested in or capable of doing the things Dayn did. She could not fathom it. He was formed completely out of another mold. *Perhaps it is the lion in him,* she thought.

There was silence around the low eating table that night and Dayn had little appetite. Gorn, who always ate like a starving wolf, but with fewer manners, scowled at Dayn through most of the meal. Moira kept her eyes averted, focused down on her plate. Thena watched them all with a tense anticipation.

Without speaking and before he had finished, Dayn got up and retired to the bedchamber he shared with Moira. The hallway was dark and he made his way forward by feeling for the walls, the soft tufts of the sheepskin that lined them running beneath his fingers as he went. At last he felt the rough wooden doorposts of their room and walked through. He lit the single candle in the copper lamp that hung from the ceiling in the center of the room, and threw himself onto the low bed with a thud.

Moira came in and stood before him, her back to the lamp so that her shadowed features were indistinguishable to Dayn.

"Dayn, I must talk to you," she said sternly.

"Then speak," he replied evenly. "I am listening."

"Your actions disturb me, Dayn. They disturb everyone. How can you be my husband, how can you be what you need to be to these people, when you act outside the bounds of custom? To guarantee the prosperity of this clan is your purpose, Dayn. It is your only purpose. Have I not taught you that?"

"Yes, Moira, you have made that clear."

"Is it then, your intent to do this?"

"Yes, it is my intent."

"Then you must promise me that you will repurify yourself, your mind and your body, and rededicate yourself to the service of Faen."

Dayn balked.

"Tell me, Moira, have the vineyards failed to produce grapes, has the wheat failed to yield grain, have the ewes failed to throw lambs, since I have been your husband?"

"No," she said with some reluctance.

"If my sole purpose for living is to insure that things are as they should be, that our people prosper, and these things are so, then have I offended Faen? Have I failed to serve her well? Or is it you I have failed?

Moira breathed an exasperated sigh.

"Dayn, you cannot ...there are both things you must do and things from which you must refrain in order to serve the goddess. She demands them all, not just one or two. She demands all of you, not just pieces of you. Perhaps her face is turned away just now. But when she turns back, she will know that things are not right. She will know that you have strayed from the path. She will know that I have allowed you to stray. She will know that I have not been the proper mother to our people and she will seek to put things right. We cannot stand before her wrath, Dayn. She will have her way."

"Moira, there are so many rules. Can they all be so important?"

"Can you be a man and ask such a question? Dayn, the mark of a true man is that he obeys. He obeys with a joy that comes from serving the goddess and the mothers. He serves from the memory of life before the goddess, when we were homeless wanderers. These things we owe to her. If not for her we would be hopeless. She is everything. Does that thought not make you wish to gratefully obey her dictates? "

Dayn blew out a long breath and pulled at the dark wool of the sheepskin beneath him.

"Moira, I will promise you that I will repurify myself to the service of the goddess. I will do it for you and for the good of the people."

Moira sat down beside him, not sure she had really heard these last words. She looked at him with pursed lips, disbelief hollowing her cheeks. Dayn looked back at her and smiled, the coyest of smiles. Moira relaxed the muscles of her face and a smile broadened her own mouth.

That night Moira took Dayn once again through the rites of purification of the goddess. This done, she anointed him with water and with fragrant oil and brought him to her bed. In the next room Gorn could not sleep. His anger for Dayn grew by the moment, and with each sound that emanated from his sister's room. On the other side, Thena thanked the goddess that Dayn had returned. She had heard that he returned upon the white stallion and her awe of him grew yet greater. She could not wait to talk to him privately, to tell him of her feelings.

92

The next two months passed uneventfully. Dayn behaved like a true man, obeying the customs of the tribe to Moira's great satisfaction and relief. His capitulation galled Gorn all the more. There was nothing this upstart could not get away with, he fumed. Moira began to feel a sickness in the morning of each day and went to the eldest mother to seek her advice. When the eldest examined her, she found that Moira was bearing a child, Dayn's child. The marriage was blessed. Now the village could look forward to many years of prosperity. All were pleased with this news and looked forward to an autumn of plenty.

That was before the hail came. Tall, dark clouds loomed out of the west in the afternoon sky. The day had been hot and still, but now a sudden wind swept through the village from the east. The clanspeople stopped and looked expectantly in that direction. One by one they pointed to the sky, inky black on the horizon, boiling blue just above the tree tops. The swollen gray-white pustules of the thunderheads, filled to bursting with violence, tilted ominously over all. The heavens spoke and their voice echoed back from the river valley. The forest inhabitants pricked up their ears as one and headed for the deepest glades.

Moira ran to the hut of the eldest and gave her some hurried instructions. Then she grabbed Dayn by the hand and led him inside their own house, all the while fearfully looking at the sky. She took him to the small altar where she started a fire and recited an prayer. While they invoked the protection of Faen for their crops and livestock a barefoot girl entered carrying a cup of fresh goat's blood. Moira dipped her fingers in it and sprinkled it onto the fire. The blood sizzled and sent up a white smoke. Moira dipped her hand in a basin of water next to the altar, wiped it off on a towel and continued to chant.

Dayn heard the first hailstones hit the walls of the house and the ground outside. It was like the sound of arrows whooshing through the air and hitting their target with a dull, penetrating thud; the sound of doom, the sound of death. He ran to the door and pushed it aside. The air was thick with hailstones the size of a ram's eye. Not even the next house was visible in the downpour. The stones came whistling down, zipping through the vegetation of the trees overhead. Small limbs already littered the ground and slices of mutilated leaves drifted down as well, imparting a sickening green hue to the air. Dayn knew that the wheat, just beginning to make a head, would not survive. The crop would be ruined. He swallowed hard, knowing in an

93

instant what it all portended. *Khol!*

Then as suddenly as it had started, the hail stopped. The ground was white as though it were mid-winter. Then the rains came. Dayn had never seen it rain so hard. Muddy rivulets instantly formed in the road beside the house joining themselves into a rushing stream, washing away the softer soil and leaving only the hard packed ruts worn by generations of calloused feet.

In half an hour, this too had passed, and the sun came out strong and bright, as if to reveal the destruction to the greatest possible extent. Dayn walked out to inspect the wheat fields. Gorn was already there. The crop was in shreds. Only here and there was a green stalk left standing. Gorn sneered as he passed by the despondent Dayn, who seemed not even to notice him. *He will notice soon enough*, thought Gorn, and headed back to the village. He welcomed with perverse joy the foulness he felt in his heart for the too fortunate Dayn. He began to plan his speech, on behalf of the people, to the Council.

Thena ran everywhere looking Dayn, for she too knew what the disaster might mean. She found him walking aimlessly through the decimated fields.

"Dayn, oh Dayn!" she called to him, taking his arm and pressing herself close to him. "It need not be. It need not happen. I will not let it. I will never let them sacrifice you!"

Dayn stopped walking and looked at the girl. Over the last year he had grown taller than she. But she had lost her girlish features as she had begun her journey into womanhood.

"What can you do, Thena? What can anyone do? The best thing for you is to go and forget about me. If they see us together there will be trouble," he said, glancing nervously about. "I have trouble enough. There is no need for you to get involved."

"But I want to be involved. I love you, Dayn, and I will not let them have you."

"Do not fear that, Thena, for I do not intend to die head-down on that cursed pole."

"What is your plan then? How do you intend to escape it?" Thena asked excitedly.

"I do not know, yet."

"Are you going away? Will you ride away on the white stallion? If you do, you must take me with you. Promise me!"

"I cannot make such promises, Thena, for I cannot yet see the road I must travel. Go now!"

94

That night the Council met in the middle of the village where the round Council Lodge stood. The Lodge was roughly a hundred feet in diameter. Heavy timbers had been placed in the ground ten feet apart in an outer circle, joined at the top by other poles of lesser girth. About twenty feet inside the outer circle was another. Here stood yet heavier timbers, taller than those of the outer circle and also joined at the top. Inside this circle was another, with still taller upright timbers. At the very center of all the circles stood an immense pole, as thick as a man was tall, rising to a great height and buried to a depth a third that height in the ground. An image of the goddess had been carved in a section of this pole, decorated with rough gems and hammered copper. A thick layer of thatch covered the entire roof and multiple thicknesses of sheepskin covered the outer walls so that the interior was dry, if not always warm in the winter or cool in the summer. Fires could be lit in the winter however, and there were vents in the roof for smoke to escape. The hides which formed the walls could be raised to admit a breeze in the summer. It was cool this evening and the hides hung to the ground.

The elder matriarchs sat in an arc around the outer wall, facing north. The people were gathered facing them, in family groups, sitting on woolen rugs and thick hides.

Gorn stood to bring his complaint, dressed in his best clothes. His thin red hair lay close against the sun-mottled skin of his head. Faen was there too. More than a carven image, she lived and breathed through Gorn and the matriarchs. Her spirit moved among them and through them, guiding their limbs and lips. Judgment day had arrived for Dayn and she pulled the strings of the actors arrayed upon her stage. Gorn began.

"Mothers, daughters of Faen, with your permission, a faithful son of the clan, Gorn, stands before you tonight. He comes to weep for the harvest. He comes to weep for the people. He comes to make known to all assembled the reason this great calamity has befallen us. The reason for our undoing is this man." He extended his arm and pointed a bony finger at Dayn who sat at the end of the arc of matriarchs with Moira at his side.

"This man came to us out of the wild, he is not of our

95

people, he is not of our custom or our belief. Yet he was chosen upon the sacrifice of Khol to be the Wine of the Harvest by my sister, Moira, the priestess of Faen. A poor decision it turns out.

"This man has continually chosen to flout the traditions of our clan and the dictates of Faen. As such, he cannot fail to be the cause of the divine retribution we witnessed earlier in the day.

"This man has gone wandering alone in the wild, without permission of the mothers. He hunts without invoking the spirit of the animals he hunts. He has gone to distant places and returned with wild beasts, horses he calls them, who have no place in the natural order of the world and who are dangerous and alarming to our people. He speaks when he should be silent. He disobeys when he should obey, like all good men. In short, he breaks all the rules. There is not one good reason he should be in this position of favor among us."

Moira stood.

"Yes, there is one good reason, Gorn. I chose him. That is the duty and the prerogative of the priestess of Faen. He was chosen for his spiritual qualities. He was chosen because Faen chose him through me."

"That can only mean that Faen disfavors you as well, for this man is an unwise choice. It is proved by the ruin of our crops. There need be no other proof."

"The affair of the crop is a trivial thing. We have had good harvests for three years now and there is ample grain to get us through the winter. There is a greater good to be considered. Our union has been blessed with the prospect of a child. Faen would not have honored us thus if she were not happy with my choice of husband." She looked back at Gorn with no little show of contempt.

"It is exactly this union and this child that lies at the heart of all our distress," Gorn rejoined. "Nothing good can come of seed, even good seed, that is stored up with bad. I have further evidence. This man, chosen of Moira to be her consort, has had relations with Thena, her daughter. The child of such an impure father cannot be blessed." Moira rose to her feet.

"You cannot prove that is so, Gorn! I have spoken with Thena about it. Nothing ever happened. It is hearsay, and a heresy, a despicable rumor you started and nothing more!"

"I saw them together in the fields today, walking arm in arm, planning yet another tryst, no doubt!"

"Liar!" Moira screamed.

"It is no lie! Ask her yourself!" Gorn shouted, pointing now at Thena. Moira shot a hard glance at her daughter whose eyes were cast downward.

"If it can be demonstrated to you that this man compromises our vitality as a people," Gorn asked turning to the assembled matriarchs, "will you grant me that his marriage to my sister and their child are also cursed, that their union should be dissolved, and the man forced to leave our village forever?"

The mothers conferred with one another in low tones. Whispers wafted through the assembly like drifting leaves. Outside, a wind began to blow from the west, parting the tops of the trees almost imperceptibly, like a lion stalking its prey, silently, like a raven soaring through the skies.

"Yes, Gorn," the Eldest said at length. "We will agree to this."

"Then there is but one thing that remains to be done. I want you to listen as I put some questions to Ulf. You all know him to be a true man, a man who obeys. Will you receive his testimony as the truth?"

Dayn stiffened.

"Yes," replied the Eldest without hesitation. "Ulf is a good man. We will take what he says to be true."

"Ulf," Gorn half-shouted over the heads of the assembly, "come forward!"

Ulf shuffled uneasily to the head of the assembly and stood before the Council. He glanced sidelong at Dayn then looked at the floor.

"Tell us Ulf, that which you told me, when I questioned you under pledge of loyalty to Faen, about the journey you made with Dayn."

"About which part of the journey, Gorn?"

"The reason for your going on the journey, the reason for which you obtained the permission of the mothers, was to make a shrine to the Old One, Eengla. Tell us about the shrine that you made, Ulf."

Ulf swallowed and looked uneasily at Dayn. "We did not make a shrine," he answered in a barely audible voice.

"You went to make a shrine, Ulf, and yet you did not make one?" the Eldest interjected. "But a good man would do what he had told the mothers he would do. And you are a good man...

a *good* man, Ulf. We cannot comprehend this."

"Tell the mothers what you did instead of building the shrine, Ulf," Gorn said almost gleefully.

"We rode horses on the beach," Ulf replied slowly.

The matriarchs looked at each other, perplexed.

"And what did Dayn say was the reason for riding horses on the beach, Ulf?" Gorn asked, barely suppressing a laugh.

"To mourn the Old One," Ulf replied.

"But that is not the way we mourn, Ulf," a grandmother spoke up. "There is a traditional way of mourning. A good man would mourn only in this way, as custom dictates. You are a good man Ulf. Yet you did not mourn in the customary way." And she shook her head.

Now the wind began to gust and swirl around the Council Lodge. It boomed against the walls of the building with the sound of waves crashing against a rocky coast. It piled up clouds over the mountains in the east. A distant thunder rumbled and rolled down the western valleys toward the little village.

Gorn felt the mood of the Council swinging in his favor. He had one more line of questions for the hapless witness. "Now Ulf, tell us about the vision that Dayn had. That which the Old One interpreted for him before you left on your journey.

"Dayn said," Ulf's words came slowly and his voice thickened, "he had a vision. In the vision ...there was ...a writing skin, and on the skin was ...the symbol for Faen ...and the symbol for Brahan. The sign for Brahan, became ...a lion. The sign for Faen, became ...Moira. Then the lion walked across ...the page ...and devoured Moira."

Dayn was still and silent. A murmur went through the Council. Moira looked at her young husband out of the corner of her eye with mounting consternation.

"Tell us now Ulf, what did the Old One say this vision means?"

"Dayn said, she told him, that the young lion ...is Dayn ...that he must kill Moira."

A gasp went up from the assembly. Moira stared at Dayn in terror and sidled away from him. The mothers wagged their heads in disbelief. Thunder crashed close by.

"Go on, Ulf!" required Gorn.

"In this way, Brahan ...would destroy ...the goddess ...destroy the old ...ways."

The people rose to their feet. The mothers became agitated. Some had covered their ears against the blasphemy.

"...and bring ...new ...ways ...the ways of Brahan, the bringer ...of ...fire."

Ulf collapsed as he finished. Dayn was unmoved. Moira had slid around behind the semi-arch where the mothers sat, some of whom were crying or chanting, some of whom were standing and shouting insults at Dayn. Others shook bony, clenched fists at him. Everyone was talking, vying to be heard, cursing Dayn, cursing Moira, cursing their bad fortune.

"There is more," shouted Gorn at the top of his voice and pointing at Dayn. "He claims to be the son of Brahan!" And he laughed maniacally. The assembly was in complete chaos now. Finally, the Eldest raised her voice above the others.

"Bind him and guard him, and wait for our return!" she shouted above the tumult, pointing a crooked and colorless finger at Dayn. The matriarchs left the Council Lodge and conferred outside while the assembly flowed around Dayn. Strong-armed men seized him and bound him with cords to the central pillar. Then they backed away. The jeweled eyes of the carved goddess seemed to regard the prisoner with disdain. There was weeping and lamenting in the Council Lodge, as keen as if one of their own had truly died. Moira knelt on the ground, weeping, praying. Ulf lay in a stupor on the spot where he had spoken his last words.

The wind now blew at gale force outside. Dust and limbs flew in the air and tumbled down the insignificant streets. Inside the Lodge the air seemed charged with an explosive ether. When at last the mothers returned, they were infuriated. They took their places and the Eldest spoke.

"Listen people, listen to the words of Faen, the daughter of the Great Mother Nyso. Dayn, the husband of Moira, must die. Faen has made it the duty of our clan to rid the earth of him. The woman Moira, the former priestess, is to be banished from the clan, but she will stay among us until the baby is born. For when it is born, it will be slain. It is of utmost importance, Faen has instructed, that the executions of both Dayn and the baby be bloodless. None of their blood must befoul our land. None of their blood must stain our hands or taint our waters. Faen has spoken!"

At that instant a lightning bolt ripped through the roof and exploded at the feet of Gorn, throwing him, twisting, sizzling, into the air. He landed against the outer wall of the lodge, fifty feet away. The impact of the bolt caused the very ground to heave and no one in the Lodge was left standing. Dayn alone remained upright, bound to the central pillar. The thatch of the roof burst into flames and burned quickly. Before the reeling people could regain their feet, it was falling in great fireballs to the ground. Screams broke from the throats of those who saw it fall, setting aflame carpets, hides, and the clothing of those who lay unconscious. The choking smoke and odor of searing skin and hair rose skyward.

Several of the matriarchs had been struck dead by the blast. Those who were still alive groped about in futility, blinded by the flash, to help the others or to maintain some order. Moira had been knocked unconscious and lay still where she had been kneeling, screened from the direct lash of the bolt by the mothers who sat before her. Ulf was jarred from his stupor by the pitching of the ground. When he opened his eyes he saw Dayn through the rain of burning thatch and rising smoke. He was first on his feet and ran toward his friend. Dayn was coughing and squinting against the heat when he felt someone behind him, untying his hands. He slumped to the ground when they were loosed. Ulf quickly ran around the pillar and caught him by the shirt, dragging him through the melee towards the edge of the Lodge.

As Ulf dragged Dayn's unresponsive body clear of the outer wall the roof fell in. The sheepskin walls were blown outward by a belch of flame which incinerated them instantly. Ulf was knocked off his feet by the scorching wind. A split second later, a momentous reversal of the air flow occurred. It pulsed back through the lodge and up through the opening where the roof had been. No one survived in the furnace of the Council Lodge. A fireball ascended heavenward, becoming a nauseating black cloud as it cooled. Then it began to rain, first larger pieces of wood and thatch still ablaze from the explosion. Next pieces of charred clothing and carpet floated downward, followed by a sooty black mist of finer particles, consisting of less recalcitrant materials. The greasy black rain fell for half an hour and covered the ground with noisome debris.

Ulf got to his feet and turned Dayn's inert body over. Tears came to his eyes. If only he could tell his friend that he hadn't meant to betray him. If only he could let Dayn know that the needling Gorn had tricked him, poor, simple Ulf, into telling

100

what Dayn had confided. He beat his breast and tore at his beard. Suddenly Dayn coughed, sputtered, and a long groan escaped his lips. Ulf bent down to put his face close to Dayn's.

Dayn parted his blue lips and whispered to Ulf, a feeble light flickering in his eyes. "The voice ...of my father, ...Brahan ...is very loud."

Part II

Chapter 11
Pirates

The ship rolled unsteadily in the waters. It was not the most seaworthy of vessels. Its hull was too round and its draft too shallow. The wood from which it was made too often became waterlogged for want of a fresh application of pitch. The one triangular sail it boasted was furled now and the ship wallowed from crest to trough amid chaotic waves.

At the base of the mast was a small altar and there a black-robed priest with a long beard burned a precious lump of incense. He chanted as he cupped the rising smoke in his hands and lifted it heavenward, as if it were unable to rise on its own. In truth, the air was so thick and the forward speed of the vessel so slight that the smoke seemed only to settle, clinging to both ship and crew. The ship bobbed up and down in it, causing the dark vapor to cascade over the sides where it lay blanket-like upon the waters, responding only to the rise and fall of the waves beneath. The crew breathed the comforting aroma of the incense and listened to the familiar prayer to Matas, the sea-god, invoking his continued blessing for their journey. One of them coughed deeply and the sound of it rang in the stillness.

Belak and his crew had been sailing for two moons, following the coastline, heading always north and west, as they had been instructed. When their store of food ran low, they would find a place to go ashore to hunt and refill the pottery urns which held the precious supply of fresh water. Whenever they came upon some unsuspecting settlement, they would don their war-gear, beach the ship at low tide and jump from it with loud and lusty cries, setting fire to houses and stealing food, weapons, precious stones and metal. But these adventures were short-lived and infrequent. For the most part, they strained monotonously on the short oars, responding mechanically to the beat of the drum which laid down a rhythm for their labor, and pushed the ship slowly ahead. When a wind came out of the south and the sail was set, they gratefully shipped their oars and watched the shoreline glide by.

Belak had wanted to go ashore today, for the last hunt had not been good. He and his men had been on the water four days now without a respite. For three of those days the weather had been good, but the rocky cliffs and crashing waves had offered no approach to the land. Last night a black fog had settled about them and obliterated the stars. The sun had come up and transformed the black mist into a dull gray fog, but had not yet been able to penetrate it, and he was afraid to come too close to the rocky headlands. Belak steered the boat northward by the occasional sound of waves breaking in the distance to his right and the feeble light which showed itself only faintly greater in that direction.

The hours passed slowly. When Belak became tired of gripping the tiller with his right hand, he would switch off to his left, cradling it against his hip. His ears and eyes and nose were alert to any change in conditions which might bespeak of danger. From time to time he let out a deep sigh, then took a deep draught of the salt-tinged air.

Toward midday the sky lightened. He looked up and saw the bright white ball of the sun through the haze. His heart gladdened at the sight. Now a breeze sprang up from the west. Soon the combination of wind and sun shredded the mist and it fled in tatters. He ordered the drumming to cease and the sail to be hauled aloft. Two of the crew jumped from their seats at his command, untied the sail, and jerked it upward. It captured the wind and billowed out. The prow of the ship dipped forward churning the sea into a white foam there. Belak could see the gray outline of the headlands now and he inched the ship in that direction.

With the fog gone the sun beat down upon each man, hot and bright. Their bronzed backs glistened with sweat. Each had a turn at the water urns then went back to his place. The priest approached Belak.

"We must make a landfall tonight," he said with authority. "We must ask Semele for further direction. We must have a

106

sacrifice to offer her. If not, it will go ill for us."

"We have done all that the gods have asked. I am sure they will show us a place to come ashore, Mithorek," the muscular Belak responded. He spoke to the priest with a mild disdain, for he had little use for gods, or for those who made it their occupation to serve them. He did, however, have a healthy respect for the sea, and when he spoke of it he often did so by using the name of the sea-god, Matas.

Both pirate and priest looked landward. Belak was hopeful. For the past half-hour he had felt a current growing in its force against the tiller. He was confident they were approaching the mouth of a great river. He asked Reyk, the drummer, to go forward and bring him a cup of ocean water. Belak put it to his lips and smiled.

"The water here is less salty. We are coming to a river mouth. The west wind holds. Matas is happy!" he said, wiping his crusty lips with his forearm.

Guided by Belak, the ship hove to the northeast, bucking all the while against the current of the river. The west wind strengthened and it bore them steadily landward. It was not long until Belak saw clearly a gap in the headlands. He steered for it. Soon he espied the mouth of the river itself. The tide was ebbing now and it wrestled with the river. The ship was caught in the struggle and tossed haphazardly among waves. Belak ordered the oars into the water. The seamen coerced the ship through the frenzied surf and sailed it onto the calm, broad sweep of the river.

The sun was low on the horizon when Belak found slack water and eased the ship onto the waiting shore. It ground to a halt on the soft sand of a bar. Several of the crew jumped from the prow and lashed it to huge water oaks that grew nearby. Others stood by, watching the woods for enemies, while the remainder of the crew donned their copper breastplates and helmets, strapped on their short swords, and drew metal tipped spears, bows, and quivers of arrows from the arms chests. The black-robed priest climbed down from a ladder in the prow carrying a box under his arm with great care. When he had gone ashore, the crew jumped from the sides of the vessel and sloshed through the murky, brown shallows onto the sandy spit.

There they made camp. The priest found a level spot, set the box down, and unrolled a small carpet. He placed the box on the carpet, untied the lid and opened it, drawing forth a flat stone blackened with the heat of many fires, and a small knife with an intricately carved hilt.

A few of the pirates went off to hunt. Two others stood by the priest and were anointed with an aromatic oil from a small flask. Thence they were sent to find a goat for the sacrifice. Two others gathered wood and stacked it near a pit being dug for a roasting fire.

Belak watched the labors of the crew with satisfaction for some time. He was a giant of a man, a head taller than any of the rest. His face was lined and bronzed from a life at sea and his head was crowned with thick yellow hair, bleached nearly white by the sun and salt air. His sun-baked arms and chest bulged with muscles enlarged by oar and tiller and were marked with the scars of many battles. He wore a short cloth shirt and a broad leather belt. On his wrists were thick bracelets of copper.

He walked to the head of the bar in the failing light and looked upriver. The twilight was giving way to darkness under the shadow of the trees which lined the further bank. A large blue-gray heron flew upriver with lazy strokes of its enormous wings. A flock of geese flew at a great height out of the north perpendicular to the line of the river, faintly honking. A chill settled on the water. The nightly ritual of the earth and its creatures taking to their beds had begun. An owl hooted, its voice echoing through the trees, and was answered by another on the opposite shore. The brown river slipped by, gurgling against the side of the ship, an unfamiliar obstacle to its well-remembered path to the sea.

It was fully night when the hunters returned. The bonfire blazed brightly, throwing the myriad shadows of the surrounding trees deep into the forest. The brown water near the sandbar gleamed reddish-gold in its light.

A deer was skewered and raised over the blaze to roast. A brand was brought out of the fire to the priest who took it and lit a small fire on his makeshift altar. The genitals of the deer were brought and he burned them in the fire, thanking Semele for the success of the hunt as the smoke rose. Following this ritual, the pirates and the priest sat patiently waiting for the sacrificial goat, but Belak walked the edge of the circle of the firelight, stopping to peer from time to time into the shadows.

Finally the two who had gone in search of the sacrificial goat returned, empty-handed.

"Well Samek?" Belak demanded.

"We scoured the nearby hills, Belak, but there was no sign of goats. We saw many small red deer, but no goats. We searched until night overtook us," the one called Samek answered.

The thirty-some men gathered around the fire grew restive. It was not good that Samek and Irmek had failed to find an appropriate sacrifice for Semele, the goddess who had sent them on this journey, the one to whom they looked for guidance. It was not prudent to fail in honoring her. A sacrifice would have to be made before they could put to sea again and they could not afford to wait too many days. Already autumn was advancing. Belak pulled a bearskin about his massive shoulders against the chill of the night.

"Then go again at dawn." Belak turned and walked away toward the fire, plainly annoyed and the failure of his men and conscious of the stare of Mithorek, the priest.

Belak awoke the next morning to the rustle of leaves overhead. The west wind still pushed inland from the ocean. The shadows of the trees were flung far out over the water by the sun, rising slowly in the southeastern sky. He raised his head and noted that Samek and Irmek were already gone. He threw his bearskin robe aside. The sand had been too soft a bed and he rose stiffly. Soon the rest were up. One by one they made their way to the deer, still hanging over the ashes of the fire, and cut away strips for a cold breakfast. They ambled into the brown water and splashed their faces. Some bent down and took long drinks. Soon Reyk had them organized into hunting parties and they were off, leaving Belak, Reyk and Mithorek alone on the bar.

"Bring out your map, Reyk," Belak said.

Reyk went to his bedroll and retrieved a bundle tightly bound in a generously oiled goatskin. He handed it to Belak who smoothed out his bearskin robe and unrolled the scroll upon it. The three men studied it.

"Here is the section showing the distance covered in the last two weeks. Here are the cliffs where the shoreline bent towards Bemil, the north star. This is the first river, Orna, this the second, Durna. Now we are come to a third. It should be located somewhere about here," Reyk said, drawing a mark on the scroll with a piece of charcoal.

"Yes," Belak said slowly. "Would you say this third river is the mightiest of the three, mapmaker?"

Reyk studied the shadows of the trees on the river. "The shadows seem to reach about the same distance into the river as those on the first river. This tells me these two rivers are roughly the same width."

"The current from this one seems stronger though," replied Belak, "and its color is brown. What name shall we give it?"

"Perhaps we should wait until Samek and Irmek return to name it. Then we can decide whether to give it an evil or a wholesome name," Mithorek said dryly.

"These gods can be a thorny problem, can they not Mithorek?" Belak said half-jokingly, taunting the priest. "Is it not enough that we burn incense and pray to them? Must they have goats as well?" Belak's frustration grew as he spoke, knowing what the priest would demand if a goat were not found before they were ready to leave. "By the gods, there *are* no goats in this land! Why don't you talk to Semele and explain that to her?"

"Semele is already angry with us, Belak. Why do you think our journey has met with so little success? There can be only one of two explanations, either she is dissatisfied, or you are no leader. Which interpretation do you prefer?

"Don't start your goading, Mithorek, or I shall snatch a *priest* from his sleep on the return voyage and sacrifice *him* to Semele. We will have our success before we return."

"This river represents our last chance, Belak. You should humble yourself and pray to Semele that our hunting is good here. Otherwise, you will have a full measure of explaining to do when you return, whether or not I am with you. Did not Semele speak in the court of Savor and tell all assembled of the riches of this country? Would you make her a liar, Belak? You had best beware of your arrogance."

"With this arm, and not with prayers, will I make good my promise to Savor," Belak spat back at the priest. For a long, tense moment they glared at each other from opposite ends of Belak's bearskin, the mapmaker on the ground between. Reyk glanced nervously from one to the other. Daringly, Mithorek turned his back to them. Belak's hand strayed to the hilt of his sword. For a moment Reyk thought his insulted chieftain might draw his blade and rush the priest. But Belak's hand relaxed and Reyk breathed again.

Throughout the day, hunting parties returned with deer. Racks were built over the fire pit and meat was cut into strips

110

and hung there. The fire was rekindled and the smoking of provisions for the homeward trip began. Late in the morning, Belak drew one group aside and bade them don their war gear. Without notifying Mithorek or Reyk where he was taking them, he set out upriver.

For hours they climbed steadily upward through an oak forest, dense with undergrowth. A few of the water oaks were beginning to lose their foliage with the advance of the season. When the wind blew their russet leaves drifted through the air. The party kept the river within sight to their left. They came upon a green pond, stranded there by the river following the last high water and surprised a colony of ducks who flew suddenly away, quacking noisily and slapping the water with their wings. Belak froze as the ducks left the trees and circled, heading off downriver. The scouting party continued to climb. Larches and pines gradually displaced the oaks and the ground became drier and more rocky.

Ahead of them on the horizon, Belak spotted a lofty outcrop of red rock. A smoke issued from the top of it and he motioned for his warriors to be quiet. Stealthily, they approached the rock face, screened by the trees that surrounded it. Belak struck a path that hugged the base of the rock and they followed him along it noiselessly. Ahead of him against the eastern face was a ladder. Belak approached it warily. Motioning for the others to follow he silently climbed. At the top of the ladder he lifted his head above the ledge enough to see the summit of the rock. Atop the rock was a circular tower built of stone. Partially hidden by the tower was a group of men.

Belak continued up and was stepping off the ladder when one of the guards came unexpectedly around the tower from the north. Belak howled and drove his sword through the man's belly. Jamming his hand in his unfortunate adversary's face he withdrew his sword and shoved him over the precipice. Pirates swarmed to the top of the rock as the surprised watchmen turned and ran to meet them. The sound of metal on metal clashed from the narrow south ledge. Suddenly Belak, who had slipped around the north side, came up behind the guards. He struck one a double-handed blow to the side of the head sending him hurtling through the air. Another turned to face him, was run through, and pitched over the edge behind his companion. The remaining guards were soon overpowered, leaving Belak's jeering warriors in command of the watchtower.

111

They entered the tower. Finding nothing except a few spare arms, food and a young mountain of dry fuel for the watchfire, they climbed down and marched further upriver. Before long they came upon the outskirts of a substantial city built of stone. Belak motioned for his men to spread out, to kneel in the bushes and observe. This they did for the better part of the afternoon. When they finally regrouped, Belak moved them out of sight of the walls to speak.

The stone city, it was reported, was situated on the south bank of the river. There were three concentric circles of stone in its plan. The first was the lowest, about the height of a man, and enclosed many houses built partially of stone and partially of wood. In this circle was a double gate. A road ran from this gate southward into a valley, high and wide, dotted with farms. The farms supported many sheep and crops were abundant. There was wheat, barley, hops, vegetables and fruit trees. The harvest was underway and the peasants were busily gathering its largess. Carts laden with produce moved back and forth between the fields and the gates of the city. There were also caves further down the slope where some of the harvest was being stored. Meat from the slaughter of domestic animals was drying in the caves as well.

The second semicircle of stone was built higher on the hill and was taller, perhaps the height of two men. Guards walked along these thicker, more massive walls with strong, east-facing gates. Some suspected that soldiers were quartered there.

Finally there was a third circle of stone, the foundation of the fortress itself, which sat partially upon this wall and partially on a huge outcrop of rock. The rock rose sheer from the river that fumed with great violence through a gorge below. The sound of the waters was a constant roaring in their ears. The stone and wood fortress, its turrets tipped with bright yellow metal, rose two or three stories above the top of the rock. The scouts' voices trembled as they spoke of the city, excited and awed by its strength and wealth. Here must truly be the City of Gold to which Semele had directed them.

When they had finished their report, Belak moved his small band of marauders back down the path to the watchtower. There he instructed a pair of them to stay and relight the fire at twilight. With the remainder he trotted away and so returned, before nightfall, to the sandbar where their main camp lay.

Chapter 12
The Well of Knowledge

Allisyn slipped quietly out a side door of the castle and breathed the fresh air deeply. Basket in hand, she pulled the handmaid's shawl closely about her shoulders and skipped down the steep stairs until her feet found the stone landing, then walked briskly down the flower-lined path to the wall. There she waited and watched the top of the wall until a rope came flying over, uncoiling and dangling in front of her. She looked quickly around, tied her basket to the end with a stiff knot, and gave it a tug. The basket inched upward by degrees until it reached the top, where it tipped over and disappeared. In another second, the basket, still attached to the rope, came flying back over the wall. Allisyn untied it, looking nervously around. Seeing no one, she ran back up the path to the stone landing, climbed the stairs, opened the heavy wooden door, and slipped back inside.

The air of castle was familiar and close compared with the wild winds that whipped the outer walls. Allisyn was seldom outdoors, except on errands with her mother, Vaalta. And then she was kept close by her mother's side, surrounded by members of the household. She thrived upon those times when she could thwart their vigilance, slip beneath their guard, and do something unexpected. She loved to see the surprised looks on their faces then. "Why are you so wayward?" they would ask. "Why can't you behave like the others? Why must you be so disrespectful to your elders?" She almost enjoyed being caught in the act more than getting away clean.

It had been a game with her for several years now. At first

her mother was blind to it. Then there was a period during which her cousin, Tandela, and the others would run to her mother Vaalta, pouring shocking news of her miscreant child into her ears, but Vaalta would not believe them. As soon as they started she would shake her head and send them scurrying away, saying she had no time to listen to such nonsense. But when the news finally reached the ears of Aefalas, her husband, she could no longer ignore it. So Vaalta talked with Allisyn and made her promise to obey. Allisyn promised, but within weeks she was up to her tricks again.

Tandela tutored Allisyn along with the other children in the extended household. But Allisyn was special, the daughter of Vaalta, Matriarch of Faenwys, the City of Faena. Tandela had always been somewhat in awe of Allisyn, owing to her favored position, and in no small part to her beauty, which exceeded Tandela's own good looks; and to her intelligence, which at the age of twelve had already surpassed that of her twenty year old tutor. But Tandela's awe was matched by a jealousy that was deeper, and darker. She delighted in catching Allisyn at some mischief and relished reporting it to Vaalta, or more recently, to Aefalas himself.

Allisyn was truly a beautiful child in every detail, from the crown of her head to the tips of her delicate toes. Her hair was of burnished gold, accented by a finer platinum color about her forehead and temples. Her skin was exquisite, the color of fresh cream, and her lips were red as overripe strawberries. She was tall for her age and slender, but with her father's naturally broad shoulders that endowed her with a regal look. Her eyes were a deep emerald green, the instant envy of every woman of any beauty who met her. They shone with a unextinguishable light and positively gleamed when she was up to some mischief.

She was climbing the stairs leading back to her rooms when she met Tandela coming down.

"You're late for your lessons, Allisyn. Where have you been this time?" Tandela probed.

"If you must know, cousin, I have been walking the outer walls and peering into the gorge," Allisyn announced.

Tandela gasped, for the walls were high and slippery owing to the perpetual mist that clung to them, and the fall into the gorge from their height was sheer. She tried quickly to regain her composure. Her eyes and lips narrowed, vexed now that she had let Allisyn shock her.

114

"Get into the lesson room, cousin. I'll be back in a moment and we shall begin," she glowered.

Allisyn curtsied dutifully, but grinned as soon as Tandela's back was turned and skipped up the stairs.

Tandela was, in her own right, extraordinary among the women of Aestri, being of uncommon beauty and intelligence. Her hair cascaded upon her shoulders in long chestnut brown tresses from beneath the prayer cap she wore. Her eyes were a deep brown, a shade darker than her eyebrows and hair. But her true beauty lay, according to the older women, in her zeal for their religion. Unmarried, she was devoted to Faena, and for all appearances, to Vaalta, her aunt.

Tandela's mother Vasana had been a Matriarch, a member of the Council, and it was only by the slimmest of chances that Tandela was not High Priestess herself. Vasana, the High Priestess Vuldroena's eldest daughter, had been groomed for the office from childhood. But she had become ill with an extended fever. When Vuldroena died, the Council of Matriarchs, fearing that Vasana was unequal to the task, appointed Vaalta. Vasana eventually recovered, married at last, and had a daughter. But with the exertion of her labor, her fever returned and her health declined further. Bit by bit, she faded slowly from the world and finally slipped into a sleep from which she never awoke.

Tandela had been raised by Vaalta as her own daughter with love and attentiveness. As Tandela was the eldest of her generation of cousins, Vaalta had placed serious responsibilities upon her to which she responded with maturity and diligence. But as much as she owed to her aunt, she could not fend off a creeping jealousy of her. Had circumstances been different, her own mother would have been the Matriarch of Aestri, the High Priestess of Faena, and she, Tandela, would now have been installed in that exalted position. As it was she had to stand by, watching as Allisyn was groomed for the office that should rightfully have been hers. Her rivalry with Allisyn grew apace with her jealous envy of Vaalta.

In her dreams Tandela would sometimes wander in the woods. There she would come upon a dark creature, like a pig, but hideous, rooting among the decayed leaves. The creature would open its mouth and whisper to her. Its breath stank and to be in the presence of the creature was to smell its repulsive filth. A part of Tandela wanted to turn away but another part was filled with curiosity. Her heart leaped when the beast opened its mouth to speak, and her lips would quiver, wanting desperately to cry out, but whether from fear or desire she could not tell. Then the pig-beast would whisper her name, "Thol-nys am I". It would show Tandela a golden trinket and offer it to her if the girl would do her bidding. When Tandela asked what its bidding was, Thol-nys would take her to a glade in the woods where there was a well. Next to the well there was a hearth, burning with a fire as bright as the noonday sun, terrible to look at. Then Thol-nys would ask Tandela to draw water from the well and extinguish the flame. Tandela would draw a bucket of water but, as she made ready to toss it on the fire, would see that the water had turned to blood. Dropping the bucket she would flee the forest, the pig creature at her heels, gnashing its teeth and slavering just behind her.

Aefalas was monarch, the King of Aestri, son of Arkalas, son of Aeolas, who was the son of Argolas the Great. His line extended back to the limits of living memory. The Kings of Aestri traced their tradition of rule back to a time before cities, before fields and harvests, to a time when the world was young, when people tended their flocks in the high mountain meadows and contended with lions for their wandering sheep. In the dawn of time the ancestors of Aefalas had been given the Holy Fire and had become its Keepers.

They became strong and fearless. And when their strength had reached its prime, they grew restless, for the tending of flocks no longer satisfied them. Organizing themselves into warring parties, they went in search of other tribes, other clans, to subdue. Everywhere they found these weaker peoples they subjugated them and exacted a tribute. Thus the family grew in wealth, prosperity and influence, and their dominion extended from the mountains to the sea.

Then the goddess Faena came, settled the people into villages, and taught them the secrets of agriculture. Wherever she stepped, springs gushed forth from the earth and where she lay down, fertile meadows were formed. The earth goddess made demands in exchange for the gifts she gave and a cult of priestesses sprouted up to attend her. The Holy Fire was tamed and became the resident of oven and hearth; no longer did it sweep wantonly through unprotected villages, no longer did it rage out of control along the borders of the realm. But the tradition of soldiery remained strong in Aestri so that the cult of the goddess never completely usurped the power of the Fathers. Thus Aestri was unique among the kingdoms of the world in that the High Priestess of Faena and the King shared the responsibilities and benefits of ruling the people. The minds of their subjects might belong to the King, but their souls and the work of their hands belonged to Faena.

In the reign of Aefalas' great-grandfather, Argolas the Great, copper metal was discovered in the hills to the south of the City and a colony of miners and metal workers established themselves there. Baklan, the god of the forge, came to live among them and instructed them in the making of many useful articles. Then, near the place where this base metal had been unearthed, Baklan showed them where new metals, rare gold and silver, dwelled and the secrets of refining them. Argolas became enamored of the beautiful things that could be fashioned from these bright bits of earth. He came to love them so that soon he no longer delighted in articles made from the gold and silver, but in the precious metals themselves. He built vaults in the caves of the nearby mountains and established vast treasuries, guarded night and day. And when he no longer trusted the guards, he himself became guard, and captive, to his golden hoard. He died in the caves along with his treasure, shriveled in mind and body. And Faenwys, The City of the Goddess, became known far and wide as Guldwys, the City of Gold.

Aefalas came to the throne at the age of eleven, upon the death of his father Arkalas. It was a time of great unrest and many wondered if one so young could rule a realm so vast and powerful. Thus, Arkalas had contrived to settle this matter before his passing. He made the High Priestess Vuldroena regent and obtained her promise that her eldest daughter, Vasana, would be given to Aefalas when he came to the throne, consolidating the power of the cult of the goddess with that of the kings. Vuldroena so promised. But when Arkalas died and the time came for Aefalas to take the throne, Vuldroena would not allow the marriage, contending that Vasana, destined to become High Priestess herself, could not marry before she came of age. So Aefalas was married to Vaalta, Vuldroena's second daughter, but four years old at the time. When Vuldroena died, because Vasana had been gravely ill, Vaalta was made High

Priestess. Thus Arkalas' original plan came to be.

Aefalas and Vaalta grew into man and woman and themselves had a daughter. They called her Allisyn and a dozen years passed. To all appearances, Aefalas was a king with all that a king might desire, abundant wealth, a powerful wife, a beautiful child, and mighty armies to command. But Aefalas had inherited his great-grandfather's eye for treasure, and not only for treasure made of gold and silver.

A few days later, Allisyn once again slipped out of the castle with a basket and made her way to the fortified wall. As she had done before she waited for the rope to come flying over. When it did, she tied the basket to its end. But before she could pull on it, giving the signal to send it back, a hand firmly grasped her wrist. She turned to see Tandela's livid face close to hers.

"Ha!" Tandela cried. "I've caught you. And what might you be up to, my pretty cousin?" she demanded sarcastically.

Allisyn answered only with the return of her even stare.

Tandela grabbed the basket, opening it to reveal a loaf Allisyn had purloined from the kitchen. Tandela stared at the bread, taken aback, not knowing what to say. How odd that Allisyn should take bread and throw it over the wall, was all she could think.

"To whom are you giving our bread?" she asked finally, derisively.

"To a peasant girl," Allisyn replied, still not having taken her eyes from Tandela's.

"To what purpose?"

"She is hungry."

"And why is she hungry? Is there not plenty for all? The storehouses are filled with grain."

"Not for them," Allisyn replied.

"What do you mean?"

"Just this, that she lives in a hovel with only her old grandmother and there is no one to provide for them."

Seeing an opportunity to catch her at something, Tandela pounced on Allisyn's words like a fox on a hare.

"It is because this family has not followed the ways of Faena that they have fallen upon hard times. Their lack of prosperity is

118

a sign that they have not been dutiful, that they have not been vigilant to keep her rituals. It is the way of Faena that the negligent ones weaken, the weak ones die. Do you not see what you are doing by giving this derelict of a girl and her grandmother bread? You are opposing the will of Faena for them. I believe your actions are those of a heretic, cousin."

"And I believe you are ignorant of what it is to be hungry for a crust of bread."

Tandela tightened her grip on Allisyn's wrist, her nails digging into the younger girl's arm. "Come with me!" she snapped.

She dragged Allisyn back into the house through wooden doors and down stone hallways lit by candles. When they arrived at Vaalta's chambers, Tandela opened the door and burst in.

"Tell her, tell her what you have done, tell the High Priestess of Faena what you have been doing!" Tandela shouted.

Vaalta looked at her daughter searchingly, her eyes suddenly rimmed with a mist of disappointment.

"I gave a loaf of bread to a peasant girl," Allisyn said defiantly.

Vaalta eyes darted toward Tandela.

"For this you make such a noise, Tandela?" Vaalta replied.

"The girl and her grandmother are destitute. It is a sign from Faena that they are cursed. Giving them bread is heresy, Vaalta. Such behavior, especially in the daughter of the High Priestess, cannot go unpunished!" Tandela debated.

"You come to this conclusion quickly, Tandela. What proofs do you have? It would not become one so well schooled in the service of the goddess to be in error in such a situation. What shall we do then?" She paused and stared at Tandela who made no answer. "I know," Vaalta continued at length, "tomorrow we shall visit the girl and her grandmother. We shall observe and question them, and then we shall make our judgment," Vaalta said coolly. "By the way, Allisyn, how did you meet this girl?"

Allisyn dropped her chin to her breast.

"I went walking," she said almost inaudibly after a long pause.

"You went out without escort?" Vaalta questioned, more disappointed than angry now. "It is so dangerous, Allisyn! You know it cannot be allowed! How can you hope to stay pure if you take such frightful chances? You will see and hear things that should not come to the eyes and ears of the daughter of Vaalta before her initiation into the mysteries of the goddess. And it is so close at hand. It is a perilous time for you!"

"She is not ready. It would offend Faena to initiate one so lacking in devotion," Tandela said with no attempt to hide the disdain in her voice, then walked away, her aim, in part, achieved.

The next morning evolved slowly. Mists from the gorge of the Mergruen, the River of Long Memory, teamed with a valley fog to form an impenetrable barrier to the sun. Leaves, rocks, everything everywhere, dripped. Allisyn found herself daydreaming by the window, watching the swirling shapes of cloud in the deep chasm carved by the ancient river. They seemed almost to speak to her; they had always seemed determined to speak, mute ghosts who came with an undeliverable message, then sadly melted into nothingness.

A knocking at the door roused her. She smoothed her skirts with her hands, walked across the room, and opened it. Her mother was there.

"Are you ready, child?" Vaalta asked.

"Yes," Allisyn muttered.

"Come then," Vaalta said tersely, attempting to suppress her emotions.

They climbed down from their rooms in the uppermost floors of the castle to a large landing further down where Tandela and three high ranking Matriarchs of the Council, Drusala, Mollaf and Maeta, were gathered. Tandela looked at Allisyn with a penetrating stare, as if she were trying to find a defect in a fabric. But the weave was flawless.

They were met at the main door by a green and silver uniformed squadron of the castle guard. These were fitted out with fine brown leather shields, boots and helmets, and each carried a short copper sword at his side in a brown scabbard. The drummer struck up a brisk beat and they all marched forward to the east gates of the fortress, two guards before and four following the retinue of women. Passing through these, they backtracked along the wall until they came to the south-facing town gates in the low outer rampart. These they also passed, walking along the Highgaet Roed until they came to a crossroads. There they took the Droemenvael Roed and followed it, bending eastward toward the jagged north rim of the valley and the belt of trees which stood at its feet.

Allisyn looked upward at the Encircling Hills. They had always seemed to her the assertive jawbone of an old woman whose teeth were fallen into decay. They grinned at her now out of the bright morning haze, mocking her diffident mood. She winced and trudged onward.

Guided by Allisyn, the group soon left the road and struck a narrow footpath which led into the wood. Above them a north wind stirred the treetops sending a shower of yellow ash leaves spinning earthward. Allisyn went forward between the guards and led them to a hovel, a house of earth and stone little better than a cave, built into the side of the mountain. Smoke issued from a hole in the earthen roof. The front door was nothing but a bedraggled and rotting sheepskin. Allisyn stood a few feet away and called.

"Bronwyn?" She paused. "Bronwyn," she called again. The weathered sheepskin was drawn back by a slender pale hand and the frightened face of a child appeared in the dim light, looking rather like a wary rabbit peering from its hole.

"It is I, Allisyn. Come out. I have brought some people," she paused here, a lump rising in her throat. "They wish to speak with you."

The girl came forward a step letting the tattered door covering fall down behind her. She wore a plain dress of spun wool, whose ragged hem came midway down her calf, and no shoes. Her ankles and feet were thin and dirty. A smoky aroma spilled from the doorway ahead of her.

"And your mother, we wish to see your mother as well," Tandela ordered.

"She has no mother. She lives with her grandmother," Allisyn replied, not deigning to turn toward Tandela as she spoke. The slight Bronwyn looked timidly about, her large and strikingly beautiful brown eyes darting from one to the next of the regal figures assembled before her.

"Have your grandmother come out, too, Bronwyn," Vaalta added delicately.

"She will ask, "Allisyn said on Bronwyn's behalf. "On some days the Old Crone cannot rise."

"Are you her mouth?" Tandela asked scathingly.

"She is dumb, she cannot speak," Allisyn added in a soft voice.

Bronwyn reentered the hut and was gone for what seemed a long time. Tandela stared at the back of Allisyn's head, loathing now more than ever each tress of golden hair. Vaalta dropped her eyes, saddened by the sight of the destitute girl and the hole she lived in, wishing that she were not here, wishing that her daughter had shown better judgment, wondering how and why Allisyn could have been drawn here. Did she not have everything life could offer, wealth, influence, position, comfort? Why come here then? Why? The guard beside her moved, shifting his weight from one foot to the other, and his leathers squeaked, arresting her reverie. The wind shifted suddenly sweeping down the hill and the smoke of the fire fumigated the group. It stung their eyes and they broke into fits of coughing. Tandela squinted and waved the fumes from before her face. When the obnoxious vapors had dissipated, she was there, the grandmother, Doena, the Old Crone.

Tandela covered her nose. Vaalta caught her breath and the guard to her right coughed. A disagreeable odor came from the woman, from her filthy, ragged clothes, from her greasy gray hair; it oozed from every pore of her mottled skin. She looked at the group but did not see them, for her eyes were covered with thick, opaque scales. Her left hand rested upon the gnarled head of a stubby walking stick at the height of her head. Her back was bowed with the weight of many years and many burdens.

"Vaalta," the old woman called. Her voice seemed to come from the earth itself.

"Yes, Mother," Vaalta replied, surprised at the hint of reverence she suddenly felt for the disheveled old woman who stood before her. Tandela noted Vaalta's tone of voice and shot an appalled glance at her.

"Why have you come?" the Old Crone asked.

"How did you know Vaalta stood before you?"

The old woman raised her skirts slightly to reveal her ponderous feet, blackened with ruptured veins, and thick yellow toenails, long and curling, like the tusks of a sow.

"Do I not walk upon the earth? Does the soil not stain the soles of my feet?" she replied. "My feet are my eyes and ears in my old age. The earth says much to those who choose to listen."

"My daughter has visited you, Mother. Why?"

122

The corners of the old woman's mouth drew into a twitching, twisted smile.

"Allisyn, Han-nys-syn, daughter of the moon, Allisyn, Han-nys-syn, daughter of the moon," she chanted, then stopped abruptly. "Yes, she comes. Can she not speak? Ask her, then! Let the moon-daughter say! Why bend an old woman's back with such a question? You dare to venture from your high walls to ask me such a thing? You brave the stench of my home to ask such a question?

"You, who can look up and see the light of the moon, have pity on me, for I can no longer see it! The moon-daughter brings it to me in her pocket. She flings moondrops around my house from the tips of her fingers. She spills it onto the floor and lets me stand in it. Sometimes I get down upon my knees and lap it up like an old dog!" She howled, then laughed, a series of deep-throated grunts, and did a gleeful dance on her stunted legs.

"How dare you speak to the High Priestess of Faena in that way, woman!" Tandela's voice erupted. I command you to show her the respect she deserves!"

The old woman stopped her dance in mid-stride and shuffled an inch or two toward Tandela. She thrust a palsied hand in her direction.

"You!" she grunted. "Mother of misery. Your words are daggers, your spittle poison. Tell them of your black dreams! Tell them! You defame even the base worship of the goddess! You bring a blight upon the earth that causes Faena to swoon. You would vomit a blackness to swallow the very sun! You..."

"Enough! Enough!" Tandela stamped her foot. "I have heard enough of this preposterous babble! Her mind is empty. Her words are empty. I demand that she be cast out! She is cursed! Vaalta!" She whirled about, her breast heaving, to look at her aunt.

Vaalta did not register the movement for her gaze was fixed upon the old woman, and she stood still and silent for a shocked moment, the words echoing in her ears. As slowly as the coming of dawn on a misty morning, she perceived in them something which led her by a shimmering thread, back to a place on the edge of memory; a space both ancient, holy, and forbidden. Then all faded to darkness. She was suddenly aware of those around her, of her position, of her obligation. At length she spoke.

"Allisyn, you are forbidden to come here again," she said sternly, avoiding the searching eyes of her daughter.

"Mother!" Allisyn started.

"You are forbidden to give them bread." Tears came to Allisyn's eyes unbidden. "Let us go now. We will decide later what must be done here. Come!"

Vaalta grabbed her daughter by the shoulders and turned her around, afraid to meet her gaze, afraid of what she might see there. She bade the women and their escort to walk away. Something fearful, revolting, compelling, alluring, was crawling through her bowels. She felt faint, but she fixed her energy on putting one foot ahead of the other until the feeling had passed and she was well away from the little earthen house.

When the visitors had gone, the old woman motioned for Bronwyn, who took her arm and helped her hobble back inside.

That night Vaalta paced the floor of her bedchamber, reassembling the events of the day. She knew in her heart that Allisyn had felt what she had felt, the strange attraction and revulsion to the old woman. But how much more strongly? And why? What was it that drew her to the hovel in the woods? Where and what was that distant, unattainable space; wherefore the longing she herself had felt to go there? It was like the sensation she recalled as a little girl, standing by the gorge of the river, wondering what it would be like to fall in, but scaring herself and drawing abruptly back, lest it actually should happen.

She longed to go to Allisyn and ask her these things, but she feared the answers to her questions. And tomorrow... tomorrow the Rites of Harvest would begin. Tomorrow she, Vaalta, must be the High Priestess of Faena and stand before the people, strong, certain and unblemished. And at the termination of the Rites, Allisyn would be inducted into the cult of the goddess. If she could only put off this bothersome affair until then, everything would be fine. She wished Aefalas, her husband, were here now. He had a better head for such things. But he was away with the army, fighting on the eastern frontier. Fighting... why did men always have to be fighting when they were needed for something important? He had promised to be back before the Rites began, to see his daughter initiated. He had better be. *Ah,* she thought, *he is as wayward as she is...*

The Heron Moon rose and its light touched the casement of her window. As the orb reached toward the zenith, its beams inched their way across the wooden floor. Vaalta stood still and watched the shadows recede, crack by crack, as the knife edge of light advanced, immaculate and pale as death. It reminded her again of the old woman's words. What had she chanted? Allisyn, Han-nys-syn? Daughter of the moon? What could it mean?

Even as her mother paced, Allisyn was climbing from her window high above the churning river. A voice was beckoning, calling her back to the hut in the forest, and she was responding to the call. "Allisyn, Han-nys-syn, moon daughter come!" it chanted.

Allisyn was cloaked in a black-hooded woolen cape. The wind from the gorge tugged at it, twisted it, blew it into fantastic shapes, caused it to pop and flap. She clung to the lip of the rock wall to prevent being lifted off and blown away. Mists curled around her. The moon shone fitfully through. A groping gust of wind clutched at her and she flattened herself against the rock shelf, closing her eyes tightly. When it had dissipated she got to her hands and knees once more and inched forward. She reached an incline, slick with mold and moisture. Turning, she crept down backwards, her knees scraping on the wet, rasping surface, her fingers grasping the lip of the capstone. Her knees slipped and she hit the stone hard with her stomach and chin, almost knocking the breath from her lungs. She wrapped her legs around the capstone and tried to ease down slowly. She slipped again, cutting the soft skin of the inside of her thighs on the sharp edge. She drew her breath quickly and bit her lip so as not to cry out, pausing momentarily. Now she continued on, her eyes full of tears and determination.

Finally she reached the inner wall. A guard paced away to her right along its broad crest. There was a drop of some ten feet on the other side, but after that she could descend the lower outer wall onto to a narrow path that threaded the brink of the gorge. She waited at the drop-off to make sure the guard's back was turned, then leaped. She landed softly on the lower wall and eased herself quickly over it. Shielded from watchful eyes, if not from the grasping wind, she pulled her hood close around her face and walked briskly along the path up the river. The wind moaned in the gorge. Beneath her skirts, blood trickled from the cuts on her legs and knees.

Once away from the wall, she ran over open stony ground, making for the belt of trees at the bottom of the grinning ridge. In the moonlight, the rocky crags looked indeed like a row of ancient teeth, this time the jawbone of some gigantic primeval carnivore. The voice called louder now and more urgently, "Allisyn, Han-nys-syn, moon daughter come!" and she quickened her pace. It seemed to come from the trees now and not from the gorge. She entered the sheltering eaves of the forest and the slender, spectral figure of Bronwyn appeared. The wraith-like girl reached out her hand, taking that of her friend, and guided her with sure steps along the dark, narrow track to her grandmother's hut.

Doena, the Old Crone, was sitting before the door, bathed in the glow of moonbeams, still and silent as a stone. Indeed if Bronwyn had not been with her, Allisyn might have taken the immobile figure for a craggy extrusion of the hill. Doena opened her useless eyes and motioned Allisyn to sit. The girl complied. Bronwyn crouched close beside her, still holding Allisyn's hand, never taking her round eyes from the older girl's face. They all remained silent for some time. Then Doena spoke.

"My child," she said, turning her unseeing eyes toward Allisyn, "a great calamity is about to befall this people. It will change everything. You must survive, for the One is coming. You must be here when he arrives. Osyn has chosen you to breathe the fire of Han-Thol; Han-nys, the sky-maiden, the transformer, the ancient and venerable Moon Goddess, has chosen you to cool the fire, to soften the burning light so that all may look upon it, to complete the One."

"I am ready to do as you tell me, Great Mother, although I do not understand what you say."

"Understanding is not so much, young one. Faith is much; it is greater, deeper, fuller, and richer than understanding. Believing in your destiny is much. Love is much. Courage is much."

"What would you have me do, mother?" Allisyn asked.

"Drink from the well," Doena replied. Allisyn looked about.

"What well?" Allisyn inquired earnestly.

Doena grasped her crutch with both hands and passed it twelve times around the circle formed by their knees as the three sat facing one another. On the twelfth time, she commanded

126

Allisyn to look at the ground before her and a circle of stones appeared. In the midst of the stone circle a dark shaft opened downward, like the pupil of an immense eye. At the edge of the stone circle was a scooped out gourd on a long slender rope. A light glowed in the depths of the well.

"Drink," the old woman commanded.

Allisyn dropped the gourd into the well. It fell only a little way before she heard a splash. She drew it up by the cord, grasped the gourd and took a long drink. The water was refreshing and cool. It seemed to her that as she drank, the water flowed not into her stomach but into her soul, carving out new channels, dredging up new mysteries, dripping into dark secret caverns, flowing into new territories and watering a newly planted landscape.

"Wash your wounds," the blind woman commanded. Allisyn complied. The fire instantly left her scrapes and bruises as she laved them, and they afflicted her no more.

"Now go where the spirit leads you," she added.

Allisyn and Bronwyn stood. The mute Bronwyn placed a kiss on the cheek of her friend and squeezed her hand. Allisyn reached into her cloak and drew out a small round loaf. She handed it to the younger girl and caressed her cheek. Then she walked away, losing herself among the slender boles of the trees.

Chapter 13
The Rape of Faenwys

Allisyn wandered alone in the woods for some time, marveling at the appearance of the well and the water that took the burning from her cut and bruised skin, wondering what other powers it might possess. But more than this she was astounded by other events of the day. It had been difficult to suppress her mirth when the Old Crone danced and spoke in riddles to Tandela. She had not known it was possible to make her cousin so angry! Then the strange call that had seemed to come to her from out of the canyon, urging her back to the hut in the forest. Had she really heard that voice? It seemed like a dream to her now, but then, then she had heard it so clearly, so clearly she had risked her life, crawling upon the castle wall in the clawing wind, to do what it had commanded her to do. She smiled at herself. She had not known she could be so brave! She felt a warming glow of self-confidence.

But what was she to do now? She thought about sneaking back to her rooms but doubted she could avoid being seen this time. Would it be any easier to go back tomorrow? Tomorrow was the beginning of the harvest celebration. What would Vaalta do when she discovered her daughter missing? Tandela would make a scene over it, of course; Tandela would insist that she be punished. Perhaps she would never go back. What then? She could not imagine leaving, really leaving, her mother and her kin behind. Where would she go? Who would love and protect her? Where would she lay her head at night?

These thoughts plagued her as she came to a prominence on the south rim of the valley where the trees thinned providing an overlook of the Chent of Aestri. Below her the farms lay in a peaceful slumber and the ribbon of the Annue'el Roed faintly reflected the moonlight. Only here and there did the dim light of tallow candles still peek out from grimy windows and penetrate the thick night air. The castle, her home, her mother and father, lay across the broad, shallow valley. All was dark and quiet there, her absence as yet undetected. From the distance came the familiar roar of the river. Nearer at hand a sheep bleated. The gusting wind tossed the treetops.

She walked on, keeping to the high ground and the belt of trees at the foot of the Encircling Hills, for what seemed like hours. She crossed the Highgaet Roed that bisected the valley, running north to the fortress and south to the mines and forges. She turned into it for a moment, even taking a few tentative steps toward home, then changed her mind and headed back into the woods. She walked on. Now the castle and gorge were to her right, away to the northeast. She had come to the west end of the valley where it dropped off into a broken hill country that cascaded to the sea. In the distance she could see the watchtower fire. She should go back home, now, she thought as she watched the dancing light. But no, something about that fire intrigued her tonight. Or was there a voice urging her to go there and climb the watchtower? She knew the breathtaking view from its summit. The broad vista of the river in the light of the full moon would be worth the walk. But the guards. Her mother would be angry if she knew she had visited them. Tandela would surely call her purity into question. What of it? She would pass the remains of the night with them by the warmth of the watchfire. Fate could catch up with her in the morning.

Fate. What was to be her fate? Doena's words at the well came back to her. She had spoken of a great calamity, one that she must survive. The One was coming. What had she meant? Allisyn knew better than to ask. For Doena's riddles were always answered by more riddles, or met by silence. Feel for the answer, she would say, reach out with your emotions, let your heart decide you, let the reaction in the pit of your stomach decide you.

There was much Allisyn did not understand. But Doena had said that was fine. Understanding will come, she would say. Understanding is nothing, she would say, faith is everything. What Allisyn *did* understand was that Doena had touched and stirred something in her being that no other human being had ever touched, ever approached, or ever even known to be there, something deep and instinctive. Since she had met Doena, all the beliefs of her childhood, all the teachings of her elders, had come into question. Doena knew something ancient and unalterable. Allisyn could feel *that*, although she could not yet access it. Yet she felt a devotion to it she had never felt for the goddess. It was what drew her back to the hut, mysteriously, irresistibly, against her own will at times, and tonight in blatant disobedience of her elders. Her stomach convulsed at the thought of her certain and impending punishment.

The thing that bothered her most was disappointing her mother. Her mother had been so good, so protective, so sheltering, so encouraging. She was throwing that security away with both hands. And her mother was so devoted to the goddess. How could it be that her daughter could reject their religion? Her mother was the High Priestess of Faena, the mother of her people. How could the people take instruction from a mother who could not even teach her own daughter? Would she lose their respect? Would she lose her position? Would Tandela become the High Priestess?

Tandela. How could she be so jealous and so cruel? She had never done anything to deserve that kind of treatment from Tandela. Why was she so eager to find fault? Father.

The image of her father, Aefalas, came suddenly to her. Aefalas ruled a strong and prosperous city, a place for himself and a place for the goddess. Aestri was a mighty realm. Allisyn admired the strength of his arms. She admired his power. What was it that moved her to suspect at times that he was hiding something; that he did not tell her everything he was thinking behind those tender brown eyes? It was like there was a secret. Like ...like with Tandela. Was there a secret between her father and Tandela. Were they hiding something? Intuitively she knew it was true. Allisyn recalled the glances they sometimes exchanged, little out-of-the-ordinary looks she had often thought peculiar. She recalled now the way Tandela's mood would change when he entered the room. If she was angry she would soften. If she was prideful she would become demure. If sullen, she would brighten. Something surely was amiss, she felt it now. "I must talk to Mother about it when I return," she said to herself.

She struck the Watchroed that led from the fortress to the

130

watchtower. Her thoughts drifted for a time. Then they coalesced again on the image of Bronwyn. What a sad, pretty little waif! In all their stolen time together she had never uttered a single word. And those eyes, large and gentle like a fawn's! Allisyn wondered at the pair; the girl who could not speak, the grandmother who could not see, but somehow they made a life together. Somehow they added up to more than one would expect; together they gave the promise of more than either could offer individually. If only the girl could speak with the voice of the grandmother, if only the grandmother could see through the eyes of the child!

Allisyn heard voices. They came from the woods in front of her. They grew louder. She sensed she should leave the path and felt an urgency to hide. On quiet feet she ran and hid herself in a thicket some distance off the track. In a moment she saw figures; men, ...men dressed for battle, men not of Aestri. She caught glimpses of their clothing as they walked in and out of the shadows and light. They were dressed in skins of animals, like wild men. Some carried spears and leather shields slung over their shoulders, some bows or short swords. Their feet were either bare or covered with thick-soled leather shoes. She counted nearly thirty of them. The sound of voices and tramping of feet died away, leaving only the sound of blood thudding in her ears. In the eastern sky a gray light appeared.

She ran back to the Watchroed and stuck out for the tower, not more than a few minutes away. She felt confident now. No one was in front of her, she knew it. How had she come by this sudden intuition? The water, the well, the calamity! She pushed her black hood back and ran with a purpose. Suddenly the watchtower loomed across her path. She skirted its bulk. The light was growing. In the bushes down the slope she saw a dark shape. Clutching at the roots and branches of stubby trees bristling from the rock, she clambered down toward it. She stopped short. It was a man, one of her father's soldiers, lying crumpled on the ground, half concealed by undergrowth. Her eyes grew wider as she covered the last few feet. There was a dark stain on his shirt. She reached out and touched his hand. It was cold. She raised her head and spied another body further around the base of the rock. Then she knew. Faenwys was being attacked! She climbed hurriedly up the face of the rock and ran back toward the city. Someone must warn the people!

131

Vaalta awoke alone, well before first light, to prepare herself for the dawn sacrifice, the first ceremony in the Rites of the Harvest. In advance of his army, Aefalas had returned in the night but she had sent him away, as was only proper. All the husbands of the priestesses were quartered in other rooms during the time of purification of the Holy Mothers, the entire cycle of the moon leading up to the Rites. Aefalas almost always found some excuse to be away during that time.

The worries of the previous day seemed remote to her now, intent as she was on the business at hand. She thought of her beautiful daughter, Allisyn, how unspoiled, how innocent she always looked lying asleep upon her pillow. All would be well, Vaalta thought. Perhaps her daughter's transgression would be forgotten in the bustle of the days of prayer, ritual and celebration that lay before them all. Perhaps when the time came to induct her into the mysteries of Faena, all would go smoothly. Tandela would relent. Surely her proud niece would see the reason in it.

Vaalta lit a candle and emerged from her chamber, walking quietly down the stairs which led eventually past the ground floor of the castle, through a rocky alcove and into a secret suite of rooms carved from the bones of the earth beneath the fortress. The others were assembling as well, women of the cult of the goddess who would participate in the Rites.

There were three rooms below the fortress, the one in which they now stood, one centrally located which was barred by a heavy door, and another small anteroom on the other side of the middle chamber. In the middle room was a thermal spring that issued from the rock and cascaded with great clamor into a large holding basin, a clear, steaming pool scoured from the rock by the waterfall. There, in that room, in the waterfall, in the pool, dwelt Faena, the goddess herself.

Vaalta lit another candle and approached the door of the middle chamber. She placed the two burning candles in copper fixtures on the doorposts then stepped back a few paces. The others had formed two lines behind her receding into the darkness, each holding an unlit candle. Tandela was at the head of one of these queues. Vaalta removed a large key, wrapped in a pure white napkin that hung from her neck, then unclasped her robe and let it fall to the floor. She unfolded the key, placed the

132

napkin upon the floor before the door and knelt upon it. All was blackness around her save for the light of the two candles. She held the key aloft in her hands.

"Faena, great Goddess of the earth," she prayed aloud, "we yearn to come into your presence on this, the holiest of your days. We grant our assurance that all who wait before you have faithfully observed your sacred ritual and are pure of body and spirit. We pray then, allow us to come into your presence, into your inner holy place, into the cavity of your body, into your earth-womb, to bathe, to cleanse ourselves in your holy waters and to be reborn of your spirit. We pray that you will renew our fields and our flocks and bless them with new life, just as you bequeath new life to us in this moment. For this, we promise you the best portion of our harvest. For this we promise you the blood and fat of the sacrifice."

She lowered the key now and placed it on the napkin between her knees. Reaching forward, she placed her hands upon the floor and touched her forehead to the rock. She arose, taking the key, unlocked the door and swung it open. The roar of the steaming waters within leaped out to her and filled the waiting room behind her. She walked on bare feet to a chest beside the door and opened it. In the chest were thin white gowns of linen. She took one and returned to the open door. The warm vapors enveloped her. With the gown draped over her left arm, she took the candle to her right and approached Tandela. Tandela unclasped her gown and it fell to the floor. Vaalta lit the candle she held. She continued this process until each of the priestesses stood disrobed, holding a light. Vaalta then went to the chest and returned again, now handing each priestess a white linen gown.

Vaalta walked into the sanctuary followed by the twelve women. The roar of the waters increased as they entered, drowning all other sound, washing away all profane thoughts. There was only the water, the crash of it, the sulfurous odor of it, the throbbing heat of it. The vapor was so dense that the candles struggled to burn and appeared as spectral lights moving of their own volition in a dark circle; no living hands holding them, no white flesh supporting them. Vaalta proceeded around the pool until all the women were in their places. Suddenly and unexpectedly, Vaalta's candle blew out. She gazed dumbly at the smoking wick for a moment, then turned to Tandela to relight it. Tandela hesitated, abruptly awakened from the trance she had slipped into, and looked hard into Vaalta's vacant eyes, dim pools reflecting weakly the glow from her hand. Hesitantly she extended her candle. *An omen,* Tandela thought to herself. The forbidden thought lingered, playing on the surface of her consciousness, then vaporized, joining the melee of the waters, contaminating them, violating the sanctuary.

Now each woman took her candle and placed it onto a copper fixture behind them on the wall. Each held the robe above her head and let it fall over her body. Vaalta stepped first into the feverish waters. The others followed. Nine times they immersed themselves in the fecund pool of the goddess, opening themselves to her, invoking her to touch them in her mysterious and hidden ways, to permeate their minds and bodies. Prayers were chanted. Ecstatic cries erupted from each throat, mingling with the primal rush of the waters. After the ninth immersion they emerged vacuously from the basin, the now transparent white robes clinging to their tingling skin, the slick mineral waters cascading in sheets from their hair, breasts, arms and legs. Once again each took her candle. Vaalta opened the door to the anteroom and they filed out of the holy chamber exhausted, perspiring, and rejuvenated.

The ceremonial robes for the dawn sacrifice were hung there. They glimmered emerald green in the faint candlelight. In this room, heated naturally by the warm rocks, their linen gowns, their skin, their hair, were soon dry. On a word from Vaalta, they donned the green robes. Each of them now took a square white napkin from their pocket and placed it upon the floor. There they knelt while Vaalta prayed once more.

"O Faena, Mother of life, protector of your faithful people, grant us your blessing now as we go into the fields of harvest. May the sacrifice we offer be pleasing to you, may you bless the harvest and renew your fields and flocks."

They reached forward now and placed their hands on the rough floor before them. Bending their elbows, they touched their foreheads to the floor in unison.

Emerging from the anteroom they were met by a retinue of young girls, dressed in brown and red, with garlands of dried oak leaves and acorns in their hair. The girls walked before them, to their side, and behind as the priestesses marched from the fortress. Before and behind them also, bearing torches to light the way, walked the personal guard of the Holy Mothers, eunuchs all, four abreast in high leather boots and red capes that

134

flowed nearly to the ground. The eastern sky swelled with a peach-colored light. As Vaalta regained the acuity of her senses and her eyes adjusted from blackness to semi-darkness, she realized that Allisyn was not among the girls. Tandela had already made note of it, this ultimate blasphemous act, this final, fatal error.

The entourage of the priestesses and young initiates proceeded through the maze of gates and walls that led from the fortress and struck the Highgaet Roed. *"Where could she be?"* Vaalta thought as Allisyn's absence began to fret her. The worried notion would not leave her, try as she might to focus upon the impending ceremony. They walked on for a quarter of an hour until they reached the Faenmoet, an ancient circle of stones standing in an open field. The circle consisted of thirteen gray stones standing erect in a compact circle with twelve portals between them. Placed before each of the standing stones were smaller darker stones laid horizontally, so that each pair resembled a chair of gigantic proportion with a very high back. In the center of the circle was a large reddish altar stone, square in plan, and roughly the height of a table. Upon this stone was laid a blade of ancient lineage. Around the circle of stones were stationed soldiers of the guard and further out, a throng who had gathered to observe the ritual. Aefalas himself stood by the altar in the center of the Faenmoet.

The Holy Mothers reached the stone circle and proceeded into it. They paraded around inside it until, one by one, they stopped at their appointed position in front of the pairs of circle stones. On a signal from Vaalta they sat upon the low seats with their backs to the standing megaliths. Vaalta took her position behind the altar. Now Allisyn's absence was starkly obvious. She should have been by her mother's side. Aefalas gave his wife a puzzled look but Vaalta kept her eyes fixed straight ahead on the westernmost stone, and on Tandela, who sat upon it. The dewy grass felt suddenly cool against her bare feet and a chill went through her. She shivered. A perfect young ram was brought to the edge of the circle from the east. Allisyn's role would have been to retrieve it and bring it to her mother. Instead, Vaalta turned and brought it herself. Aefalas followed her with his eyes, scarcely turning his head. As he brought his attention back to the circle he met Tandela's gaze. Her eyes seemed on fire from some inner source.

Aefalas grabbed the ram and threw him onto the altar stone,

binding his feet with leather thongs. Vaalta took the knife and held it aloft, just as the sun was emerging over the top of the mountain ridge and the easternmost stone.

Belak and his men had watched the procession from the castle with great interest. He split his marauders into two groups. One group he sent off in the direction of the castle with orders to break in once they heard the sounds of battle from the fields. With the other group he shadowed the procession to the stone circle, being careful to stay far enough away as to be invisible in the dusky first light. A thin gray mist had risen from the fields in the night, aiding his purpose. As the procession pierced the crowd of onlookers and entered the circle of stones, he and his men went onto their bellies and crawled to within thirty yards of the bystanders, leaving dark streaks in the dewy grass.

Suddenly, as Belak lay in the wet pasture, he heard the sound of running footsteps. He flattened his face to the ground and lay motionless to avoid detection. A shape rushed by him. Allisyn was running through the Browse toward the crowd. "Mother!" she screamed. The crowd parted as she ran through them. "Mother!" she shouted again at the top of her voice. Belak raised himself up, seized an arrow, and bent his bow. As Allisyn reached the edge of the stone circle Belak sent the shaft flying toward the middle of her back, but she stumbled and fell face down into the soggy moor. The arrow whistled over her and found Vaalta's heart, passing cleanly through her with its force. The knife fell from her hand as she lurched forward onto the altar. Aefalas heard a sound but saw nothing until his wife fell. He leaped to her side as Belak and his men came to their feet with cries of war erupting from their throats.

Aefalas lifted the limp body of his wife from the altar. The fleece of the ram was stained with her lifeblood. Allisyn crawled unsteadily toward her father. The crowd of onlookers fell to the ground in a panic, caught suddenly between the stone circle and the advancing invaders. Hearing the cries, Aefalas jerked his head in their direction. In the next instant, he looked instinctively to the guard and realized to his dismay that they carried only ceremonial spears. *Eunuchs!* he thought with disgust and panic, *and the army is still far away in the*

136

Droemenvael. Aefalas' thoughts returned to the business at hand as arrows fell among them. Several of the eunuchs fell.

The ferocity and suddenness of the attack caught the guard completely unprepared. It was some moments before Aefalas could rally and organize them. A few he managed to send forward to meet the attack. The remainder he pulled back to protect the priestesses who had run to the center of the Faenmoet to attend the fallen Vaalta. In the meanwhile deadly shafts continued to rain among them. Two priestesses fell. The women gathered wailing upon the ground. The guards formed a ring around them. The pirates rushed the circle, swords drawn, unsatisfied to prick their victims from afar with arrows.

Belak had made up his mind to take the head of this king back to Savor on the bowsprit of his ship. He ran forward, bellowing. A guard lunged at him with his blunted spear but Belak hewed it off with a stroke of his sword, knocking him aside, and charged ahead unabated. Belak planted his sword in the belly of another. As he did one of the guardians drove a spear into his side. Belak roared, wrenched the weapon from the soldier's hands, and pommeled his face with its butt end.

Had some of the peasants not come forward with their short shearing knives drawn, Aefalas himself might have fallen. One of them grabbed an attacker from behind and stabbed at his chest. Another drove his knife deep into the back of the pirate just next to Belak, who whirled and hacked at the peasant with his sword. Now the guards, eager to die in their sworn duty to protect the Mothers, sprang forward. Some of the pirates stood and fought, giving ground slowly, while others retreated hastily to the edge of the stone circle. From there, they again shot among the women lying at the base of the altar, forcing the guards to stay and protect them with their shields while the pirates made their escape.

Meanwhile, the second group of pirates had encountered little resistance at the castle. They slew the gate wardens and ran through the city to the tall fortress, setting fires as they went. They broke the main doors of the castle and rushed inside, indiscriminately slaying the surprised inhabitants and servants. Finding the treasuries in the uppermost floors, they broke in, hurriedly throwing whatever they found of value into rough loot bags. Gold and silver plate and goblets they took, swords with jeweled hilts, necklaces and bracelets of immeasurable worth, heirlooms of inestimable price. Then as swiftly as they had entered, the pirates vanished. Gone in a heartbeat were the guttural calls and haughty laughter of the invaders. Only the crackling of fires, the moaning of the injured and dying, and the shocked cries of onlookers remained.

Belak and his marauders regrouped at the base of the watchtower. There was no pursuit. They howled at their success. Some of their comrades were left behind in the fields, it was true, but it was a small price to pay for the plunder they had taken, for the honors they had gained. The injured Belak stuffed a handful of grass and mud into his wound to stop the bleeding. He showed the gash to his men and they cheered him. Belak raised his sword above his head and bellowed with delight. Such was the glory of taking a wound in battle to the pirates of Bera. The only greater honor was to die.

"My brothers," he called to them. "Today we have fought bravely and taken much booty. My heart swells with pride of you. Let us go now, back to the ship, and sail home in glory. We have left our blood here. We have made the ground holy with the bodies of our fallen. When winter passes, we will come back, in greater numbers, with more ships, and take the rest of what these weaklings have to offer." With that, he motioned his warriors back to their ship and they set off in high spirits.

Chapter 14
The Ruined City

As the shouts of the raiders grew faint, the groans of the stricken rose to the ears of Allisyn. She lay on the ground, feeling the weight of a body atop her. With one arm she reached up and touched the smooth, cool face of the altar stone. She pushed herself up with her other arm. The dead guardian who had fallen upon her rolled to the side, his lips ashen, his unseeing eyes staring blankly skyward. The thin light of dawn slowly, painfully, revealed the extent of the carnage among the stones.

With her hands upon the edge of the altar stone, Allisyn pulled herself upward. When her eyes reached the level of its surface, she saw her mother, chest down upon the stone of sacrifice, the pale face turned toward her. A trickle of blood painted the dying woman's lips. They closed involuntarily, then opened again, as if she were attempting to utter some final word. Vaalta's eyes were locked in an animal stare. Aefalas knelt behind her, in shock, clasping her legs with his powerful, useless arms. Tremors of weeping wracked his body. Allisyn pulled her face close to her mother's. She smelled the blood on her breath. Tears welled into her eyes and overflowed their banks in a flood of grief.

Vaalta's lips moved again, activated by something deep within, a potent force that would not let her expire without finding release. Allisyn brought her ear close and placed her cheek in her mother's blood, chilled upon the cold stone.

"Watch ...for ...me," she whispered, almost inaudibly, and exhaled her last breath into Allisyn's ear.

139

A shadow suddenly came between the girl and the weak light of the sun. Allisyn lifted her head to see Tandela towering in silhouette above her. The sun had thrown her shadow across Allisyn's back, along the ground, and out beyond the edge of the stone circle like a great dark finger. Its rays touched the Browse, coaxing thin wisps of vapor from the dews. Tandela raised her arms and spoke.

"Arise, my sisters, for the sacrifice is here. Faena stands before us, Faena calls to us. Do you not see her, do you not hear? She awaits the ritual. Our duty is still at hand, to invoke her blessings upon the harvest and new life, new beginnings. Arise, gentle sisters. Tandela will lead you now."

She allowed her hands and eyes to drop and opened her arms to her shocked sisters. Those of the priestesses who were alert sat up. They raised their eyes to the one who spoke, the one who saw what they did not see. They reached upward instinctively with their hands, hands spattered with blood, smeared with mud, and touched her fingers. In their desolation they reached out for a pillar of strength, clinging to her like the wet grasses to their clothes. Those who could helped their sisters to rise. Even Aefalas relinquished his grip on the body of his wife and stood. Of the living within the circle of stones, only Allisyn lay inert, beside her dead mother.

Tandela looked down at the pair. Her eyes, devoid of pity, regarded them coldly. She motioned for Aefalas to remove his daughter and for the sisters to clear the altar of the body of Vaalta. They laid her aside with gentle hands, obediently awaiting Tandela's next command. The fettered ram that had lain silently on the altar, reddened with Vaalta's blood, smothered by the body of the High Priestess, benumbed by the smell of death, bleated. Allisyn kneeled on the ground beside the altar, her trembling shoulders supported by Aefalas' hands. Tandela raised the sacrificial knife and plunged it downward into the animal. Reaching into the belly of the young sheep, she cut away a lump of fat and split it. She rubbed it against her forehead, feeling the warmth of the oil, and in turn, anointed the foreheads of the priestesses with the oil of life. Then she turned to Aefalas. In simple obedience to the fiat of ancient tradition, he knelt and raised his eyes to Tandela, who smeared the oil onto his forehead.

"May your reign never cease, your arms never falter, your realm never fail. May the desires of your heart be granted and

140

the words of your mouth become law. As these things have been, so will they continue to be. According to the will of Faena, so be it!"

So Tandela completed, without flaw, the remainder of the ceremony. When she had finished, she was moved to speak further. Once again she lifted her arms and eyes heavenward.

"Faena, all hearing, all seeing, all knowing. You bring your righteous judgment upon those who err, upon those who stumble along your path. The candle of Vaalta has been extinguished. The blood of her body is shed. It runs out to nothingness, a stain upon the earth, a trifling flow. Your sign is clear; her time, her line, is ended. With our lips and our hearts we praise you for this holy and righteous verdict. Bless then, those who remain, who stand before you in purity."

She lowered her eyes and looked deeply into those of each priestess with a probing stare, as if to read the thoughts of their hearts. Satisfied, she cut a portion of the ram's fat for each of them, opened it and placed it in their hands.

"Go now and bless the fields with the largess of life, the fat of the harvest. Return a portion to the fields and herds. Renew and remake them. Seed them. Fulfill them."

The circle of priestesses began to revolve, joined by the young girls. They sang as they walked around the altar stone, each circle becoming larger than the last, spiraling outward toward the stones. Twelve times they circled and then departed, each passing through a portal of the stone circle and out into the fields, accompanied by one of the initiates.

Tandela, Aefalas and Allisyn were left in the Faenmoet. The dead littered the theater. The silence was tomb-like. Aefalas called for six of the guardians to bear the body of Vaalta back to the city. They came and laid their spears down in pairs, parallel to one another, then laid the body of their Mother upon them. Grasping the ends of their weapons, they lifted her up and bore her away on the bed of spears, as they would a comrade who had fallen in the field. Aefalas called the remnant of the guardians and helped Allisyn to her feet. Tandela paid them no heed. When the guard was formed, she followed them to the castle. The King and his daughter fell in behind.

Aefalas saw the smoke from the burning city long before they had reached it. He walked as if in a trance until he reached the outer walls. There he met the small detachment of soldiers, left behind in the city, who had assembled awaiting his return.

141

Taking command of both his senses and his charges, he set them about the business bringing the blaze under control. There was little they could do except to pour the contents of the cisterns on the parts not yet burned, in hopes that the waters would turn back the flames. Little was saved. By midmorning the city had been reduced to a skeleton of blackened walls. Faenwys, the city of the goddess, the city of golden splendor, was a smoking bed of cinders.

Aefalas and Tandela walked through the rubble together, surveying, pondering. Neither of them spoke.

Aefalas felt a great weight on his shoulders. He had never faced a task of such enormity. How would they rebuild the work of so many hands, the hands of generations long passed, who had labored with such effort to construct it? The autumn would soon deepen and the waning days hurry the season along into winter. Where would they live? How would they survive? He thought of his wife lying upon the grass at the entrance to the city. The first job must be to prepare her for her funeral. He tried to imagine her face and her hair, her slender body, but all he could see was the blood-stained lips, the unblinking eyes, the pallor of her dead face. In the midst of his musings, he heard stones grate and the rubble shift. Tandela was there, walking ahead of him. She bent to inspect something that lay among the ruins. Aefalas caught himself staring at the outline of her hips beneath the emerald-green gown.

In an instant he remembered the night she had surprised him on the balcony. All were asleep but he could not rest. A dream had startled him awake. He had sat upright, trembling. He had thought to awaken Vaalta and tell her of it, but he had not. Instead, he got up and walked across the room to the double doors, opened them silently, and stepped into the hallway. He could hear Vaalta's gentle breathing and was glad he had not troubled her. Closing the doors behind him, he paced the hallway for some time. Although his footfalls were inaudible, his weight caused the timbers of the floor to creak beneath him.

Not knowing why, he had gone down a flight of stairs to the floor below that housed his extended family. At the landing he had peered down the hallway. All was still. He turned and strolled out onto the balcony at its eastern end. The moon was rising and a breeze off the snowfields of the mountains was freshening the airs of the valley. To his left, the falls pulsed like the slow beat of a gigantic heart.

He pondered the dream. He had been walking in the woods with his spear, tracking a boar. He was standing in a soft bog when he heard a shoveling, rooting, ripping sound ahead of him. Suddenly the boar was there. It bristled and charged with a grunting roar. He threw his spear but the rampaging beast swerved and the throw missed. He wanted to run but found himself mired up to the knees. The boar came on, launching itself into him, slashing at his stomach with his tusks, spilling his entrails onto the ground, then gorging himself upon them. Aefalas was madly trying to fend off the boar and reclaim his lost insides when he awakened in a sweat.

At that moment he had felt a pair of soft hands upon his shoulders. His first thought was that Vaalta had awakened and followed him to find out why he was pacing when he should have been asleep, to comfort him and bring him back to bed. He stood there while her hands massaged his shoulders. He closed his eyes and felt his muscles relax. She wrapped her arms around his waist and squeezed him. Her hands moved to his chest, then back to his shoulders, then up his neck, squeezing, warming, caressing him. When he turned around to thank her he discovered Tandela standing there instead.

He brushed her arms aside and took a surprised step backwards toward the balustrade. Unabashed, she came forward, placing her arms about his neck and kissing him, pressing her thinly clad body against his. He smelled her hair, scented with lilacs. He felt her warmth, dangerous and arousing. In a moment of weakness, he leaned forward to return her kiss. Now it was Tandela's turn to act surprised, but her surprise was feigned, calculated to draw him on. She backed away, pushing aside his arms. She turned and walked through the archway leading into the hall, but stopped to look back over her shoulder, teasing him. It was then he saw the outline of her hips beneath the compliant gown. The moonlight had burned the vision into his mind, a vision he had struggled long to forget, but could not. Seeing her now, even in the broad light of day, this day of death and destruction, the memory of the touch and sight and smell of her came rushing back. It had been over a month since he had been near his wife. What a pity that she had refused him on the last night of her life. How ironic that Tandela was here, now...

He thought again of his wife and the last moments of her life on the altar, but his eyes remained firmly fixed on Tandela. She was there still, poised in the same position, as if she knew that he watched, haunted, enchanted, and frustrated.

She straightened, turned, and walked toward him, looking directly into his eyes.

"We will rebuild it... together," she pronounced, the faintest hint of smile widening her lips, her hand touching his face. He nodded hesitantly, vacantly, in affirmation, and watched her amble away.

Allisyn sat by the body of her mother until the sun was high. From time to time she reached out to take hold of the dear hand, feeling the skin become cool and firm beneath her fingertips. The day wore on. All was in turmoil. People ran here and there on urgent errands or staggered about in dazed confusion. Still Allisyn sat by her mother. Still the guardians stood by her. Toward evening Tandela and Aefalas emerged from the gates. Aefalas reached down to take his daughter's hand. Tandela stood by, stridently unmoved and reticent.

"Come Allisyn," Aefalas said, almost pleading, as if he had asked before and she had not responded. She took his hand and stood, noticing for the first time that her mother had been laid upon a light couch and covered with a black sheet, all of which now rested upon the hafts of spears. Garlands of late summer blooms had been placed around her and she had been anointed with sweet perfume. She wondered that she had not seen her mother handled or prepared in any way, aware that she had not left her side. The guardians took the body now and marched through the inner fortifications toward the gaunt walls of the fortress. Where the rubble had been cleared away on the east side, they halted. The priestesses stood around the clearing dressed in deep black. Tandela made her way into the lower vaults of the fortress and retrieved a flagon of water from the spring of the goddess. When she returned she handed it to Allisyn. Allisyn, knowing her role, dutifully prayed over the body of her mother and poured a few drops of the holy water on her head.

This done, the guardians lifted Vaalta once again upon the palette of spears and the entourage filed out of the east gate. Tandela went before them. Aefalas and Allisyn followed behind. They passed through the outer wall and turned east onto the Droemenvale Roed. Crowds gathered as the people came to offer prayers, to see their Mother for the last time. A great wailing went up from the assembly as they made their way by the gorge. The sun was sinking into a thick bank of clouds on the horizon as the tearful multitude came to the high bridge that spanned the river. The Bridge of Vapors it had been called, since time out of time. The winds gusted and moaned. Below them, the gray-blue fume rose and fell, undulating in a macabre dance of death. Tandela stood aside as the bearers took the body onto the span. Allisyn and her father stopped and waited together. On an unspoken command the bearers lifted the body high upon their shoulders and tilted the bier on which it lay. The body of Vaalta slid in a series of uncertain jerks from the platform, then tumbled stiffly, blown like a twig in a gale, and was swallowed by the mists and tumultuous waters.

Chapter 15
Voyage Into Darkness

Belak's raiders make their way triumphantly back to the sandbar where the ship lay. Mithorek, the priest, watched as they debauched from the woods and sprang onto the flat sandy spit. He had been waiting anxiously with the few men designated to guard the ship. He exhaled, long and deeply, but otherwise did not show the relief he felt.

Belak was the last to come onto the bar. Walking through the ranks of his men, grinning and spreading his arms expansively, he approached Mithorek.

"The gods have smiled upon us today! We have burned the city! We have brought a portion of its treasure and left glorious dead upon the field. I myself have taken a wound!" he announced, speaking both to the priest and to the crowd of men gathered around him.

"But now, we must leave," he added. "The tide will be running soon and we must go with it. See how the sun passes into the western sky? Winter is coming! See how the fists of the trees open and the leaves tumble from their fingers? Let us prepare for our departure!" he shouted, turning to his warriors.

"No, Belak," Mithorek countermanded. "We cannot yet leave. We still have not found an acceptable sacrifice. To leave now would be to further anger Semele."

"You and your sacrifices!" spat Belak. "We cannot give Semele her goats. There are no goats. The gods will have to do without their precious goats!" Belak answered, full of himself. "Come Mithorek, the northerners we have just attacked will soon be here to singe your beard!"

"You know the law, Belak. If no suitable animal can be found then Semele requires a human sacrifice."

"And I tell you I will not do it! I have seen these men fight bravely against a mighty army and prevail. They have shed their blood to make the prophesy of Semele come true. They have brought back treasure for Savor. It would be a blasphemy to these men to take the life of one who has fought so well."

"You speak of these *men* as if *they* were gods, Belak. What audacity! They are nothing. If one of them has to die in order to insure our safe return to Bera, then so be it. Any one of them would be glad to die for the others. They have already proved that today. Have you not witnessed it yourself in the field, brave men dying for one another?" He turned to the assembly of warriors.

"Who is here that would not lay down his life for his fellows?" he shouted.

"They died for gold, not for gods, Mithorek. These men have found, I have found, a higher purpose. Our strength is our purpose, our might is our god. And what of you, Mithorek, what of you? Are you willing to die for the others? Are you willing to be the guarantor of our safe return? Are you willing to lay open your belly and have your own entrails burnt upon the altar? Would you have it so?"

"You speak blasphemy upon blasphemy, Belak. Who would burn the incense? Who would offer up the prayers? Who would..."

"Silence!" Belak roared. "I care not for these things. I defy the gods. I curse them. I dare them to hinder my passage. The gods have given me nothing and I owe them nothing. Everything I have I possess because of these." He raised his arms and flexed his copious muscles. Veins stood out purple and thick on his neck and face.

"Then you are cursed, Belak. I pronounce this upon you. That you will never see Bera again, that the sea will drink your blood, that..."

Mithorek's words were cut short as a spear, hurled from behind Belak, slammed into his ribs. His eyes grew round and he staggered backward toward the ship. He had taken only a reeling step or two when he lost his balance and toppled over.

Belak whirled around and stared at his raiders, who fidgeted under his stare.

"Who did this?" he inquired roughly.

147

All were silent.

"What did you see?"

Again there was a long silence. Finally Reyk, the mapmaker, spoke up.

"He fell from the ship... there was a monstrous fish... with teeth. It tore him open... and swallowed him."

"What about the rest of you? What did you see?" Belak probed.

"It is as Reyk said," Samek said. "That is what we saw."

"Yes, yes. You have seen well," Belak asserted, speaking to all. "You have seen as I have seen." His grin returned and a laugh broke from his throat. "Let us make ready to leave."

Now the men fell to the task of preparing the ship for departure. They placed the booty in the hold alongside their provisions. The newly cured meat was placed in boxes of salt brought from Bera. Casks were filled to the brim with fresh water. When all else was accomplished, Belak ordered the body of Mithorek to be brought aboard. Someone whispered that he was still alive.

The few men remaining ashore threw off the ropes and dug at the hull where it had planted itself in the sand of the soft shoreline. When the ship floated free, they climbed the dangling ropes and hoisted themselves aboard, rejoining the others to pull at the oars. Reyk shouted commands. Belak manned the tiller. The ship eased away from the bar, turning and slipping down the current as it went. The tide was slack as they emerged from the mouth of the river. The wind favored them and they set the sail.

The pirate chieftain looked at the body of the priest in disgust. *"How dare you oppose me? You were so certain of your precious gods. Where were they now? Surely they did not come to your rescue. They are impotent, just as you are."* He saw the dying priest shudder and he called to him.

"Mithorek, where are your gods now? In the sea? Perhaps. Perhaps you would like to be there with them, eh?"

He summoned two of his cutthroats.

"Tie his hands together and make fast a line to them. Dump him overboard and drag him behind the ship, but keep his head up out of the water. We would not want him to drown."

The men did as their chieftain instructed.

As they prepared to throw Mithorek into the wake of the ship, Belak called out again to the unfortunate priest.

"So, Mithorek, the prophecy comes true. He fell overboard, and was torn to pieces by a gigantic fish!" Belak howled with laughter. "I am a god too, no? One who can tell the future and then make it so. Is that not the province of the gods?" He laughed again, then motioned for the pirates to throw Mithorek over the side. The priest's body hit the water but the line was too long and Mithorek went under. They sported with him for a moment, pretending they had caught something. Then they hauled him up by his hands, his head and shoulders visible, the rest of his body trailing in the water.

"Is he still alive?" Belak called, looking over his shoulder.

"Oh yes, Belak. He is alive, but he leaves a bloody trail in the water from his wound. He will not live long!"

"Perhaps long enough," Belak replied.

The sun hung above the western horizon, a great orange ball growing moment by moment more dim and bulging at the edges. Then it plunged into the depths. The wind turned now and followed, pushing them briskly down the coastline. Belak steered. He looked down at his fingers. They sensed no danger through the tiller. He felt the ponderous drag of the body as a fisherman might feel a mercurial tug on his line. Occasionally Belak would feel something hit the body, like a fish hitting a baited hook. Then he would allow himself a sardonic smile in the darkness. All was going well, very well.

Belak lashed himself to the tiller and slept for most of the night. With the following wind and a smooth sea they made good time. He awakened as the first light softened the eastern sky. Untying himself from the oaken arm he stood and roused the others with a call. In turn, they each went below and took their portion of salted venison, then returned to their stations by the oars to eat. When the first two had finished, he singled them out.

"Vassak, Droeg, pull up our friend and see how he fares this morning." Belak ordered, indicating the stern of the ship.

Belak stood and watched as the two hauled Mithorek up. The lower half of his body was gone, eaten away by sharks or other sea predators in the night. His flesh was white as a fish's, every last drop of blood having been drained away. His eyes were open. Vassak and Droeg pulled him up near the deck.

"Your gods did not protect you last night, Mithorek. Did you forget to say your prayers, or was Semele's will no match for mine? Where is your haughty tongue now, priest?"

149

"Cut him loose," Belak said at length. Droeg cut the rope and the remains of the priest splashed down into the water. What was left of the body was spun and tossed on the waves, intermittently riding crest and trough, now visible, now hidden from view, with each undulation receding further from sight as the ship sailed away. It was a gray-blue speck in the distance when finally it slipped beneath the heaving surface and was gone.

The following wind held until late afternoon when it suddenly died. The sail, which had propelled them toward home and safety abruptly relaxed and hung useless from the mast and halyard. Belak felt a change in the current. He summoned Reyk. The cartographer checked his maps and their position, confirming that they were drawing close to the mouth of the second river, the Durna. Belak looked to the west. They had waited too long to begin the return trip. The slashing winter storms would soon overtake them. Ominous clouds loomed on the horizon. Lightning flickered in their blue-gray bowels.

The ship was not becalmed for very long. The great shapes filled their lungs and blew their chill breath over the face of the waters. Large raindrops spattered on the deck of the ship. Belak lashed himself to the tiller once more. He ordered Reyk to beat a cadence and the sailors to grab their oars and tie themselves to their benches. They would make for the mouth of the middle river where they might hope for shelter. The sea rose now, inky and turbulent. The ship pitched, snared in the surge of the waves.

As the storm overtook them, the sailors began to wail and call out to Matas, frightened now that the insolence of their chieftain might lead them to their sure deaths, suddenly afraid that they might cross, accursed, into the Otherworld. Belak hurled insults at their weakness over the voice of the churning ocean.

Hailstones rattled on the deck, drowning out the beat of Reyk's drum. Belak shouted orders but they could not be heard. Waves broke over the ship, inundating the deck and washing away anything not secured. The sailors were suddenly awash amid the violence of the crashing seas. Belak stood knee deep in the surf, resolute as an oak tree.

Night came but still the storm did not abate. If anything, it increased in intensity. The sailors had ceased to row. Many of the oars were broken or washed away and the rest were useless

150

in the hands of the weary seamen. Lightning seared the skies revealing the rocky shoreline, too close to the ship. Belak shouted to his men to untie themselves and jump overboard, but his words never found their ears. He felt the hull shatter. He reached for his knife and cut the cords which bound him to the tiller, slicing his arm in his haste and the darkness. The ship lurched sideways and he jumped overboard. He swam strongly but was overpowered at length by a monstrous wave. It picked him up threw him headlong toward the shore, as if the sea were vomiting some loathsome object it had been forced against its will to swallow. It slammed him against the rocks, lifted him up, feather-like, and slammed him there again. Then Belak yielded before the vengeance of Matas and passed from consciousness.

When he awoke the light of morning was slicing through the tops of the trees at the edge of the dunes, throwing shadows across the breakers. Belak lifted his head and rolled over. He felt a knife blade of pain in his ribs and caught his breath, wincing. Lying on his back now, he looked up the beach to the north. There he saw a form, like a man, lying face down in the sand.

He looked the other way and saw Reyk walking toward him, holding something under his arm. The beach was littered with timbers and pieces of the ship he recognized. Here and there, tattered bits of sail clung desperately to rocks. He looked oceanward, where he could barely see the ragged outline of the broken hull above the white caps.

"Belak, it is good to see you alive!" Reyk called. "I have been walking the beach since the sun came up. I found many of our men drowned along the shore, ...and this." He removed the bundle from under his arm and held it out. It was his map scroll, still wrapped tightly in the oiled goatskin, which had survived the transit of the waves and washed up high upon the shore. "It is safe. We can come again, and bring others," he added grinning. Belak motioned for Reyk to help him stand. Reyk grasped his chieftain's wrist and pulled him up. Belak stood, bent with pain. His chest hurt and the wound in his side was throbbing.

"First we must get back," Belak whispered. "It is far by

151

ship and still further on foot."

"I have found none alive but you," Reyk said.

"What does it matter? We had better start if we are ever to get home."

"Over there is where the Durna flows into the ocean. Should we follow it inland, or ford it and follow the coastline?"

"What does it matter?" Belak repeated with disgust. "Let us go inland, I am sick of this briny water and these screaming sea birds."

They wandered down the beach slowly. Walking was difficult for Belak. He stopped frequently, out of breath, caught in the grip of his pain. Reyk watched him with concern. It would indeed be long until they arrived home with Belak in this condition. They had no food or weapons and winter was closing fast behind them. How would they survive? He thought of going on without Belak, but discarded the idea. He waited. They had barely made it into the trees when he turned back to his chieftain.

"B... Belak," he stammered, shivering. "You are hurt badly. You cannot walk far. Perhaps, you should wait here. I will go on and find a village, ...bring back someone to help you. Sit down here and wait."

Belak went slowly to his knees and sat down gingerly, placing his back against the bole of a great oak.

"Yes," he whispered. "Yes, find someone, anyone. Find a place where we can rest. These gods, curse these gods," he added through clenched teeth.

Reyk walked up the river until nearly nightfall. In the gloom before him, he fancied he saw dim lights and he stumbled toward them. His stomach growled. A blacker shape rose up before him, a wall. He strode eagerly forward, touched it, then followed its rough-hewn curve until he came to a gate. He called out.

A woman sitting in the gate tower heard the call and leaned out to see who it might be. The torch lights revealed a stranger.

"Who are you?" she asked curtly.

Reyk did not understand her speech, but guessing her question, answered in his own tongue.

"I am a merchant seaman. My ship was wrecked last night

152

in the storm. I have a friend. He is wounded. We are hungry. Can you help us?"

The woman understood nothing. She called a companion to watch the man while she went to get assistance, climbed down the wooden ladder and headed for the center of the small city. Arriving there, she entered the most conspicuous of the houses.

"Mother," she said approaching an aging woman, dressed in a thick woolen robe, deep burgundy in color. "There is a man at the gates who speaks in an unknown tongue. What shall we do with him?"

The old woman held her for a moment in her glassy gaze.

"Stay here, I will return."

She shuffled her way back into the house and knocked upon a set of double wooden doors. One of them was opened noiselessly from within by a girl. At the other end of the candlelit room sat a young man of perhaps twenty years, engaged in a conversation with two women. His hair and his robes were black and unadorned. The women were clothed in loose robes of a deep scarlet. The three of them sat on the floor on a carpet before a dais. A carved wooden chair stood behind them. The young man's dark eyes flashed when he saw the old woman enter.

"What is it, Grandmother?"

"There is a man at the gate, Barthol. The wardens want to know what you would do with him."

"Ah, the mariner. Bring him before me. I have foreseen his coming."

His grandmother, Meyde, hobbled out of the room.

"Go now, you two, I have work to do. We will finish this matter at another time."

The women bowed low to him and left by another door. Barthol got up and walked to the dais, where he sat upon the chair to await the arrival of the seaman.

In a moment Reyk came in, accompanied by two slim, muscular women who stood on either side. Despite their rather masculine appearance, Reyk thought them of surpassing beauty. Indeed they were. Both had long black hair that would have hung past their waists had it not been braided. Their faces were sternly handsome. They wore short, finely woven tunics of wool revealing their firm legs from mid-thigh to the ground. Over these tunics were short, fitted jerkins of thick leather. But even these trappings could not hide their shapeliness from

Reyk's famished, roving eyes. They wore broad bracelets of copper like those a warrior would wear to turn the blade of a sword. Each of them carried a staff tipped with a copper point.

One of the women motioned Reyk to his knees. He dropped down, fixing his attention on Barthol as he did, who now rose and walked forward a few steps. Reyk's eyes darted to the athletic legs of the woman to his left. Then he looked back at Barthol. If he wanted to, he thought, he could grab one of the spears, kill this boy and take these women to Belak. What pleasure this pair could bring two marooned seamen.

"What is your name?" the Dark One asked.

Even though Reyk did not understand the language of the young man, the meaning of his words formed in his mind.

"Reyk," the pirate answered tersely.

"What brings you to our city?"

Again, the meaning of the unrecognized words formed in Reyk's mind with startling clarity.

"M'lord," answered Reyk, "I am the mate of a merchant ship. We were plying our trade along this coast when a storm came out of the west and drove us upon the rocks. My captain lies wounded near the shore. I have come to ask, nay, to beg, for your assistance. He has taken wounds and cannot walk. He needs food, a place and a time to mend."

"What is your trade, Reyk?"

"M'lord, we are traders in cloth, but alas, we have lost all our goods. We are ruined," Reyk lied.

"With whom were you trading?" Barthol asked.

Reyk was growing weary of questions. He was hungry, for food and for the women who stood beside him.

"What is that bundle beneath your arm?" Barthol demanded.

Reyk gripped his maps tightly. Of all his possessions, they were the most precious. Now, in this strange land, they were all that he owned outside his own life.

"They are navigation charts. They would mean nothing to you. Only I can read them."

"We shall see. Give them to me!"

"What business are they of yours, boy?" he grunted.

"Do not be impertinent with me, Reyk. And tell me no more of your lies! I am Barthol, the son of Thol-nys. I know your mind. And I know your trade. You are no merchant. You are a pirate. Your business is death and your joy is plunder. All this Thol-nys has revealed to me! Give me the charts!"

Unmasked and desperate, Reyk lunged at the young man. In the same instant, the warrior-woman to his right twirled her spear and caught him under the throat with its shaft. The other threw herself between Reyk and Barthol and thrust her spear to within an inch of his heart. Reyk dropped his bundle to the ground and grabbed the spear instinctively, forcing it away from his throat, testing the strength of the woman. The woman crouching before him put her hand on the bundle and dragged it away, still keeping her spear pointed at Reyk's chest.

"I do not fear you, Reyk, nor your chieftain. But I do have business with you. You are to lead a troop of my soldiers to him and come back here, the two of you. We will make him whole and send you on your way. But you must pay me in return for my hospitality."

"And what might that payment be, Barthol?"

"It is of no concern to you, Reyk. You are in no condition to barter. You have no alternative but to accept my terms. Unless of course you wish to die now. That alternative is always open to you. You have only to tell me that you wish to die and I will have Tama here accommodate you." He paused. "No? Well then, I see that you choose to see reason. Good.

"Tama, feed him. He will be our guest for the evening. Let him sleep in the barracks with the soldiers." He turned his attention back to the pirate.

"Reyk, you will find that all of my soldiers are women. In fact, you will find only women in this city. There are no males, besides myself. That is a curiosity to you I see. Do you want to know why? It is because all the men are executed. It is the law of Thol-nys. These are my women; she has given them to me and me to them. I am father, husband and son to the women of this city. We are well versed in death here, Reyk. Do not try to run from my soldiers, do not try to fight them, do not try to handle them; for they will kill you without a second thought. Men are detestable to them. All men but me. We are one, with each other, with Thol-nys."

With that Barthol turned his back and stepped up upon the dais. The warrior-woman, Tara, raised Reyk to his feet, her spear still under his chin and tight against his throat. The other, Tama, pressed the tip of her spear against his back and they escorted the pirate from the presence of their master.

155

Chapter 16
The Taming of Reyk

Reyk awoke before dawn of the next morning in the barracks of the warrior-women. They were quartered in a long, low wooden hut with spartan accommodations. Each woman slept in a space upon the floor, just as Reyk had. Wheat straw was piled in each place and a sheep skin thrown atop each pile of straw to make a bed. The arms of the women, spears, short swords, bows and arrows, hung upon the wall at their heads. They slept in their woolen tunics; their leather vests hung on the wall along with the rest of their battle gear.

Reyk did not move but lay, in the middle of the barracks, surveying the sleeping forms all around him, listening to their slow, measured breathing. He cursed his situation; a man alone in a hut with scores of lean, beautiful women and death as his reward if he so much as touched one of them. They had not even bothered to bind him in the night, so confident they were in themselves and in the effect of Barthol's words. When he lay down, he had not gone to sleep instantly, for many thoughts passed through his mind. He thought of bolting and running for his life, killing and breaking through the gates. He thought of sneaking past the sleeping women and slipping silently away. But how would he escape over the high wooden walls unnoticed? Finally he thought of reaching out and touching the sleek, sun-bronzed, thigh of the woman sleeping next to him. But judgment prevented him from doing so, overriding his instincts for now. The night was half spent when he finally drifted off into an uneasy sleep.

The women began to stretch now, rolling this way and that,

yawning as the first light of day found its creeping way into the barracks. One by one they sat up. Now they stood, brushing the straw from their tunics and combing it from their hair. At the end of the room the woman he recognized as Tama and several others were arraying themselves in their panoply of battle. Reyk lay yet motionless. Tama came to his place and with an upward flick of her drawn sword ordered him to stand. They marched away as a group with Reyk in their midst, out the back of the barracks, following a well-worn path through thick-trunked oaks that led to the river. Here while Tama and her two companions guarded Reyk, the remainder of the guard removed their tunics and took their morning baths. The sight of all these well-tuned female bodies was too much for the frustrated Reyk. He lay down and closed his eyes until the bathing was over.

He was still sleepy and dozed until he was surprised by the blunt end of a spear in his ribs. He got up slowly, addled by his sudden awakening, and marched with the women back into the barracks. There they were joined by others. When they left the barracks again, about a tenth of the warrior-women were in the body that followed Tama. With Reyk in their midst, they walked to the main gate of the city. Eyes burning from lack of sleep, he watched as the strange city came to life.

It was almost midday when Reyk led the women to Belak, still lying beneath the tree where they had parted company. The surprised pirate sat up painfully at their approach. Tama halted her troop and examined him from a distance. She motioned for several of the women to cut branches roughly four feet in length and an inch in diameter. They laid them on the ground and wove them loosely but expertly into a sturdy mat, lashing the ends together with leather thongs. Tama motioned for Reyk to help Belak onto the mat. Belak looked at Reyk, and the female soldiers, with wonder. But the wonder left his face when he tried to get up and the pain in his chest and side returned. Reyk helped him as best he could onto the wooden lattice. When he finally lay there, each of the women grabbed the protruding end of a stick and lifted Belak from the ground. In this fashion, they carried him all the way to the village, stopping only once for a brief rest. Reyk was amazed at their strength and endurance. Belak lay as one dead upon the bed of sticks, having passed out from the pain that wracked his chest as the women jostled him over the uneven ground.

When they reached the village, the two captives were placed

157

in a pit near the barracks. A lattice, not unlike the one upon which Belak had been borne into the city, was placed over the top of the hole. Large stones were placed around the perimeter atop it and four soldier-women were left to guard the prisoners. When bread was thrown to them, they ate greedily. It was many sweltering hours later when the retiring sun began to lose its strength and cast the bottom of the pit into shadow, much to the relief of its inhabitants.

It was early evening and the sweating prisoners were dozing wearily when the cage-like cover of the pit was abruptly thrown aside. Reyk was ordered out and a old woman crawled into the pit with Belak. She examined him, looking carefully at the wound in his side. He had a raging fever. She opened the wound, washed and bled it, then dressed it with a poultice. When she had gone, Reyk was ordered back into the pit where he passed the night with the delirious Belak.

Within the week, Belak's wound had begun to heal and the throbbing pain in it subsided. His fever broke one afternoon in a cold, drenching sweat. Food and drink took their effect and strengthened him. Soon he could sit up and talk. The pain in his ribs persisted however, making it difficult for him to breathe, and lingered in his chest until his dying day.

Days in the pit passed slowly. One morning when Reyk awoke a rime of frost had covered the ground. He watched Belak shiver in his sleep as he lay on the earthen floor of the pit. Reyk wondered what was going to happen to them. What were the conditions, the bargain, the terms that Barthol would demand in exchange for harboring them? They could not live in this pit forever. How many weeks had they been imprisoned here? He had lost track of the days. The stench of their own filth was unbearable in his nostrils. Flies harassed them by day and rats scurried across their bodies at night. The weather was growing cold. Would Barthol turn them out now that Belak had recovered? Would he allow them to stay in the city through the winter and then send them home? Or did he mean to let them die in this stinking hole? Reyk pondered these questions this morning, as he had each morning of their captivity. He was heartsick. He longed for freedom. He longed to stand once more on the rolling deck of a ship with the sky stretched to each horizon above him. He felt he would do anything to be free once again. He would humble himself. He would promise anything. He would do anything Barthol wanted. How the thought of freedom burned him!

Sometimes when the monotony of the hole became unbearable, Reyk would become angry. In those times he fantasized that he and Belak would break free from the pit to take Barthol's young, impudent life. Then the city of women would be theirs! How marvelous that would be! They would bend the arrogant women to their will. They would call the women whenever they chose to call them, do with them what they would, and send them away when it was their pleasure. Their lust would know no bounds! Never again would they feel the sharp tip of a spear against their chest, held there by the thin arms of a woman. Yes, Reyk and Belak would have revenge on their captors. It would happen. Knees would bow. Heads would roll. How gloriously gory it would be!

Hearing a noise above him, Belak stirred and raised his head. Something was afoot. Scraping sounds announced the removal of the stones from the lattice cover. With blurred vision he saw the warrior-women heaving them away. The cover was lifted off. Tama was there with an armed escort. She ordered them out of the pit with a gesture of the spear in her hand. Belak and Reyk rose to their feet.

"No matter what happens, Reyk," Belak whispered into the ear of his comrade, "I am not getting into this hole again. If they try to put me back in I will fight, I will die, but I will not spend another day in this pit."

Reyk nodded in confident agreement but his eyes darted uncertainly about. A rough-hewn wooden ladder was lowered into the hole and Belak climbed out, followed by his haggard companion. The soldier-women led them along a narrow path through the woods away from the river. They climbed a craggy slope, Belak watching constantly for a chance to run or fight his way free. Cresting the hill, they came at last to a rocky shelf. A steamy trickle emerged from the rock face behind it and gathered itself into a deep pool. The slippery rocks of the pool were covered with orange, yellow and green lichens and mineral deposits. The smell of hot sulfur hung in the air. Above them were more of the trim, taut-muscled women. Their bows were strung and each held an arrow at the ready. Belak realized there would be no escape short of death.

159

Tama came forward, gesturing for the men to remove their clothes and get into the pool. Belak's nature was to resist, to follow no one, nothing, except the dictates of his own mind. He stubbornly refused. Tama barked an unintelligible order at him and made gestures with her hands. Reyk eyed Belak nervously. When Belak did not move, a group of soldiers came forward and grappled with him. He fought, but in his weakened condition was bested and thrown to the ground. The sentinels stretched their bowstrings to the limit, muscles rock-hard, fingertips imprinting their cheeks, and trained their arrows at his heart. A spear was thrust into this face. Ungentle hands grabbed his clothing and forcibly removed it. Then he was made to stand. One of the women examined the wound in Belak's side. Tama shouted her order at Reyk who began ashamedly to remove his own tattered garments, never taking his eyes off the stern woman. When the two men were disrobed, they were forced at spearpoint into the steaming pool.

At first the hot water stung their skin, but they became accustomed to it and relaxed under its soothing influence. Belak placed his head under the surface, scrubbing his hair and beard with his fingertips. Reyk followed his lead. They had been in the bath for a quarter of an hour when Tama ordered them out.

Belak wondered what would happen now if he didn't comply. Would they come in after him? He sat without moving. Tama gestured for them once again to get out. Reyk started up but Belak caught his forearm and pulled him back.

"Stay," he demanded.

The incensed Tama ordered two of the women into the pool to retrieve Belak. They waded in. Belak moved back toward the rock face, watching them like an animal at bay. The women lunged forward unafraid and he wrestled with them, churning the waters of the once quiet pool. Reyk backed away involuntarily. Belak captured a lock of hair of one, twisting it into a rope, and pulling it tight. Overpowering her, he forced her head beneath the waters. She struggled desperately. The other flung herself on his back and clutched at his throat with an animal-like growl. Belak swung a massive fist at her, still holding the head of her frantic companion beneath the steaming surface. Tama watched the fight, her eyes subtly widening. Reyk's own eyes darted to hers. It was the first hint of uncertainty he had ever seen on her face.

Tama reacted quickly, ordering two more of her warriors

160

into the pool. They waded in, waist deep, brandishing spears. One of them jabbed her weapon into the beleaguered Belak's shoulder. Blood flowed and he stifled a cry. Enraged, he let go of the woman he held beneath the waters and wrenched the arm of the other from around his neck, tossing her aside like chaff. He stood upright now, chest expanded, roaring a challenge. The blood from his shoulder flowed in rivulets down his arm and dripped from the ends of his fingers, staining the waters of the pool. The women drew back, all except one. She had never risen when Belak released her. Now her lifeless body drifted slowly downward and came to rest on the rocks at his feet.

Tama turned and whispered in the ear of one of the warrior-women who stood beside her. The woman nodded and sprung down the path back toward the village. Tama allowed a smile to cross her lips as she stood, resolute, waiting, watching Belak to see what he would do next. His chest heaved. Then, not having yet realized that he was wounded, his eyes went slowly to his shoulder. He placed his hand there, applying pressure to stop the bleeding. The blood seeped from between his fingers.

"Come on then, you dog of Barthol! Come in and fetch me yourself!" Belak shouted angrily at Tama. "Or go yelping back with your tail sweeping the dirt to lick your master's feet! Tell him to come and fetch me out himself. I will tear his miserable head off!" he added and sat back down. Reyk said nothing. In all the struggling, he had not moved, had not lent a hand in aid to his chieftain. His hesitation had not gone unnoticed by Belak, nor by Tama.

For three days Belak and Reyk stayed in the pool, burning during the day, shivering at night. For three days they neither ate nor slept nor spoke. And Tama did the same. She stood by the pool, eying Belak, neither eating, drinking or sleeping, challenging him, through the darkness and the light. Others came and went and changed the watch, but Tama stayed, locked in a contest of will and endurance with the pirate chieftain. *One of them must relent,* thought Reyk. They could not go on forever.

On the morning of the fourth day, Reyk broke the silence and slid over to Belak's side.

"Belak," he whispered weakly. "I am hungry and this water drains the very life from me. Come, let us go out. You have made your point. You have beaten them. They are afraid of you now that they see the strength of your will and your arms. You

161

did not allow them to overcome you. Come," he said, taking hold of Belak's arm. Belak jerked it away and shot Reyk a fierce, crazed look.

"No," he said forcefully. "We have not beaten them, not her," he said pointing to Tama, "not this pig. She means to beat me in this waiting, starving, thirsting game. But she will not. I will not go, not until she falls down or takes leave of the pool."

"I must go, Belak," Reyk whined. "I have not your strength, nor your will, nor your desire to persevere. I am hungry," he repeated. "I must go."

"If you go, Reyk, you will forever be a slave to her, to Barthol, to this moment."

Reyk tried to think about Belak's words, but he could not force himself to do so. He could only think of getting out, of eating, of drinking cool water. He dragged himself to the edge and crawled out. When he did the warrior-women bound him and dragged him away.

Now there was only Belak, Belak and Tama. He looked at her through eyes half-closed, squinting against the reflection of the sun off the glistening waters. She was beautiful and strong, strong of mind and body. Such a mate she would make for a man like himself! Together no one could vanquish them. If only he could make her see how foolish was her allegiance to this pup, Barthol. Together they could rule the city. He stood up and walked to the edge of the water on the slick rocks.

He reached out his hand to her, bringing it within inches of hers. As he flexed the muscles of his shoulder his wound seeped blood.

"Come join me in the pool, Tama," he taunted. "I see that you are a fine, strong woman. What such woman could resist a man like me?"

Tama's eyes remained fixed on his. She was unmoved. Belak laughed, returned to the water and sat down, pushing the bloated body of the dead woman out of the way with his foot.

"With a few more days of this stewing, she will be done and I will have myself a feast. What will you eat Tama, my girl?" He laughed again.

In the afternoon red clouds appeared in the west. By nightfall they had blanketed the sky. The weather turned cold. The wind rose. Belak was glad to be in the warm waters, but his stomach gnawed at itself. He was beginning to weaken. But he would die before he would let this vixen outlast him.

The sun rose the next morning but could not penetrate the woolly clouds. Everywhere lay a mantle of white, except in the pool where Belak sat. The flakes fell sporadically but did not affect him, dissolving with serpent-like hisses into the steaming waters. Belak turned to see Tama still standing beside the pool, her shoulders and her hair rimed with white. He was amazed that she stood so firm, unaware that it was not the strength of her own mind and body that had sustained her, but the perverse will of her master. He began to wonder for the first time if he could hold out, if he really could beat her.

The snow fell throughout the day and night. In the afternoon of the next day, Tama sank to her knees. Belak's hopes rose and he laughed weakly. By evening Tama was sitting on the ground in the snow and mud. The next morning when the sun rose, she lay unconscious. Belak crawled to the edge of the pool. Standing on uncertain legs, forcing them to uphold him against their own weakness, he stepped out of the pool over the body of Tama. He started down the path toward the city but had only gone a few steps when he was apprehended by the soldier-women. They bound his hands and half-dragged him down the path. Behind him, others lifted Tama from the ground and carried her off in the same direction.

Belak was led to a clearing in the woods. There he saw Reyk, his arms pulled behind him and tied around a large elm. Before him but beyond of his reach lay a plate of stewed venison, a loaf, and a flagon of wine. The emaciated Reyk was leaning forward, asleep, or unconscious. His head was nearly between his knees. He drooled involuntarily and stood in his own filth.

The women lashed Belak to a tree nearby, facing his comrade. Belak resisted meagerly but his strength was almost gone. Night came and the naked men shivered. The rough integument of the trees wore sores in their skin and the acids in the bark made the abrasions itch and swell. The next morning steaming fresh food was brought and set before them. Its aroma rose to their nostrils. But Belak was beyond hunger. He seemed not to smell at all. He grew weaker. Day passed into night and darkness mingled with the light until all was a gray blur.

On the morning of the next day, Barthol, surrounded by his guard, strode purposefully into the clearing. He addressed the prisoners in a proud voice, filled with derision.

"My friends!" he said expansively. "I have come to save you. Are you ready to parley?" Neither of the captives responded. Their heads remained bowed. "They are asleep, Tama. Perhaps we have arrived too early!" he jeered, looking around at his women for their reaction. A convulsive spasm of laughter passed through their ranks.

"Tama, get their attention for me."

Tama, who had been nourished back to health, walked to Belak and jerked his head up by a greasy lock of hair. His eyes were vacant.

"Belak, do you wish to serve or to die?" Barthol demanded.

With his remaining strength Belak formed his last words as mortal man.

"I choose... death... over... serving... dogs," he said loud enough for Barthol to hear.

"Very well, Belak. Tara, lift the head of Reyk so he may watch his friend go to meet his gods," Barthol said without emotion.

Tara walked to Reyk and jerked his head up, pointing his eyes straight at Belak.

Tama removed her sword from its scabbard with a ring.

"The penalty for being too much awake, Belak," pronounced Barthol, "is to sleep forever." With that Tama swung her sword. Belak's head rolled to the feet of Reyk. It came to rest, face up in front of him, the eyes in the head darting about in terror, the mouth moving as if to speak, but no words came. Then the mouth was still and the eyes frozen open, staring blankly at the sky.

"And now you, Reyk. Will you serve?" Barthol asked with a twisted smile.

"Willingly, Master, my lord... Barthol. I would have... sooner... if... you had... but... asked," he wheezed. Then darkness overcame him.

Within a week, given food and drink, Reyk had recovered from his forced starvation to the point that he could walk on his own. Still very thin, the deep hollows in his cheeks gave him a ghastly appearance, and his eyes protruded a little more than normal. A color of a sort had returned to his skin and a light, or rather an unearthly glow, like that of smoldering embers veiled

164

by ashes, simmered in his eye. When he was finally summoned to Barthol, he went enthusiastically.

Barthol met him in the same room where they had first spoken. Tama and Tara ushered him in. Reyk threw himself abjectly onto the floor as soon as he saw Barthol and stayed there until his master summoned him to rise.

"Reyk, I am glad to see you are well. Come."

Reyk approached the dais. Barthol studied him carefully.

"I am glad that you take such delight in my service now, Reyk. I can bestow many gifts upon the faithful," he added.

"Yes Master. You can reward and you can punish. I know this well."

"Reyk, I want you to come and sit beside me, here, in this chair." Barthol pointed to a chair to his right. There was a small table between the two chairs and on the table was Reyk's bundle. "I want you to tell me all about your journeys, where you have been and what you have seen. Come, my friend, do not be afraid!"

Reyk approached the dais with much bowing and fawning and sat down.

"With your permission," he said before reaching out with his hand toward the bundle. Barthol nodded.

"This is a map, Master," he said, untying the bundle and removing the goatskin cover with difficulty, "a drawing of the coastline, a drawing that shows the way from my homeland to the furthest extent of our journey," he added as he unrolled the scroll, placing it between them upon the table.

"See, here is my home. I live on an island, called Bera. The king of the island is Savor. He is very powerful. As long as we have lived upon this island, we have been a people of the sea and of ships. Savor has many ships. There are other ships too, ships owned by fishermen, but Savor commands all the warships."

"What does Savor do with his warships?" Barthol asked.

"Master, if you please, he sends them out to raid the coastal villages in other lands. They bring back gold and slaves."

"And is that why you were near our shores?"

"Yes, Master. The villages near our home we plundered until they were bled dry. Then a shipbuilder in our country made a discovery that would make the ships lighter and stronger and faster. That meant we could sail further."

"Tell me more about your homeland, Reyk."

165

"In our country, we worship a goddess, as you do. Her name is Semele. She is..."

Reyk saw Barthol's eyes kindle and he stopped short in abject fear.

"There is no divinity other than Thol-nys, Reyk. She is the Originally Begotten, the All Powerful. Do you understand?"

"Yes, I know this lord, this Semele, she is a minor goddess, of no great importance, hardly divine at all. Please lord, I did not mean to misspeak. I am an ignorant man. Please do not be angry with your most humble servant, please lord, please..." Reyk almost cried and a thick white spittle dotted the corners of his mouth.

"That will do Reyk, but never mention her name again in my presence. Do you understand?"

"Yes, Lord Barthol, yes."

"Go on then."

"Yes, lord, with your permission. Savor has an oracle who speaks for this, this, false goddess, and the oracle told of a land, a city, to the north, where there was much gold, strong men and beautiful women that would make excellent slaves. So Belak, the best sailor and warrior in Savor's service, was told to go and find this city. We sailed from here, at Bera, all along the coast to the west for many weeks," Reyk said, his finger tracing the outline of the coast. "We passed the mouth of the great Vinsa. We raided many villages along the way, but we discovered no cities of gold. We came here, to this point, and then the coastline turned north. We passed a river, the Orna, we called it, which means 'first river' in our tongue.

"Then we came to another river, the very river that flows by your city, lord Barthol. And we named it the Durna, which means 'the second river' in our language."

"The Iechryn, in ours," instructed Barthol.

"The Iechryn, yes, lord, the Iechryn," Reyk said with some difficulty. "We had sailed all the summer and were about to lose hope of ever finding the City of Gold, when we came to the third river, this, the Trona. We sailed up and beached our ship. Belak led us forward on foot. We came to a strong city, we saw beautiful women and strong men, and we found gold there too. We sacked the town and made off with some of the plate and jewelry. It lies on the bottom of the sea, not far from here."

Barthol leaned back in his chair and laughed.

"Then this is our bargain, Reyk. In the spring you shall

166

leave this city. You may build a boat and sail home or you may walk, but you shall return to your home. There you will tell them this tale of the golden city and make them hunger for it." Barthol leaned forward as he spoke. "You will lead them back with your maps, but you will not take them to the City of Gold. You will bring them here, to me. Then together we shall all come to Guldwys, and we shall conquer it. The gold we will melt down and forge into an image of Thol-nys, the Indestructible Destroyer, and the people will become her slaves. There will be many men to sacrifice to her, and we will prosper, and the women will become ours, just as the women of this city have become mine. This I promise you, Reyk."

Barthol looked at Reyk with an intensity the unfortunate man had never before experienced. There seemed to be a fire in the Dark One's eyes that burned the message indelibly into the map-maker's brain. The look forced him downward, to his knees, then to his belly. It weighed upon him like a great crushing boulder, pressing him to the ground.

"I will do... everything... you ask, master," Reyk replied, gasping for breath.

"Good. Now, that you have made your vow I will give you a gift, Reyk. I will give you a woman, a woman of my own."

Reyk looked at Barthol with a sudden combination of lust and fear.

"Among our people there are two classes of women, Reyk. There are the warriors like Tama and Tara, here. We call them the *Dorni*. And there are the women of my harem. These women we call the *Anyllonde*. The purpose of the *Dorni* are to protect me, the son of the all-powerful Thol-nys, the Divine Calamity. The purpose of the *Anyllonde* is to bear children. When they are too old for my pleasure and for child-bearing, they work the fields and tend the flocks. The female children grow up to become *Dorni* or *Anyllonde,* as their skills and fortunes dictate. The male children are given to Thol-nys for sacrifice, for she lives upon their blood."

Reyk, still prostrate on the ground, felt a shudder run through him and moisture bead on his lip and forehead.

"Arise now, Reyk."

Barthol clapped his hands and a young woman came through curtained doorway from an adjoining room. She walked silently to the place where Reyk lay. As he picked himself up from the floor he took the whole of her in, her small feet, the tantalizing

167

curve of her thigh, the slender waist, the abundant breasts. He smelled her perfumed aroma. He looked at the pleasing features of her face, the dark, fiery magnificent eyes, the finely wrought nose with its sharp-rimmed nostrils, the generous blood-red lips. Her head was crowned with a mane of jet black hair that trailed to her waist.

Reyk immediately felt, in stark contrast, ashamed of his gaunt appearance, his skinny legs, his hollow cheeks, his bulging eyes. He seemed dried up and impotent in her presence. A new thought rose vaporously into his mind, condensed and wormed its way about like a viper inside his brain. With his inner eye he watched it slither about until he recognized it. Suddenly he was afraid of what Barthol might ask in return for this gift. In the next instant he was afraid that Barthol might know his thought. His hands trembled with longing and fear.

"This woman... is a gift of surpassing excellence, Lord Barthol," he said when he could speak. "Please, do not give her to me, I am not worthy."

"If you do not take her I will not be pleased," Barthol rejoined.

Reyk had to swallow hard before he could speak again. The lump in his throat seemed to be in the way. The room and everything in it faded to shadow and he saw the head of Belak lying on the ground before him, or was it his own? Why had that picture come? This vision faded and another appeared. He was free again, sailing in a strange ship on a dark, wild, unfathomable ocean. Abruptly, the wind shifted and his sail hung limp against the mast. He knew there was only one reply he could make.

"Yes, master. If it please you, I will take her."

Chapter 17
The Enchantment of
Aefalas

There was both sorrow and confusion in Faenwys following the raid of Belak's marauders and the funeral of Vaalta. What normally would have been a joyous and fulfilling harvest festival was thrown into chaos. The Council of Matriarchs was convened to seek the will of the goddess in the appointment of the new High Priestess. They met, as ever, in the rock chambers below the ruined shell of the fortress. This holy place had been untouched, undefiled by the hands, the feet, the breath, or the fire of the raiders. Never had its stones known or felt the footfall of a man.

The Council did not go smoothly. The matriarchs were divided as to whether Tandela should assume the office. There was concern that she was unwed and childless. Would Faena approve that her chief attendant had not been proven fertile? Still, Tandela was faithful and knowledgeable in the ways of the goddess. Had she not received visions in which the goddess spoke to her? What were the alternatives? Who was more qualified? In addition to these arguments, she was Vaalta's niece, which made her by kinship the ranking matriarch of the Council, though youthful in comparison to the others. Still, the older women were unconvinced. Though they had entreated Faena and offered many sacrifices, no clear sign was forthcoming from the goddess on the matter.

After a day of much debate no decision had been reached. Meanwhile, time was passing and the rituals which should have been performed for the benefit of the people were neglected. When it looked as though the tide of opinion might turn finally against her, the frustrated Tandela decided on a desperate tactic. As ranking matriarch and the one to whom the others had turned in the recent crisis, she suspended the proceedings. She had called the council and she could adjourn it. She decided it was time to see just how useful her *uncle*, Aefalas, would be to her.

Evening found him meeting with the city magistrates, a group of officials who performed minor duties necessary to the efficient functioning of the town and the Chent. Aefalas had recruited them to serve as the leaders of the rebuilding effort. They were gathered in a ground-floor room of the castle which had been left a shell by the flames but still had four standing walls. The roof was open to the sky and the door was a charred ruin. Aefalas stood as Tandela entered the room. She paused in the blackened doorway.

"Tandela," he saluted, turning toward her, "it is good that you have come. We have been discussing the clearing of the city, the housing of the homeless, and the rebuilding. We need the advice of the Council."

"Aefalas, I must speak with you, now," she parried. "These other matters can wait."

Aefalas acquiesced with little hesitation and dismissed the others. When the last man had filed out, she drew closer to him and spoke in a whisper.

"Aefalas, the Council has not confirmed me. I want you to intervene on my behalf."

"What are you asking, Tandela? The affairs of the Council are not within my authority to influence. There is nothing I can do."

"There is, dear uncle. There is something you can do. You can marry me. As your wife they would have no choice but to confirm me."

"But Tandela, I cannot marry you. You are my niece."

"It matters not to me."

"But it will matter to others."

"What are the others to me, to us? Their opinion counts for nothing. Besides, there is no civil law that says we cannot marry. There is no dictate of Faena that forbids it. It is only convention. People such as we can flout convention. We *make* the conventions that others follow," she said haughtily.

"But there is a law concerning the time of mourning. The

king may not marry until the mourning period is completed. The king must wait a year following the death of his wife before he can marry. This *is* written. And we must have a High Priestess before that. She must carry out the harvest rituals or all will suffer."

"*You* can change the law. You *are* the law Aefalas. You *can* do this!" she added growing agitated.

"I do not wish to change it, Tandela."

Tandela took a step backwards.

"You do not wish it? What do you mean, Aefalas? Do you not desire me? Am I flawed? Would I not make you a good wife, a dutiful one, a regal one, a wife who would be the envy of other men, Aefalas? Am I not beautiful enough?"

Tandela dropped her head to her chest and feigned tears. The light of the room grew dimmer by a degree as the falling sun dipped lower into the bruised sky. Aefalas stepped toward her and she burst into tears. He reached out to put his hand upon her shoulder. Feeling his touch she pulled away and ran to the other side of the room, sinking into the corner. He watched her as she retreated. She was beautiful enough, he thought. He considered walking away, he should have walked away, but he did not. He walked toward her instead, drawn on by some mystical force, against his better judgment, if not against his desire. He kneeled beside her.

"Tandela, I..."

She turned her face bringing her lips close to his. He felt her breath rolling in shallow pants across his face. She placed her arm about his neck and drew him into a long kiss. When she had finished she spoke.

"Now, my love, my strong Aefalas, will you not decree that we may marry?"

Aefalas wavered.

"I will... consider it. All this comes too quickly and amid a thousand other responsibilities to the people."

"Yes, Aefalas, think of the people. You must think of their needs. And what do they need now? They need a High Priestess, a strong woman who can take them through this trouble. Will they have that need met? Put aside your doubts Aefalas. *I am* that woman. Who did they turn to when Vaalta was pierced? Who kept her head and was a pillar they could lean on. What other choice, Aefalas? What other choice is there? None that will withstand logic. I alone can give them

171

what they need. I alone can give you what *you* need, Aefalas,"
she said, her lips brushing against his as they moved to form the
words.

"If I did not know better, I would swear that you are a
sorceress, Tandela, so potent is your spell," he said with some
difficulty. Tandela smiled inwardly.

An echo of her recurring dream; the clearing, the swine, the
well and the water turning to blood involuntarily rippled through
her mind. Then it was gone.

"A sorceress I would be, if only to conjure you tonight, my
love."

He reached out to place his hand on her cheek and to once
again press his lips to hers. But knowing well her craft, she
suddenly stood, as if there were a pressing need to go. "Meet
me at midnight, Aefalas, at the shrine of the goddess," she
whispered hurriedly, and ran out.

Aefalas stood in the charred room alone now, his palms wet
with perspiration and his knees aching from kneeling on the hard
stones. Had she really asked him to meet her at the shrine of the
goddess? Madness! It was forbidden for a man to enter there!
The law was death to the man who defiled that place, and he was
not above the law. No man had ever died for it because no man
had ever dared to do it. Insanity! He shook his head to cast off
her spell and walked from the room out into the twilight.

He strode away from the ruins of the castle and continued on
until he came to the scorched gates of the outer wall. Here he
paused. Everywhere people were settling down for the night in
makeshift quarters, either in tents or the fragments of burned out
buildings. His mind was clear now, like the sky. He gazed up
at the flawless heavens. The guiltless stars were beginning to
burn brightly there, pinpoints of light strewn in a milky swath
across the vaulted arch of blackness. He decided to go on.

He passed through the outer ramparts into the broad valley
of the Chent. He came to the Faenmoet and paused for a
moment. The memories of the day before flooded the recesses
of his mind, floating up images of the bloody fighting, the
shouting, the whistling of arrows, the smell of fear, of Vaalta,
now standing erect and stately, now falling heavily upon the
stone, bleeding, panting, expiring, of her eyes, vacant and still.

172

His throat tightened. His thoughts ran to Allisyn. He wondered that he had not seen her all day. Then they turned once again upon his wife. No more would he hear her voice, touch her hand, feel her breath upon his face.

Her breath upon his face. The face of Tandela appeared close to him. His pulse quickened. How was it that he felt as he did for her? She... she was his niece. How could he think of marrying her? It would never do. What was it about her? When he was not near her his thoughts were lucid and firm. But when he came within her sphere, his purpose seemed to falter, his resolve to weaken, his will to bend, until he was caught in her net, as surely as fishermen catch the shimmering piscines in theirs.

And now she wanted him to meet her at the shrine of the goddess. If it was such lunacy to go there, why then was he contemplating it? The scene appeared before him. He stood at the doorway to the cavern. Overhead the moon rode, bathing him in its light. The doorway was a black void before him, beyond it the heavy rumble of the waters. A pale hand extended out of the blackness, white as death. It opened upwards to him and beckoned him to enter. He passed through the plane of the doorway, out of the light and into the the cavern. She was there. He could feel her breath on his face again.

For hours he wandered the fields, hills and woods with this picture in his mind, walking on and on into the void, the pale hand always before him. The moon rose. The wind rose. He thought he heard someone call his name. He turned around to face the ruined city. He stepped in that direction. One foot followed another until he stood at the entrance to the shrine. The subterranean waters roared. He stood immobile, not knowing why he had come, not knowing why he did not leave.

Tandela inched forward from the blackness into the revealing moonlight. It touched her forehead, her cheekbone, the tip of her nose, her shoulder. Her hand reached out to him.

"Come inside, quickly!" she whispered. And he did.

She shut the door behind him and locked it. Now it was utterly black.

"Why have you come, Aefalas?" she asked. The question caught him off guard. He groped to answer the voice of the invisible sorceress.

"Because you bade me," he replied stupidly.

"Do you not know it means death for you to come here?"

173

"Yes, I know."

"And yet you do so upon that risk, why?"

"Because I no longer command my will. Because I belong to you. Because I am prepared..."

"Prepared for what, Aefalas?"

"To die... to die for you, if need be."

"Then come, Aefalas. Come die with me, and be reborn of me."

She reached out in the darkness, leading him with seductive hands to the door of the font. She pushed it back. Sulfurous vapors rushed out darkly, ominous searching shapes backlit by the dim glow of thirteen candles arrayed about the sacred pool. Tandela stood in the doorway facing him now, her beguiling figure barely distinguishable for the swirling of the vapors. She seemed unreal, untouchable, immaterial. She pushed her cape off her shoulders then unclasped her robe. It fell in slow motion to her feet. She reached out and took Aefalas' hand once more, drawing him toward the holy basin, profaned now. He moved forward like a blind man, the roar of the pulsing waters filling his ears, his mind, his innermost being. Tandela let go his hand and he stopped. She walked around behind him and shut the door, pressing her back against it, feeling its heat, then stepped forward and placed her beguiling hands lightly upon Aefalas' shoulders. The over-bearing weight of his complicity settled there, immovable as a mountain.

The sun rose next morning into an empty sky, untroubled by the misfortunes of those humans below who began to stir in the broadening dawn. Tandela walked through the rubble to the Council room, the scene of their debates the day before, the scene of her tryst with Aefalas. She addressed the group of eleven gathered there.

"I will both open and close our deliberation this morning with a short statement. Aefalas and I are to be wed." A shock wave circled the room. "Confirm me as the High Priestess of Faena, so that we may go on with our lives, so that we may rebuild our city, so that Faena will smile upon our people."

Drusala, one of the older women, stood. Her countenance was stormy and angry clouds brooded about her eyes. "Although the Council does not govern the land in civil matters,

I must object to this marriage. Aefalas is your uncle, and even if he were not, the law forbids him to marry until a year has passed following the death of Vaalta."

"Aefalas is this morning rescinding that law," Tandela countered. "He believes I am the best hope of our people. He is willing to change those laws and to answer the dissenters. I have his vow that he will challenge anything or anyone that stands in the way of my confirmation."

"The marriage of the High Priestess is no civil matter, good sister Drusala," spoke Maeta, another respected member of the Council, to the older woman. Then she turned to Tandela. "What trickery is this, Tandela? These are not Aefalas' words. There is some mischief here." The room suddenly hummed with whispered conversations. "Let Aefalas come and speak these words himself, then I will believe them," she added over the rising din.

"He will come, if that is what you require," Tandela rejoined, calmly, but with firm voice.

Another aging matriarch stood now and a silence fell upon the gathering. Mollaf did not speak often in Council, but when she did, her audience listened. And though her body was withered with years, as the dried fruit of the orchards, her words were full with wisdom.

"What of Allisyn? What of Allisyn?" Mollaf repeated, piercing the silence. "As the daughter of Vaalta we have an obligation to consider her."

"Allisyn cannot be considered," Tandela replied. "She is not of age. She has not even been initiated."

"She was to be, even this harvest!" Drusala blurted out.

"But she is under suspicion," one of the younger women predisposed toward Tandela interjected. "She is not eligible due to her impurity..."

"That was not proved," Maeta interrupted. "That was not proved. We were to debate it, but alas, fate has intervened. Vaalta is dead. The city is burned. Such a thing has not happened in my lifetime. We have had no opportunity to debate it. There have been more pressing matters."

"Perhaps now is the time," Mollaf concluded.

"Enough of this talk!" Tandela shouted. "The rites must be performed. We must act now. Confirm me!"

Everyone spoke at once. Some added their voice in support of Tandela; others staunchly backed the older women.

175

"Wait. Perhaps there is a solution to our dilemma," Drusala interjected, her voice rising above the rest. "We could confirm Tandela for the purpose of performing the harvest rites. At the end of that time, we can talk to the girl. Perhaps then Faena will show us whether she favors Tandela or Allisyn."

"But she would not be ready," Tandela objected. "She would not have gone through the initiation. It would be another year before she would be eligible!"

"Then so be it," the aging Drusala replied. "We have served the goddess all our lives. What is one year? We can wait for Allisyn, if she is the choice of Faena."

Tandela, momentarily without a response, fumed quietly. Behind the doors of the inner chamber, the waters of the goddess rumbled.

"No" she said at last. "It is unprecedented. I will not permit it!"

"*You! You* will not permit it, Mistress Tandela. Do not attempt to pinion us with your false authority. You are not Aefalas' wife yet."

"Not as Aefalas' wife, Drusala. As a member of this Council I will not agree to Allisyn's investiture. The opinions of all must be considered, and all must agree. That is the way of the goddess."

Having organized the people and seen that they had commenced the activity of clearing the streets and pulling down broken walls, unsafe to leave standing, Aefalas looked for his daughter. He had not seen her since the funeral of Vaalta and her absence perplexed him. All morning he ardently searched but found her not, asking all he met if they had seen her, finding not one who had. He walked the byways of the city, entered broken buildings, and sought for her among the rubble heaps, but to no avail. Late in the afternoon, Tandela found him shuffling about among the ruins. She was still heated from the Council session.

"Aefalas," she called sternly. He looked up, then distractedly continued his search. Tandela walked to his side and spoke to him in a demanding tone.

"I have announced our marriage to the Council but still they resist me. We must be married soon. Did you sign the order to

176

rescind the mourning law?"

"No Tandela... but I... I will do it," he muttered.

"That is not what you promised me last night, Aefalas."

"Allisyn... I cannot find her. She has disappeared. No one knows her whereabouts," he replied, nearly frantic with anxiety.

"What of it? She is a trouble maker, that one. We have no use for her," Tandela hissed.

Aefalas looked at her askance.

"That is no way for you to speak to me, Tandela, or to speak of my daughter."

Tandela's exasperation ripped the boundaries of her patience. "No, you have it all wrong, my love. That is no way for *you* to speak to *me*!" Her look hardened.

"Do you not recall what you did, what *we* did last night? You set foot into the sacred basin. You... you defiled the holy place of the goddess. Do you recall the penalty for that? The penalty is death Aefalas, death! You would not want the Council to hear of your misdeed, would you? But I tell you plainly, unless you do all that I ask of you, I will make it known to them. Do you understand me?"

The shocked Aefalas suddenly realized the magnitude of his folly. He whirled and looked at her.

"You would not dare!"

She did not answer, but looked him squarely in the eye, challenging, defying him.

"It would be your word against mine!" he blurted.

"Then you would be a liar as well as a blasphemer! As you wish it, so be it!"

"You tricked me!"

"No, Aefalas, you finally took from me that which you have long desired!"

Aefalas turned away quickly, burning with loathing, shame and fear. When he had controlled his emotions, he turned back around to face her.

"Help me find my daughter," he demanded.

"I know where she is."

"Where, Tandela?"

"She needs punishing, Aefalas. If you want my help in finding her you must agree to punish her."

"Witch!"

"Fool!"

"Command the Council to confirm me and I will welcome

177

her back, with open arms, my *sweet* love!"

"Curse you! I cannot. I have not the authority!"

"Then do what you must. Threaten them."

"I shall not!"

"And I say you shall. Choose Aefalas! Your life, or theirs."

For the rest of the afternoon, Aefalas again wandered alone. Ostensibly he searched for his daughter, but could only think of himself. How could he have been so deceived? How could he have done this insane thing? His weakness clutched at him. He prayed to whatever gods would listen but found no sympathetic ear. He rambled until night fell.

High in the cirque of hills cradling the lofty Chent, the heart of his realm, he threw himself down, exhausted, on a rocky shelf and wept. A lone stunted pine clung there to a bit of poor soil in a narrow wedge in the rock. The wind bent it down over the king and it sang a song both wild and lonesome, a song of one dispossessed, of one friendless, of one chosen to suffer. Yet it was a song not without hope. It was a song of gripping the rock with one's last shred of strength in the face of cruel winds and lashing rains, a song of standing firm in the scorching heat of day with only a drop of water to cool a feverish tongue. The wind took up the song and played it among the chinks in the rocks.

Aefalas fell asleep. The song of the gnarled pine faded from his hearing. All was quiet now. He had a single, vivid dream in which he met Tandela in a clearing in the forest. There was a well. He fell in accidentally and she grabbed for him. At first he hoped that she was trying to save him, but to his dismay, he came to realize she was holding him under. He struggled desperately to free himself but could not. Beholding her through the rippling surface, her head became that of a great and hideous sow. The pig sang a song of forgetting, of sinking into deep, dark, cold waters. Finally, he ceased to struggle, closed his eyes and breathed deeply. The waters entered his body through every portal and pore and he passed into a deeper sleep.

178

Chapter 18
Voice of the Prophetess

Days later, days which for Aefalas had been seemingly unattended by the rising and setting of sun or moon, the King of Aestri approached the Faenmoet in the vestments of a bridegroom. They were of a pure white linen. Tied about his waist was a silver sash. He was barefoot.

Tandela was dressed in a wedding gown of pale green. About the shoulders it was studded with small polished droplets of jade, each held in place by a delicate golden clasp. Around her neck was the seal of the office of the High Priestess of Faena. Upon her brow she wore a circlet of gold in which was set an emerald of remarkable size and beauty. Her feet were bare as well. They passed through the stone portals, Aefalas from the north and Tandela from the south, and met in front of the altar stone. Drusala was there, against her will, to perform the rite of marriage. The other matriarchs were gathered as well, some willingly, some under threat of death. An immense crowd had been summoned. Every person in the city and in the Chent had been served notice to attend the wedding of their king and future queen. They dutifully came. A chill wind blew out of the north, hammering the stones.

Drusala began a chant.

Faena, thou giver of life,
Holy Mother of mothers
Faena, goddess, omnipotent,
of the healing waters,
Faena, of the living river

179

in the earth below
Hearken now to our petition,
your will that we may know.

We stand beseeching patiently
In awe of your divinity
Awaiting now your blessing,
Expectant of your passing,
Humbly in your pastures
Aware of our earthly natures
We raise to you our flocks and lands
Touch us with your fertile hands.

Here now is your chosen one,
Your High Priestess, Tandela
Here is your blessed one,
Aefalas, King of Aestri.
Now with all bowing before you,
May every heart pledge to you,
May every mind know you,
May every tongue praise you.

At these words the people nearest the stones sank to their knees, followed by those further out in successive ranks. The ripple migrated outward from the stones through the sea of humankind as though a pebble had been dropped in a still pond. Drusala waited until all were kneeling before she continued. Unnoticed by her, three figures remained standing near the back of the throng; Allisyn, Bronwyn and the Old Crone.

As Drusala recommenced her singing, one of the figures called out. It was Doena.

"Pagans!" she cried. "Pagan rites for pagan people! Who among you knows the true God? Who among you knows the ancient story. Into the sea Osyn fell with Thol-nys and there he vanquished her. Why do you worship her and her dark brood. Why do you stand here like cattle before the shrine of the Great Pig?"

Within earshot, heads turned toward the old woman. Many whispers were sent in her direction, urging her to be silent, but she would not relent. Louder and with greater vehemence she hurled her profanities at the King and the High Priestess. Shouting into the north wind, Doena's voice was not heard at

180

Mollaf, the wise old thinker, spoke up.

"But what might happen to this old woman? Might Tandela not take some rash action against her if she continues to speak out?"

"Possibly," Drusala commented. "But what of it? What is the life of one when weighed against the lives and well-being of the many?"

"Much, when the life is your own," said Mollaf. "And what of Allisyn? She is connected with this woman now. What might Tandela do to her? You know that she does not love the girl. And the roots of her discontent are deep, planted in the soil of generations. How can we protect the daughter of Vaalta?"

"We will make her a ward of the Council, surely that will suffice," Maeta announced.

"It may suffice for today, and tomorrow. But what of the future? What if Tandela's powers grow rather than diminish? What if our own abilities to protect the girl fail? What might happen to her then?" Mollaf questioned.

"We will initiate her next autumn. Then we can sway the Council to confirm her as High Priestess. A year is not long to those who have known many years," Drusala answered.

"But we know not what Tandela may do in the interim. Already she has seized much power and she may harbor further plans," Mollaf continued.

"We could send the girl away, beyond Tandela's influence," Maeta suggested.

"To where, sister?" asked Mollaf. "We could not hide her anywhere in the realm that would be safe. And I think we can not trust our neighbors. We either know little of them, or they are openly unfriendly to us. There is little security for her outside the Chent."

"Well, we cannot sit idly by and let Tandela have her way with us all. Something must be done, and soon," Drusala fretted. "I suggest we protect Allisyn while we can, and as best we can, keeping our eyes and ears and senses open for signs of trouble. At the first sign, we will remove her to a secret place. If Tandela discovers her whereabouts, we will move her again. We will keep her in hiding until the year is up. Meanwhile, we will let the crone speak out."

"Perhaps we can find someone close to Tandela, someone who we can trust, to tell us her thoughts. In that way we might keep one step ahead of her in the game."

"A spy can be a sword with two edges, Maeta," Drusala said. "I suggest that we employ no one in such work. The Council is divided in support of Tandela. We do not know who we can trust and who we cannot. We had better not reveal our plan to anyone outside this room."

"All right, but where will we keep Allisyn now?"

"I will keep her," Mollaf answered. "I think she will be safest with me."

"Yes, with you," the other two agreed.

"So," Drusala said, "we are all of one mind. We will set the old woman free. Under pain of death we will tell her to go home. It is a hollow threat, I know; still we may protect ourselves if Tandela questions us. But I fancy the old woman will not go home. She believes herself a prophetess, and she will have her say."

Mollaf lived in a sturdy farmhouse in Ostwyn, a hamlet only a few miles from the city. They removed Allisyn to a room there, under cover of darkness. She went silently. Doena and Bronwyn were told to go home and not to return to the city. Allisyn took her leave of them tearfully.

"What attraction does that wretched woman hold for you Allisyn?" Drusala asked. But Allisyn gave no answer.

The very next morning as the anxious light leapt into the eastern sky, Doena was at the door of the pavilion where Aefalas and Tandela had slept. The prophetess and her granddaughter had gone there immediately upon their release, not even feigning to go home, and had huddled outside, insensitive to the weather. Already the cold nights were stalking the autumn, chasing it further south. When the old woman stood, she left a circle upon the ground where her body had rested. All around it was a hoary frost. Doena took a deep breath and shouted so that she might be heard plainly inside the pavilion.

"Tandela, Mother of Misery, Queen of Darkness, listen now to the words of Deus, the one true God. Lay aside your emerald of green. Lay down your scepter. Arise from your incestuous bed. Put aside the worship of the earth goddess. Bring your people out of the darkness and into the light.

"Your dreams have been blighted by Thol-nys the Destructress, the ancient enemy, and you sink into the mire of her hatred. Step into the light of Deus and throw back the veil of darkness. Pray for your soul, Tandela, even as we pray for it.

"Give up your marriage to Aefalas, for it is unlawful. You have made it unholy, too, because of your deceit. Pull him from the well of unconsciousness, pull him up into the air. Drown him not in the darkness. Let not the great sow rend his flesh. Do not drown the people in their own blood, for this is what Thol-nys will ask of you. You know not the deadly nature of the path you walk! Come out, repent of your wickedness and seek the favor of Deus."

Within the pavilion Tandela awoke to the raucous voice of the old woman. The anger she had felt on the previous day came rushing back, flooding her senses, unlocking the hatred in her icy heart. She sat up in the bed. Aefalas slept on by her side. Her new-found contempt for him mingled with her loathing for the old woman and became a writhing dragon of hatred within her. She sprang from the bed, drawing her robes about her, and went to the doorway. She threw back the flap to behold the Old Crone and her granddaughter.

"Why are you here?" Tandela shouted. "Go away and leave me in peace. I know what I am about, old woman. I am indifferent to your lies and curses. Your cries are impotent. They will not affect me. Go!"

She swept back into the great tent. The old woman raved on. Tandela went to Aefalas and woke him.

"Wake up, Aefalas, and open your ears. It is that stinking hag! Listen to her insults! This is your doing. You would not let me deal with her. You had to give her over to the Council. See what the Council has done with her? Nothing. They have let her go and she has found her way back to my door, flinging lies before her. Deal with her!" Tandela shrieked.

Aefalas arose and went to the doorway, as Tandela had. The old woman was still there, berating them for their wrongdoings, predicting their downfall. He said nothing to her, retreating quickly into the pavilion. There he whispered to a guard to bring Drusala to him. The guard went with haste and returned within the hour with the matriarch. Drusala could hardly suppress a smile as she approached, hearing the cries of the Old Crone grow louder with each step. She entered the tent and was brought before the King.

"Is this what I asked of you, Drusala? When I released the old woman to your safe keeping, I did not expect her at my door

187

this morning. It is not a pleasant way to start the day, I can assure you. And worse than the old woman's rantings are the demands of Tandela to get rid of her. Please, take her away and do not allow her to return."

"Aefalas. You bring this upon yourself," Drusala whispered boldly in her sovereign's ear. "Rid yourself of Tandela and the old woman will be gone. You must strike at the root of the weed, not at the top, if you want to rid your pasture of it."

"You know not what you ask, Drusala. Silence the old woman."

"We told her to go home and not to return. But she did not listen. Her belief is stronger than the love of her own life. But we fear to silence her, she has the people on her side against Tandela."

"What are you saying? The people do not know what is happening. They have no reason to suspect Tandela. Silence her, unless you want Tandela to do it for you."

"Tandela cannot touch her. The old woman is under the protection of the Council. To defy the will of the Council in this matter would be to lose her office as High Priestess."

"Tandela may yet do many things she is forbidden to do. She has no respect for the law."

"We will ask her to desist, Aefalas, but we cannot control her. She has broken no law. She only speaks her mind. If her mind is set against Tandela, so be it."

"She blasphemes Faena. Is that not your concern?"

"Yes, but I tell you, she has the ear of the people in the matter of your wife and your marriage. They believe Tandela has enchanted you. To silence her would be to create unrest among them."

"Then know this, Drusala, if you do not act on this matter, you walk upon the edge of a knife."

Outside, Drusala drew the old woman aside and reasoned with her, urging her to prophesy to the people. Little chance was there to reach Tandela, or even Aefalas in this matter, she said. To stir the hearts of the people was the way to accomplish her purpose. Aefalas would be rid of Tandela soon enough, if the people rejected his queen.

And so it was that Doena roamed the Chent that winter, led by her mute granddaughter, finding an ear wherever she could and filling it with her message. They lived as beggars, exchanging a crust of bread or a cup of soup for words that many were intrigued to hear.

But Doena was indeed a sword with two edges. For wherever she planted seeds of doubt about Tandela with the people, she also scattered other seeds, the message of the one God, the knowledge of Deus. And the people listened with great interest. Thus she prepared the way for the one who was to come.

Tandela herself was not idle during this time, seeking at every turn to further consolidate her influence over Aefalas. For the most part, it was an easy matter. From time to time, he would appear to awaken, to emerge from her spell and show signs of independent thought and action. He would do something unexpected, something that caught her off guard, something that made her doubt that her strangling web was intact. Then she would redouble her efforts to control him, finding some new way to compromise him.

She kept spies abroad who reported to her on the whereabouts of Doena. They brought back news of what she preached among the people. Whenever some new gossip came to her ears, Tandela fed the fires of her malice with it.

As she stoked the furnace of her hatred, the Great Calamity drew nearer and nearer to her. She often dreamed of the horrific sow. Often it spoke to her in those dreams in its grunting, gnashing voice. The voice had even begun even to invade her waking thoughts. One night she dreamed that the sow had a litter of piglets, horrible and misshapen. She rolled her great bulk upon them and smothered them, grunting with satisfaction. When the sow rolled away Tandela found the three troublesome matriarchs, together with the Old Crone, Bronwyn, and Allisyn, among the dead piglets.

In one dream there was a pure white piglet and the sow caused Tandela to murder and slaughter it. When the queen cut it open she found twelve pearls. These were no ordinary pearls, Thol-nys told her. They were the pearls of Deus' thought. Yes, Deus did exist, the great enemy and usurper. He had made the pearls, The Twelve Pearls of Wisdom, he had so haughtily called them. What folly and nonsense! The wisdom of Deus was but a mockery of her own, the Great Destroyer, the One who had been since the beginning, and would be always. The pearls had been planted in the white pig, sown there to hide from Thol-nys on the earth what could not be hidden from her in the Otherworld. They must be found and destroyed. Then there would be no more hope for Deus. Then there would be nothing. Then the world would fall under the inevitable influence of herself, the Great Calamity, and be cast into eternal darkness, to wither and fade, to decay until it was no more. Then all the false works of the arrogant Deus would be destroyed and Thol-nys would reign supreme. She bade Tandela to seize the Pearls for her, to take them to the clearing and throw them into the dark well.

Tandela constantly sought to know the whereabouts of Allisyn. She found from time to time that her enemies among the Council would move the girl. Then she would seek her out again. She rather enjoyed this cat-and-mouse game, knowing the time would soon come when she would deal with the threat Allisyn posed to her authority; the time to pounce, to pin her down until she struggled no more, and then, to end her menace once and for all time.

Over the course of the winter stone masons and carpenters worked diligently to rebuild the castle. In the valley, Doena undermined its very foundations. The winter solstice came and went. Now each day the sun mounted higher into the sky, the days lengthened and winter retreated to its northern home. The equinox came and Tandela led the matriarchs in the observance of the rites of planting. When the rites were past, the castle was once again ready for occupation.

The first morning Tandela awoke in her newly completed lodgings there was a commotion in the courtyard below. Doena had returned, crying her prophesies to the stones. They rebounded and echoed and found their way to the open window of the queen, high above. From her aerie, Tandela looked down, regarding the old woman and her granddaughter with cold disdain. She had given ample thought to what she would do if her detractors returned. Now she would hatch her plot.

"The Council is dissolved," Tandela announced when it met later that same morning. Her words were met by a chorus of dissent. Even those who supported her had not expected this.

190

Soldiers came and arrested Drusala, Maeta and Mollaf. The others were sent away and told, upon pain of death, to say nothing.

"So, Tandela, you have grown very sure of yourself! Queen of Aestri. Ha! That is nothing to Faena. She will seek you out. She will bring you low. The Council is sacred. Never has such an abomination been carried out. You will pay for your insolence. The goddess will not stand for this!" Drusala spat as she was ushered out.

"Silence, traitor! Where is the girl, Allisyn? You have kept her hidden from Aefalas, her father. You have conspired to turn the girl against the King and me. You shall no longer be the source of enmity between us. Where is she? Tell me or you will die."

"No doubt you know already where she is. We know that you seek her life. You will not be satisfied until everyone who threatens you is dead. My mouth is shut. I will not give you the satisfaction of hearing it from my lips. You will kill me at any rate."

"You proclaim your treason from the rooftops, Drusala. You build the case against your own self. Remain silent then! It is of no consequence to me. I have given you the opportunity to cooperate. If you choose not that option, so be it! Take them away!"

Upon the dissolution of the Council and the arrest of Drusala and her accomplices, Tandela moved to arrest Doena and Bronwyn. The next morning when the prophetess returned to berate the queen, the guard of eunuchs that Tandela commanded were waiting for her. When the Old Crone opened her mouth to speak they arrested her and Bronwyn; they bound them, handled them roughly, and took them to the dungeon which had been constructed beneath the castle, of the very rooms that were formerly devoted to the worship of Faena. There they were thrown into a cell opposite the three matriarchs. The angry springs which flowed behind the cell walls made the atmosphere of the prison hot and stifling.

In a few hours the eunuch guards returned, striding fervently through the thick wooden door of Doena's cell. From the adjacent cell, Drusala and the others heard the parlance.

"Old Woman, Queen Tandela orders you to recant. You must publicly renounce the things you have spoken against her and swear never to speak them again. Swear now that you will do this and you may avoid her sentence."

"I care not for the orders and the sentences of the whore of the Great Destroyer," Doena began. "She is a worshiper of the darkness. She will bring destruction upon all of us. Your sons will die upon the golden altar, the altar of the Great Pig. Go back and tell her to turn from the darkness, to repent of her worship of Thol-nys. Deus will have compassion on her, even now. It is not too late. Tell her..."

Doena never finished the sentence. The guards seized her and pinned her to the floor. The chief among them forced his hand into her mouth, caught her crevassed tongue, and with a swift motion, cut it out and threw it upon the stones. Blood streamed from Doena's mouth and nose. Bronwyn eyes bulged and she uttered a deformed scream. The old woman writhed upon the floor, wailing.

The guards turned and fell upon the girl.

"Queen Tandela has decreed that even as the tongue of the old woman has been silenced, so shall the lamps of her 'eyes' be extinguished," he pronounced.

Those who had held the old woman now took hold of Bronwyn. Their chief grasped the hair of the frail girl with one hand, and with the rough fingers of the other, gouged out her eyes. Bronwyn sank to the floor in shock. The soldiers left hastily, wiping the blood from their hands. The screaming woman and girl groped desperately in the blackness of the cell to find one another. Across the passageway, Drusala and her companions huddled together, offering frightened, fervent prayers for the suffering ones and for their own deliverance. Behind the oaken doors, the waters boomed, raging against the confines of the rock.

Chapter 19
The Pearls

Within the week Allisyn was found and brought to the castle. She was not allowed to see her father. She was locked in the topmost room of a high tower, its one window overlooking the raging gorge of the Mergruen. The furnishings of the room were spartan, consisting of little more than a bed and chair. Food was brought to her once a day. Outside her door, guards were perpetually posted.

She became angry, but her anger did not last. Then there came a creeping void, a space bereft of feelings and emotion, a haunting listlessness. After a time, her languor turned to despair, for there was nothing to capture her attention, nothing to distract her from her loneliness and the boredom of her incarceration. Bare walls stared back at her dumbly. The bed became too familiar to lie upon, the chair too wretched to sit in. She became fretful and she paced. She sat upon the floor. She went to the window. Outside the mesmerizing vapors danced, billowing up ceaselessly from the cavernous depths of the gorge. Only occasionally did they lift, allowing her a glimpse of its sheer sides far away and the verdant draperies that clung there, watered by hot springs that spouted and plummeted steaming into the spume below.

When she thought, she thought about those she loved. She sorely wished to see her father and wondered why he had not come. This disquieting thought both vexed and saddened her. Had Tandela's influence over him reached the point that he feared to see his own daughter, or worse yet that he himself wished this fate for her? In her more hopeful moments, she imagined he was not aware she was being kept in the high tower of his own house. But the more she thought of him, the more hopeless she became.

When she was not thinking of her father, she thought of Doena and Bronwyn. What had become of them? She had not seen them or heard from them for months. Had Tandela locked them away too, or found some, more cruel way to rid herself of their annoying presence? Or had they simply forgotten her? How many times had she risked the wrath of Tandela to bring them bread? Is this how they had chosen to repay her kindness to them, to desert her when she needed them most?

Months passed. In time the room became dreamlike to her. It lost its definition, like copper loses its brilliance when a patina creeps over its surface, spoiling its ability to reflect the light. Sharp edges became blurred, outlines obscured, colors faded. She seldom noticed when her food was brought. She ate little. Her skin paled and her green eyes lost their brilliance. But even as the outer world receded, something seemed to be gaining strength within her.

She was drawn more and more to the window. Sometimes she sat for hours watching the never ending play of the vapors. One day as the sun set, a rainbow coalesced before her, majestic, still and radiant. The sun set and the rainbow melted away. Gazing into the darkling depths, something seemed to be drawing her, calling to her. Was it the voice of the waters, of the goddess? They spoke of death. Her death, she mused. She thought of walking to the window, climbing upon the ledge and casting herself into the melee of the waters. The thought shocked her. She began to tremble. For the first time since she had gone to the tower she bent her head and cried. She poured out her heart to the stones and watered their parched surface with her tears. Overcome with grief she lay on the floor and wept uncontrollably, for her father, for her friends, for herself. Then she slept.

The Hawk Moon rose. Its free, soaring light came creeping across the room, illuminating the stones near Allisyn's face, nudging her gently awake. Exhausted from mourning, she opened her burning eyes. All was blurred at first, then, by degrees, her vision cleared. She saw the stones, wet with her tears. Further away, the soft line of the moonlight partitioned the chamber floor. Beyond it a shape appeared. At first she dismissed it as illusion, the play of her fancy. But as she looked

194

more closely, focusing her attention on its roundness and the light and shadow upon it, the illusion took form. The shape was a foot, a beautiful foot, small, bare and exquisite. She dwelled upon the toes, then let her eyes caress the soft concavity of the instep, the petite ankle. The hem of a dark garment allured her. She rolled onto her back and saw the image of her mother, Vaalta, stoop to place a pale hand upon her forehead. The hand was soft and comforting, like cool water to a burning throat. A breath emanating from the apparition stirred the airs of the room. A vision of her mother lying on the altar stone flashed through Allisyn's mind, and Vaalta's last breath brushed against her face once again. It seemed to lift her off the floor until she stood upright. She reached out to her mother and they met in an ethereal embrace. Allisyn felt as if she were a child once again, felt the joy of being rocked in her mother's loving arms. Her cares melted away and were absorbed by the night.

"Take courage, my beloved," Vaalta whispered in her daughter's ear. "Your destiny is a lofty one, your purpose high. This suffering is but a doorway. There will be other trials. Your destiny lies beyond them. Greet them as teachers. Embrace them, not for what they seem, but for what they are. Awaken now and come. I will show you that nothing is as it seems. These walls are but a vapor, these barred doors but a mist. Only believe in love, only commit to love for all, even those who neglect or misuse you, and you may pass through them like a thought. No wall made by the hands of man may imprison that kind of love."

With that Vaalta took her daughter by the arm. With the brush of her hand the door to her room soundlessly opened and they passed noiselessly over the threshold. Down the winding stairs they glided. They walked across the sky, using the clouds as their stepping stones. They wended their way through forests and stood on mountain tops. They laughed as the surf washed their feet and left their footprints on the sands of the ocean.

Morning found Allisyn lying upon her bed, remembering her vision. She ran to the window where the mists churned. There the voice of the waters throbbed as ever in her ears. But there also was the memory of her dear mother, her love, her joy, her strength and her confidence. She strode across the room to the door and knocked upon it.

"Open the door," she called to the guards on the other side. "I wish to see my father."

The eunuchs looked at one another. In all the months of her captivity they had not heard Allisyn speak. Her voice seemed commanding now beyond their ability to resist. One of them bolted down the stairs and sought out Aefalas. He found the king in his morning rooms, pondering a dream of the night before. Vaalta had come to him. She had placed something in his ear. He could not remember anything more.

"Sire, your daughter. She calls for you."

Aefalas looked at him impotently, fidgeting. From the adjacent room Tandela heard the guard and burst into the room.

"No!" she commanded. "I forbid it Aefalas."

Aefalas stirred at her words and felt a challenge rise, unbidden, within him. But his feelings stemmed less from the love for his daughter than from the affront to his power.

"I am the king Tandela. You cannot forbid me to see her!"

Tandela was taken aback by his forwardness. She jumped to the attack.

"She is a blasphemer and a traitor. She is dangerous, Aefalas. We have spoken of this before. She must stay there until she dies!"

Aefalas softened his approach. Perhaps Tandela would respond. Perhaps there was some remnant of decency left in her. "She is a child, she made a mistake. The old woman deceived her. Have pity on her, Tandela!"

"Pity! My dear husband, pity is what saved her!" Tandela lied. "I have shown both of you mercy in far greater measure than you deserve. She should have been executed for her impudence and her part in the treasonous plots against me! She alone lives, might I remind you, of Drusala, and others of the Council that sought my death!"

"Has she not suffered long enough, Tandela? Let her come forth. Even if she was involved as you say, perhaps her suffering has cleansed her of her wrongheadedness. Perhaps she has repented. Perhaps she would be willing to prove her repentance."

As he spoke, a black thought took form in the witch's mind. Maybe there was a way to be rid of Allisyn once and for all. And at the insistence of her father, no less. Now it was she who softened her tone.

"It may be that you are right, Aefalas." She looked at the guard, still standing by, visibly relieved by the change in her temperament. "I would believe, if Allisyn were to submit to a test; a test to prove her innocence in the matter. But it must be a test of my own devising. Would you agree to it, Aefalas?"

Aefalas looked distrustfully at his conniving wife. Her penchant for evil frightened him. He swallowed dryly. He thought of his daughter, forever wasting away in the tower of cold stone. Surely he still had the power to save her, even if he could not save himself.

"I would agree. But if she passes the test, she must be restored to her rightful place among us. Would you agree to that, Tandela?"

"Of course, Aefalas. But if she fails, she *dies*. Tonight I will think on it and tomorrow I will put her to the test."

Aefalas walked the groaning wooden stairs to the tower where his daughter was a prisoner, his heart heavy with the burden of her life. Tandela no doubt would invent some task impossible to accomplish and her life would be forfeit. He would do whatever he could to help her. He knew that. Even if he were to die trying, he would do what he could to win back her freedom. Allisyn must pass the test. Her life, his life, were no good as they were, locked in prisons, prisons of their own making, or of the making of others, prisons with walls, and without. Allisyn must triumph. If she did not she would die and Tandela's victory would be complete. Allisyn was all that stood between Tandela and her complete domination of Aestri. Aefalas was not strong enough any longer. She had stolen his power and broken his will. He could not stand up to her. His legs ached as he climbed the final steps to the tower room.

"I wish to speak to my daughter," Aefalas said to the guard.

The guard opened the door and admitted the king to Allisyn's chamber. She stood with her back to him by the open window.

"Allisyn," he said. Almost the name did not cross his lips. It seemed so long since he had spoken it that the word hesitated in his throat.

Allisyn turned to him with tears in her eyes. She walked across the room and embraced him. He felt her tremble as she began to cry. He held her at arms length and looked at her. She had changed in the last months since he had seen her. So like her mother she looked now that he paused, surprised, before he

197

could speak. Her face had matured. If her eyes had lost their sparkle, it had been replaced with a deeper, stronger, more constant light. Like moonlight it appeared, as if the very beams of the Orb had come to reside there. If her skin had lost its girlish softness, it had been supplanted by a firmness that bespoke her womanly constitution.

"I should have come before, Allisyn. It is not that I do not love you. It is Tandela. She... I cannot..."

"You need not say more Father. Truly, we all have made mistakes. We have slept when we should have kept watch. But that is no matter now. We must do what we can. How is it with you? Are you well?"

"My soul is sick, Allisyn. I am unable to cope with her sorcery. It is all her doing. Ever since... nay before, Vaalta's death she was plotting, scheming and I was blind to it. Even now, I come to you with tidings I would not bear."

"What is it then? Has she decreed my death?"

"Perhaps. I have agreed with her that she may set you a test to prove your innocence in the claim of treason she has made against you. If you pass, you will be reinstated to your rightful position in Aestri. If not..." His voice faltered.

"I understand."

"I thought it better that you stand the test than to waste away in this tower, where I am powerless to help you."

"Not powerless, father... loveless. You have lost the love for yourself and thus you cannot love me, you cannot help me. The love of your own life has grown cold. I see it in your eyes and feel in your heart. You come to me now not out of love, but out of pity. Pity you have in great store, pity for yourself, pity for us. Pity but not love. I do not need your pity father, but I do need your love."

Aefalas bent his head and stared at the stones of the floor.

"I want you to have it Allisyn. But I know not where my love has gone. I know not how to find it. Perhaps I need your help more than you need mine."

Allisyn did not speak immediately, letting these last words sink in and settle, uncomfortably, in her conscience.

"What is the test, father?" she asked, when the silence had been cultivated long enough.

"I do not know. Tandela has said she will decree it tomorrow. Will you accept her challenge?"

"It is time."

198

Allisyn was brought before the King and Queen in the Great Hall of Aestri the next morning. The massive copper and wood doors, newly carved and hung, inlaid with gold, silver, and precious stones, opened to admit her. There was a rumbling of voices within. Her heart, which had been calm, leaped abruptly into her throat. Her mind, which had been certain, was gripped with a sudden doubt. Having never seen the hall and familiar of late with only the small space of her room, the girl was intimidated by its proportion. Standing at the east end, she could barely make out the details of the west. The ceiling arched high above her.

She walked forward now between two colonnades of pillars, black as ebony, shimmering like starlight on deep waters, that supported the expanse of the roof. Between the pillars and the walls in oaken boxes were gathered a mass of people. They hushed now at her approach. In the growing silence, her footfalls echoed across the length and breadth of the space, to come ringing back in a jumble of staccato shocks that seemed to stab her very breast. High windows in each wall admitted slices of sunlight that did not yet reach the floor. In the shadow at the end of the hall sat Aefalas and Tandela.

Allisyn and her guards stopped short of the dais where sat the royal pair. Tandela, dressed in a deep emerald robe, edged at the throat and wrists with black lace, stood and called her forth.

"Daughter of Aefalas," she cried out, loud enough so that all gathered there might hear. "You have been charged with treason! Out of my great tolerance, you have been heretofore spared the fate of the others who were involved in this intolerable plot, this bestial attempt to undermine my authority.

"And now, I understand you have consented to face a test; a test that will prove, for better or for worse, if you did, or if you did not, willingly participate in this deception and treachery. And I, in my concern for this people and as a testament to my justice, have consented to let you face this test. Will you then agree to it, to its conditions, and submit to the finality of its outcome?"

"What is the test, Tandela?"

"Will you agree to be bound by it, will you swear an oath

199

before this assembly and before the goddess?"

"Swear to what, Tandela?"

"To whatever I please, impertinent girl! The nature of the test matters not, for you have it not within your power to accomplish it. Only by the will of Faena will you be condemned or freed. Do you agree to it? If you do not, then know that you condemn yourself already in the presence of these people."

"I will agree and so swear, that my innocence may be proved."

"Then be bound by your oath to this. You will bring me the Twelve Pearls of Wisdom. Find them and give them to me so that I may reign immortally on the earth and in the Otherworld, so that my power will know no limits, so that my name will forever be remembered, so my divinity may be unveiled, not only queen, but goddess. This I require, bring me the Twelve Pearls. You are bound to return to this place within one cycle of the moon, whether you have found them or not, to face judgment.

"And this further is laid upon you," Tandela added in a whisper, approaching Allisyn so that only she could hear. An evil light was in her eye and she glared at the girl, taking a perverse delight in what she now would say. "No one must tell you where they are, no one must show you where they are. You must find them without aid of the earthly *tongues* or *eyes* of others. You will do this alone. I have seen to it. No one else must know the secret of the Twelve."

Allisyn was completely at a loss. Tandela's words were beyond her comprehension. They made no sense. She might just as well have asked her to discover the secret of the moon's light and why it waxed and waned. She looked at her father. His eyes were averted, cast down to the floor. For all his words of support, Allisyn realized he was useless to help her. Hearing Tandela's words he too had despaired, for he himself knew not what they meant. He had no words of comfort or advice for his daughter, not even any pity. When he finally looked at her, he saw one already dead. Resignation and death were in his own eyes.

Allisyn turned in silence and walked from the hushed assembly, her footfalls soundless now. The massive doors closed behind her and the Great Hall of Aestri erupted in talk.

Allisyn was suddenly free, free to go where she chose, free to live life and spend the time left to her as she pleased. For she felt already in her heart the sentence of her death, and that thought set her free from the uncertainty of many months of imprisonment. But the hopelessness had returned. She had been so bold, so certain when her mother had come to her, so sure of herself when she had entered the Great Hall. Now she realized her faith in herself had been misplaced. What had Vaalta said of her lofty destiny, her high purpose? It was nothing. What had she known? She was dead as well. All around her was death and despair. She had just as well go to the gorge and throw herself in, as she had considered so many times, a fitting end to a life not worth the living. In this dimension, bereft of light, of hope, she wandered without direction, or so she thought. But as surely as her heart still beat, she was drawn toward the Encircling Hills, to the band of forest that stood at the tumbled feet of the great cirque of mountains at the eastern end of the valley. Without consciously knowing it, she was being drawn again to the hovel of the Old Crone.

It was not until she was nearly upon it that she realized where she was. The veil of despair lifted for a moment and she was aware of the familiar path. She called out to Bronwyn at the door of the hut but there was no answer. She drew back the curtain and looked inside but no one was there. Her thoughts raced back to Tandela. Had she done something to them? Had they been put to death along with the others whom she had suspected? Allisyn realized suddenly her own error. She remembered how she had longed for her father, the touch of his hand or the sound of his voice, for any sign that he still cared for or loved her. Perhaps they had felt the same way about her. Perhaps they had felt abandoned by her. Perhaps they had needed more from her than she had needed from them. She decided then and there to find them, no matter how long it took, no matter that it would take her away from her quest for the Pearls. She would find them and tell them that she loved them. And no one could ever take that away from the old woman or the frail child.

For days she wandered about the Chent. Everywhere she went people turned their backs on her. Neither would they speak any word or show any sign to aid her. But a strange thing happened. The more she was turned away, the more she was neglected, the more that her own people spurned her in fear of their queen, the stronger her determination grew. Her love reached out to her friends and she knew that it would find them. Finally, in the lingering twilight of high summer, on a lonely road under the eaves of the forest, she met a woman coming home from gathering mushrooms.

"Good mother," Allisyn called out to her while she was yet a distance away. The woman stopped and seemed to hesitate. She looked up and down the road, then ran to Allisyn and drew her aside into the trees.

"Princess, I know who you seek. But I am afraid. I am afraid of what they might do to me if they catch me speaking with you. I have three little children and my husband is no more. My concern for them has kept me away from you. The other day I overheard you ask the whereabouts of the Old Crone and her granddaughter. I saw the look in your eyes, the look of one who has lost her children and cannot find them. I heard the love, the caring in your voice, and my heart went out to you. But still I feared, and fear sealed my tongue." The woman covered her mouth with her hand and broke into a fit of weeping.

As Allisyn watched her, she caught a glimpse of moonlight reflected in Vaalta's eyes.

"Come mother, do not cry," Allisyn comforted. "But tell me, where may I find those whom I seek. My days are but a few and I know that I must spend them in service of the ones I love. Before my time comes, more than anything else, I want to make sure they are cared for. For though they are unlovely and imperfect, I love them all the more."

When the darkness was complete Allisyn and the woman left the shadow of the trees. She led the princess across a field of ripening corn. They flitted watchfully across a lane and through another field until they came to a low farmhouse. In the rear of it was a low barn. The woman stopped short.

"Princess, surely you know..."

Allisyn waited for her to speak again.

"Surely, you know what has happened to them."

"I know not."

"The... the queen," the woman stuttered. "Oh, I cannot speak it!" And she began to weep again.

Allisyn rushed forward and found Doena and Bronwyn huddled for shelter in a crevice where two barn walls met. Doena reached out with palsied hands for her darling Allisyn

202

when she recognized her voice. In her excitement the old woman unleashed a babble of incomprehensible sounds. Allisyn fell to her knees and hugged the ragged prophetess.

"Doena, Doena, praise be to Deus I have found you at last!" Without a pause she turned to throw her arms around Bronwyn, but stopped short, surprised by the dirty rag wrapped about her head, covering her eyes. She reached out with her hands to touch the delicate face of her young friend. Bronwyn responded by reaching up and grasping Allisyn's wrists, weakly, the princess thought. Allisyn turned to the woman.

"The queen... had the tongue... of the Old Crone... cut from her mouth... and... the eyes... of the young... one... put out!" the woman said through her stifled sobs.

Allisyn raised the cloth that covered Bronwyn's eyes. She tenderly put her fingers into the empty sockets, wet with Bronwyn's tears; tears not of sorrow or self-pity, but the joy of reunion. Allisyn took Bronwyn's head in her hands and kissed it. She turned back to Doena in the darkness placing her left hand against her crevassed lips with its bristling hairs. Gently she opened the Old Crone's mouth with her fingers, probing the cavity where her tongue had been and feeling the stump that was left. When she withdrew her hand she leaned forward, placing a kiss on the forehead of her maimed friend, praising Doena for her courage. Then taking Bronwyn and Doena by the hands, she bade them stand and led them through the blackness back to the hovel that had been their home.

In the days that followed Allisyn thought of nothing but her two charges, nearly spent from want and exposure. Bronwyn was emaciated. Doena was bent nearly double with the pain in her ancient joints. Allisyn went to the forest, gathered mushrooms and dug roots for them. She cooked and cared for them until a blush of color had returned to Bronwyn's cheeks. But the old woman continued to decline. When she tried to speak Allisyn would quiet her, brushing her soft hand over the agitated lips and throat.

One night when they were resting peacefully, she crawled out of the hovel and walked to the edge of the forest. In the sky, the Sow Moon was waxing to full. That image brought back forcefully the fact that her time was fleeting by. Tomorrow she must return to the court of her father and confront Tandela. Tomorrow she would stare death in the face once again.

Her heart was lined with concern. Who would care for her friends when she had gone? There would be none. They would be forced to beg once again or eat among the animals, as she had found them only a few nights before. Sorrow overcame her like a cloud drawn across the face of the sun. She could not bear for them to suffer. How could she insure that they would not? She thought of taking them away, of running and hiding, of giving up her birthright, of disregarding her oath to return. She could evade death by running, but how long, how far, could she run? And if she ran she could not care for her friends, for surely they could not run with her.

A fog was rising from the forest floor. She stood in the moonlight with her head bowed. Its beams illuminated her bare foot, causing it to glow with a pale blue light. She studied the toes, the shadow at the instep and the knobby ankle. She was allured by the hem of her dress. Suddenly she realized it was the foot of her mother. She raised her eyes and Vaalta stood before her once again.

"Allisyn, my beloved. Because you have loved with a sincere love, a hopeful love, you have saved yourself. Go and wake the Old Crone and tell her what you seek. She will show you the way." Then as suddenly as she had appeared, Vaalta was gone.

Allisyn ran into the hut and sat beside Doena who breathed in a slow, rattling rhythm. She seemed asleep. Allisyn placed a hand on her shoulder.

"Mother," the girl spoke. "I am to seek the Twelve Pearls of Wisdom. When I find them, Tandela has caused me to swear that I will bring them and give them to her. You, who have drunk from the Well of Wisdom, can you help me now?"

Doena rose and walked with difficulty to the entrance of the hut. Sensing that something was happening, Bronwyn awoke and followed. The three passed out of the hovel into the still evening. The pines towered silently above them. Sitting upon the ground they formed their circle. Doena traced it with her hand. Twelve times she drew it. Then, as before, the well appeared and a light glowed in its depths. Allisyn took the hollow gourd from the edge and threw it in, letting the rope run through her fingers until its knotted end was all that remained resting in her palm. Then she drew the vessel forth. The light

204

grew brighter. When she held the dipper at last in her hand she found that the source of light was in the hollow of it. The well itself was dark now. She looked into the gourd, nearly blinded by the brilliance. She put her hand in to feel along the bottom. There was an object, smooth and hard, but flexible. She drew it forth, a string of pearls, twelve pearls, the Twelve Pearls of Deus.

They were dazzlingly bright, as bright as the sun but with a blue-white light, like that of the moon. With reverence, Allisyn placed them in her lap. In the pail, she noticed there was still a glow, softer and dimmer, as if the necklace of pearls had left an echo of its own light there. Inside she found there were yet two more pearls. She reached in and scooped them up. They weighed heavily in her hand when the water had drained away. Allisyn looked at Bronwyn and found that she had taken the cloth from around her head. The empty sockets of her eyes rested darkly upon her cheeks. Allisyn looked to her hand, then to the dark vacancies in the face of her friend. Not knowing why, she reached out and placed the pearls, one each, into the gaping sockets of Bronwyn's eyes. They seemed to come to life as Bronwyn looked once again at her friend. A smile bent her lips. Bronwyn reached out for the ladle. Taking a long drink, her tongue, the tongue which had never spoken in her life, was suddenly loosed.

"My Allisyn," she said in a voice that sounded eerily to Allisyn like Vaalta's, "because you have loved with a sincere and selfless love, you have saved yourself. Take the Pearls and go to the house of your father. But do not give them to Tandela. They are not for her. They are for the One who is to come."

Allisyn could scarcely comprehend that her dear friend Bronwyn could see and speak again, but she believed it. She believed it all now, her mother's words, the potency of love; love, the first and highest attribute of the one true God, the essence of Deus, love the healer, love the omnipotent, love the unblemished and the true.

She took the Twelve Pearls, wrapped them in a soft cloth and placed them inside her dress. The light faded as if the moon had been eclipsed. Bronwyn's eyes still shown with a gentle aura. Their light fell upon Doena lying inert on the ground. The Old Crone, the prophetess, the voice of Deus, had passed into the Otherworld. The Well of Knowledge closed and the waters that had given up the Pearls and were hidden.

Allisyn and Bronwyn buried Doena in the hovel that night. They pulled the down walls around her and raised a cairn of stones above her, a crown upon the hill. All night they mourned her and labored until their act of veneration was complete. In the early morning light, they rose wearily and walked over the hills to the east, down to the Mergruen where they bathed in a quiet eddy-pool above the falls. They washed their clothes and hung them on nearby branches to dry. They lay in a grassy summer field to dry their hair. Refreshed and laughing, they drained the dews of honeysuckle flowers and perfumed themselves. When their garments were dry they dressed once again and walked arm in arm to the city.

In the Great Hall the people were once again assembled. It was the appointed day. Once again Allisyn stood before Tandela, this time with Bronwyn at her side. Tandela had a disquieting feeling that she knew the younger girl, but could not guess her identity. The queen stood before the assembly and a silence fell palpably. Aefalas sat expectantly on the edge of his seat, staring at his daughter.

"So the time has come, Allisyn, to judge your innocence or your guilt. Have you the Twelve?"

Allisyn reached into the breast of her simple gown and withdrew the soft cloth wallet. Tandela watched with growing interest, licking her dry lips. All eyes were on Allisyn's fingers. But before she pulled aside the final fold to reveal its contents, she stopped short.

"I hold in my hands the Twelve Pearls of Wisdom, the Twelve Pearls of Deus, the one God. They have come into the Now from beyond all, the seeds of His thought, His very essence. Deus has set them in the world beyond the reach of the Great Calamity, to serve mankind.

"Therefore I must take back by oath, Tandela. Now that I know their nature, I know that you must not have them." She pulled them from beneath the last fold of cloth and they shone forth, luminous orbs of great beauty. The sunlight itself was dimmed by their brilliance. A collective gasp went up from the assembly, whether at the sight of the pearls or at Allisyn's words, no one could reckon. Tandela was mad with the desire of them.

"Give them to me!" she demanded. "They are mine." She walked a few swift steps down the dais toward Allisyn. Allisyn held the strand up by it ends and draped the Pearls about her neck. Bronwyn stepped in between her and the approaching Tandela. She looked at Tandela with her smooth white eyes. Tandela recoiled as she saw them, no iris, no pupil, no color, only an egg-white luster.

"You may not have them, Tandela," spoke the slip of a girl. "These pearls are the property of humankind, sent by Deus to heal our wounds. And now, Tandela, know me. For I am Bronwyn, the girl you blinded. I am the granddaughter of Doena the prophetess, the girl who has not spoken from birth until this day. My vision and my voice have been restored by Allisyn, the bearer of the gifts of the Twelve. She and no other is their keeper. She has paid the price of them. Deus has chosen her to honor Him by bringing their gifts into a needful world."

"Stand back, wretched girl!" Tandela shouted. The end of the hall became dark, as though night were falling. Tandela seemed to grow taller and swallow the light. The light from the Pearls beamed all the stronger. Tandela reached for them. From the end of her hand, fingers stretched out to grasp the Pearls, like the dark claw of some menacing raptor. In the very moment she touched them, Allisyn fastened the clasp of the strand.

The Pearls flared yet brighter and began to revolve, slowly at first. Tandela recoiled. They gained momentum and soon they were moving in a whirl of light about Allisyn's neck, like a comet streaking through dark heavens. The swirling circlet of light moved upward over her face and to the top of her head, where it gleamed as a halo. The light migrated outward in fine tracery from the halo until its threads reached the floor. The halo descended and grew larger in diameter as it migrated past her chest, her waist, her hips. When it reached the level of the floor it had formed a shimmering, translucent wall around her. Allisyn herself seemed to glow from within. A brilliant white light shone from her eyes. It streamed forth as though it might never more be contained. It flowed from the ends of her fingers, and from each strand of her hair. It spilled from her nostrils in frosty vaporous clouds. The light filled the chamber, rolling back the darkness as it did. Tandela stood panting. Aefalas rose slowly to his feet.

"Behold," called Bronwyn, with a voice that shook the very

207

walls of the castle. "The gifts of the Twelve are bestowed. Never shall you possess them, Tandela, and never shall you give them to Thol-nys. They are safe now as is their bearer. No longer will you threaten her while she wears the Pearls! Allisyn of Aestri shall never die by your hand!"

Part III

Chapter 20
The Brotherhood

Dayn and his band rode swiftly over the Dacon Plain, a herd of wild kine before them. Soon the hunters were among the stragglers, launching arrows and spears, bringing their time to a stumbling, bellowing end in the buzzing summer grasses. When the hunters had killed several aurochs they dismounted. Carcasses were stripped of their hides with sharp knives and meat cut into strips for drying. Some of the men set themselves immediately to the work of tanning the hides, hides which would be turned into clothing, into saddles and bridles for the horses and into quivers for their arrows. Others lit fires and began roasting portions of meat. Still others gathered riderless horses and corralled them using a makeshift picket.

Dayn surveyed the efficient industry of his brothers with pride. It had been a long, frustrating process to bring these men out of their darkness. Many of them had only known the ways of the goddess, of the mothers, of bleeding into the earth to produce the next crop like his step-father Khol. How fulfilling it was to see these men now, astride powerful horses, galloping unchecked over the wide, treeless plain. For nearly ten years now they had lived in this way, free to go where they pleased, free of the conditions and the constraints of towns and flocks and fields.

The first followers had come from Dayn's own village. Ulf had helped persuade many to join in the aftermath of the great conflagration and destruction of the Council House in which they had lost their families and all their reasons to stay. Perhaps twenty had come away then. Bit by bit, Dayn and Ulf had accustomed them to the unnerving herd and taught them to ride. As they traveled the valleys and plains of their homeland, they came upon other villages. By ones and twos, they recruited young men of promise.

Dayn could tell almost immediately who would follow when his band arrived. Most of the onlookers would shy away or cower at the order of the matriarch of the village, still others would gaze in wide-eyed terror and wonder at the strange and audacious men who rode the fantastic beasts. But some, when Dayn came prancing up on Mataforas, nostrils flaring and snorting, hooves pawing the ground and raising a cloud of glorious dust, would look at him with admiration and longing. He knew that longing, that desire to be free, to think and choose for one's own self, the desire to break away from the plodding, uncomprehending flock and ride like the wind sweeping through tall grasses.

To learn the art of riding had become a ritual of sorts to Dayn and his band. Dayn had come to realize that the darkness was more easily lifted from the minds of the initiates once they had learned to ride. So he began the training of the new ones in that way. First they had to lose their fear, but not their respect, of the intimidating animals.

For these were not horses of just any kind. They were the first horses, formed out of the struggle of Osyn and Thol-nys in the depths of the ocean, bred of fire and water. They were as strong and enduring as the breakers that hammered the ancient rocky headlands of the shoreline into the sands of young beaches. They were as swift as a storm slashing down from the north, as graceful as curling waves, as restive as flecks of foam on the rolling surface of the waters, as wary as the shadows that played across the shallow, sandy bottom near the shore. In color they tended to be gray with black manes and tails, often with white flecks mottling their hips and feet. Their eyes were either blue or green and they were beautiful to look at, but fearsome, for they burned with the unquenchable fire of creation. They stood at the shoulder easily as tall as the tallest man. Their hooves and teeth were potent weapons, hard as stone and quick as lightning.

Once the men became comfortable around the magnificent beasts, Dayn would have them stroke and pet the animals and speak to them in comforting tones, gaining their allegiance by degree. Having accomplished this, the horses would suffer the

212

men to mount them. By slow stages they gave themselves to one another, the proud horses allowing themselves to be tamed, led and directed, and the timid men allowing themselves to be elevated, leaving finally the level of the earth, the flocks, the fields, and the mothers, with an uncertain but opening confidence.

It was not easy for these men, with consciousness so infant-like, to sit astride these tall towers, these powerful engines of flesh, and proclaim, "I am". The blood of the very womb of the earth resisted it, the darkness of the hollows of caves and the ocean depths pulled at them, beckoned to them, pleaded with them to sleep, clawed at them when nothing else would avail, always attempting to pull them irrevocably back down.

The love between man and beast grew with the passing days, seasons and years. As each rider fed and groomed his mount, as they lived, slept and traveled together, they became inseparable, developing a bond that could not be broken except by death.

As the confidence of the individuals and the band grew they went further afield, traveling in ever widening circles from the place their brotherhood had been born, the protected Vale of the Cyryn. They traveled the length and breadth of the Dacon Plain, from the west where the Vahlen River, brief but swift, plunged from the mountains to the rocky coast, to the north and east where the broad, slow-moving Sothmont skirted the mountains and carved the steppe, to the long sun-drenched coastline washed by the Gulf of Imden.

But these borders did not hold them long, and beyond there was nothing to restrain them. They lived to discover the unknown and explore new territories. Out of the Dacon they crossed the Sothmont and found a wider, wilder, land. To the north it seemed limitless. To the east it was many a days ride until it rose to a high range of mountains. To the south alone did there seem to be an impenetrable barrier, the mysterious and frightening ocean, where the lapwings scurried from the tide on foaming beaches. The long line of its coast eventually led them eastward to a wide river. Beyond it they saw a fertile sloping plain and they longed to explore it. The Fallon they named it, because it was beyond their reach.

Inherently they were peaceful men. As prisoners recently escaped from sentence of death in a dark dungeon they wished more than anything to be left alone. They were in love with their

213

freedom and breathed it in great gulps, like one who has just managed to break through the surface of the waters and save himself from drowning. Therefore they went without fear because they had not caused others to fear them.

At twenty, Dayn had grown handsomely into manhood, tall and thin like a cedar sapling and as tough. His sandy hair was cropped short and he had dark brown, thoughtful eyes. In summer, most of the brothers wore short tunics and Dayn was no exception. On his feet were sandals that laced up over his muscular calves. At his side he carried a short copper sword and slung across his back was a bow and quiver of arrows. He was not the fastest nor the strongest of the brothers, but he was the most intelligent and that set him above the rest.

Dayn and the brotherhood thrived on adventure and they were quick to leap at the chance of one, whether it was to find the highest mountain to climb or the swiftest river to cross. They devised contests to see who could ride the fastest, shoot the straightest, and defeat his brothers in wrestling and mock combat to prove their strength and prowess. But these adventures and games did not completely assuage their hunger for glory. In the back of their minds, there always loomed the need to face a true test, one in which they would actually face death and conquer their fear of it. This would be the authentic proof of their might and their ascendance, of their ability to stand on their own, without the mothers, and be their own men.

Such a test did finally come. They had ridden far to the eastern fringe of the plain where the flat steppe gave way before the wooded slopes of purple-shouldered mountains beyond. Dayn and his fifty brothers jostled along in the heat of the sweltering plain, the declining sun selectively deepening the color of the skin of their backs to a dark umber and lightening their hair to gold. Sweat pasted the dust of their riding to the bodies of man and horse and their throats cried out for water. At last they came to the fringe of the forest, where a stream issuing from a fold in the hills had gathered itself into a broad, shallow pool.

The brothers dismounted and drank the cool clear liquid, letting it run down their hands and trickle from their elbows in ale-brown droplets. The horses walked easily into the pool, drinking as they went. Mataforas gave Dayn a playful shove while his head was turned and sent him headlong into the water. The sputtering Dayn leaped up off the sandy bottom, sending a shower of water at the pearl-white stallion. The horse responded with a neighing laugh and vaulted at Dayn, causing him to jump out of the way into the path of Draek. Draek joined the melee and soon the entire band of fifty horses and riders were soaked and exhausted with play.

Unknown to the exuberant youths, a pair of eyes watched them from behind a fallen tree on the opposite bank.

The band emerged dripping from the water and made camp. Soon there was venison to roast. While their supper cooked, they each took turns boasting of their mastery in the water fight. When they had eaten their fill and the tales began to repeat themselves, they dropped off one by one into a smoky, heavy-lidded sleep. From outside the circle of firelight, in the woods, the eyes kept their vigil.

Dayn awoke to the frightened neighing of horses. The brothers were on their feet in a disoriented second, running in the direction of the picket with weapons drawn. The moonless night was dark. Dayn saw the white specter of Mataforas and navigated by it until he reached the side of his stallion. Mataforas was quivering with repressed anger and he startled at Dayn's touch. Dayn whispered comforting words while the others inspected the herd.

"Herid's Elieda is missing," Ulf reported at length. They searched the thin forest roundabout for the truant mare but the blackness made it impossible to find her. Returning to camp, Dayn placed a consoling arm around Herid's shoulder.

"Do not worry brother. We shall find her in the morning," Dayn comforted. And find her they did.

In the sodden dawn after a cold breakfast, they circled outward from the camp, searching and calling, but no sound came to Elieda's ears. They found her lying on the ground, entrails spilled. One of her hind legs had been torn away and there was gaping hole in her back. Herid came running and fell to his knees beside her. A few insects buzzed around the still warm carcass.

None of them had ever seen the like of it before. They had thought themselves, their horses, to be indestructible. The wanton slaughter of the animal shocked them. No one spoke for a long while.

"What does this mean?" Ulf asked at last. "Is it an omen?"

"What... who could have done it?" Draek wondered aloud. They all looked at Dayn who stood now after examining the wound.

"It looks as though she were *bitten*," he said incredulously, "and the leg as if it were torn from the body." None of them could comprehend it. It was some time before Fremd suggested that they bury the young mare. The river was a good distance away and it took many hours to bring enough heavy stones to raise a cairn over her body. By the time they mounted and rode away, the day was well advanced.

Their shadows were still short when the shaken band came to the outskirts of a village. A little girl, playing on the edge of a field where her mother bent to work, saw the strangers. She ran, grabbing onto her mother's legs and hiding behind her ankle-length flaxen skirts. Caught in the open, the woman stood, trembling slightly, took a few stumbling steps backward over the undulating furrows, and watched with growing terror as the mounted riders approached. There was nowhere to run. She picked up her daughter and covered the small head with her soil-browned hand.

Seeing her fright, Dayn dismounted and walked slowly toward the woman, holding his hand out, palm upward in greeting.

"Do not be afraid, mother," Dayn soothed. "We will not hurt you."

"Who... who are you?" the woman asked, unassured by Dayn's mild words.

"A band of adventurers, interested only in finding out about the world. What can you tell us?"

"To leave, and quickly," she replied curtly, anxiously. "We have nothing that you seek. If you have any sense, you will leave."

"Everyone, everything, has something to offer us," he said and stepped closer. The woman misinterpreted his intent and backed away again. Her quaking increased.

"Why are you so frightened, mother? Honestly, we mean you no harm."

"What are those?" she asked, pointing at Mataforas, then quickly retracting her shaking hand. Dayn looked around and invited Mataforas to join him. The great horse walked forward. When Dayn turned back to face the woman, he saw that she had

216

swooned. He lifted her head from the ground, pulled the sable hair back from her face, and brushed the soil from her clothes, noticing that his heart was beating strangely faster. She was not unlovely and she felt soft to his touch, like Moira had felt. The woman opened her eyes to Dayn's concerned gaze and seemed to relax. Dayn sat her up and steadied her until she could stand once more. Assured now that Dayn could be trusted, she led him and the brothers unsteadily toward the village, holding the hand of her little girl.

An old man met them at the bounds. The little girl broke away from her mother and ran to his side, whispering something hurriedly into his ear. Dayn hailed the man.

"Good day father." The man said nothing, ambling to the side of the young woman and speaking to her in hushed tones. Although Dayn could not hear their discourse, the woman seemed to be explaining the presence of the strange visitors. The man eyed them suspiciously as she talked. Finally, the woman returned to face Dayn while the old man hobbled off toward the heart of the hamlet. The fear had left her dark-brown eyes but she still kept her distance from Mataforas.

"Why are you so afraid?" Dayn inquired. "You act as though we were some sort of monsters!" he joked.

"That's no joking matter," the woman countered. "And you wouldn't be so smug if you had ever seen Ghrunth!"

"Who, or *what*, is a Ghrunth?" Dayn probed, half-amused.

"Ghrunth," she replied, "*is* a monster. Truly!" she added seeing Dayn's disbelief break into a smile. "You don't believe me, do you?"

Dayn did not believe her.

"Of course I do!" he lied good-naturedly. "Tell me about him!"

"Well, first of all, its not a *him*. We don't *think*. Well, at least she never bothers with us women, only the men. No one knows why."

"What do you mean?"

"None of the women ever go missing. Of course, we stay pretty close by. It's always at night. The hunters will not spend the night away from the village any more, it's too frightening. Still every now and then, one of them turns up missing. Sometimes we will find a piece that she didn't eat. I remember when we found the remnants of poor Wymm, it was terrible. I'll always have nightmares about that!"

217

Dayn's thoughts flashed back to the previous evening.

"You say this Ghrunth, steals your men... and eats them?"

"Well, at least that's what happened to our unfortunate Wymm! There have been others..." her voice trailed.

"Last night, mother, we were camped not far from here. One of our horses was stolen. We found the remains of her carcass. She had been torn apart."

The woman looked suspiciously in the direction of the horses. "Ah, that would be Ghrunth alright. It's been a while since she's eaten. We've become much more careful of late."

The band were invited into the village and sat near a wellspring in its paltry square, where the local matriarch plied them with stories of the monster. It had not always been this way, she insisted. Before Ghrunth came, they lived in prosperity and without fear. She came out of the east, the mother claimed, waving her arms vaguely in that direction as she spoke, out of the Mountains of Eversnow, hungry, and seeking revenge. For legend had it that she was once a beautiful woman, a princess of her race of giants. But her fantastically rich husband had been killed and robbed by a human, an adventurer who had somehow crossed the mountains. Finding the killer and avenging him became an obsession to her. Her obsession turned to hatred and her hatred turned her into an ugly hag, bent ever on killing. Due to her great size, she had a great hunger, but because of her ugliness, no one would come near her. She had no recourse but to eat her victims.

The brothers sat in rapt attention as the matriarch told her tale. Ulf's mouth had gone dry and Draek noticed that his own heart was pounding. Dayn saw the look of uncertainty in Draek's eyes and his competitive spirit suddenly got the better of him.

"I'm not afraid of her," Dayn, who sat a little apart from the others with his back to a spreading elm, blurted out.

"You... not afraid?" the matriarch said in disbelief, looking him straight in the eye. "Why you're only a boy."

"But there are fifty of us!" he remarked.

"Immaterial," the matriarch shot back. "She would catch you all and have you for breakfast, one at a time."

"I think you underestimate us, Mother!" Draek spoke up, his wounded pride wresting control from his common sense.

"Humph!" the old woman snorted.

"We'll find this Ghrunth and kill her for you," Draek half-shouting, standing both to shake his own fears and to rally the brothers. He stared at Dayn, who seemed to be having second thoughts now.

"You'll never find her. But she'll find you. Oh yes, she'll find you if you go looking for her!" the matriarch tempted.

"We'll find her alright. Just tell us where she lurks, and what she looks like. We'll find her and rid your village of her pestilence," Draek boasted.

"What she looks like?" the matriarch replied. "Why she doesn't look like anything. She's made herself invisible, and that's the truth of it. Her ugliness was even too much for her own self to stand, so she's made herself invisible. You can't see her, or hear her, or smell her. First thing you know you're bitten clean into. That's how you know, when it's too late, when you're in her jaws! But they say when the wind blows, that's when she's walking, that's how you can tell she's coming for you."

Draek was taken aback. The prospect of fighting a monster that he couldn't see or smell or hear cowed even his audacious swagger.

"They say there's only one thing can make her visible, and that one thing is fear or pain. But she fears nothing and nothing can wound her because she can't be seen. So there's an end to it. There's nothing to be done."

The matriarch left them and retired to her dwelling. There was a profound silence. One by one the villagers filtered away to find their unfinished chores. The brown-eyed woman sat with her daughter in her lap not far away from Dayn, and now she sidled closer to him.

"I suppose there *is* no hope for our village then. Alas for my own husband Wuerth who was gobbled up last year. Alas for the father of my Little Ara." She looked at Dayn with tears beginning to run down her upturned face. Some foreign emotion swelled his heart.

"I will find a way," he declared in a thick voice.

As fantastic as she seemed to the brothers, Ghrunth *was* real. But she was no giantess, no beautiful princess that had been turned into an hag by black magic. She was a daughter of Thol-nys, spawned in the beginning of time of the blood of her

219

fearsome mother, ever thirsty for the blood of men, and utterly evil. For this was a time when monsters still walked abroad upon the earth, before they crawled inside the heads of men.

Ghrunth sat upon a rock at the entrance to her cave, high up in the thickly forested hills, gnawing upon the thigh bone of Elieda and picking bits of gristle from her teeth. She perceived Dayn and his band of adventurers long before they were anywhere near. She belched. The horse flesh had been satisfying and the morsel she had brought back to her lair had made her a nice snack for the following day. But meals could be few and far between. She could ill-afford not to lay by stores when the opportunity presented itself. And here were a half-dozen tender tidbits about to knock on her front door.

She raised herself off the stoop and wove her spell. First the tip of her tail disappeared, then her massive, horny feet and legs. The scaly arms, which hung almost to the ground were the next to go. Finally, her loathsome head with its protruding lumps of bone faded from view. The last thing visible was the lumpy tongue, licking her beak-like lips in anticipation of dessert.

Dayn and his avengers dismounted and left the horses untied so that they might run if Ghrunth attacked. They headed up the mountainside as quietly as they could, which was not nearly quiet enough to fool the keen-eared Ghrunth. The forest was very still and each step they took proclaimed their foolishness.

"Let's go over the plan again," Draek said, stopping them in a deep ravine. "The four of us," he said, pointing to Frax, Sarn and Truenn, "will draw our swords and frighten her. When she shows herself, Herid, Dayn, the two of you will shoot her. When the fear and pain make her visible, we will all rush her and make an end of it. Agreed?"

"Yes," they all nodded, licking dry lips.

Dayn and Herid fanned out to the left and right respectively while the others climbed forward out of the defile. Draek clashed his sword against his small round shield and shouted.

"Come out, Ghrunth! We have come for your blood! Show us yourself and your fear! We know your secret. Come, quench the thirst of our blades!" Dayn smiled at the sound of Draek's proud words boldly breaking the stillness of the woods.

Ghrunth chortled as Draek bantered on and sat down to watch the antics of the insignificant humans. Far from being frightened, she was mildly amused and stretched herself out upon a hillock to watch.

Seeing that their clamor was producing no effect, Draek brought his foursome up short.

"Perhaps she is not here," Frax said. Suddenly a wind stirred the treetops.

"We should go back," Sarn said nervously, feeling the breath of the breeze against his face and remembering the words of the matriarch.

"No!" Draek answered. "Don't be a whelp, Sarn. You are not afraid, are you Frax? What about you Truenn?"

"We are with you," Truenn proclaimed. "Let's go on."

The four of them pressed ahead under the pressure of Draek's chiding, hurling ineffectual threats at Ghrunth. When the odious creature had heard enough she heaved herself from the ground and marched down the hillside toward the frail band, still cloaked in her spell of invisibility.

On the left flank, Dayn was watching the four. Doubtful of their plan, he wondered what might give them the advantage they needed to defeat the monster. The monster. The invisible ogre. It suddenly occurred to him that it was all a hoax, that the matriarch had been making fools of them all. Perhaps there was no monster at all and she had sent them chasing shadows. But the woman, she had seemed sincere...

Suddenly Truenn left the ground, lifted by an unseen claw. His head and shoulders disappeared and there was a crunching sound. The surprised Herid shot wildly where Truenn flailed helplessly in the air. The body flew back to the ground. Draek stared in shocked disbelief. Dayn grabbed his sword and strode to where his brother lay writhing on the ground. Unknown to him, he was coming up behind the monster.

Ghrunth leaned forward and swung her huge arm, sending Frax head over heels down the slope. Herid fired again, hitting nothing. Ghrunth stood and raised her arm above her head, poised to flatten Draek with a massive fist. The backlash of her swing snapped off a branch and the hornet's nest attached to it fell to the ground between her feet. Simultaneously, she felt a presence behind her and hesitated. The angry hornets swarmed and rose into Ghrunth's face. As she whirled about to face the unknown menace, snapping a young sapling off with her tail, a hornet stung her in the eye. The pain was sudden and sharp. For a brief second, the spell that made her invisible collapsed. Dayn saw the outline of her swarthy leg and stuck his sword deep into its ethereal sinews.

221

Ghrunth screamed. Now her outline was clear to be seen. Herid's third arrow found its mark in her thigh. The hulking monster, who had never known pain or fear, turned and fled, trailing blood behind her as she ran. Dayn lodged another arrow deep between her shoulders. She fell, plowing the mouldy earth in her agony. Draek jumped upon her back and when he drove his sword between her ribs, the monster convulsed and lay still.

A shout went up from the warriors and they all began to talk at once. Draek and Herid dragged the severed head of Ghrunth back to where Dayn was helping Truenn to his feet.

"Ha-ha! Look at this, lads! Look at what we have done! We have killed the beast and saved the village! What a day! I knew we could do it!"

"Ghrunth is dead!" shouted Herid. "Let's go back and tell the villagers!"

"I think my arm is broken," Truenn said, not overly exuberant.

"A battle wound!" shouted Herid. "That *is* lucky. I wish *I* had been wounded."

"Look here!" cried Frax. "My face! It's all scratched where the monster pummeled me!"

"A broken arm is better!" argued Truenn. "Isn't it Dayn?"

"You saw me, didn't you Dayn? You saw me fighting the beast too, did you not?" added Sarn.

"You wanted to turn back!" Draek accused.

"Not really. I dealt the beast a blow!" Sarn insisted.

"She was already dead!" Frax taunted.

"Did you see Dayn stab it in the leg?" Herid asked. "What a stroke! That blow was her undoing. That is when her spell began to unravel and she became really visible and I shot her. Hurrah for Dayn!"

"I finished her off, though. Did you see me leap upon her and stab her through the heart?" Draek reminded them.

"That was marvelous, Draek. Dayn shot her, though. That's what made her fall!"

"Enough, enough, friends," Dayn interjected. "You are all heroes. You are all very brave, and I am very proud of you. This, my brothers, is how we were meant to live! Let us go back and tell the mothers!"

The villagers crowned them with laurels. The brown-eyed woman placed a kiss on Dayn's blushing cheek and was reluctant to let him leave.

222

Chapter 21
Trials

The excitement over the slaying of Ghrunth lasted well into the autumn. It was discussed around the campfire each night and the tale grew with each telling, the monster becoming larger and more hideous, the deeds of the warriors more death-defying and glorious. It was the crowning achievement of their lives. But in the end it was not enough. The need for the brothers to prove themselves, each to himself and to the others, became a never ending game. And they went in search of new perils. Life was magnificent and filled with excitement. They did as they pleased and went where they wanted to go. There were no others to consider but themselves and no consequences if they erred. It was perfect.

But as the brothers ventured further and more frequently from the Dacon, they came to the lands of people who were different, who grudged their coming and mistrusted them. They did not want the horsemen interloping in their territory and did not approve of their nomadic lifestyle, nor of their leading the young men away from the tribe, their ways, and their culture. Dayn's band had swelled to more than a hundred and if their intentions were unchanged, their needs had grown. Provisioning a hundred men and horses was no minor task. Where they camped they hunted and foraged, and their circle of fires and trampled grass made a lasting impression on the land and the minds of men they encountered. As they retraced their journeys, they often found these people to be less and less hospitable. Some became openly belligerent. The design of the brother's weapons evolved from that which made for reliable hunting, to that which made for better defense, and finally, to that which made for efficient attack and killing of other men. Uncertainty, if not fear, began to dog their footsteps.

That Dayn's band was mounted was a significant advantage if they encountered hostility. But their numbers were still small and strengthened only now and again by young men who risked all to join them. There were no women among them, and thus no offspring, for they shunned women as symbols of the matriarchy and their former shackles. So they looked for some other advantage, something that would elevate them in battle above the others. Something that would make them so feared that they would need no longer fear for their own safety. They found this thing quite by accident.

Ever the Fallon called to them and ever they longed to set foot upon its shores. Upon a time they were hunting far to the east along the shores of the Moravon River, a land abundant with sweet grass and unharried game. They had traveled far up its estuary when they came to a deep ford. Then they did what they had never been so bold to do; they crossed it, the horses up to their flanks in the cool, swirling waters, the feet and legs of Dayn's warriors wetted to their thighs and hems of their tunics. Their copper breastplates and tips of their lances gleamed in the sun. The water drained in sheets from the horses as they climbed up the further bank.

Dayn split the troop in four squadrons. Each would ride away for two days then seek once again the ford, where they would regroup, sharing reports of the land and its inhabitants.

Dayn's own group, flanking the others on the left, rode south and east. The country was much to their liking, wide, firm, and gently sloping. They sang as they rode, such was the joy of their hearts. A warm wind arose in the south and blew toward the river as twilight fell. In the dimness of the failing light, they discovered a path, broader and more evenly worn than the tracks of deer and wild kine. Dayn dismounted and studied it.

"This path has been made by men," he observed. "We must be wary." Mataforas, Dayn's white stallion, tossed his proud head in agreement. Dayn led the muscular horse off the path to the east, with the others following him to camp for the night.

They were in their saddles once again at dawn, still riding south along the broad path. To the east as the sun rose, a low line of hills was revealed, gathering the rising plain about their feet, and further on, the blue silhouette of taller mountains. The ground began to break into broad ridges with deepening rills between, like many fingered hands pointing back toward the plain and river. The road traced a line up over one of these fingers and thence onto the back of the hand. Dayn stopped his squadron. This land, more broken, stony, and less suitable for swift riding, made him uneasy. He was about to turn his riders in another direction when he saw smoke on the southern horizon. His curiosity aroused, he led the others forward at a wary trot. They climbed the steep face of the ridge and came out onto its wide crest, dotted with stubby, spiny bushes. Further away to the south, the ground rose yet again to a series of smooth-topped hills, warmed now by the mounting ardor of the sun's fire. In each of the intervening valleys, a dark swath of forest lay in shadow, yet untroubled by the light. A small clear brook issued from the feet of the nearest copse.

Dayn led the troop on toward the pillar of smoke, screened by a line of dark firs. Bidding his brothers to halt behind this cover, he and two others alone went forward, coming eventually to the end of the line of trees and to the edge of a small clearing. Ahead of them, a barren pit of substantial dimension had been scraped in the earth against the side of the hill. On the steep upper slope, dark caverns opened back into the hillside and men came and went from them, hauling burdens on their backs. Dayn traced the line of their march to discover a cluster of small buildings. In the midst of the buildings, the pillar of smoke issued skyward. On his signal, he and his two companions rode toward it. They were challenged by sentries as they approached; small, squat men with thick arms, legs and chests, and round, bearded faces. Each of them carried a pike tipped by a metal that gleamed like the golden rays of Hanthol himself. Dayn walked Mataforas forward.

"Who is master here?" Dayn called to the sentries.

"Who wishes to know?" came back the hasty reply.

"I am Dayn. I come from a country many leagues away, across the Moravon and the plains that lie beyond. We are travelers and discoverers, adventurers who seek the truth and knowledge of the ways of men." One of the sentries trotted away toward the buildings and returned with another man.

"I am Harf," the newcomer said. He was short and burly, nearly as broad as he was tall, and looked as though he had been quarried from the stone of the earth itself. His broad face was

225

accented by a determined jaw. His sinewy arms terminated in stubby-fingered hands. He wore a short, black apron. "My people are miners of the ores of the hills and makers of metals," he continued, eying the short copper sword that hung at Dayn's side and the copper breastplate he wore. "We make our living in their trade. We exchange our metal goods for our neighbors' cloth and hides and food. We are a peaceful people, given to commerce rather than fighting."

"This is good. I would learn more of your metalcraft. Can you tell me aught of it?" Dayn inquired.

"I can and will if you will sup with me and tell me of your travels. I desire to learn of other peoples who might have an interest in our craft."

"Yes, but I must first attend to my brothers. Stay but a moment and I will return."

"How many of you are there?" Harf asked, his good-natured tone hiding the concern in his question.

"Enough," Dayn replied.

Dayn trotted back to his two companions giving them instructions to camp where the stream leaped from the wooded cleft between the hills. When he returned, Dayn dismounted and followed Harf to one of the low buildings. It was a simple edifice, and somewhat primitive. Its low rock walls were laid dry and atop the walls were rafters of round logs. These, in turn, were covered with a thatch of gorse and grasses from the dry hills. Dayn had to bend over to get through the door. Inside, in the center of the hut, was a square fireplace. Above it was an opening to allow the smoke to exit. A fire was smoldering there now and a small animal, a hare or large squirrel, was spitted and roasting. Everywhere were tools and scraps of metal. A bin of shiny coal stood in the corner.

Harf drew up crude benches for himself and Dayn beside the fire. He tested the meat by slicing away a morsel. Seeing that it was done, Harf offered a piece to Dayn, then drew them each a mug of cool ale from a barrel in the corner. Thus they sat, slicing off the flesh, eating it with their fingers, savoring both meat and drink.

"How much copper can you smelt in a day at your forge?" Dayn asked when he felt his host had eaten enough to smooth the burrs from the edges of his hunger. "In the village I come from copper is refined, but the quantity is very small, only enough to satisfy the wants of the villagers for simple farm tools. Some small diggings and a small furnace is all the smith can manage. But the work is of good quality."

Harf continued to chew. Finishing his generous mouthful, he washed it down with ale, wiped his lips with the back of his calloused, forge-blackened hand, and stood.

"Let me see your sword," he coaxed.

Dayn unsheathed and handed it, hilt first, to the metalworker. Harf placed it upon the table and walked through a doorway into an adjoining building. In a moment he returned, carrying another short sword. Dayn noticed that its blade was brighter and that it gleamed like sunlight on water. He remembered the tips on the pikes he had seen the sentries carrying outside. Harf gave the sword to Dayn, who looked at it with the admiration of one who sees and appreciates the skill of another. It was simple but beautifully shaped, not pitted like his own, and its edge was smooth and hard. His eyes betrayed his delight in it.

"Here we mine an ore, Cassiterus, or tinstone. From it we obtain a white metal we call tin." Harf reached into a satchel that hung at his side and produced a small bar of tin, in length no greater than his short forearm and about the thickness of his finger. He placed it in Dayn's hand who held for a moment, feeling its weight, then returned it to the smith. Harf bent the bar and it produced a strange, deep-throated squeaking sound, like the croaking of a frog.

"The copper comes from another mine on the other side of the hills," continued Harf. Here we take the tin and copper bar and melt them together. When they cool they form a new metal that we name bronze. This sword is made of bronze. I am always trying new ways of blending these two metals in order to make bronze of varying qualities. Now let me show you something!"

He took Dayn's copper sword and set it on two blocks of wood, its hilt upon the one and its tip upon the other. He raised the bronze sword above his head and brought it down with a swift, clanging stroke. Dayn watched in amazement as the bronze sword cleaved his own copper weapon easily in two. Harf's eyes gleamed and a smile brightened his face. Dayn's own eyes went round with wonder. The implications of what he had just seen were quick to dawn upon him. Harf returned the bronze sword to Dayn's hands and tossed the shards of the copper sword into an oaken barrel of scrap in the corner.

227

"There, it is yours."

Dayn ran his fingers along the sharp, polished edge, captivated by this new toy.

"I want each of my riders to have one," he said. "How long would it take you to make a hundred?"

"A hundred swords? How will you pay?"

"What do you require?"

Harf looked hard at Dayn, sizing him up before he answered.

"Mining is hard work and our own people disdain to do it," began the diminutive smith artfully. "We are a people of high craft, making objects of great beauty and utility and we are loathe to labor in the caverns. We take our joy, and our profit, from manufacture. And we could do yet more; we could make a wider variety of useful objects, things of greater value, if only we were free of the pits, if only we had help to work the mines."

"You should hire someone to work the mines for you."

Harf laughed. "Hiring is expensive. It would cut too dearly into our profits."

"Then what would you propose?" Dayn asked innocently.

"We need people who will do what we ask of them, without objections and without demands."

"Where would you find such people as that?"

"Oh, we have found them before, here and there. Some people are farmers, some are shepherds, and some are miners. It makes no difference, it is all work. If a farmer who raises a sheep for his overlord becomes a miner and hauls ore for me, what is the difference? They work, they eat, they sleep, and they get up the next day to do it again, like cattle."

"I'm not sure I understand you, Harf. What exactly is it that you want me to do in exchange for the weapons?"

"I want you to bring me those farmers and those shepherds to work in the mines, my friend. Can I be more plain?"

"What if they don't want to be miners? How will I convince them to come?"

The smith swore an exasperated oath under his breath. "You seem a man who could think of something clever," Harf said sarcastically. "Look at you, a vigorous man, a *leader* of vigorous men. You ride upon beasts and you have weapons. Soon you will have better weapons, if you bring me workers for the mines."

"You mean bring them here against their will, as slaves?

228

You mean to take away their freedom?"

"Freedom? Look, Harf has seen some of these villages where the mothers run the men about like dogs. Why do they put up with it, eh? It's because they don't know any better. Would they not be better off here, doing an honest day's work, than beating their heads against a stone for the likes of those? If they knew what a drudgery their lives are, they would come willingly. All I am asking you to do is give them a little help. Just bring them here and let them see how they like it. You'll be doing them a favor. I promise you."

Dayn was perplexed. He was not sure he believed the smith. He had seen the labor of slaves and the thought of it rankled him. One who valued his freedom so highly should value the freedom of another. Yet he himself had experienced the villages of the mothers. He had seen the red blood of Khol on the snow. He looked again at the bright sword. This bronze was a thing beyond all value. It was the very thing he sought to insure his own safety and allay his fears that his own freedom might somehow be taken away. Here was truly a great prize, a mighty tool for mighty men, a proud weapon for proud men.

"How many would you require?"

"Fifty, at first, then more."

Dayn swallowed hard. Harf had snared him, his own desire for the bright new toy had bound him.

"I will speak to the others," he said at length.

"Speak to the others? Are you not their leader? Are you not able to make a decision for their own good that they will follow? Speak not to them, sir, command them!" he urged Dayn, his eyes sparkling.

"If I bring you workers, and they do not like the mines, will you let them go?" Dayn asked, trying hard to justify to himself the enslavement of his fellow man.

"I'm offering you power, man. Will you throw a gift such as that away over the lives of a few miserable wretches?"

Dayn wavered.

"Here give it back," said the smith grabbing at the sword. "Go away. I will find someone else, someone with backbone, a man who is not averse to doing a man's work!"

"No, wait. I want it."

"Not nearly enough!" the frustrated Harf roared. "You don't deserve a sword such as this. I will save it for a better man. You're not up to the task."

229

"I am!" shouted Dayn, stung by the insults of the blocky smith like sparks from a forge hammer.

"Are you? Then prove it to Harf."

"So be it!" roared the young lion.

Dayn and Ulf lay flat against the ground, just on the far side of a low prominence, raising their heads cautiously to observe the procession from the village. There were perhaps three hundred people in all, walking slowly, singing songs of praise to the goddess, thanking her for the bounty of the pastures and the abundant new calves among their kine. Walking knee deep in fragrant, blooming timothy, the people followed their priestess and the icon of the deity she carried. Dayn and his band had ridden far north of the Moravon and east to where the plains splintered and rose in disjointed blocks to the Etsinn Mountains to find these victims of grim chance. Dayn motioned Ulf to bring forth the riders, who were bivouacked below them, while he remained on the hilltop to watch.

The people were a mile away from their village when Dayn's warriors broke from behind the low ridge. Seeing the horsemen, they bolted toward their homes like a flock of startled birds but the swift steeds had soon cut them off, forcing them to run back the other way. The riders circled the fear-stricken folk who pressed in hard against one another. Then the riders stopped and Ulf spoke to the crowd.

"We want fifty of your strongest men," he shouted at the High Priestess. "Choose them and let them stand forth, and none will be harmed."

"By what authority do you make this demand?" she shouted back angrily.

"By this," Ulf drew his bright bronze sword and held it aloft. The light of the sun glinted off it throwing a long bright bar across her neck and shoulders.

"No!" she shouted. "You shall not have them. You have no right to take them!"

Ulf kicked the flanks off his horse and walked him a few steps into the circle, looking sternly all the while at the woman.

"Hand them over, mother, so there will be no bloodshed. We do not wish to hurt you."

"We will not. The gods curse you if you do such a thing. Away!"

One of the riders sent a shaft from his bow into the ground near her feet.

"Reconsider, mother!" Ulf insisted. "There is no other way for you. Send out your men before our weapons speak too loudly for you to withstand."

The High Priestess stood her ground, defying the mounted warriors to make the first move. Out of the press of captives a knife flew. With a thud it found its mark in the side of one of the riders. Thirty bows answered instantly. Thirty arrows flew into the crowd and thirty people dropped, some screaming, some clawing at the ground or at the shafts embedded in them, some lying motionless. The riders rearmed their bows. A woman in the crowd panicked and tried to break through the line of horses back to the village. A few others followed her. More arrows whined and the little group fell. The crowd came alive with screams of terror and curses. Twenty of the riders dismounted and began to collar and bind men among the captives while the others held their bows, fitted with arrows, strings pulled taut, fingers against their temples. In time, fifty or sixty strapping men were taken, bound in six groups with strong leather thongs and led away across the blossoming fields. Women and children cried, and called out to their husbands and fathers in despair. Over all the priestess shouted her curses.

Dayn had seen everything from the top of the hill. He rolled over, turned his face to the sky, and stared into the sun. He placed his hands over his ears to smother the cries from the meadow below and shut his eyes tightly, but the light and the sounds still assailed him. When he could stand it no more he rolled off the crest of the hill and whistled for Mataforas. The white stallion came trotting. Dayn jumped upon his back and loped away down the hill toward his men. The whole business bothered him. Fifty lives, fifty slaves, fifty sorrows, fifty and more broken hearts, all for fifty swords, he thought. He looked back at the huddled, frightened mass of bleeding people but turned quickly away. He looked down at the bedraggled, confused men destined for the dark mines and tried not to remember their faces.

Winter was hunting in the wide steppes of Dor between the Icy Mountains and the westernmost thrust of the Etsinn. Dayn and his warriors, now nearly two hundred strong, all with bright bronze swords at their sides, spears tipped with bronze and breastplates of the same strong metal, rode north following an immense herd of red deer. They were clad in fur-lined robes of wild kine, deer, or bear, with boots of the same materials to warm their feet. A light dusting of powdery snow lay upon the ground and the gusting wind whipped it into slithering, stinging waves. Dayn called a halt for the night and the riders pitched their light tents, making fires for warmth and cooking.

Dayn shivered as he lay in his bedroll. Tomorrow they would go south again. In the failing light he drew letters with a piece of charcoal on a skin stretched over a frame beside him. As he did, memories of his former life drew near. He thought of the young Thena who had taught him to write, and of Moira who had taught him more. He wondered about the people of his village, if they still trod the same paths, still worshiped the same goddess. He remembered his nights with Moira, her soft skin, her gentle touches and a familiar longing seized him. He thought again of Khol, his stepfather, and was saddened, saddened by the loss of one so venerable and so kind. His thoughts revolved upon the faces of the men he had led to slavery in the mines of Harf and he tried again to forget them. They had not liked the mines. Harf had broken his promise. But Dayn loved the bright metal, and the brothers needed it.

Yes, tomorrow they would go south. But where would *he* go, what would *he* do to escape these memories?

The next day they did indeed turn to retrace their northward journey. With evening closing once again, they saw the lights of an insignificant village to the west. Dayn suggested they go there the next day and talk to the people. Perhaps they would find something to bring them back this way again.

The sun rose out of the frigid east, bathing the sky and the snow-dappled steppes in a rosy light. Following a cold breakfast they turned their backs to the sun and approached the village down the track of a narrow ravine. No one was abroad in the outlying fields. Smokes arose from the primitive houses but among them, they found only silent streets. Odd, thought Dayn, that in such a village no one had hailed them. Just then, the spaces between the huts came alive with arrows, wooden spears and flying stones. Just ahead, Dayn saw one of the

232

brothers fall with an arrow bristling from his back. A stone glanced obliquely off his own forehead and knocked him from Mataforas. He fell, hitting his head sharply on the frozen ground. He rose to his feet uncertainly, just in time to see a bellowing, dark-haired, wild-eyed man rushing him with an axe. Something hit the man in the back and he slid, face-down, to the ground at Dayn's feet. The axe flew past and tumbled to a ringing halt. Dayn drew his sword. All around him the brothers were under attack, being pulled from their horses and beaten with clubs or stabbed with sharpened staves. He jumped back onto Mataforas' broad back and shouted for the brethren to retreat. Riding swiftly away, they regrouped about a mile distant, where the narrow ravine ended and the plain rolled away unbroken to the east.

"By the gods!" Dayn shouted. "How dare they attack us! How many are missing?"

"By my guess, twenty," Ulf half-shouted. "Frax and Deen, Aban, ...let me see, ...Horn and Sarn, Doen and Foerg, Ludd, Semm and Samor. Who else has fallen?" he cried.

"Evin is wounded," someone shouted, jumping from his mount to catch Evin, who reeled and fell from his saddle.

"By the gods," Dayn shouted once again. "We shall not let this attack go unrequited! Who can ride? Who can ride?"

"Dayn," Ulf said, "let us turn aside. We will only lose more men. It is not worth it. Let us go."

"No!" Dayn shouted above him, angered by Ulf's timidity, or perhaps the logic of his brother's argument in the face of his own irrational pride.

"Who will ride with me to avenge the slain?"

All shouted and dashed their swords against their breastplates, making a sound like a failing hillside.

"Draek, lead a third around to the right and come down upon them from the north by the river. Herid, you lead a third up from the south. I will lead the rest back down the ravine. Go now!" Dayn shouted. Horses and riders exploded away raising a fine cloud of icy needles, shouting as they rode. Into the village among the trees they crashed. Dayn's charge was imprudent as the houses and hedges and other obstacles made fighting from horseback difficult. But the fury and superior weapons of Dayn's warriors took their toll. Though the villager's put up a stiff resistance, they were finally forced to fly into the forest. Some of the riders wantonly chased fleeing

233

groups of the townsfolk, killing not only men, but women and children in their wounded pride and rage. When they had regrouped once again upon the plain, Dayn found that they had lost another fifteen brothers. A cold mist came to his eyes as Ulf called out the names of those who would ride no more, but whether from anger or sorrow he could not tell.

Following the attack, the band moved slowly south, taking care for the condition of the wounded among them. In a day or two they had left the frost behind. The weather turned warmer and they camped for a time in the lee of the western mountains. While they were encamped, Evin died of his wounds. Doubt stalked Dayn.

Ulf came to him while he sat alone in his tent. Outside the bonfire burned bright. The brothers sat or stood around it, still talking of the battle, of who had killed and how, showing off their wounds. The stories grew more fearsome, more exciting, and more gruesome, with each rendering. Dayn began to loathe their bragging.

"It was a bitter stroke," Ulf said at length, "one we must forget. Those who are gone can be brought back neither by our tears nor our desire."

"Why, Ulf, why? Why did this happen? We came in peace. They did not even try to understand us."

"They did not care to know us or why we came. They were fearful, and fearful men can do fearsome deeds. I cannot blame them. It was bound to happen. Perhaps they had heard of the slaving. Perhaps they are simply stiff-necked. Who can say?"

"We must become stronger. If such a thing can happen to us, if people will attack us unprovoked, we must be more prepared. We must have more men, and better weapons. Perhaps we should subdue all the people of this land, show them our might, make them serve us, take away their weapons so they cannot strike back," Dayn emoted.

"That would take many men, many more than we have or could ever hope to have. You have never liked the slaving, Dayn. Would you make a whole country of slaves?"

Dayn bit his tongue and did not answer.

"Warring is not the answer, Dayn. Warring will only make us more enemies and increase our fear, and our fear will force us more and more to take up arms. We would forever more be fighting. No, I think we cannot end warring by making war."

234

Chapter 22
The Triumph of Fear

Dayn and his band wintered in the southern reaches of the Plain of Dor, hunting for their subsistence, and constructed the most permanent camp they had yet made. But with the coming of spring the brothers grew restless. They began to wonder about their leader. All through the winter he had been sullen, laughing little and keeping mostly to himself. Where would he take them now? Would they look for battle? What new adventures would they find? Many began to think of leaving, of going their own way. But where would they go? Not back to the mothers, not back to the boredom of tending flocks and fields, not back to that sleepy half-lit world.

The spring rains came and still Dayn gave no indication of moving. For days on end he sat in his tent drawing characters and writing. What he composed he showed to no one, not even to Ulf.

Finally there came a day, when spring was already well advanced, that he came forth from his tent and summoned the riders. They stood by eagerly awaiting his words. When he addressed them, all ears were trained to hear him.

"My brothers," he began. "We have been together long, some of us as many as ten summers. In that time we have seen and done much. From our small beginning our numbers have swelled and we have become both known and feared on the Dacon and the Plain of Dor, even across the Moravon and in the Fallon. We have learned much. We have mastered horses. We have broken the domination of the mothers over our minds. We have learned, each of us, to be our own. And we have learned

235

to trust, to depend on one another. Without this we would never have awakened. Individually, under the influence of the mothers, in the tribes and villages from whence we came, we would still be asleep, still awaiting the call to thought and reason.

"Yet, my brothers, I feel there must be a purpose for this call. There must be a reason for our awakening, else what good has it brought us? Must we not use this gift for a higher purpose than riding the plains for our pleasure, taking slaves for our gain and killing when we must to keep these freedoms? It must be so. And yet, I admit to you I cannot discover the purpose. I have thought on it much and still it evades me.

"I know that many of you have questions, many have doubts. Many of you look to me for answers. I have come to a place from which I know not where to lead you. My heart grows restless and I know that yours do as well. My searching keeps me awake in the night. And thus far it has kept me roaming the plains and far-flung lands. My heart desires to know at last what it is that I seek. For if I know this not, how will I know when I have found it?"

The riders gazed from one to another with confused looks. To some, it was as if Dayn spoke to them in an unknown language. To others, his words appeared as fleeting spectral lights in the dim margins of their minds. To a few, including his friend Ulf, who had journeyed further than the rest, Dayn's meaning was vaguely comprehensible, but my no means clear. Geffon, spoke up.

"Dayn, we are your people, your brothers. We have left all for you. It is enough for us to be here. It is enough to ride with the wind in our hair in the first light of dawn. We will follow you wherever you lead us."

"Yes," replied Herid. "We are forever yours, Dayn. You have given us great gifts, gifts beyond all measure. You have shown us that we can be as we want to be. You have shown us the might of thought and the might of arms. Lead us on to great deeds! Lead us on to adventure! Let us seek conquest, the conquest of men and of knowledge. It is enough to *be,* Dayn, and to be led by you. Never will we desert you!" He kneeled and offered his sword hilt to Dayn.

"I agree with Herid," said Draek. "We need only to ride and to eat. We need only to conquer and to possess and be free. For in these acts of doing we find our being. Not by thinking

236

will we find the answers to the great questions, but by doing. We will be what we do. Our task is not to question what to do, Dayn, but to do. Whatever we do, that then, is what we sought to do. What use are these questions? I have no such questions."

Many others remained silent, lost in this labyrinth of new ideas and words, but in their hearts they knew they would follow Dayn, wherever he might take them. To follow him was all they knew, and all they wanted to know. To have their freedom was enough. Dayn was both disappointed and inspired by their response. He knew he had crossed a bridge that someday they would cross as well, but not yet. They were not ready. Was it his destiny ever to be alone, to be the one to break new ground, and thus to have others always depending upon him? It was an honor, and yet a burden.

Another month found the brothers back upon the Dacon Plain, camping close to where the Vahlen fumed from the mountains in a last burst of white-capped frenzy before its bed found the gentler slopes of the coastal plain. It was a warm spring afternoon and the riders were enjoying a game of stamina and physical prowess they had invented for themselves. In this gambol the bladder of a young auroch was filled with air and stitched together. Around it was a closely fitting cover of leather. The ball was kicked or carried by the men. The one who held the leather ball played against all the others. The object of the game was to get the ball outside a large circle which had been marked off in the grass. They laughed and shouted as they played.

In the distance, Fremd, one who was quieter and enjoyed his solitude more than the rest, played a simple tune upon an instrument he had devised. Having taken several shepherd's reeds, some longer and thicker, some thinner and shorter, he had stitched them to a leather bag and lined it with an auroch's bladder to make it airtight. To this he had attached another reed to act as a mouthpiece. He blew into the mouth reed to inflate the bag which, when pressed in between his arm and his side, forced the air through the other reeds. The sound created was at once a low buzzing sound, like insects among the meadows on a summers eve, overlain by the melodic strains of the played

237

pipes. The sound came from a hidden hollow to Dayn's ears, hauntingly beautiful in its mournful simplicity. It reminded him of the song of birds heard over the low sighing of wind among the grasses, and moved him almost to tears.

Warily attracted to this music was another man who emerged from the thin forest among the hills. One look would suffice to tell that he once had been a mighty man, broad of shoulder and strong of sinew, now emaciated through hardship and deprivation. He walked with a stick and a pack slung upon his shoulder as if he were on a journey of considerable length. He hid behind a boulder for some time, listening to the music, watching the musician intently. From some distance away, he heard shouts of confrontation which turned uncharacteristically into bursts of unrestrained laughter. He skirted the hollow where the musician sat and rounded the hill behind it to the south. He spied Dayn sitting at the door of his tent and the playing field beyond. His quick eyes went to the picketed horses and he made a rough count of the strength of the band of nomads. Dayn detected the motion from the corner of his eye and saw the man before he had time to conceal himself again.

"Greetings friend!" Dayn shouted, standing as he spoke. "Welcome!"

Discovered, the man drew himself up to his full height and strode forward. He wondered at the youth of this one who had addressed him with such authority. For his part, Dayn was surprised to find such a man wandering alone, far from hearth, home and the security of his people. *Perhaps he is one who has heard and seeks the fellowship of our company,* Dayn thought.

"Greetings, brother," Dayn said again as the man stood before him. "I am Dayn, the leader of this brotherhood."

The man looked through Dayn at the company, surprised to see that there were no women among them, as Dayn's words had implied.

"I am Reyk," he said slowly in a voice thickened by disuse, speaking in the language of the Ieche, a parlance akin to Dayn's own.

"It is unusual to see a man like yourself traveling alone. I wonder greatly to see it. What is your destination?"

"I am going home," Reyk said.

"Ahh!" Dayn replied. "And where might that be?"

"It is far away, many moons of traveling on foot."

Dayn's amazement grew.

238

"It must be far indeed. How came you to be so distant from your home?"

"I was among the crew of a ship wrecked off the coast to the north. I alone survived. And now I must walk home," Reyk answered.

"And what might be a ship?" Dayn asked with perfect naivete. Reyk looked at him and laughed.

"A ship ...a vessel with a sail ...and oars."

Dayn missed his meaning and it showed in his eyes. Reyk continued.

"Men get inside, and it floats on the water, on the ocean."

Dayn now indeed showed his wonder and innocence. Suddenly he understood. Taking Reyk's arm he motioned for him to come. Dayn led him to the horses. "These are our ships, ships of the steppes."

Now it was Reyk's turn to be amazed as Dayn untied Mataforas, climbed onto his back, and paraded the tall white stallion before him. But Reyk had wandered far and seen much, and he did not reveal his surprise as Dayn had. Involuntarily his thoughts began to revolve on battle, strategy and the obvious advantages of being mounted in a world of those who fight on foot. These thoughts he also hid.

Dayn dismounted and returned to his new acquaintance. He had noted the man's gaunt features at first glance. Now he gave thought to hospitality.

"Come," he offered, "I will give you meat."

All day Dayn spoke to Reyk and told him much. Reyk asked many questions but gave few answers. Dayn spoke of his men, their travels, their discoveries and innocently showed Reyk his bronze sword. In this, Reyk's interest was keenly aroused. Dayn spoke on, unaware. When he had finished Reyk asked him probing questions about the maker of the bright swords and where he might be found. Dayn felt a sudden reluctance to divulge this secret. That Dayn did not tell the whole truth of this matter was not lost upon the clever Reyk. For he had been trained by Barthol, The Master of Lies, and could tell when Dayn was hiding the truth.

That night when Dayn's riders gathered around the great fire to cook and eat their evening meal, Reyk stood by expectantly, his mouth watering. Ulf saw the hunger in the hollow of his cheeks and eyes.

"We will gladly give you food in exchange for a story. Do

239

you have a tale?" Ulf asked.

"Verily," answered Reyk, "but the telling would be much abetted by a full belly!" And he laughed as merrily as the rest.

When the meal had been consumed and the fire was dying, Reyk stood in the midst of the riders. The sun sank into the sea beyond the mountains setting the undersides of the clouds ablaze with a yellow light and forming ranks of alternating light and shadow. Reyk's haggard face was lit with striking similarity by the bright glow of the fire.

Throughout the day Reyk had been discomfited by whirling images that rose, unbidden, from his unconscious, as if warring factions were struggling for mastery of his soul. Visions of the prow of a ship breaking glassy waves into foaming chaos would come and he would think of Belak. He would remember his lord Savor and his mission. His hand would touch his scroll of maps, and he would recall his obligation and desire to bring this knowledge back to his land, for the status and reward it would bring him. Then Barthol would appear. The woman he had taken at the request of his avowed master would appear, beckoning, drawing him rapturously on into a cavern where there was no light, no thought, no life. There was pleasure there, and sweet, lingering death. Then once again his thought would break into the light, free of the darkness; he would vow never to return to the city of women unless as a conqueror. Never would he return as minion, as slave to the will of Barthol. But the darkness would always return and he would feel himself falling back into the black pit of obedience to his hateful master.

These factions warred within him now as he stood before the brothers, gathered about the fire upon the Dacon. As he told his tale, these competing influences wove the threads of his thought and speech into a fabric of lies.

"I come," Reyk began, "from a land far to the south, across the sea, so that one may only come there by ship. In the building of these ships we are instructed by the gods, so that none save us may make them. We are hunters of the seas, as you are hunters of the plains. We are questers for knowledge of the great oceans and the lands that lie upon their margins. This I believe you can understand.

"Upon a time the gods told us of a City of Gold, a city of great riches, in the north. They said to our king, 'Go, find the city, and bring back tokens to show us what you have done. Remember the road, so that others may follow. Do this so that a

240

brave and mighty people will become yet more mighty and feared.' So the king gave me command of a ship and crew, the bravest sailors of our land, and we set sail. After many months we found the City of Gold. There were indeed riches there and women of great beauty. There was one, my friends, one of surpassing beauty, a goddess perhaps. Her hair is like copper and her eyes like the emerald green of the sea. Her feet are like the wind and her coming and going like the waxing and waning of the moon. And she fell in love with me. Gold she gave me as a token. But it was nothing to her, for in the midst of that city there flowed a river of gold and the very streets were paved with it. There is so much gold there, my friends, they count it as a burden. They give it away freely and do not guard it. But alas for all others, one may come there only by ship, and I alone know the way.

"The golden woman laded our ship with treasure and bade us sail home, bringing the gold to our king as a token of friendship between our lands. But, alas, laden as we were, a storm came out of the north and overwhelmed us. Our ship foundered and we were driven against the rocks. The gold sank to the bottom of the great sea. I alone survived, for the gods threw me into a deep sleep, and when I awoke on the shore, all about me were the faces of women, beautiful women, but fierce. They carried shields and lances, bows and arrows, a great warlike tribe, black of eye and of hair, but fairer than fair to look upon.

"They carried me to their village thinking me a god, who had come out of the sea. Never had they seen a man before, for their whole race is of women. They lavished me with attention. They swore their fealty to me and promised that if I would stay and govern them, they should be my tribe and I their master. They enticed me using their every device. They gave me women of great beauty for my own, to command as I might please. If I said, feed me, they would bring me food. If I said, serve me, they would serve. If I said, die for me, then they would fall upon their swords. It was only by the greatest strength of will that I left there, for I was sorely tempted to stay and be their prince.

"In the end I had to leave, for my allegiance to my people was stronger than the voices of the sirens. I am going home now, back to my people. In this goatskin I carry the memory of the road, written in characters that only I may read. When I

241

reach my home, I will get another ship. Then I will return to Guldwys, the Golden City."

The men who sat upon the ground looked at Reyk as if he indeed were a king or a god. As his tale had progressed he had become taller and more princely, his gaunt features changed from lines of destitution to traces of wisdom and his listeners sat in awe. Some had been stirred by the tales of easy gold, and some by the passion of the dark-haired tribe of amazons.

"Tell us, Reyk," one of them said at length, "how can we come to the City of Gold and to the City of Women? For you have made us desire them."

"It is not for you to know. You cannot go there. You asked me for a tale, and I have given you one."

"Is there not something we might barter for the memory of the road. Is there nothing we have that might make a fair trade."

"No, friends," Reyk replied, "there is nothing."

"What about the bright metal?" said another. "It is the best thing we have. Would that not be a fair trade?" Reyk's heart leaped. Dayn rose to his feet. The conversation had gone far enough.

"No, friends, the bright metal is not enough," Reyk said. Dayn's anxiety diminished.

"Then what of a horse, a ship of the steppes to carry you home."

"A horse would be a great prize," Reyk said, rubbing his chin. "But alone, it would not do."

"Then what of a horse," bargained another, "*and* the secret of the bright metal? Surely that is barter worthy of your consideration?"

"Ahhh!" sighed Reyk. "Now you begin to tempt me. For these things, I could tell you the whereabouts of the dark-haired tribe of warrior women. What would you say to this?"

"Yes, yes!" they shouted together.

"No!" Dayn said, striding forward into the firelight, addressing Reyk, then turning to his men. "No, my brothers! These things are ours alone. You told me yourselves that your freedom was enough, that your horses were enough, that the bright metal was enough. 'These things *are* ourselves, the things that make us who we are,' you told me. Would you then give your very selves away? Would you sell yourselves for gold and for women? We have no use of these. What would we buy with gold that we do not have already. You cannot buy

242

freedom with gold! What use have we for women and for their darkness? We have thrown off their yoke, would you harness yourselves to them again? They have no power over us! Let not this wanderer seduce you with his tales."

"What would you have us do, Dayn?" asked Draek in agitation. "Would you deny us this adventure? Then you would deny us our freedom. Freedom means that we are free to choose what we will do and where we will go. When you are truly free, everything is permitted."

"Everything is permitted, Draek," answered Dayn, "but not everything is wise. You must learn the difference. Everything can be had, but each thing comes at a price. You must be sure it is a price you are willing to pay."

"Let them speak for themselves," Reyk interjected, glaring at Dayn. "Are they not also men like you?"

"I am only trying to help them see..."

"You are only trying to control them," Reyk shot back. "If you are what you claim to be, you will let them make their own decisions. Or can you not give that up? How fitting it would seem that this tribe of men should conquer the tribe of women; why not now master them when mastery is within your grasp? You have made yourselves free of the mothers, you say. But I say you have only run away because you are afraid of them. If you are truly men, then you must conquer your fear. Conquer the mothers, and be slaves to your fear no longer!"

"Often one becomes the slave of that which he seeks to master," Dayn rejoined coolly.

"The words of a coward!" Reyk countered.

"We are no cowards!"

Ulf, watching the conflict build, stepped between Dayn and Reyk, setting his hands upon their chests to keep them apart. He spoke up now, addressing the riders.

"We have joined together of our free will, out of a common need to form a common bond. Anyone is free to go as he chooses, as it has always been. But consider this, as we have grown, we have grown to trust one another. He who betrays that trust will break the bonds of brotherhood. So let us decide. Either we must all stay together or we must *all* go our separate ways. I say there is no middle ground. Liking it or not, knowing it or not, we have pledged a trust by sharing certain secrets among us. If one of us gives those secrets away, he does so not only for himself, but for all."

243

"What you have said is true, Ulf," replied Draek. "But as we are bound, so are you, so is Dayn. If the brothers want to do this thing, then you must decide whether you will depart or go with us. The will of the brotherhood must rule the individual will of the brother. Let us decide the will of the brotherhood in this matter."

"Who would turn aside with the faint-hearted when renown and gold are to be won?" Reyk interjected.

"Not I," someone shouted.

"Let us follow Draek!" shouted another.

"Yes! Let it be as Draek says!" the men clamored.

"So be it!" cried Dayn to the riders, quieting them with his outstretched arms. He turned to Reyk.

"How can we be assured that what you say is true?"

"I swear that it is," replied Reyk.

"Then cursed be your flesh if you have lied!" Dayn said sternly. "How many of you then," Dayn asked, "will consent to give this man the secret of the bright metal and a horse in exchange for knowledge of the whereabouts of the City of Women?"

The warriors raised their swords as one and cried in a loud voice. Dayn looked at them indignantly, whirled around, and with a tormented mind, sought his tent.

Reyk was told the whereabouts of the tinstone mines and of Harf the Smith who forged the bright metal; the sharp, hard bronze. In exchange he told Dayn's warriors how to find the City of Women. The next day, Reyk was taken to the pickets to choose a horse from among those not paired with any rider. He chose a beautiful, timid young mare, barely a year old. Her face and shoulders were golden, like the sands of the beach. The gold faded, mottling to a light gray on her back, hips and legs, thence darkening at the knees and intensifying to black on her legs. Mareff, for thus she was called, was a magnificent animal. The riders held her as Reyk tried to mount, but in vain, for she would not let him ride. Other horses were tried, but none would suffer Reyk to mount them. In the end, feeling cheated and vowing revenge, he turned away and sought his homeland on foot.

The riders were eager to break camp and to find the village

of the warrior women. Once more Dayn tried to dissuade them but they would not listen. All winter since the battle, they had languished for action. Now they had set their minds upon going to this village. Reyk had taken advantage of their pride, their fear, their longing for adventure, and fueled it with dark thoughts, twisting their courage into cunning. They wanted nothing better now than to ride to the village and steal away these fiery women, fitting mates for a brotherhood of warriors, to serve new masters.

So they mounted and rode singing into the west, the lust of adventure upon them. Dayn was at their head, but his heart did not ride with them. In the end, he had not believed Reyk nor his boasts of easy conquest. He went for the sake of keeping the brotherhood together, and the hope that he could teach them a lesson, at least to those who might come through the ordeal unscathed.

Chapter 23
Bitter Blood

The brothers rode north, quickly leaving the plain, following the trace of the Vahlen to where it penetrated the hills. At the end of the first day of riding, they came to its headwaters. Following Reyk's instructions, they headed east across a cool mountain pass, thick with fir trees, and found the headwaters of yet another river which would lead them to the coast. Dayn knew these waters, for they joined the tributary which fell away from the mountain of Brahan and flowed by his old village, forming the Cyryn, thence running through its forested vale to the sea.

The evening of their second day of riding brought them to the shore. Here the strength and spirit of the horses seemed to swell, for it was here, among the surf and climbing dunes, that they had first emerged from the sea. Dayn and Ulf spoke quietly together that day as they rode, remembering their first sight of the white stallion and of the herd. Here among the outcrops of scaly rock and expanses of smooth flowing sands they had learned to ride, here the unquenchable fire had begun to burn. Was it about to burn out of control? Dayn wondered.

By noon of the next day they were in unfamiliar country. They found the outwash of the Iechryn, as Reyk had foretold, then turned east and so approached the village of the warrior women. Now that they had come, a vague uneasiness haunted the band, and instinctively, they looked to Dayn for guidance. At first he was reluctant to give them any, perhaps because his pride had been wounded, or perhaps because he felt his own uncertainty. But finally, as they enjoined him, he found that his concern for their well-being would not allow him to refuse. With Dayn once again leading the council that night, the brotherhood planned their attack.

The morning opened hazy and warm under the influence of a moist southerly breeze that had invaded the lower reaches of the Iechryn. Dayn and his band rode boldly forward. By mid-morning the haze had broken into pockets and lay only in the deeper hollows. It was into one of these dells that Ulf led the main body of horsemen, to await nightfall. A smaller group, some twenty, under Dayn's guidance, rode nearer to the village.

When they were still some distance away, Dayn and Draek left the others behind and cantered on alone, passing through a forest studded with oaks of great girth, and thence into a small clearing, one of many interspersed among the stately groves. A woman gathering firewood there espied them as they appeared through the trees. She gave a shrill raptor-like call and another younger woman, clad in a light tunic and armed with a copper-tipped lance, leaped up and sped away toward the village. The others fled into the woods.

Dayn and Draek rode on, feigning disregard of the stares that followed them from the shadows of the trees. They saw no other women in the successive clearings. Finally, as the sun reached midday, they came to the rough-hewn gates of a wooden stockade. To Dayn, there was an eerie familiarity about it. Here and there, the ground was mottled with a patchwork of filtered green light, but a single, intense sunbeam fell white upon Dayn. He called out.

"Good people, open your gates and let us enter. For we are weary travelers, come from afar, who seek your hospitality."

A woman's voice answered from the gate house above them.

"We would allow you to enter, sirs, but we are only a village of women, with no means of defending ourselves against such men of might. Therefore, as is our custom and law, we ask that you lay down your weapons and surrender them to our fair sister. Will you so do?"

"We will," Dayn replied, dropping his bow and quiver, sword and lance to the ground. Draek did likewise. Thereupon the gates swung inwardly open. A sleek, muscular woman, followed by two others of her kind, but not so tall or handsome, picked up the discarded weapons. The two were obviously in awe of the horses, keeping as far from them as they might and still perform their duties. The tall one, the warrior-maiden Tara,

247

betrayed no such fear or wonder, and motioned for Dayn and Draek to dismount. On the ground, Dayn found himself face to face with the black-haired woman. She was taller than he, though less broad, and he was struck by her stature and proud bearing. She motioned for the travelers to follow. As they did, other women fell in behind them and led the horses away.

The gates closed behind them and they were suddenly surrounded by armed *Dorni*, arrows aimed at their throats and spears at their hearts. Thereupon they were bound and blindfolded and led through a low doorway. Within the darkened lodge, the smoke of old fires rankling their nostrils, they were led further along through a narrow hallway, which eventually opened out into a larger room. Here their blindfolds were removed. They stood, as Belak and Reyk had before them, before the dais, before the low, unadorned throne. The throne was occupied by a dark man, dressed in black. Draek was surprised to find him here, a man, when Reyk had told there were only women. It was not the last surprise he would find. The Dark One turned a ring upon his finger addressing the adventurers, but staring only at his ring.

"Who are you?"

As he spoke, even so few words, an odd feeling crept over Dayn, a sensation at once familiar and frightening, as if he looked upon death itself, but was compelled to run forward and embrace it as the mother he had never known. Draek stared at the dark man, stunned and disturbed by his likeness to Dayn, yet struck by the differences.

"I am Dayn, a wanderer. This is my companion, Draek. We seek shelter for the night, your hospitality, and answers to questions of our own."

There was no surprise in this meeting for Barthol. For Thol-nys had shown him the coming of his brother, the sunrise of a day that knew no night, and his hatred for him itched and swelled like a festering wound. Thol-nys had instructed Barthol to kill him. Dayn was a threat to her, to them, she had said. Unless he died, a terrible struggle would come, leading perhaps to the undoing of all they had planned together. Here was a doorway that Barthol must pass through, the murder of his own brother, for her sake, in order to prove, once and for all time, that he was worthy to serve the Great Calamity.

"Welcome then," Barthol said with a broad smile, flashing white teeth from behind thin, purple lips. "Unbind them, Tara."

The amazon did so, sternly, betraying no emotion. "Show them the city, then bring them to dine with me this evening, at the table we have prepared."

"Please, tell us the name of our gracious host," Dayn said with all courtesy.

"I am Nyad," Barthol answered and the strange death-longing swathed Dayn once again, as unmistakable as the vapors that emanate from the cave-tombs of the dead.

Evening fell on the Vale of the Iechryn. Dayn and Draek could have asked for nothing better than to be shown the village with the chance to make observations of its defenses. When they were alone they conspired together. When the moon was at its zenith, they would climb the walls and take the gate wardens by surprise, open the gates and let the army ride silently in. Fifty of them would surround the barracks of the warrior-women, while the remainder would enter the harem and capture as many of Barthol's *Anyllonde* as they could carry away. The first hundred would keep the *Dorni* at bay, giving them battle as necessary, and form the rearguard for the escape of the victorious captors of the harem.

When they had freshened themselves, Tara came for them with an armed escort, leading them to Barthol's private chambers, where they would partake of their last meal.

When they arrived, Barthol was seated opposite the door, reclining amidst cushions arranged in a wide circle on the floor. He welcomed his guests with a broad smile and bade them to sit down beside him. He clapped his hands and a group of twenty women of his harem filed into the room. His two guests watched in amazement.

The women were all beautiful beyond the ability of their language to express, each in her own way. Their hair ranged in color from golden to sunset red to nightshade black, but the black-haired ones were the most beguiling. Some of them wore short linen tunics; some were bare-breasted and wore only short skirts. They were adorned with gold and silver bracelets and earrings. Some had pulled their hair off their shoulders with strands of polished gemstones. Their bodies were oiled and glistening and the fragrance of their varied perfumes fell in wave after enticing wave upon the guests as they glided by. But Dayn

249

noticed behind the luster of their eyes a vacancy, as though they walked but were already among the dead. Having made their entrance they kneeled before Barthol and his guests.

"My wish is that you should enjoy the company of these women for the time you are my guests. May that be your pleasure, and may your pleasure find no boundaries," Nyad gestured.

Draek was overwhelmed by the offer. His lustful eyes greedily sampled the women before him, anticipating one amorous encounter after another. Barthol's gaze had only to flicker across Draek's to know that he had already fallen under their spell. Then he looked at his brother. No such fall had occurred there; the detestable Fire still shone from the lamps of his eyes. No doubt it would be extinguished before the night was done, Barthol thought confidently. He could be patient. His game was for Dayn to spring the trap of darkness knowingly, willingly. For that would be a pleasure to Barthol greater even than his brother's death.

Barthol clapped again. The first group of women left and others came bearing food and wine. They arrayed themselves around the three, feeding them, holding their cups, and attending to their every need. The eating and drinking went on until the three men were filled. Draek's head reeled from drink. Dayn had been more cautious with the wine, which had been noted by his host.

When the meal was over Barthol clapped his hands yet again. Musicians appeared, some bearing drums, some holding cymbals of varying sizes. They sat down behind the men facing the circle and began to beat out a rhythm. One by one, dancers entered through the door. They circled the room, gliding like birds riding the heavens on warm currents of fragrant air, in flowing robes of sheer nothingness intended both to hide and to reveal, and with hair that flowed out behind them like a horse's tail in the wind of its flight. Their faces and limbs were painted brightly in fantastic patterns, some like birds and some like creatures of the forest.

The beat became faster and the dancers whirled, flashing seductive smiles at their master and his guests. Faster they danced as the drummers quickened and amplified the beat. Above all, the cymbals chimed and crashed. To Dayn, the dance was a summer thunderstorm, the drums, the thunder rolling over the plains, the cymbals, the ear-splitting crash of lightning, the dancers, frightened little birds and animals fleeing for nest and safety before the onslaught of the pelting rain. Now the drumming became a torrent gushing from the hills, the cymbals became the white spray leaping from rock to rock. The dancers flew wildly through the air and rolled in abandon upon the floor. The drumming reached its climax. As one the dancers leaped into the air with an ecstatic cry and fell to the floor in an exhausted heap, still now except for the heaving of their chests. The drumming abruptly ceased. The silence rang in Dayn's ears.

Barthol cast a glance at Dayn and thought he saw the Fire flicker and depart. He honored the dancers by rhythmically slapping his hands upon his knees, then rose before his besotted guests.

"Now friends, choose. Choose one or choose many. For everything is permitted," Barthol said, looking down at Draek, who seemed beyond the ability to lift his head. "For those who may no longer be capable of choosing, I will see that you are accommodated." He turned to Dayn. "Sleep long, if not well, my brother," he said, then left the room. Dayn felt a tremor go through him.

The dancers got up slowly. Some crowded around the reclining form of Draek and some around Dayn, who still sat upright. Dayn watched as Draek was lifted up and carried into the next room. Dayn looked around him now at the expectant faces. His eyes became locked in a stare with one of the dancers. Her eyes were round and yellow, like a cat's, and her face was painted in vertical streaks of tawny yellow and green; a lioness, crouching in the grass. Try as he might, he could not resist watching her. The lioness smiled back resonantly. Seeing this, the other women drew aside, slowly got to their feet, and returned to the harem. Then the two of them were alone. Dayn's emotions oscillated between desire and wariness.

The lioness crawled away from Dayn, the lean shadow of her body moving cat-like beneath the gossamer fabric of her costume. Slinking about on all fours, she circled the room then sat in a corner, mimicking with her every movement, the behavior of a lioness. Dayn, transported back to another place and time, watched, fascinated, as she rubbed her head with her forepaws. She licked her hands and arms, imitating the cleaning ritual of the great beasts after they had killed and eaten. Her mood suddenly changed. She leaped around the floor, bounding from cushion to cushion. Before Dayn knew it she had leaped atop him and sat astride his chest, intensely looking into his eyes, mesmerizing him with her gaze. Now she leaped away again, returning to her den in the corner. One by one, as if she had willed it, the torches lighting the room began to sputter and go out. The extinguishing of the last one plunged the room into sudden darkness, and only its fading red glow made it possible for Dayn to see.

The lioness came out of her corner again, purring and prowling around the darkened room. She circled Dayn, ever closer, stalking him like prey. He began to fancy the game. She stopped a few feet away. He saw the reflection from her yellow eyes for a moment unlidded. Then the pale lights disappeared and she pounced.

In that instant a thin wand of moonlight appeared through a high window and glinted off the cold edge of the knife the lioness held in her plunging hand. Dayn rolled away, foiling the executioner's stroke, and jumped on top of her with a force that knocked the breath from her lungs. His hand went to her mouth to keep her from crying out while his free hand grasped her wrist and forced it up between her shoulder blades. From the next room, he heard Draek's last mortal cry, betrayed unto death. Dayn was desperate. His stomach knotted. At anytime the others might rush in. He did not want to kill the girl beneath him, but he dared not release her. If so, his escape was doomed. This murder was not her doing. It was Nyad's doing; he knew it. Betrayed! Inside himself, Dayn felt his visceral urgency to flee do battle his impulsive lust for revenge.

His eyes went to the window. The moonlight was fuller now and a breeze brushed his face. He let go of the girl and bounded toward the high portal. He grabbed the tapestry, pulled himself up, and squeezed through. His feet were already on the ground outside when the lioness found her voice and screamed an alarm. Her prey had escaped and was loose in the village.

Dayn stood pressed against the wall. He must think quickly and surely. A false move would mean his certain death. He must get to the gate tower and warn the others away. But how? As if to aid him, the moon dodged behind a flying cloud bank. If only he could leap upon Mataforas and ride far away, never to return. Suddenly he heard cries. The *Dorni* had been alerted and were running through the village in small bands, intent on hunting him down.

Dayn stood listening to the drumming of running feet and the beating of his heart in his ears. Into the midst of his panic, came a vision. He saw himself wrapped in the purple cloak of his father, casting no shadow, leaping onto the back of the wild, white horse for the first time. Far away he heard the muffled neighing of Mataforas and the rhythm of his hooves. Then there was a pause as if the ground had disappeared beneath the steed, and so it had. Mataforas flew with a single bound over the stockade fence. The pounding of hooves resumed, louder and nearer now, drawing all in the direction of their sound. Suddenly, the mighty horse rounded a corner and rushed to his master's side. Hardly had he stopped before Dayn pounced upon his back. He reached for the purple cloak. As he swept it over his shoulders, horse and rider disappeared from mortal eyes. Tama and her band of warriors rounded the corner and came into the street just in time to see them vanish.

Dayn rode to the stockade wall and jumped from the back of his mount. He climbed the steps unperceived and surprised the gate warden, her eyes and ears trained on the melee within the village. Grabbing her shoulders, he threw her from the wall. He leaped down, his feet barely touching the ground before he was again on Mataforas' back, pulling open the gates and riding through. Outside, Ulf saw the gates turn on their great hinges. He looked for Dayn and Draek but no one was there. Perplexed, he held his riders back for an instant. Suddenly, Dayn appeared in the midst of the clearing before the gates, the purple mantle of Brahan flying from his shoulders.

"Fly my brothers! Draek is dead!" he cried. "Leave this evil place!"

But pride and greed had ensnared the riders and would not allow them to turn back.

"No!" someone shouted. "We have come to conquer the women and we will not turn back. If Draek is dead he must be avenged!" Two hundred swords were drawn with a rasping ring. Booted feet kicked the ready flanks of the horses and they leaped forward. Through the gates and around the village they circled in a cloud of pale, silver dust. Roving bands of the warrior-women contested the riders, maddened with greed and revenge. They rode recklessly through the village streets, hewing at whatever threw itself across their path, slaying and maiming.

As the defenses of the village weakened, the riders

dismounted and broke into houses. A dozen of them broke into Barthol's harem. Screams erupted from the huddled *Anyllonde*. More riders came now, drawing the battle along with them. Fighting broke out at the doorway. Tama was there, valiantly defending the defenseless women with whistling thrusts of her long spear. But she and the few others who stood with her were no match for the overwhelming numbers arrayed against them. She fell with a cry as the marauders burst into the room. The riders came on, grabbing the nearest, the most beautiful, of the women. Across the broad backs of their steeds they threw them, mounting behind and riding away into the night.

The fighting raged on as Dayn rode reluctantly back through the gates. He wanted no part of this. Why had they been so eager to listen to the lies of Reyk? And why had he allowed the brotherhood to talk him into leading them here? Death was here, he knew it now, the fatal stroke to freedom and the life they had known. He had not been strong enough to save them and the taste of his own weakness was bitter in his mouth.

Sitting upon Mataforas at the gates, he suddenly remembered Nyad. He ...he was to blame. This was all *his* fault. He saw now that Reyk's words had come from Nyad, it was *Nyad's* lies that had led them there. But why? Why would he bring destruction upon himself and his village? He did not dwell on this question for long, for he swept aside his untenable self-pity in an instant and in its place found the refuge of blame. He blamed Nyad, not himself, for the evil, for the death they had found, and set his thoughts upon revenge. He would kill Nyad and exonerate himself in the act. He would wrap Nyad in the shroud of his own weakness and kill them both together.

Cloaked once again in the purple mantle and filled with malice, he urged Mataforas purposefully on toward Nyad's throne room. Arriving there he dismounted, burst through the door, and came to stand before the empty black chair. The shadow of a shadow, he stalked the dark Nyad, unseen, from room to room. From outside came the sounds of retreating hoofbeats, the wails of captured women and the echoes of diminishing battle. But even as Dayn searched for the deceitful lord of the city, Barthol was climbing the bank on the far side of the Iechryn with Tara and a band of her warriors, heading for their secret refuge in the hills.

Failing to find the object of his deadly passion, Dayn's bitterness swelled into anger. He knocked over crockery and

254

lamps, he kicked over furniture and slashed beds with his sword, lashing out, unwittingly, at himself. At last he stood in the center of the throne room, his neck and back arched, his face to the ceiling, and screamed out Nyad's name in frustration and rage. Tears came to his eyes and he fell on his knees, covering his face with quivering hands.

With the suddenness of a sword thrust, he was jerked to a new level of awareness. He perceived clearly now all that had transpired and realized the depths to which he had fallen. He understood that in seeking to conquer evil, he himself had been conquered by it, blaming, raging and seeking vengeance against Nyad, all to spare himself from himself. In that instant, Barthol turned toward the village and laughed from the depths of his black heart.

Dayn left the house of Barthol in confusion, no longer knowing who he was. He mounted Mataforas and led him through the ravaged streets. The smell of death was everywhere. He stopped before a tangled heap of strong, brave women, pawns of treachery, who had fallen in battle, their slender hands still clutching their weapons, their skin so white, their wounds so dark. Riding on, he passed at last through the gates, the very gates, had he known, through which Carthyn had carried him to escape death for the first time. He followed the remnant noises of his legion as they rode away through the forest to the place they had appointed to regroup.

There they passed the night. Those who had taken captives dragged the women recklessly to their tents and sated themselves upon them. Dayn slept fitfully. In the morning he awoke to a wailing cry. Emerging from his makeshift lodgings, he discovered that forty of the brothers lay dead in their tents, their eyes and mouths closed, their throats gaping. The women of Barthol's harem were nowhere to be found. Hidden knives had drunk the blood of vengeance in the night, and they had run back to their evil master.

Chapter 24
Commutatus Primus

Dayn's world was in turmoil. Devastated by his failure and the gnawing weakness that had allowed it, he felt the remorse of one who has not lived up to his own standards of conduct. He felt great sorrow at the senseless loss of life, not only of his own brothers, but of the women who had so bravely defied them. At least he had the satisfaction of knowing that, in the end, he had shouldered the responsibility for the whole sorry affair, and had been man enough not to fold under that weight. In the end he had been man enough not to blame his misfortunes on Nyad or Reyk. Temptations would always be there. He alone was to blame if he succumbed to them.

Still, he had little heart left for leadership. Perhaps he should slip away quietly. When he was gone they would find another to lead, perhaps Ulf; he had grown wise enough. But Dayn had been alone before and he did not relish it. Perhaps he could slip quietly to the backwaters of the brotherhood and remain there, causing no one grief and following the lead of another more qualified than he.

But most of all he wondered why this misfortune had come to pass. He had been the leader of a band of adventurers, a brotherhood of strong and intelligent men. Now he had fallen to so low a depth. How had it happened? Why had he fallen? In his village, Moira and the mothers would have had an answer. He had not sacrificed to the goddess, he had defied her and denied her her due. That is what they would say. But he did not believe it. There was no power of this world mightier than a man of intelligence, of this he was more than ever convinced.

Such a man needed no deities to lean upon. Why, his own father was a god, or so he had been told. Where had he been when his own son was beset by troubles and foes? A purple cloak, was that all the assistance he had to offer? If so, then the race of men had better figure out how to get by on their own.

After a morning of gathering the dead, of building and lighting the funeral pyre, the remnant of his legion came to him. A few of the outspoken ones wanted Dayn to help them find the women who had wronged the brotherhood, in order to seek retribution. But Dayn refused and they backed down, unwilling to take it on themselves. Others advised that the brothers should go back home, back to the Dacon where they could live as they pleased, unmolested. But Dayn knew that things had changed. They would not be happy there for long.

In the end they decided to go on, away to the north. They were in new, untried and unexplored country. Perhaps they were happiest when they were searching. Something within Dayn urged him to try again. Perhaps it was their lot to search and never find answers; perhaps it was the lot of humankind. So he stirred the cold, powder-gray ashes of his soul, seeking the glowing spark that had not died.

The brothers rode slowly, inching their way out of the accursed Vale of the Iechryn. By nightfall they stood saddle-weary on a low ridge. Behind them dark mists gathered. Blackness seemed to lurk in the hollows there. Ahead the land sloped gently down into yet another river valley. For the first time in his life Dayn was afraid of what he might find ahead. He shivered slightly as the wind picked up and found its way, with clammy fingers, through his garments. One by one, the cold, immovable stars lit the firmament. He recalled how he used to lie at the mouth of the lion's den and gaze in joyous wonder at these minute lights. Now he wanted only to hide from them, from their light, any light. He felt some comfort as the wan sun finally plunged into the sea. Now no one could see him shiver, and he could be alone in his self-doubt and misery.

The next morning Dayn led the brothers westward. He had an urge to see the ocean again. Perhaps it, if anyone or anything, would understand the churning restlessness within him. Just when the sun had climbed to the zenith and begun its slow journey across the gulf of the untainted afternoon sky, the wind shifted around to the southeast. A line of clouds appeared on the eastern horizon where there had been only an untroubled

257

blue. Unnoticed by the brothers, the clouds grew darker and more turbulent as they were piled up over the mountains by the searing summer heat of the plains. A large thunderhead tilted above, blocking the sunlight and casting the riders in shadow. As Dayn turned around to look, a bolt of lightning crackled downward, rending the atmosphere in its fury, striking him as he sat upon Mataforas. The shock of it knocked the nearby riders from their mounts. Steeds were thrown neighing to the ground, their hooves pawing the air. The roar of the discharge was deafening. The earth recoiled and heaved, hurling fragments of blackened rock skyward in response. In a split second the blinding flash became an insensible void. Soil and shattered stone fell in a pelting brown rain. There was no other sound. Ulf felt an acute ringing pain in his ears and reached up to place his fingers there. When he withdrew them the tips were stained to a deep scarlet with his own blood. Dazed, he sat up. All about him others were getting to their knees or sitting about numbly. But some did not get up at all. For an anxious instant, Ulf searched the smoking earth for Dayn.

But Dayn was not among the stricken. He was still sitting on Mataforas, quite unharmed and unmoved, his head erect. A light was on his brow such as Ulf had never seen, as if the sun itself had come there to reside, and a large raven sat upon his shoulder. Ulf groped forward toward his friend on his hands and knees, finally pulling himself to his feet against the legs of the white stallion. The raven cawed loudly.

As for Dayn, he had felt nothing. He had only seen a whirlwind come out of the cloud, descending slowly, as one might perceive a flock of birds approaching from a great distance. At the center of the funnel was a light. When the light had drenched him with its brilliance, he heard a voice saying, "Dayn, why have you forgotten me?" Then the light was sundered into a rainbow of colors, crimson, green and violet. In the next shimmering instant, his father, Brahan, the Bringer of Light, stood before him.

"Fa... Father," stammered Dayn. "Where have you been? I... I have not forgotten you. I have been searching, all these years Father, it is just that, ...only now, ...I realize what I have been seeking. You... why did you desert me?"

"I did not desert you, Dayn, I have been near, and I have given you many gifts. When you were born, I rescued you from death. I gave you a home among the lions so that you

258

might learn the lessons of the wild, of the way life was before I gave man the gift of fire. I led you to the village, to your grandmother, so that you might learn the ways of the goddess, so that you might see that which must remain and that which must be changed. I gave you my cloak so that you might tame the white horse. I rescued you when you came back to the village with the herd and you were put on trial. I have given you your freedom Dayn, so that you might lead others to freedom. What have I held back?"

"Your counsel, Father, your wisdom, your time. These things I have so needed. You have given me everything except yourself. I have been on a dark road, Father, in need of a lamp."

"Had I stood in that road before you, Dayn, you would not have known me, so wrapped up in your own affairs have you become. You cannot see everything at once, Dayn, that is the fate and sorrow of man. When your eyes are trained on the things of this world, you cannot see the hidden things of the Otherworld. But now Dayn, now is the time. I will give you yet another gift, and you will be forever changed. You will see new things, with new eyes. That is my gift. Some things will fade from your vision. That is the price of this new insight. But do not be saddened, for the vision I give you now will serve you best. Some things are not worth your time, Dayn, and it is better that you do not see them. You must not be distracted by them any longer."

"What do you mean, father? What things will I be able to see, and what things will pass from my vision?"

"Patience, Dayn. Be comforted. Know that old things must pass away, to make way for better things. Much that you have perceived to be outside of you will be inside once the gift is bestowed. One of these things, Dayn, is me. Never again will we meet in this world. The time of the lesser gods has passed and the time of man has arrived. I will lose this incarnation, this body, and come to dwell within you. Then only Deus, and one other, will remain."

"Who is Deus?"

"Deus is the Father, your Father, our Father. When Osyn, for so he was then called, defeated the Great Destroyer, Tholnys, in the depths of the void, he rose out of the sea as Deus, the One God, the master of all. Then he brought forth Hanthol, the light that comes out of the darkness, the symbol of his

259

ascendancy, and set it in the heavens to burn. This same fire was destined to be set into the minds of men, there to burn until the Last Day when Thol-nys is overthrown and the Darkness is conquered forever. I am Bra-Han, the bringer of the light, the bringer of the Fire of Han-Thol.

"In the Beginning, Deus decreed that the lesser gods, the offspring of Himself, should rule the Now until the time of men had come. But the offspring of Thol-nys appeared to vie with the sons of Deus, to wither all that he had created. That conflict is the source of all strife and discord in the Now. Deus decreed that when the time of man had come, as his sons were taken back to him, so the daughters of Thol-nys would lose their power. Thol-nys knew this. So even though she could not breed a human child herself, she found a way. When I lay with Yvanna, your mother, so that you might be, Thol-nys managed, using her dark sorcery, to place another seed in the womb. And so you have a twin brother.

And so, today, we must make our next move and hope that Thol-nys cannot find a way to confound us. Today, I come to live within you. We have had a narrow brush with disaster, we very nearly failed, but for now, we have thwarted her."

"What do you mean, Father, that we have very nearly failed? Speak plainly to me!" Dayn pleaded.

"Two days ago you attacked a village, the village of your birth. The dark one, Nyad, is your twin brother. But he did not tell you his other name; he is Barthol, the son of Thol-nys by your mother, Yvanna. He is the servant of the Great Calamity in the Now, the one who sent Reyk the pirate into your camp, the one who put the lies in Reyk's mouth and seduced the brothers to raid the village. He is the one who plotted the murder of your body and soul, together with his demon-mother, and he very nearly succeeded. When you walked the village, searching for him with the anger welling up inside you, feeding upon itself, he very nearly accomplished his purpose. Had you succumbed to the will of Thol-nys, killed Barthol, and so become her servant, all would have been lost."

Dayn stood silent for a moment, letting the unbelievable words of his father soak in, like water into a stone.

"I desire the light, Father. I desire your wisdom. I wish to become as you are, the man-son of Deus in the fight against darkness. But I do not want to lose you, now that I have found you at last. I need you, Father."

"As I have revealed, Dayn, many things will not be as they were, but I will be with you, always. I will live inside you, I will be the channel through which you may speak to Deus. I will quell the conflict between your Self and Otherself and bring them together at a new level of enlightenment. You will gain wisdom and clear vision into the hearts and minds of men.

"And I will be with you yet in another way. When this incarnation passes I will become once and for all time a raven, bound to the earth and skies. I will be the prince of the race and will rule them from the western sea to the fences of the Utlai. I will become Brahan of Dor, the raven-god, and Brahndor, the first Prince of the Ravens, and finally Randor, my son, for you, and never in life will I leave your side.

"Now, before I am changed, there is yet one more thing to tell. There is a city to the north and there you must go. It is the other city that Reyk spoke of to you, the one he called the City of Gold. It is not as he said, Dayn, but there *is* treasure there, one more valuable to man than all the gold of kings ever unearthed. You must go north to the next river, the Mergruen, and follow it until you come to the city that sits at the head of the gorge. There you will find a young woman. Her name is Allisyn, the daughter of Aefalas, King of Aestri. You will make her yours, and she will make you hers. She holds the Twelve Pearls, the essence of the true nature of Deus, and she is fated to bestow them upon you. She will complete you and you, her. Armed with the Wisdom of the Pearls, you will be ready to receive the World Dream of Deus."

"Wait, Father, before you go... answer me a question. When I was young I had a dream. In it I was a young lion who devoured Moira, the keeper of the old ways. Grandmother interpreted it for me. She said I was to destroy the old ways and bring the new. I thought my destiny was to conquer the mothers, to destroy the ways of the goddess, yet now you wish me to find this woman and join with her?"

"You still have much to learn, Dayn. Ever Thol-nys uses the perception of man to twist the truth. Destruction and violence are not the only means to bring about change; neither are they the best ways. They are the ways of Thol-nys, the ways of Darkness. My aim in bringing you to the Village of the Cyr was that you learn the ways of the goddess, integrating them into your consciousness, not destroying them and disregarding their wisdom. But it was not to be. Now there is another chance,

261

another hope. Allisyn is the bearer of the Twelve Pearls. She was chosen by Deus to discover them, just as you were the chosen to receive them of her. Deus wishes that there be peace among his children and that man and woman live in harmony. It has not yet been so. That is the legacy of Thol-nys. She divides, and by division, seeks to conquer.

"To walk the path of Deus is to venerate the qualities of both man and woman. When Deus first became, he was nursed by Han-nys, the Good Mother, the good offspring that followed from the death of Nyso, the Great Mother, just as Thol-nys was the Terrible Mother, the evil offspring that came of that calamity. In reverence to his sister-mother, Han-nys, Deus decreed that the Pearls should come first to woman and that woman would nurture man with them, just as Han-nys nurtured Deus with the Divine Milk. Han-nys is the Moon even as Deus is the Sun. The moon takes the light of the Sun, so bright and terrible that it cannot be beheld, and transforms it into a thing of beauty and joy. Thus will Allisyn, the Daughter of the Moon, take the Fire of Han-Thol that burns upon your brow, soften it, transform it, and make it a lasting gift for mankind. Just as the blade, hot from the forge, must be tempered by water to make it strong, so must the fire of consciousness be tempered by the waters of the spirit to create the whole human being. Do not be afraid, Dayn, for wondrous things are about to befall you. Your union with Allisyn will end your searching, if alas, not your sorrow."

"What do you mean, Father, that she will not end my sorrow?"

"That is for the future my son, that is for the future. All will be revealed in good time, in Deus' time. Some things cannot be taught until the pupil is ready.

"Now send these brothers back to the plains and let them be guided by Ulf. When you are ready, when they are ready, you will gather them unto yourself once more. For now, let us be away. You and I will wander for a year and a day. We will travel far. I will show you many places and many things that you have not yet experienced. During that year, I will instruct you and prepare you to receive the Twelve. Then we will go to Allisyn and with her, your life will truly begin.

"And now, hence forward you shall not be Dayn. You shall be Brahannetus, the one who comes after the fire, the seed of Brahan, and Ravennetus, son of the raven, the champion of Deus in the Now. Go forth and fare you well, my son!"

Brahan reached out and embraced Dayn, kissed him on the forehead and was transmogrified, becoming as a light upon the brow of his son and a beautiful raven also.

So it was that Ulf beheld Ravennetus, only seconds after the lightning strike, still astride Mataforas, with the light shining upon his brow and the great bird, born of the thunderbolt, sitting upon his shoulder. For though much had passed between Brahan and Ravennetus in the Otherworld, only seconds had transpired in the Now.

Chapter 25
The Retaming of Reyk

Reyk stood before his lord Savor, the pirate-king of Bera, maps in hand, and bowed low. Upon a long table he rolled them out. The pictures and characters drawn there spoke of a voyage to the north and things that had befallen the command of Belak. The whole of the voyage was recounted with accuracy until Reyk came to the encounter with Barthol and the City of Women. Belak, it said, had died in the water. Reyk alone had survived, was taken in by the women of the city and brought before their ruler, a man of some influence but with little bite for all his bark. It would be easy to take the city. Many of the women would be suitable slaves and could be sent back in ships. Others were beautiful and would make excellent wives for the soldiers as payment for their service.

Next they came to the matter of the bronze swords. The swords, Reyk said, were made by a colony of smiths in a small country rich in mineral deposits called The Fallon. The smiths made swords and other items of bronze, selling them to whomever would pay the highest price, or bartering them for food and slaves to work the mines. The colony, for all practical purposes, was unprotected. Reyk's recommendation was that they sail up the Moravon and offer gold for the bright weapons. Then they would attack the Gold City. On the way back they could in turn conquer the colony of smiths, enslave them, and take back the gold.

"You have done well, Reyk," said Savor. "When do you suggest that we set sail?"

"My lord," Reyk answered, "the seas are alive with storm

264

serpents in winter. We should prepare the fleet using the time from now until the Crow Moon. Then we can leave. We will reach the land of the smiths during Sow Moon and come to the City of Gold in the Moon of the Hawk. We can be back here at the latest in the Hound Moon, and thus escape the bad sailing weather."

"How many ships will we need?"

"We should take four ships, two unladen. In one we shall send back captives from the City of Women and in the other, booty from the Gold City. We will meet no resistance greater than we can overcome with two ships of warriors. To take more men would be a waste."

"Good, Reyk," said Savor. You shall spend your time from now until we sail assisting the shipwrights. Tell them of the improvements you have suggested to make the ships more fit to sail the northern waters. I want you to report to me every seven days on their progress. You shall sail back to the north with the fleet when it is ready.

"Thank you Lord Savor."

"I have taken a great interest in this expedition Reyk. I shall lead it myself."

"We would be honored, my lord," Reyk fawned.

"Very well, then. Look to your duties."

Reyk had traveled all during the summer and into the autumn to arrive back in Bera, the island home of the pirates which lay to the south of the long rocky coast of Basoland in the Gulf of Vinsa. All throughout that long and consuming journey he had dreamed of the woman Barthol had given him. He was loathe to leave her and was in haste to get back to her. Things would be different when he did. Savor would hang Barthol and the woman would belong to him alone. Hatred for Barthol had festered in his mind until it had become an open, oozing sore. The thought of Barthol hanging from a mast pleased him greatly. Perhaps he would have some sport with him while he hung. Or perhaps the horseboys had already tickled his throat with a blade. That would make things all the easier. He had been concerned about his woman after telling the horseboys about the city. Well, small loss if she died. There were others, and more beautiful; he had seen them. No doubt Savor would reward him with any one or several of his choosing. And if the horseboys had taken them away his pirates would find them. With bronze to equalize things, they could be overcome with certainty. Things were going very well to his way of thinking, very well indeed. If he could only get home! Walking was a curse and he cursed the horses that would not bear him. Filthy beasts! He and his mates would kill them too, and feast on their flesh.

The winter was a mild one and the work of outfitting the fleet went smoothly. In the middle of spring it was assembled. The High Priest of Semele invoked her blessing for their journey. The High Priest of Matas prayed for his cooperation and for calm seas. The sea-going brigands set out under fair skies. Lord Savor was in the first ship with Reyk. Following them in the convoy was Tarcon, a man as fierce as Belak had been, but less cunning. With the king were fifty warriors and with Tarcon another fifty, lustful men, heedless of life and full of desire for the spoils of the voyage. Reyk had not spared hyperbole in telling them tales of the lands they would plunder. This art he had honed well.

They sighted the estuary of the Moravon after sailing for a month. The winds were with them as they sailed up the river. With Reyk's aid, they found the colony of Harf the Smith and straightaway concluded a deal for arms. There they waited for three weeks, until the swords, spear tips and shields were all prepared. Stunned at the sight of the pirate gold, Harf danced greedily.

Savor and his band of cutthroats set sail again. The fair weather held but the westerly winds challenged as the ships tacked their way toward the setting sun, out of the mouth of the Moravon and along the unbroken coast which formed the southern boundary of the Dacon Plain. It was another several weeks before they rounded the craggy headland where the coastline of Aestri veered abruptly to the north. Now they passed the mouth of the Orna that boasted no villages. They came to the Durna, which the men of Aestri called the Iechryn. Savor decided the plundering of the City of Women would wait until they should return from their main objective, the sacking of the Guldwys.

Watching the mouth of the Durna slip by, Reyk felt suddenly

and unaccountably ill. He had a mysterious and profound urge to wrest command of the fleet from Savor and sail up the river. A brooding darkness settled in his mind. Standing behind his king upon the deck, Reyk's hand went involuntarily to the hilt of his sword. He surveyed Savor's back, his eyes coming to rest on a spot between his shoulder blades. Then just as abruptly, the darkness passed and Reyk was himself again. But he noticed that his hands and brow were sweating, as though a fever burning inside him had just broken.

In only a few more days they sited the mouth of the Mergruen. The pirates began to stir at the thought of murder and gold. Stories circulated once again of the wealth and the beautiful women for the taking.

The ships were sighted long before they felt the surge of the Mergruen against the landward heave of the tide. Although Aefalas had been distracted by many things, not the least of which were dealing with his difficult queen and the rebuilding of his city, he had vowed that it would never again be surprised and sacked by pirates. A watch had been set along the coastal approaches. Outposts were manned with swift runners to carry any word of passing vessels or interlopers. The guard of the watchtowers had been redoubled and the towers themselves fortified. It was with the utmost confidence that he sent the armed strength of a thousand soldiers against the fly's-bite of the pirate force.

Savor and his raiders made landfall later that same day, just as the sun was snuffed out by a dense finger of fog lingering on the horizon. They put in to a small bay just down the coastline from the river's mouth, for Reyk had correctly guessed that following the previous year's attack, the river itself would be watched. They slept that night aboard the ships, waiting patiently for the light of day to reveal the most advantageous landing area. But in the night Savor had changed his plan of battle. He consented that a force would land in the bay, but only a small one for the sake of diversion. The main force would be sailed around the point and up the Mergruen the next afternoon, weather and tide permitting. It was true that this maneuver put the diversion at risk; if the main force could not be landed in time, those first ashore might be discovered and cut to pieces.

But if the diversion did work, Savor's main force would attack the rear of the defenders, instead of their stiff-necked front.

Early next morning, with the tide low and the sea calm, they drove the boats close to the sandy sloping beaches. Led by Tarcon, a company of sea-raiders jumped into the water and struggled through swell and undertow to gain the shore. Once the invaders made land, the ships turned and sailed west and north. The fog, which had come ashore in the night, masked their passage. They entered the mouth of the Mergruen on the afternoon flood tide and had waded ashore by early evening.

The diversion worked well. As soon as Aefalas' runners sighted the troops coming ashore in the morning they sent their urgent message to their king with haste and without looking back. His force, which had set out downriver, was diverted to the south.

Meanwhile, Savor's first landing made its way through the woods, deliberately and with as much noise as possible. The pirates shouted insults at the invisible defenders, blew horns, and clashed sword upon bright shield. Aefalas' soldiers met them in late afternoon in a thin pine forest atop a broad ridge overlooking the sea. The pirates, under Tarcon's command, were vastly outnumbered. They feigned an attack, then withdrew to a denser part of the wood, drawing the soldiers after them.

Bors, the chief of Aefalas army, was unconvinced that he had confronted the main menace, so he set a small detachment to harass the invaders while he sent runners and waited for news. Soon he was rewarded, at least on one count; the ships were no longer in the bay to the south. But the runners he had sent toward the mouth of the Mergruen did not return. He was reorganizing for the threat he suspected would fall upon his rear, when the screaming pirates burst out the woods upon his ill-formed troops.

The strength of his numbers was not as much to his advantage in the woods as it might have been in the open, but his army was vast indeed in comparison to the attacking force. And the woods could be turned to his advantage as well, for Bors knew something of the art of war. He divided his force into thirds. The first counterattacked the pirates, while the second and third contingents were sent in wide circular flanking movements, beyond the sight and ken of the brutes to his immediate front. Soon they had the pirates surrounded. Day was fading fast now. In the deepening gloom of the woods, the soldiers of Aestri waited for Bors' horn-blast. When it came, they jumped up with a great cry and fell upon the unsuspecting seamen. The surprised pirates rallied and fought with unanticipated fury, driving the soldiers back initially in all directions. But as night fell, the force of numbers began to tell and the pirates were subdued. Those who were not slaughtered were taken prisoner. A few managed to hide under cover of darkness in thickets and thus prolong their lives until the following morning.

Bors sent a force of a hundred soldiers to the ships at anchor in the Mergruen. A few in the vanguard bore torches. As Bors had planned, Savor mistook them for his own people returning from the field with victorious tidings of the battle. When Savor realized his error, it was too late. In the deepening night the rest of Bors' force arrived behind the torch bearers. They threw grappling hooks onto the decks of the ships and held them fast to the shore. Although the small body guard that Savor had kept with him shot effectively from the deck at the attackers, even killing some, more hooks came flying. Then the bravest and the swiftest among Aefalas' soldiers ran in close with torches and sent them flying into the ships. Whoosh! came the fire sticks. As they landed, the pitch-smoothed seams of the decking caught fire. The flames spread rapidly, licking and curling with red tongues round the masts.

Savor came on deck with death in his eyes. Reyk was there, watching in terror as the hooks rang against the planking and the torches swished by, fierce young comets in the outraged night.

"So!" Savor cried, seeing the conflagration and the surprised Reyk. "So this is what comes of your advice! Stupidity! By the gods, if we all must die then you shall die first!" Brandishing his blade, he lunged at Reyk. As he did, another torch came whirling over the deck and hit the pirate-king squarely in the head. Savor fell, dazed, then stumbled back to his feet, the left side of his face withering in flame, his hair and beard evaporating, his skin crackling. He ran blindly at Reyk who, seeing the rage and horror on Savor's melting face, leaped over the side into the rushing black current.

The reeking dawn revealed the smoldering ruins of the four ships. Two were still drawn up fast on the sand bar; the other two, having broken loose, had drifted downstream and sunk, portions of their blackened hulls visible like grimy rocks above the surface. Aefalas' soldiers rounded up the straggling remnant of the raiding party. Reyk was found hiding near the rocky shore, his clothes in tatters, his beard knotted with seaweed.

Along with six other prisoners he was brought before the tribunal of Aefalas the next afternoon. Tandela was there. The seven were made to kneel.

"State your names," the bailiff called.

One by one the pirates gave their names, which were recorded in a judgment book. Tandela studied each of them with keen interest. Aefalas began the questioning.

"Tell us from whence you come," he demanded. All maintained their silence with heads bowed.

"Look at me!" Aefalas half-shouted. "This is no jest. If you do not loosen your tongues they will be loosened for you!" He glared at them. The pirates looked from one to the other. Then all eyes turned to Reyk. Aefalas noted their movement.

"You there, on the end," he said, pointing to Reyk, "tell me from whence you come."

Reyk's only thought was to save his skin. "Lord," he began, "we come from a land far to the south. We are only poor sailors, pressed into service by the king of another land who had gained dominion over us. We did not know his intentions. Please do not kill us, we are only frightened, unwitting slaves. Please, lord, have mercy on us."

"There will be no mercy. You will all die for the attempted sacking of our city. You have but one decision, to go to your gods with truth or with lies upon your lips." Tandela lifted her proud head at Aefalas' words and her face flushed with a sudden and passionate thrill.

"Lord," said Reyk with bold demeanor, "I speak the truth. May your life be long and your name be honored, and may you not go to your gods with the blood of innocent men upon your hands."

"You rabble. What do you know of innocence? What do you know of honor? It is neither innocent or honorable to be in the service of murderers. You could have cast yourselves into the sea. You could have revolted against your overlords. But you did not. What say you of this?" Aefalas questioned.

"If we have committed a crime, lord, then it is but the crime of survival. What man would not serve, however onerous his master, in order to survive, in order to avenge the death of his family, in order, perhaps, to accomplish some greater good by and by?" the crafty Reyk rejoined.

"Have you ever been here before, on these shores, in this city?" Aefalas asked.

"No, never Lord," Reyk lied.

"Then explain this!" Tandela interjected holding out the scroll of maps, still sheathed in goatskin, that had been taken from Reyk's person when he was captured.

"I thought it was a wallet of food," Reyk countered, thinking quickly.

"It is a map!" Aefalas said, addressing the group of seven and unrolling the scroll. "Last year Faenwys was sacked. Many were killed, my wife among them, and our city was burned. How did you come by this map?"

Reyk started to answer.

"Silence!" Aefalas roared at Reyk. He pointed to one of the captives, a cabin boy, a mere youth, who was trembling. "You!" he pointed, "you will answer me this time!"

The youth began to weep. Reyk shot him a hard look. He was shaking violently.

"Lord," he started, between sputtering gasps, "the map... the map..." He looked out of the corner of his eye and saw Reyk glaring at him. Caught between the hawk-like gazes of Aefalas and Reyk, he fell to the floor in a blathering heap. Soldiers pulled him back to his knees.

"Speak!" shouted Aefalas, rising, intimidating.

"Lord, Lord, ...it is his map. It is Reyk's map. He led us here! Have mercy, lord!"

"He is crazy, Lord. The strain has been..."

"Silence!" shouted Aefalas at the top of his voice, his face contorted in a blood-red rage. "Take them away. We will find out all they know later."

It was night when Tandela slipped out of the royal bedchamber and tiptoed down the stairs. Down and down she descended until she came to the rocky grotto beneath the fortress. There she ordered the guard to open the dungeon and

271

bear her a light. The door opened. The heat throbbed. Tandela was led to the cell where Reyk was being kept. When the cell was opened, she took the torch from the guard and entered alone. Reyk was lying on his side against the far wall. He awoke squinting in the light. Behind it he saw sumptuous, richly ornamented skirts, but the face of the one who held the bright ball of fire was hidden from his view.

"Sit up," she commanded haughtily. "I am curious about you. You have a look that intrigues me. Tell me about yourself."

Reyk was surprised. Jolted out of sleep, he took a moment to get his bearings. Tandela waited impatiently.

"Great queen," he said, recognizing her as his eyes adjusted to the light. "I am only a poor sailor. My accuser... he is a stupid, frightened boy..."

"No!" she interrupted. "That is not what I mean. I do not care that you have come to do murder here. I am indifferent to that. So let us get to the point. You have the look of one who has gazed into the dark well," she half-whispered, drawing closer to the cringing sailor. "I know that look. Tell me the truth of it and I will set you free."

Reyk was drawn magnetically to her. She dropped the torch downward so that he might see her face more clearly. Seeing in the dark pools of her eyes the same look of death and cold malice he had seen in the eyes of Barthol, he gasped inwardly. He trembled as he sat and rattled the chains that bound him, the sudden memory of the Dark One flooding back. Tandela smiled.

"Leave us!" she shouted at the guard back through the doorway. The warden obsequiously obeyed.

When they were alone, Tandela pulled out the scroll-map and unrolled it upon the squalid floor. She pointed to an ink mark on the map, set inland from the coast, by a river called the Durna. "Tell me about this!"

Reyk was struck with a stomach-wrenching terror. In that moment of abject fear, he knew that this was all Barthol's doing. He knew now that Barthol knew everything, even about this woman Tandela. He thought he had been wise and strong-willed, that he had shaken off Barthol's enslaving bonds. He realized in that instant that Barthol wielded a power over his mind beyond anything he had imagined possible. He knew that the attack had failed because he had failed to bring the fleet to

Barthol as he had promised. He knew the purpose behind his capture. He knew why this woman stood before him now. Lies would not help. He looked upon his death as surely as he sat in a putrid, rat-infested dungeon far from his homeland.

"There is one in that place whom we were born to serve. If you let me go, I will bring him here," Reyk replied.

Tandela felt her breast burn as if hot metal had been thrust inside her. She felt naked, as if suddenly she had been shown her true nature, a nature against which the last semblance of denial had been swept away. An engulfing darkness settled on her.

"It will be so," she said, trance-like. "But tell me, tell me *his* name," she pleaded, her voice quickening.

"His name, witch, is Barthol. May the gods truly have mercy upon us now," he added under his breath.

In the dead of night, Tandela had Reyk released. He was escorted to the limits of the city under solemn oath to find Barthol and fetch him. But she needed to extract no such oath, for Reyk was bound by destiny to do her bidding. It was impossible for him to do otherwise.

Supported by the people, Allisyn had again taken up residence once again in her father's house. At once there was an undeniable tension between herself and Tandela. Allisyn was as good as Tandela was black-hearted and her presence polarized the household, the soldiery, the town and the realm. Tandela felt it, an enemy lurking on the borders of her hard-won territory. Allisyn was forbidden to go near Aefalas, whom Tandela had bound in the very heart of her twisted knot of control. She would not have those bonds undone.

Allisyn did not provoke her. She kept to herself and with Bronwyn, who was always by her side. They moved about the castle bestowing kind deeds and gentle words that seared Tandela like scalding oil whenever she observed them. They hovered in the halls, to the queen's way of thinking, like two specters, benign for the time, latent in their motives, yet potentially deadly to her cause. Slowly, imperceptibly, they revolved Tandela's wheel of fate in the opposite direction with their displays of love and kindness. If Tandela gave them an order, they meekly obeyed, blessing her even if her command

273

discomfited them. This burned in the queen with the hottest flame. She would fain have had them throttled in their sleep, but the conflict was too visible and too sensitive for boldness. What was called for here was subtlety, all the guile that she could call upon, and something that did not suit her well, patience. She had never been possessed of that quality and she loathed to demonstrate it now.

Once she had seen Reyk and learned of Barthol, she immediately took new hope for her degenerate cause. Here, it seemed, was help unlooked for. Here was someone in whom she could confide her evil plots; here indeed was an accomplice. Together they would find a way to do away with her troublesome cousin and the despicable, white-eyed serving girl. Together, she felt, they could shake Aestri, yea, even the world, to its very foundations. Together they could kindle the fires of her power to a new height. Together they would take command, and then she would dispose of him. He too would burn in her cauldron of hate.

Allisyn knew something was terribly wrong when Reyk was discovered missing, along with the dungeon warden on duty during the night. She suspected Tandela but could prove nothing. Nor did she want to. Somehow, she felt that it was meant to happen, that Reyk was meant to escape. She could not see what would come of it, but Bronwyn predicted it would serve them ill.

For his part, Barthol knew that Reyk was coming. He felt it even as one feels the approach of a storm on a close and sultry summer day. Indeed, he directed Reyk's coming, guiding his very footsteps over unfamiliar paths to his abode by the Iechryn. Reyk grew more anxious with every step closer to his evil master. He could feel the heat of Barthol's rage from afar. He could read Barthol's thoughts; that he, Reyk, had disobeyed and was being called home to take his punishment. Reyk knew he would die unless Barthol had further use for him. Whatever he was commanded to do he would do, for he knew that no shred of his own will remained. If Barthol's command was for him to fall upon his own sword, he would gladly do it. Gladly indeed, for then he would be free of this misery. Or would he?

As he approached the village, his anxiety grew, until it raged like a fever within him. His heart felt like molten lead in his chest, his blood like hot quicksilver flowing though his veins. He came like an unwilling slave, escaped, but drawn inexorably back; fearful of his master's wrath, but unable to sustain himself without his master's support.

To Reyk's surprise, Barthol welcomed him like a lost son, sat him down and spoke compassionately with him. Under the influence of Barthol's lies, Reyk confessed all. He opened his mind to Barthol's probing. He told him of Tandela and Allisyn and the City of Gold, Faenwys, the city of the goddess. And Barthol told Reyk he had done well, that he, Barthol, would be going to Faenwys, and that Reyk should remain by the Iechryn to rule in his place until he returned. Reyk was taken in like a fawning dog, at once afraid of his master's blow and grateful for the morsel he had been given.

Then Barthol did a thing most unexpected. He summoned Reyk's woman and she came to him, as desirable as ever. Reyk could not believe his good fortune. He took her greedily that night, thinking that perhaps things had gone his way after all. After exhausting hours, after his white-hot passion had run its course, Reyk fell asleep. Then his dark-haired love reached for her blade. Swiftly she ended him, then turned the knife on herself, just as Barthol had commanded.

Barthol arrived in Faenwys on a moonless night in high summer. So deep and so utterly black was the creeping mist about him that he passed through the gates unseen. Doors that were closed and barred inexplicably opened to him. He walked on, winding upwards, street by silent street, until he stood in the courtyard beneath Tandela's window. There he bent his thought and stirred her in her sleep. She opened her eyes, staring into the impenetrable blackness. A breeze drew her attention to the window. She stepped toward it and put her hand on the latch, her eyes drawn irrevocably downward. There, in the courtyard, stood a dark figure, a shadow blacker than the night, staring up at her with the cold, pale light of death in his eyes. Her heart leaped and beat fast even as a sudden chill clinched her breast. She ran heedlessly, expectantly, downstairs and opened the doors to receive him. When Barthol's foot crossed the threshold, Allisyn abruptly awoke and sat upright in her bed.

275

Aefalas awoke alone the next morning. He called for his wife but there was no answer. He drew a robe about himself and searched the adjacent rooms. Still there was no sign of her. Perplexed, he walked downstairs and called for her. Only his echo returned to break the silence. He entered the Great Hall and saw two figures sitting at the far end upon the dais. One of them was Tandela, seated on the steps at the other's feet. The other was a handsome young man, dressed in black with a short black beard and obsidian eyes. He sat upon the throne of Aefalas.

"Who is this?" Aefalas demanded of Tandela. She responded only with a vacant stare.

"He is master," she finally muttered.

Aefalas did not like his look, too confident, too haughty, he thought.

"Come down from my throne," Aefalas demanded. Barthol contested his will. Aefalas fought back with what powers he still possessed, but these had been so eroded through his complicity with Tandela that they amounted to little. Finally he demurred and cast his eyes downward.

"You may sit here now, Aefalas," Barthol replied at length, and he stepped down.

At that moment Allisyn and Bronwyn ran into the hall. The girl with the hair of burnished gold stood in the sunlight streaming through the high windows, and the aura about her shone like moonlight on new snow. From the moment he saw her, Barthol wanted her, wanted to control her, wanted to take her, to possess her, to use her. His lust for her was as boundless as her goodness, and his avarice was kindled. Here, as Thol-nys had told him, was his next challenge and sure prize. But such a light could not merely be covered up; such a light had to be extinguished from within. Such a light must be devoured by the Great Sow, the Great Calamity herself, through him. This was the only way. For the existence of Twelve Pearls, the essence of Deus, forever gnawed at her belly.

Bronwyn advanced first, standing between Barthol and Allisyn, trembling, seeing the stare from the vacuous depths of Barthol's and Tandela's eyes, four dark pits swallowing all the light that entered them. She trembled for Allisyn and for the world. She turned to Aefalas and addressed herself to him.

"Aefalas, who has come here? Who have you allowed to enter your home, the place of your fathers and the heart of your

276

people? Alas, Aefalas, that you have fallen so low! Now all will wither in the autumn of our year."

"Stand aside, girl, that I may behold the Jewel of the City," Barthol sang. "For truly you misperceive, it is not the autumn but the spring. I see the opening bud and smell the fragrance of its perfume. How can you speak of withering in the presence of such a flower?"

"A fair wood may harbor a foul serpent," Bronwyn shot back.

"And insolence is often the fruit of a uncertain heart, Bronwyn," replied Barthol. "Be wary!

"I am he," Barthol said, speaking now to Allisyn, without words, *"the one for whom you have waited. I have come for you, Allisyn, and you alone. I am that one to whom the Twelve belong. Surely you see that. One day you will give them to me. It must be. You will see. I will show you. Yes, that day will come, yes."*

"I see with greater clarity than you deem, Barthol. Not for you, not for you, are the Twelve destined," Allisyn replied, speaking her thoughts to his mind.

"You are my great quest, Allisyn, not to be denied me forever. In time all things will evolve into night. Even the sun, one day, will not rise. Darkness is the final resting place of all. Here is comfort, the end of longing, the end of uncertainty and the burden of consciousness, here, Allisyn, where I wait for you."

And it seemed to the others that the light about Allisyn inexplicably and momentarily dimmed, as a candle that falters in the wind.

Chapter 26
Web of Deceit

Barthol walked freely in the City. Everyone who met him felt a vague uneasiness and often a morbid mood settle upon them. Arguments broke out among friends where he lingered and enmity festered in old wounds. But he was not suspected. Barthol's mind was shrouded in an impenetrable mist and no one could know his mind or his purposes. Only those to whom he revealed his thoughts, as he had to Allisyn, might read them. He had taken up residence in a high tower of the castle and from that lofty place sent out his brooding, wicked thought.

One day shortly after his coming to Faenwys, Tandela knocked upon his door. Of its own volition seemingly, it opened, and she entered. He held out his hand in greeting. Hesitantly at first, she took it in her own and kissed it.

"Greetings in the Great Darkness, my sister. We have many things to discuss. Come!"

"My Lord Barthol," she began, addressing the younger man. "Long I have waited your coming by the well of Thol-nys. Long I have prepared for your arrival."

"You have done well, and Thol-nys has seen. She can bestow great power, and give great gifts to her loyal followers."

"Yes, Great One, still I have much to accomplish and my desire is that you will aid my purposes. I assure you that they are one in the same with your own."

Barthol looked at her long, as if to read her deepest unrecognizable thoughts, fragments of yet uncongealed notions in her mind. "Yes, sister, our path lies together for a long while and we would do well to tread it side by side. What would you yet accomplish here, Lady Tandela?"

"Long have I labored to consolidate my power so that I might, without contest, build an altar to Thol-nys here, worship her openly, and bring the people to her. I began with Aefalas. That was all too easy. He fell for lust of my body in the forbidden pool, the penalty for which is death under the laws of the matriarchs. After that, he was under my control. My sister, Vaalta, his wife and High Priestess, was killed by marauding pirates. I seized the opportunity to take control of the Council. Those who resisted me, I murdered. Now I have all but destroyed the worship of Faena. The matriarchs no longer have any power."

"Good, Tandela, good. The Great Calamity smiles upon you."

"But even as the old order was being swept away, a new threat arose. An old woman came, half-blind with her mute urchin granddaughter leading her about, denigrating me and preaching a new religion. She seemed to know my dreams, my thoughts, my purposes, my deeds, and she proclaimed them to expose me. My cousin, Allisyn fell in league with them. I had them arrested and thrown in the dungeon. At length, I had the woman's tongue ripped out for her heresy and the eyes of her urchin gouged. They wandered off, impotent, but Allisyn followed them. The old woman died, but when Allisyn returned, she had the girl, Bronwyn, with her.

"Allisyn was changed, more despicably pure and more dangerous. By some trick, the girl's eyes had been restored and her tongue, silent from birth, had suddenly been loosed; her grandmother all over again. Everywhere this 'miracle' was on the lips of the people. They venerate Allisyn and her serving girl. In this only have my plans gone awry. Whereas I sought to reduce Allisyn, to drive her out of the realm and the minds of the people, she has grown stronger, much stronger than ever. It is a bitter cup I drink, Barthol. And in this, I most desire your help; to utterly destroy her, to break her and see her ended. But I cannot do it while the people worship her."

"A dilemma, indeed, my corrupt one, but not such a difficult task. We have only to offer them something more desirable than Allisyn. Humankind are so easy to deal with, my pet. They venerate the beautiful and the high so long as their base needs are met. When they are hungry or cold they forget those things soon enough; then they become depraved and will do anything.

"Here is my thought, Tandela. We will tax the people. We will take everything they have. When they are desperate, we will give them some of it back, and they will be ours forever. They will be grateful, you will see. They will do what we command, they will worship whom we worship. They will forget Allisyn, because she will have nothing that will meet their needs as we can. Men are indifferent when they are fat. But when they are lean, they can be worked like metal in a forge, shaped into our shape and bent to our purposes.

"Then we will build an altar, Tandela, to Thol-nys, a great golden goddess. And they will revere us who fashioned it. They will give themselves and their sons and daughters to be sacrificed there. They will even offer Allisyn up, if that is your desire. They will throw themselves into the gorge at your whim. You will have power greater than you ever have imagined. Grappling with Allisyn for their favor will not work while they are fat. First we take away. When the time is ripe, we will dole out a pittance to them, and they will be ours completely."

The lust of Tandela's heart swelled as Barthol revealed his plan. She imagined herself clothed in the richest garments and the finest of jewels with slaves of her will to serve her the finest food, unquestioning. Deep within her, she thought she heard a grunting laugh that was not her own.

"There is only one condition, Tandela, if you want my help. You must give yourself to me. Aefalas' wife, and queen of Aestri you may be, but never again will you give yourself to him. You will be mine, undeniably, unwaveringly. You must agree to this."

"I will, gladly, my Prince," Tandela assented without doubt, but inside she thought, *"My body, mind and soul are my own, ...mine, and I will do with them what I will. That, Barthol, is the first principle of darkness. Whose pit will be the blacker?"*
And she placed a fervent kiss upon his lips to seal the bargain.

With Tandela in hand, Barthol sought out Aefalas. He found him early one morning walking in the gardens high above the gorge of the Mergruen. Gray mists thrown up by the swirling waters below had collected on branch and flower in the night. The light and heat of the sun, still waxing over the

280

ramparts of the eastern mountains, had not yet driven the droplets under leaf and they dampened Aefalas' shoulders and legs as he walked. Barthol came up behind the king, at first but a shade drawn over his heart and mind, next a long shadow that cleaved the sunlight about him. Seeing someone approach, Aefalas turned and looked up. Barthol bowed low, the hem of his ebony garment sweeping the ground, soaking the dews into its fabric.

"My lord Aefalas," he said. "May I walk with you? I have found little company since coming to your fair City and I desire your conversation above all others."

Aefalas said nothing but did not hinder his guest. He turned and Barthol joined him along the path.

"Lord, this is a city of many wonders. Never have I seen its equal in splendor. It truly astounds me that in so few lives of men you have created such a place. And not only is it marvelous, it is strong, and it is rich. I have gazed in awe at the girth of the pillars of the gates, the height and thickness of its wall and the number of its soldiers. I have seen the goldcloth tapestries and ornamentation of your palace. I come from a poor village where we are unaccustomed to such majesty. You are a great man indeed."

"And why have you come?" Aefalas asked. "Do you come merely to envy, or do you come to take away what I have amassed by my strength and wits?"

Barthol laughed. "You mistake my purposes, lord. I have come only to Tandela. She sent for me. I have come to give counsel, where it is sought."

"And what counsel would you give *me* concerning my wife?"

"I know not, Aefalas. A counselor always seeks to understand before he gives advice. If you would have my help, tell me what is on your mind. Only then can I assist."

Aefalas looked him straight in the eye. At first he was reluctant to open his thoughts to Barthol. Then a sinking coolness descended upon him, a chill that seemed unaccountably familiar and compelling. Dark arms seemed to rise up out of the ground, wrapping themselves about him, urging him to speak.

"Tandela... how do I begin? She is the cousin of my first wife, Vaalta. Vaalta was the High Priestess of Faena, and she was beautiful. Her hair was the color of corn silk, of bright copper, newly refined and polished. Her skin was soft as the fleece of a newborn lamb and as white as cream. She was everything to me, and yet... not enough.

"Tandela never liked her, because she was beautiful, because she was powerful, because she was my wife, who can say for certain. The strife goes back many years between them and came to a trial too sore. I was caught in the middle. Tandela seduced me and led me woefully astray. When Vaalta was killed in the pirate raid, little above a year ago, Tandela fixed her mind on replacing her as High Priestess, as queen, as my wife. I was weak in spirit and I was vulnerable. And when I fell, she caught me so fast in her net, I could not recover. Since then, she has ruled me, and alas, the realm. Sometimes I pity myself and sometimes I hate myself for my weakness. Now I have no control of her, not even in the matter of my own daughter, Allisyn.

"Tandela despises her too. Not only because she is beautiful, more beautiful even than her mother, but because she is Vaalta's daughter, and she fears her rivalry. She fears, and loathes, any rival, and she bends her malice upon them; they suffer, and they break. I do not want my daughter broken."

"It is a cruel fate," Barthol consoled. "You have cause to be the happiest, proudest man on earth. Yet this woman has brought you to your knees. Such a shame."

Aefalas eyes fell toward the earth at Barthol's last words and they walked on for a while in silence. Suddenly Barthol turned to Aefalas.

"What would you give me, Aefalas, to be rid of Tandela's hateful presence? What would you give me if I broke her sway over you?"

"What do you mean?"

"What if I made her to disappear, to vanish from your life?"

"I will not have her blood on my hands. If I were one to deal in murder, I might have done it long ago, but I do not, although, by the gods, ...I have condoned it. To protect my secret, others have died." The weight of his own words bowed his great shoulders. His hands went to cover his face and his frame shook tremulously.

"Not then, by murder, Aefalas, but I would have the freedom to use any other means at my disposal. What would you give?"

"I would give anything that I have to the man who could rid me of her."

"Then it shall be done."

"What payment do you ask in return?"

"The prize I ask, Aefalas, is your daughter, Allisyn. For now that I have seen her, I cannot help but desire her. In that I do not differ from any other man. Other men will come to seek her hand, to take her for themselves and thus break our bargain. You must not let them. You must stand by me and keep tryst until I can fulfill my part of the bargain. For I will surely give you your desire."

Aefalas looked at him coldly. "You ask much, Barthol."

"But do I not also offer much, Aefalas?"

"Of a truth. If you do this thing, then you shall have your desire," he said. But inwardly he thought, *"Yes, rid me of Tandela, then I will rid myself of you, vile serpent, and recover my daughter. No one will mourn your demise. I will be rid of Tandela and have my daughter back as well. For I would have all things ordered as I will them; that is my pride and glory."* And even as Aefalas made his pledge, Barthol knew his deepest, most secret thoughts.

Barthol continued to move among the people, spreading discord, sowing seeds of bitterness, pitting one against the other. It was his great delight to draw shadows over the hearts of men. One day as he walked among the barracks of the soldiers he came upon their chieftain, Bors. Bors was not a man of the City, nor was he of Aestri, the great sculpted valley west of the mountains and east of the sea. He came from beyond the mountains to the east, the son of a wild northern tribe of nomads conquered in Aefalas' eastern forays. He was a man of great physical mien, and stern. Aefalas had noticed his strength and proud demeanor and brought him to Aestri. There he had proven the strength of his arms and his loyalty, graduating by degrees to finally lead Aefalas' army.

Upon their first meeting Barthol sensed a dissatisfaction within him, an ambition to be coddled, and anger to be unleashed, beneath the seemingly flawless exterior. Now in this chance meeting, Barthol unleashed his hounds, crying on the dissonant trail, searching for the one weakness that would open Bors to their rending jaws. They sat in a guard room along the southern wall. Outside, the sun was at midday and the grasses

283

wilted in its heat, yet here, inside the great wall of stone, the cool dampness of twilight held court.

"I have heard your story, Bors. It is the mark of a great man that he may be conquered and not seek vengeance, that he join with his conqueror for the greater good. Lesser men would have frittered away their lives in a dungeon for their insolence, or lost their lives in a vain attempt to prove the the sovereignty of their will. But not you, no, you are too prudent. You have humbled yourself when humility was required, bent to your new master, seized the opportunity afforded you, and thus have risen high among the mighty and the wise."

Bors made no comment, but looked evenly at Barthol over his tankard of wine, waiting to see what direction his comments would take next.

"But to what end? Surely not to a life of servitude. No man wishes to serve. It is not his nature. A man may will to serve only so long as it serves his own purposes, and no longer. I wish to know your mind on this Bors. What is your purpose? Perhaps we can join forces."

"Perhaps I have no purpose, and perhaps, if I did, I might not share it with you. Tell me, what is *your* purpose, Master Barthol? I came to Aestri in chains. You came, so I hear, of you own free will. I have shaken free of my chains by honorable conduct. You, on the other hand, shackle yourself with dishonorable words. Why would a man thus enslave himself?"

"You read me falsely, Bors. I am a free man who may use his words, and pick his friends and enemies, as he chooses. I came here at the invitation of the queen, as her counselor. Such a man as I, in such a position, might be valuable to his friends and a scourge to his enemies. Which would you choose to be?"

"Neither, if the truth be known."

"The truth? The truth belongs to the strong, Bors. The weak, those who serve, have no truth. You say you are a man of honor, a man of truth, but your truth is only the truth of your master. If he declares one day that you die, you will die. That is the truth. It makes no matter if you deny it and proclaim your own truth. The fact is, your head will roll. Who speaks the truth, then, the master or the slave?"

"Aefalas brought me from the wilderness to this City. He has given me opportunity and done me great honor by recognizing by abilities. If I am to be a slave, then I will be the slave of such a man."

284

"Listen to your words, Bors. You speak of opportunity, and honor. Deceit! You have been deceived! Masters give their slaves such opportunity and honor as suits them. You have no opportunity, no honor, unless he gives it to you! Men of renown, Bors ...men of renown make their own opportunities. They wait not on others. Men of renown seize their own honor. They do not stand meekly by to have it thrown to them as scraps from the table by those less honorable! A man must take what he needs, what he desires, when he wants it. Men of renown do not lick the boots of their masters; they are not dogs, Bors!"

"I like you not, Barthol! Yet your words trouble me. I sense that many a good man has been trapped in your snare, and I would not number myself among them. Yet my mind is no longer clear on these matters. Perhaps it is but the influence of the wine. But I would trust to my own thoughts, and not to yours."

With that Bors drained his cup and stood, placing his helm upon his head, and swept out of the room.

It was some weeks before Barthol deemed the time was right to ply his subtle craft with Allisyn. Tandela had fallen easily and Aefalas simply, under his spell. For to those who have done evil, greater evil more readily comes. The determination of Bors had tested Barthol's abilities. Yet these forays were just precursory to his main objective. And it was against Allisyn that he would exert his most cruel effort and use his greatest guile.

He had revealed himself and his purposes to her at their first meeting. For not by trickery would he have her succumb. No, her fall must be complete. She must have no regrets. She would come to him in full knowledge of what she was doing, utterly damning herself, sealing her fate and his success.

He caught her unawares one afternoon, she having sent the ever-present, ever-meddling Bronwyn away on an errand. Allisyn was seated in a window alcove, watching the play of misty shapes in the gorge, thinking of her mother and the tragedy of her death. Barthol threw himself at her feet, thinking to have some jest with her. He lay prostrate upon the floor until she uncertainly bade him to rise.

"Master Barthol, your jest poorly masks your intent. Still I would not have you debase yourself. Rise."

"It is my honor to do your bidding, Lady Allisyn."

"You have no honor, Barthol, and my bidding is that you go away and leave us to heal our own wounds. For the poison that your administer in the guise of a balm, the death that you deal in the guise of life, that which you seek to take in the guise of giving, is apparent. Your sorcery is wasted upon me."

"I, a sorcerer, Ma'am? You give me too much credit. I am but one who is cursed with keen insight into the hearts of men. If I use that to my advantage, who can blame me? Men use less gentle tools for their selfish purposes, yet you do not deprecate them for it. Why then, do you single me out? I have a gift that could be used for great good. Alas that I had not been led astray as a child! For with better upbringing, I might have been a better man. I had as wicked a mother as man may know, gentle Allisyn. But a man may change under the auspices of good influence. And those who know the true value of a man know that. If not, what hope is there for any of us? For we all, alas, wear soiled garments, do we not?"

"It is true that one may change, Barthol, yet one must want to change. Are you ready for that?"

"What must come first, Ma'am, the change or the change of heart, the change of heart or the change of influence? You could change me, if you would but undertake it."

"I am afraid I do not have the power to change you, Barthol even if I had the desire to do it. That which controls you is a power both ancient and great. It clutches at your heart and your soul with mighty talons. To set you free would be to destroy you. And though my desire is that you would change, I do not desire it at the cost of your life."

"You are too gracious, Ma'am, and I value that above all the rest of your qualities. But you misperceive me. For I am not sent to be your undoing, but your great gift and opportunity. You are the vessel of the essence of Deus, the Twelve Pearls. Are you unaware that their purpose, at the end of all things, is to conquer evil finally and forever? Would you withhold their blessing from me? For who indeed needs it more? And what greater gift could you give to the world than to transform me, here, now. Save the world from long ages of suffering, Lady! I am the one for whom the Pearls were intended, that is the meaning of the old woman's words! What good would it do to give them to the good? If your purpose is to use them to change the world, then start with that which most needs changing. Or do you deny the gift? Do you choose to hide it? Do you falter? Do you deny your destiny? Perhaps Deus has misplaced his trust. Perhaps he has erred in his judgment. Would you prove Him wrong, your Infallible One, your God of the Truth?"

"Your words are like serpents, Barthol; twisted as always, but their bite has no power to poison me. To give you the Twelve would be to cast their light into the pit of unlightable darkness. You are false and utterly evil. They are not for you. And they are not for me, not yet, so do not tempt me! I am but the keeper. The one who will come will take them and reveal their secret to the world. I have a part to play, Barthol, but my part is not to use them as you would have me use them. This much I know."

"Yet you cannot see the end of all things, sweet Allisyn. For surely one day even the sun will burn itself out. All will be reduced to ashes and cinders and darkness will reign for eternity. As it began, so shall it end. If you pity mankind, give me the Twelve now and let the darkness fall, early and completely. All your strivings are in vain. You will only increase the struggle and the suffering for a little while. Life is not as good as you would believe it to be, Allisyn. Look at your own life up to now; neglected by a licentious father, your mother violently killed, you and others around you suffering at the hands of your ambitious cousin, Tandela. Is life so good that you should want more of it? There is more sorrow to come, Allisyn, more suffering, if you keep up these pretensions, this delusion, that somehow Deus will make all things better. He cannot. If he could defeat the Great Calamity, would he not have done it long ago? The evidence is all around you that things will only become worse. Is my being here not proof of that?" And with those words he laughed malevolently.

"So deluded and pitiful you are," he added. "Yet I would not have it so. Let me enfold you in a blissful end to your suffering. Let me but place that one kiss upon your lips, my golden one..."

Barthol heard the sound of footfalls racing down the hallway as he drew his face close to Allisyn's. Bronwyn burst upon them and Allisyn stood quickly, leaving Barthol bowing over an empty chair.

"Allisyn, come quickly!" she said between gasps. "The One has come!"

Chapter 27
The Challenge

Ravennetus had ridden to Faenwys from over the mountains in the east at the coming of morning. He saw there a sight rare to behold, the rays of the sun surging forward along the valley floor until with a magnificent flourish they climbed the walls of the city and struck the gold pinnacles of its towers, transforming them into pillars of flame. He sat astride Mataforas, his spotless white stallion, the gift of Brahan that he alone had tamed, and observed the sign. A dream he had dreamed, that he would know the city of his destination by the flames that leaped from the roofs, a city burning but not consumed.

Upon his shoulder sat Randor, the size of a great eagle and beautiful to behold, whose eyes saw keenly all that stirred in the waking city. Ravennetus pulled the purple cloak of Brahan around his shoulders and the three, man, horse and raven moved forward, cresting the jagged rim of the hills and loping down into the Chent of Aestri. Into the shadow they rode, but the light raced swiftly to meet them. They emerged from the band of trees at the foot of the hills and burst into the sunlight, yet invisible to mortal eyes beneath the magic mantle.

Ravennetus rode to the gate, removed his cloak, and called out to the wardens.

"Brothers, open the gates of the City to receive the traveler who comes home."

"Does this vagabond bear a name?" the warden called back mockingly.

"Tell the Lady that the One has come!"

The guard, mistaken of Ravennetus' intent, sent a runner to

the queen to inform her of the visitor, eying all the while with wonder and trepidation, the great white horse beneath the traveler and the immense bird upon his shoulder. Bronwyn, walking through the courtyard, heard Ravennetus' voice as the faithful hound hears the sound of the hunting horn and immediately recognizes its call. She ran to tell Allisyn.

The messenger took some time to find Tandela, albeit through no lack of diligence, for she was ensconced in her chambers. He knocked and was admitted. The door swung open and there, lying upon her couch, was the queen. Barthol stood behind, bent over her, whispering into her ear. Her hand was upon his cheek.

"M'lady, ...there is a man at the gates ...seeking your permission to enter," announced the runner, clearing his throat and speaking with obvious hesitation. "What is your pleasure?"

"Turn him away, do not let him enter. For we know what he wants and we are not pleased at his arrival."

The messenger bowed low and left quickly.

Meanwhile, Allisyn and Bronwyn had run to the gates. They stood for a moment, expectantly, but the gates remained shut.

"Why do the gates not open?" Bronwyn called up to the warden.

"We await the instructions of the queen in the matter of her visitor," he called back.

"He comes not for the queen but for the Lady Allisyn, and she is here! Open the gates!"

At that moment, the runner came from his audience with Tandela.

"The queen forbids his entry. He may not pass!" the runner cried.

Ravennetus heard the pronouncement from within.

"Begone!" cried the gate warden. "The queen forbids you to enter."

"My business is not with the queen, but with the Lady Allisyn!" Ravennetus shouted.

"You have no business here at all!" the guard shouted back. "Off with you!"

Ravennetus dismounted and ran to the gates. Randor rose into the air then settled upon Mataforas' back. With all his might, Ravennetus pushed against the gates, attempting to force them open. The posts groaned and the timbers bulged, but he strove in vain. In frustration, he drew his sword and struck a blow upon them with its hilt. From high above, the wardens laughed at the young man's futile attempts to break the gates but marveled at the strength of purpose that kept him attacking them again and again.

What happened next seemed a miracle. Ravennetus retreated from the portals and ran to the stallion. Randor flapped his great wings once again, rising into the air and coming down onto Ravennetus' shoulder. Ravennetus drew his sword and with it drew a circle round his head. A bright light shone from man and horse and raven that dimmed the sun. The guards drew their hands before their eyes to shield them against its intensity. Amidst the brilliance, the three figures before them melted, like metal in a forge, into one, the torso of the man becoming the neck and head of the horse, the wings of the raven growing to immense span and issuing from the flanks of the luminous apparition. With the sound of a rushing wind the horse ran toward the wall, wings spread. A shout came from the throat of Ravennetus that echoed though all the valley. The guards watched incredulously as the soaring shape passed over the high wall. When the vision was earthed again and the light had retreated, Ravennetus sat upon the white horse with Randor upon his shoulder. Before him stood Allisyn and Bronwyn.

He slid his right leg across Mataforas' pearl white back and dismounted directly in front of Allisyn. Beautiful she was, more beautiful than he had imagined, strong yet soft, wise yet meek, shimmering like the gliding surface of the ocean but underlain by a fathomless depth of character. He spoke first.

"Lady Allisyn. I am Ravennetus, called from my journey to your side, called to fulfill the prophecy of the long ages, propelled here by the will of Deus." He went down upon his left knee, bowed his head, and offered his sword hilt to her.

Allisyn spoke as one entranced.

"Ravennetus, long have I known of your coming and joyful I am at your arrival. Look now upon the Twelve."

Her hand glided upward and where the delicate fingers alighted he looked. There for a brief and glimmering instant, the Twelve Pearls were revealed at the base of her slender neck, curving over the transept of her shoulders and draped upon her breast, glowing like living fire.

"The Pearls from the Well of Knowledge," she continued, speaking, it seemed from the Otherworld, "the essence of Deus incarnate. Twelve are their number. Twelve, the number of searching and the number of completion, the number of the neverending dance of the seasons, the number of death and life renewed, the number of descent and of the light coming out of the darkness, the number of the spiral. By us alone, by the joining of our natures, are they made manifest in the world. Only then will the end and means of Deus be known. Only through them will humankind be blessed. Only through them will the Everlasting Light conquer the Eternal Darkness, only then will Life conquer Death."

Aefalas ran into the yard, followed, from another direction, by Tandela and Barthol.

"You there," Aefalas cried, "get away from her!"

Ravennetus took a step back.

"Who are you and what do you seek?" cried the king.

"I am Ravennetus and I seek nothing, rather, I have found what it was destined that I should find."

"Do not speak to me in riddles, boy. Tell me plainly why you have come, in this manner, with these!" He pointed to the wondrous animals.

"He comes as a thief to take what is yours, Aefalas! He comes to change all things, to tear down what has been built, to strip clean what lies hidden. He comes for your daughter, Aefalas!" cried Barthol.

"Silence!" roared the king. "Let him speak! In truth, boy, why do you come flying over my walls like a sorcerer? Speak!"

"I come not as a thief, King. But I do come to change all things, not to tear down, but to transform; to reveal what lies hidden, yes, to expose dark things to the light, to drive out the poison and to heal. That is why I have come."

"More riddles! Answer me true, if you can, what have you to do with my daughter?"

"She is to be mine, and I, hers."

"That, boy, is a mighty presumption!" Aefalas contested, pointing at him and growing more agitated with each exchange of words.

"Stop!" shouted Bronwyn. "Stop this bickering! Open your ears to wisdom, Aefalas. Your daughter, Allisyn, and this man, Ravennetus, are the blessed of Deus. Believe, then, that they hold the keys to the future of humankind and do not thwart them. For if you do, you contend with the will of Deus himself!"

291

"You wicked and perverse girl," Tandela shouted at Bronwyn, her face contorted by rage. "Just like your grandmother you are, always interfering, always causing trouble. Curb your tongue! You speak of mysteries that are too deep for you. Deluded liar, power-mad little imp! You but ride in the train of my cousin for your own gain. Be silent or feel the breath of my wrath!" She lurched forward but Barthol caught her by the arm.

"Quiet, Tandela," Aefalas said staring rigidly at her. "Save us the drudgery of your exhortations. And yours!" he said whirling about and pointing at Bronwyn. Then he turned to face Ravennetus. "I want answers from you, boy, and now!"

Allisyn lifted her arms and silenced them all. Then she spoke.

"Am I to be excluded from this debate? Or is the voice of the one over whom you prate so unimportant? It strikes me exceedingly odd that those who have disavowed me should suddenly be so interested in my life, so interested in those I choose as my friends and companions. Long have I desired your love, but you withheld it. But, hear me, I have not suffered your repudiation for naught. I have walked through your fire not only unscathed, but unscathable. I do not blame you, for such was my destiny. Deus has called me and Deus has prepared my path. Nothing you might do can change that. Repent of your evil, and perhaps you may save yourselves. But let me go, I beg you, give me my life."

"No man's life is his own, and no woman's, Allisyn," said her father. "You are no exception. For good or for ill, you are bound to us, to this City, to this realm. You are bound by our laws, our customs and by the blood that flows in your veins. You are bound ...you are bound by promises, by oaths."

Allisyn looked at her father with a burgeoning fear. A thin smile curled Barthol's lips.

"What oaths have you taken, Father, concerning me, that you have not made known to me? Is it not enough that I am humiliated in my own house, by my own kinsmen, that you choose to barter my life away behind my back?"

She hung her shoulders and wept. Ravennetus unsheathed his bronze blade and pointed it at Aefalas' chest.

"What treachery is this?" the young stranger demanded. "Tell her the fate to which you have bound her!"

Fire leaped into Aefalas' eyes.

292

"You dare to question me? You dare to make demands of me? I am no witless bumpkin that you may cow and carve, lad. You have let your arrogance outpace your good sense. You shall visit the dungeon! Guards, arrest him!" Aefalas cried and stepped toward him, his chest flung out in defiance.

Suddenly Ravennetus found himself in a ring of bright metal. He whirled about, placing his back to his horse.

"Seize the beast, seize the beast!" shouted Barthol, pointing to Mataforas.

"Kill the bird, shoot the bird!" Tandela screamed.

Ravennetus leaped unto Mataforas' back and kicked his flanks but strong hands grabbed the bridle and held him fast. Randor beat the air with his wings, rising, then falling upon one of the soldiers with his rapier talons. The white stallion reared, pawing the air. One of the soldiers fell beneath his flying hooves but another jumped in to replace him. Ravennetus' sword sang and cleaved the shoulder of another. Mataforas swung about. A strong hand grabbed Ravennetus by the leg, pulling him downward, and he fell from the high back of his steed. When his head hit the ground, he knew no more.

Ravennetus awoke in a dark cell below the fortress to the miserable reek, the oppressive heat and the throbbing of the waters. Above in her chambers, Tandela spoke with Barthol.

"The game is afoot sooner than we expected, is it not Barthol? What then shall we do? The slow plan which you devised has come to nothing."

"Tandela, my dark beauty, there is an important concept that you must grasp, a lesson that you must learn. My plans never come to naught. We will proceed just as we designed."

"But what of this interloper, this bird-boy? Does his arrival not change the situation?"

"Of course, my love. All we need do is rid ourselves of Ravennetus and give our plan time to work."

"And how will we do that? Rumor of him and his association with Allisyn have spread already like wildfire throughout the city. Soon he will be untouchable, as *she* is. We cannot murder him."

"Oh no, no, ...we will have to set him free, of course. Allisyn will not let him languish in the dungeon for long. But

293

when he goes free, he must be powerless to affect her further," Barthol muttered, thinking aloud as he paced. "That is the issue. Leave it to me, my pet. I will find a way."

"You have done well, thus far, Aefalas," the Dark One said to the king. "By your actions you show that you are a man of honor and that your promises are firm. This is good."

"Yes, I am committed to fulfill my oath to you, but only as long as you fulfill yours to me, Barthol. I will do what I can to make sure that this Ravennetus does not interfere with your plans for Allisyn. But what shall I do with him? I cannot hold him long. Allisyn will not stand for it. The people will not stand for it. Neither will I allow you to murder him. We could not get away with it, in any event. What then, is your counsel in this matter, in the matter of this boy, Ravennetus?"

"Of course we cannot allow their union to take place. But we must allow him to go free, do you not agree?"

"And if we do, how shall we keep them apart?"

"I have thought upon it, and I have a plan that will keep him out of the way for a long while, perhaps forever."

"Go on," Aefalas said evenly.

"The world is wide, Aefalas. This realm, with all due respect, is only a small part of it. Beyond the mountains, as you know, there is a broad plain, many a day's journey in breadth. And beyond that lie yet more mountains. To the east of those mountains lies a land yet broader, and a river so wide that one cannot see the other side, a river of such breadth that it makes the Mergruen seem as one thread in a fabric of cloth. Beyond that river, the plain stretches on until it reaches yet another mountain range. These mountains, the Utlai, are a great fence, beyond which are monsters terrible to behold, spawned in the dawn of time, at the beginning of all things. For in that time, before time began, there was a great battle of the gods. And Osyn fought with Thol-nys. And he wounded her in the thigh. And where the drops of her blood fell upon the earth, gruesome creatures sprang up, hideous to look upon and covetous of the flesh of men, killing and eating them with impunity. They are immense and powerful, utter demons. These creatures were herded together by Osyn, behind the fence of the Utlai, a range of mountains too high and inhospitable for even the monsters to cross. Thus they are kept separate from men.

"There is one so immense that the tallest tree is to her like a blade of grass. She is so grotesque that her gaze alone may slay the faint-hearted. Her skin is covered with scales of armor and her long arms terminate in many fingered hands, each finger with a claw. Her breath is befouled with decay and the stench of her body goes everywhere before her, withering and suffocating. Her name is Magor and she is deadly.

"In the middle of her head is an immense horn, in aspect like that of an auroch, but huge, in proportion with her own size. She might plunge it into the side of a mountain and split the earth asunder.

"As Allisyn's father you may ask any gift you wish in exchange for her hand, and one so dear should be dearly purchased, do you not agree? Give her freely to Ravennetus, so long as he brings you the Horn of Magor for your prize."

Aefalas looked at Barthol, appalled by his plan to send Ravennetus to certain death, yet charmed by his knowledge and cunning.

"How do you know this?" he asked, not sure that he wanted to know the answer to his own question. Barthol laughed. "Some things are better left to the imagination, Aefalas," he responded, chortling with spiteful glee.

The next day, Ravennetus was brought from the dungeon, blinking and soiled, into the Great Hall of Aestri. Tandela and Barthol loomed behind Aefalas upon the left and right arms of his throne. Allisyn rushed to Ravennetus' side as he stood before the three. Then, before the free assembly of the people, Aefalas made his pronouncement.

"People of Aestri, this man, Ravennetus, has asked to be joined with my daughter Allisyn. Such permission is not lightly given, especially to one whose origins and lineage are so obscure. Yet my daughter says that she desires it and I would not be heavy-handed in my judgment. Therefore I make this proclamation, that they may be joined together when Ravennetus brings me a prize. This prize is none other than the Horn of Magor, the monster of fable that dwells in the east beyond the great mountains."

Allisyn drew close to Ravennetus and clasped his hand.

"Do you promise to be bound by my request, Ravennetus?"

"I do not quail before any challenge, not matter what it might be. The hand of Allisyn is beyond the value of any earthly

295

prize. Yet I do not doubt that this horn has little merit of its own and that you do but send me to my supposed death. So be it. For I was not chosen of Deus to die at the hands of a beast, whatever my fate may be," the proud young man replied.

"You have heard his oath. So let him be bound. Return with the horn, and you may have her hand."

"Then give me my horse and weapons and I will go. I ask but a word alone with Allisyn before I depart. I release her to your safekeeping while I am away. Guard her well, Aefalas, for there is great evil in this house."

Mataforas and Ravennetus' weapons were brought. He stood with the girl he had known so short a time beneath a spreading elm beside the wall overlooking the gorge. For a moment only they were alone together. He reached out to her, and gathered her into his arms. She laid her head upon his chest and listened to the slow beat of his heart.

"I grieve to leave you here, Allisyn; so brief has been our time together, so few our words. Yet do not despair that I will return, for I will surely do so. Our fate is to be joined and to walk the path prepared for us by Deus. Of this I am certain. That which I fear most lies within these walls. The one they call Barthol, I know him, and he is capable of any evil. For I am the son of Brahan, the son of Deus, and Barthol is my brother!"

Allisyn gasped, gathering the folds of his tunic into her fists. She looked searchingly into his eyes. He told the truth, she knew it. And yet she could scarcely believe.

"That?" she asked benumbed, trembling.

"That," he replied. "He is the son of Thol-nys, out of the womb of my mortal mother."

"Then I fear him all the more. For he is evil incarnate and means not only to defeat us but the will of Deus himself."

"Yes; that is why I tremble to leave you here, my love. But I am bound by my oath and my honor to do your father's bidding. There is no other choice. Keep well and be on your guard for treachery. My thoughts will be with you every day."

Then he kissed her lips and turned sorrowfully away. In her mind, Allisyn had already made a choice of her own.

Chapter 28
The Wild Nature

In the twilight, Allisyn and Bronwyn emerged from the castle, hooded and cloaked against recognition. Initially taking the Droemenvael Roed, they followed its arching line as it bent north toward the river. When they were out of earshot of the gate wardens, they paused. The waxing Stag moon rose above the jagged eastern skyline.

"Now I must go, Bronwyn," Allisyn explained. "I must follow him. If I do not go now, I may never see him again."

"You are right to go, Allisyn, for he will need your gifts to accomplish his quest. But still I am determined to go with you," Bronwyn asserted.

"You cannot, Bronwyn! This path leads to death. I deem that only he and I are doomed to walk upon it. I love you Bronwyn, and I would not have you suffer."

"I will suffer if I cannot go with you. I will suffer when they find that you have gone and they torture me to tell them where. Please, let me go, at least a little way," Bronwyn pleaded. Allisyn looked on her with compassionate eyes.

"I am moved by your love and loyalty, Bronwyn. Come then, let us find Ravennetus. When we do, together we will decide what is best for you. But you must be bound by that decision. Do you promise?"

"I promise."

"Then let us be quickly away."

With that they walked on, going silently in the lee of the wall. The raw wind rose, buffeting them as they approached the river, and they pulled their cloaks closely about their shoulders.

297

They left the road, striking the path that threaded the margin of the gorge, and ascended to the high bridge. At the crossroads before it they halted, looking this way and that through watery eyes. Seeing no one, they ran across the arching span to the north bank of the river. Beneath them the waters roared, drowning out all other sounds. Once across, the road narrowed and began in earnest its ascent into the hills. They labored along until they stood in the pass where they paused and looked back into the valley of the Mergruen.

"It looks so peaceful from up here, the glowing fires, the twinkling candles. Listen! Can you hear the bleating of the sheep in the distance, Bronwyn? It seems the very dream of tranquility. Sad that it is not so. Sad that I must leave Father bound in the webs of Tandela and Barthol." A tear rolled down her cheek, catching for a moment a moonbeam that slanted across her face. "But I can do little there. It is with Ravennetus I must go, for there lies the greater good."

"Do not be so sad, Allisyn. I believe you will see your father again before the end," Bronwyn prophesied.

They turned their backs upon Faenwys and continued along the road. Here it was broad and well worn, a thoroughfare that connected the Chent with the long, lush Valley Droemen to the north. Here were settlements of people, subjects of Aefalas, and far along the length and breadth of the valley their farms and fields extended. Allisyn had always thought this the fairest part of the realm. It was higher and cooler here. Here were orchards that filled the spring air with the fragrance of apple and pear. Here were emerald pastures, crisscrossed by low stone fences that swept up from the valley floor and clung to the wild fells of the mountainsides, where bloomed the bright yellow gorse. Here were streams that leaped in chains of splendid falls from the stony heights. But tonight all was washed to shades of gray in the dim moonlight. As they walked, the roar of the river behind them diminished to a low hum.

But now they were in need of a decision. Where was Ravennetus and how would they find him? Indeed how could two, on foot, catch up to one who rode, not knowing the direction he would take. Perhaps not even Ravennetus knew that. Allisyn had watched him take the Droemenvael Roed when he left Faenwys, had watched his figure fade from her desperate last view from atop the east wall of the castle. But where he had gone beyond that, Deus only knew.

298

From where they stood, the Droemenvael Roed led to the northwest, bifurcating the valley and eventually becoming but a track that meandered to the desolate coastline far away, where the unbridled wind blew incessantly and the salt-grasses hissed like snakes among the undulating dunes. If Ravennetus meant to go east, this way would lead him in the wrong direction.

He might have decided to go cross-country, trekking out of the valley and cresting the broad spur of mountains which formed its northeastern border. Allisyn could not guess how long or difficult a journey that would be. But she did know that beyond the mountains lay a wide plain where fierce nomadic tribes roamed. Her father was often there, bringing order and peace he claimed, but always his stories were of fighting and war. She shuddered to think what might become of her and Bronwyn in that hostile country. What would they do if they did not find Ravennetus soon?

The last choice, which was really no choice at all, was to follow the Mergruen to its source, an arduous journey of many days that led southeastward into the Ice Fields of Ninn. They could not go that way, for they would die of exposure in those climes that knew no summer. Hopefully he had not gone there, Allisyn mused. In the face of uncertainty, they kept to the road.

For his part, Ravennetus had taken this same road. He had come this way into the City under the guidance of Randor, who seemed to know all roads, from the broadest market thoroughfare to the least forest track. He was far ahead of the two women now, on the verge of one of the outer settlements, camped in a spruce wood just off the road. There he had lit a fire and was roasting a hare. Randor dozed in the trees above. Mataforas stood nearby, pulling up tender shoots of green grass with his strong teeth and making crunching noises, familiar and soothing to his master.

The women walked on. In the late hour the lights in the nearby farm houses were extinguished, one by one. A dog sensed them from a distance and heralded their passing. The road glimmered faintly in the moonlight. An owl hooted in a tree overhead.

The moon set and the night deepened. The stars spread their glorious pale of light across the heavens. The path dimmed and narrowed and still they walked on, guided as much by intuition as by sight. Bronwyn noticed a faint glow that seemed to come from her mistress, a light both comforting and soft, and though

299

all about her was foreign, she felt secure.

Night revolved toward morning and the two women began
to feel the effects of their sleepless ambulation. The night
approached its deepest and coldest. Allisyn drew her hood close
about her cheeks and shivered.

High in the hills above them, lying upon a crag before her
den, a lioness awoke. She raised her head and listened, hearing
the soft snoring of her growing cubs from within the cave. But
another sound ruffled the sensitive hairs of her ears and she
turned them toward the noise of soft footfalls far below in the
valley. She flicked them yet again, drawing in the soft rush of a
nearby stream as it cascaded from rock to pool. Sensing the
coming of dawn, she stood and stretched. It was time for
hunting. She jumped silently down from her high perch and
wound her way through a thicket, in a defile between two huge
boulders. She entered a meadow, crossed it quickly, and
plunged into the trees on the other side. Suddenly she froze, for
she heard something more, unusual at this hour; the voice of a
human. She lifted her nose and pressed it into the breeze, the
slightest of airs, advancing up the valley from the distant sea.
Yes, a human was there. She padded away, her empty stomach
growling, to investigate.

Allisyn and Bronwyn had come to the limits of habitation in
the Droemen Vale and stood upon the frontier of Aestri. The
road, now a mere cart track, cut a narrow swath through an
untamed meadow, tall with the fronds of summer grasses. Here
they sat down to rest their weary feet and legs.

Out of the trees, the lioness entered the meadow, parting the
vegetation imperceptibly as she walked. She lifted her head and
heard the voices more clearly now, the tender voices of two
female humans, not the grinding crush of male voices of the
species. The lioness was perplexed that they should be here at
this hour, but pleased with the prospect of an easy kill. As she
inched forward, the voices became louder, effectively masking
whatever little noise she herself might be making. The breeze
rustled the grasses. Good, she was still downwind of her prey.
Coming to within an effortless bound of them, she gathered her
legs beneath her and pressed herself against the earth.

The women talked on, unaware they were being stalked, that
one of them was about to nourish a family of lions. Had they
turned, they might have seen the yellow eyes of the cat shining
through the stems of the grasses. But they did not. The lioness

300

tensed to spring, her eyes dilated. She splayed her toes and pushed them in the soft earth. The muscles of her jaws tensed and she forced her ears down flat against her tawny head.

At that very moment the lioness felt another presence in the meadow. She stiffened, senses alert to the sudden danger. What was it? She looked but saw nothing, sniffed but detected no odor. To her ears came the sound of a song, or chant, which produced a mystical and charming effect on her entire body. She relaxed and sat up. The chanting came nearer. She sensed an invisible hand being extended toward her, turned her nose toward it, and recoiled slightly as it touched her. She saw nothing, yet some unseen hand was stroking her head, now her neck, now patting her firm flanks. In the next moment, a voice spoke to her. It spoke to her of cubs, of play, of tomorrow-kill. Improbably, the lioness stood, turned, and silently retreated through the meadow. Bronwyn and Allisyn sat unaware, talking still of moonlight, of starlight, of traveling at night, of aching muscles and weary backs, until they drifted off to sleep.

Allisyn awoke about midday. High above a great bird circled, now riding the warm updrafts, now spiraling slowly downward, flapping, climbing, swooping, a dark shape against the bright sky. She sat up and looked at Bronwyn who slept on beside her. Eventually feeling the weight of Allisyn's stare, Bronwyn opened her colorless eyes, yawned, and stretched. Allisyn opened the pouch she carried and produced a small loaf of bread. A smile broadened Bronwyn's features as she thought of days long gone by, days when she would come begging at the castle wall, and Allisyn would toss stolen loaves to her. They shared their bread in silence. Then Allisyn spoke.

"Well, my faithful Bronwyn, which way shall we now turn? This road leads away west, not to the east where my heart lies."

"Yes, but do not forget the old saying, 'he who desires to travel east may need to travel west to get there.' The shortest path is not always the surest and the road may twist and turn. We may wander many paths before we come again, at last, to the house of your father. What does your heart tell you?" asked Bronwyn.

"To go forward in faith that Deus will reveal the way, and shelter us upon it!"

"Never was a more wise answer spoken! Let the day bring what it may!"

The two women walked along the cart-track for the better

301

part of the day. The playful, growing becks of the valley had gathered beside it to form a shallow river, flowing sprightly over a brown bed speckled with white stones. Everywhere they searched the soft earth for signs of the great white horse, but found none. Toward evening they stopped again. Allisyn pulled out the remainder of the loaf they had shared at breakfast.

"I do not wish to go to the sea, Bronwyn. I fear that would take us far from the one we seek. Look! The eastern mountains are lower here. We might travel toward that pass there, and so come to the plain beyond."

"My concern is not for our direction, but for food. We left with little and now we have less. We figured to find Ravennetus quickly and have not eaten as sparingly as we might. But now I despair of finding him soon."

"Bronwyn," Allisyn said with difficulty, "there is still time for you to go back. I do not place this hardship upon you. Let me go on alone. You can find a place to live in one of the villages until I return."

"Speak no more of it Allisyn, for I have pledged to go with you, at least until you find Ravennetus, and I shall not turn aside."

They ate the remainder of their bread in silence and went to sleep early, just as night fell. The Stag Moon rose again, one night fuller and rounder. Allisyn awoke toward midnight to the splashing of the river. It seemed extraordinarily loud. Filled with curiosity, she got up and walked toward it. Something within its narrow banks caught her eye, a flash of silver, then another flash, and another. Pulling her skirts above her knees, she waded in the stream. To her amazement, it was filled with shining, wriggling salmon, so thick that she could reach down and touch their mercurial backs as they swam. "They are going home," she thought, "following their instincts, just as I am. Going home to a place they have never been, going home to give birth before they die."

She grabbed at one and attempted to toss it onto the bank. It was halfway out of the water when it shook free and dived back into the teeming school of its brothers and sisters. Surprised by its strength and impressed with its determination, Allisyn waded back toward the shore and grabbed another. This time she was successful. On the shore, the fish flapped its nimble body, beating down the grasses, longing for the water, gasping for its liquid, life-sustaining breath. Allisyn tossed up several more behind it. Some of them flipped and flopped about until they found their way to the bank and slid back into the abundant waters. Allisyn called Bronwyn, who came running.

"Quickly!" Allisyn called, "pull them away from the edge! I'll throw some more up to you!"

Bronwyn did as she was asked. Very soon Allisyn stood beside her on the shore, gazing down at the silver flanks of the fish heaving rhythmically in the pale light, their scales sparkling like gems, their mouths working in a silent chorus.

"This is a gift from Deus, Allisyn. He is surely providing for us!" Bronwyn said fervently. Allisyn, her dampened skirts still knotted about her thighs, kneeled down beside the fish and whispered a prayer of thanks.

In the middle of the night they scaled and cleaned the fish, enough for many days provision. They lit a fire and smoked the largest of them on a wooden grill woven of green willow branches. Then they ate, and a merrier meal neither of them could remember. The next morning, they smoked the rest of the fish and by midday, were prepared to set off once more. Although the delay had put them further behind Ravennetus, now at least, with their remaining bread, they had food enough for a week. Spirits high, they continued on arm-in-arm.

For two days they clambered among the boulder-strewn eastern hills. At night the howling of wolves drove them to sleep in the trees. Now they had come to the verge of civilization itself. They crested the pass which had been their landmark and looked upon a country at once wider, more magnificent, and more frightening in prospect than any they had known. Away to the northwest, they could make out the fuzzy blue line of the ocean. To the east and southeast stretched a broad plain, fertile and limitless. To the south, the line of mountains faded away to infinity.

"We must find a point upon the horizon each morning just below where the sun rises and walk toward it. In that way, we shall keep upon a steady course," said Allisyn.

By evening they were upon the margin of the grassland. Bronwyn suggested they eat and sleep in the trees one more night. On the open plain, they would find little shelter from storm or beast.

Sunrise came with a splendor that Allisyn had never before beheld. The orange ball of the sun rose out of a sea of mist above the level, unbroken horizon, tinting her skin, the trees, the grasses, with its brilliant glow, and she wept for the beauty of the dawn.

After breakfast, they set out across the plain. What had appeared to be level ground from above was in fact an undulating sea of grass, like rolling waves of the ocean frozen in time and space. Up and down they climbed. Eventually the surface flattened and the grasses became shorter. While they welcomed the easier walking, they realized this new terrain afforded them less concealment.

Toward the middle of the afternoon Bronwyn suddenly fell to the ground, pulling Allisyn down beside her. Rising to her elbows she pointed across the plain to the southeast. At first, sighting along Bronwyn's outstretched arm, Allisyn could see nothing.

"There, there!" Bronwyn whispered urgently. Allisyn looked at her egg-white eyes, wondering at the miracle of her sight, or intuition, then gazed back at the horizon. There a band of nomads was indeed making its way, ant-like, across the plain, with carcasses slung on poles between their shoulders.

"We must be more wary," Bronwyn warned, her colorless eyes beseeching Allisyn.

They walked on, seeing everywhere herds of deer and wild kine. Now and again, great flocks of birds would rise from the ground, wheel as one, then resettle to the earth further away. That night they camped beside a small mere. Its water was not as fresh or cool as that of the mountain streams of their homeland. They made a small fire to keep predators away, for there were no trees in which to sleep, and still they heard the scream of lions, the barking of foxes and the howling of wolves, most often far away, sometimes startlingly nearer at hand.

Allisyn kept the uneventful first watch. She woke Bronwyn when the moon had run half its race and Bronwyn watched for the remainder of the night. Towards dawn the girl heard a muffled sound, like a twig breaking under a heavy foot. Her heart raced. She peered intently into the gloom, seeing nothing. She heard the sound again, closer now. Picking up a bundle of grass she had woven tightly together, she lit it and held it aloft, walking courageously toward the sound. She gasped, for in the fringe of the torchlight was the retreating shape of a man. She ran back to the fire and woke Allisyn. Together they watched expectantly as the night gave way before the dawn, but neither saw nor heard anything more.

Six more days they traveled and still the plain stretched on before them. Allisyn found her thick woolen dress uncomfortable in the humid autumn heat of the lowlands. She cut off the bottom of it at mid-thigh with the kitchen knife she had brought along. With two wide bands of material she made herself a pair of knee-high leggings to turn the prickly nettles. She cut away the sleeves and midriff and made a belt to keep her skirt up. The remnants she tied up in a bundle with her hooded cloak. Her unblemished, rose-white skin, the wonder of the City and the envy of those who saw her, turned red, then brown. Her hair was bleached to a whiter blond. Her arms and legs, which had tended to be lean, blossomed into round, bronzed curves of new-formed muscle. More than the priestess-daughter of the King of Aestri, she began to resemble the wild huntress-daughter of a nomad chieftain. Bronwyn thoroughly approved of the adaptation.

After a time, the bread and fish, which they had eaten sparingly, were consumed. Still the plain stretched on before them. Occasionally they found a mere or small stream where they washed their faces and cooled their throats. On the banks of one of these, Allisyn found a long branch and tied her knife to the end of it, making a barely-effectual spear. She impaled a frog, but this provided only a brief respite from their growing hunger. They knew that soon they must find food or die.

They had just lay down by their evening fire, in a rill formed by a stream gurgling along its muddy bottom, when the howling of wolves broke out, frighteningly loud and close by. They reached out instinctively and hugged one another for a shocked moment. Reassured, they sprang into action, throwing fuel onto the fire. The brighter light illuminated a circle of eyes gathered about them. Bronwyn gasped. One wolf, lean and tall, prowled restlessly back and forth, darting, pacing, just beyond the circle of the firelight, his tongue lolling from side to side in his slavering jaws. He stopped, threw back his shaggy head, and emitted a long, tremulous howl. The rest of the pack joined the chorus. It was then Allisyn realized how desperate their situation was, for the deafening howls surrounded them on all sides. She felt fear grip her stomach. Bronwyn pressed herself to Allisyn's side and together they backed up to the precipitous bank that formed the wall of the rill.

The large wolf advanced into the firelight. Allisyn stabbed at him with her makeshift spear. Bronwyn picked up a burning stick from out of the fire and lunged recklessly at the pack. They darted away but came on again, this time closer, bolder, their lupine instincts bent now on the inevitable kill.

Suddenly a large raven flew into the firelight, talons extended, beak open, straight at the head of the lead wolf. The daring wolf scampered backward, growling and snapping at the intruder. Behind and above them on the plain a horse whinnied, so loud that the wolves flattened themselves to the ground, yipping in pain. Allisyn and Bronwyn covered their ears. In that instant Ravennetus jumped from the bluff above their heads, landing in front of them, clashing his sword upon his shield. The wolves retreated. Other men ran to the edge of the circle of light armed with pikes and wooden pitchforks. Some boys among them, armed with shepherd's slings, flung rocks among the pack and dispersed them. In a moment the insolent howling broke out once again, but at a distance. Ravennetus turned to Allisyn. Changed she was, he thought, wilder, freer, and yet more beautiful than ever. She ran to embrace him.

"Allisyn, my love. Why have you come?" he asked.

"I could not stay behind fearing that I would never see you again. I could not wait; it would have been the death of me. Father meant to give me to Barthol, of that I am sure. And I would rather die in the jaws of a wolf than to live in the den of a jackal."

"I am glad you are here," he responded with all sincerity. "And you have brought another I see," he continued, turning playfully to Bronwyn. She flinched slightly as Ravennetus touched her cheek with his calloused hand, then smiled broadly and returned his greeting, resting her hand upon his arm.

"She would not stay behind, either. And how could I force her, when her reasons for following were as good as mine? But I did make her promise to turn aside upon finding you, if we deemed it prudent. For I fear to take her where we must go."

"Perhaps, then, it has been for the best. For I would not have you wandering alone in the wild," Ravennetus said. "I see that you have learned much," he continued, holding her at arm's length. "The innocent girl has died and the wise woman has been born."

"Life is not easy in this country," Allisyn stated. "If you had not found me, I would have turned into a perfect amazon!"

"Do not say that," warned Ravennetus, "for I have known their kind and they are deadly."

"Tell me, Ravennetus," interjected Bronwyn, "How did you come to find us this evening, in this wide world?"

Ravennetus laughed heartily.

"I did not find you this evening, Bronwyn. I have been following you since the first night you took to the road, when you almost became the breakfast of a lioness! I spoke to her and she left without doing you any harm. But I thought that I should stay close by, in case you needed me again."

"Was it you, then, I saw just before dawn several nights ago?" Bronwyn asked.

"Yes, I almost came too close! You nearly discovered me!"

"What?" exclaimed Allisyn. "Do you mean that you have let us roam about this wilderness, in danger of our very lives, when all the time you were nearby and could have saved us these trials?"

"Ahh, ...yes," Ravennetus answered reluctantly. "At first, I thought you might turn back, and I could not have borne another goodbye. So I did not reveal myself. I waited, and watched, and as I did, I began to see the transformation in you. I watched as your self-reliance, your courage, your spirit, grew. Yes, you have faced trials. But there are worse ones ahead. You have profited from this experience. I believe we were meant to be together in this quest, to face adversity together, to forge our bond in the fires of tribulation. My admiration for you grows with each passing day. Now I realize I cannot face this trial alone. I need you, Allisyn. Yet I would not place you in danger."

"I was in danger from the moment I met you, Ravennetus. For we are engaged in a struggle against the very forces of Darkness. In this fight there is no safe haven. It is better to be together in danger than apart. I will cast my lot with you, for better or worse, in life or in death. I will not fail you."

"Nor I you," he added. "I will always honor you." Then he kissed her brow and turned to the circle of men gathered around them with a grin.

"These," he indicated with a wave of his arm, "are men of the village Horen. They are friends of my wandering days and have rallied to me in my need. They have driven the pack away and we owe them a debt. Yet they have invited us to be guests in their village tonight. Come, let us go with them. We will share their fire and spin them a tale in exchange for their hospitality!"

Chapter 29
The First Quartet

Ravennetus was up and away before dawn and returned with an immense deer draped across the shoulders of Mataforas, staining him crimson to the hocks. He made a gift of the slain animal to the village for their help. Greatly pleased, the men roasted the venison and entreated Ravennetus and the women to feast with them again that night.

Days went by before Ravennetus made any signs of leaving. At length he came to Allisyn to discuss their journey.

"The Heron Moon is almost upon us. Soon it will be bitter cold upon the plains. The journey to the Utlai will take months, thus we will be caught traveling in the very depths of winter if we leave now. At any rate we cannot pass those mountains in winter. We will be forced to stop short and cross in the spring or early summer when the snows have melted, unless we can find another way. Then we must find the beast Magor. The question is whether to leave now and endure the winter on the plains, or wait here and set out in the spring."

"I fear to delay the start of our journey. For if we do not go soon, we may never go."

"And what of that?" Ravennetus asked. "We are together now. What need have we to go back to the house of your father? I would have gone back to claim you. Now I have no reason to go."

"But I do," answered Allisyn. "And so do you. They will say that you have stolen me away. If you return with me, and the Horn, then your name will be cleared. Otherwise, you will forever be an outlaw in Aestri. And I need to go back for

309

Aefalas, my father. I have left him, I fear, in a desperate situation, caught between the wiles of Tandela on the one hand and the utter evil of Barthol upon the other. I fear what they might do to him, to Aestri and my people. I must go back, and as quickly as I may. Thus, haste *is* needed.

"And there is yet another reason, Ravennetus. We have been joined to fulfill a prophecy and our destiny. Our work lies there, I deem. We must confront Barthol and bring about the end of the influence of Thol-nys. For if Barthol establishes her worship among men, then many will suffer and darkness will fall quickly."

"You speak with great vision, Allisyn. I see all the more clearly why I need you so. Without you, I fear to fall short of my calling. Bless you, my love!"

In the end they decided to move on sooner rather than later, and that Bronwyn should stay behind in the village of Horen. She was sad to see her mistress and Ravennetus depart without her. But deep inside she knew it was not her fate to take part in the wresting of the horn from the head of Magor. That task was for those of bolder and stronger constitutions. "Your task is to wait, Bronwyn," Allisyn said, "to be patient, and to be here when we return." And Bronwyn found no argument to offer.

They rose on a brisk morning, a thick frost upon the ground and a rime of ice on the branches of the trees. Mataforas was waiting, well-fed and strong. They slung their provisions of loaves, dried fruit, and venison, sufficient for a journey of several weeks, on his back and stole away into a white mist. The sun's rays warmed the frozen ground, driving the cold vapors into the air. Ravennetus and Allisyn sat in tandem on the great stallion and Randor flew overhead. Due east they rode. The men of the Horen had described the way they should travel and they made for a pinnacle of rock, a landmark they could not miss. The villagers had called it the Graf.

These were ecstatic days for Ravennetus and Allisyn. They rode freely over the broad plain; free to be and do as they wished in the youthful ardor of their love, a love filled with promise and wonder, as yet unblighted by hurt or sorrow. There were no other lives but theirs and no other world but the one in which they moved.

310

In two days riding they espied the Graf looming on the eastern horizon. There was no mistaking it. The rock jutted boldly from the ground, as if a god had forced a gigantic fist up through the crust of the earth. They must climb it, they decided. So they forded the fuming river which thundered down the mountainside, littered with ponderous boulders and the gray-brown trunks of fallen cedars. On the further bank they found a track, narrow but plain, made by the slender feet of countless deer that had passed that way over the millennia. All about them the unspoiled forest stood in the majestic stillness of the dawn of creation. They climbed for half a day before they stood at last upon the wind-blasted peak.

From there they surveyed the wide lands all around; to the west the plain they had crossed, to the northwest, a rolling country crowned by a thick wood, to the north a mighty river formed of two tributaries that came together at the very knees of the Graf, and to the east, another endless plain. Far away in the east, they could barely make out another range of mountains, crowned now with snows of the advancing winter.

"There are the Etsinn Mountains, and there," Ravennetus said, pointing to a low gap in the ridge, east and slightly north of where they stood, "I am told, is a pass; there the mountains narrow in breadth considerably, though they are no less lofty."

"And who has told you this?" queried Allisyn, for those lands lay beyond the reckoning of people of Aestri or the villagers of Horen.

Ravennetus lifted his arm and cried aloud the name of Randor. From far below, where he had been riding the currents swirling round the mountainside, came the great raven. He landed with a rush of wings upon the leather cuff of Ravennetus' outstretched arm.

"My father did," he said, looking with pride and love at the bird. As they picked their way down the western flank of the Graf, Ravennetus told Allisyn the story of his days, of his youth among the lions, of his time in the village by the Cyryn where he learned the ways of the goddess, of his Grandmother, the taming of horses, the brotherhood and the freedom of riding the plains, of his meeting with Barthol and the attack on the village of the amazons. Finally he told her of his father, Brahan, and his transmogrification, of Brahan's spirit entering him and becoming one with his own, of his father's body changed forever into the raven, Randor, who sat upon his shoulder.

311

Then Allisyn told Ravennetus her whole history, of her sheltered early life as the daughter of Aefalas the King, and her mother, Vaalta, the High Priestess of Faena, of her mean and spiteful cousin Tandela. She told of her first meeting with Doena, the Old Crone, and Bronwyn her granddaughter, and how she came to know the true nature of Deus. She told him of the death of her mother and the usurpation of Vaalta's power, of Tandela's marriage to Aefalas, and her ascendance to the head of the Council of Matriarchs. Allisyn told of the maiming of Doena and Bronwyn by the wicked Tandela and of her own wandering to find them. She told him of the Well of Knowledge, of the finding of the Twelve and finally, the irrevocable bestowing of their power and wisdom within her. She told of the old woman's prophecy that One would come, One who would join with her to do the work of Deus in the Now. She told of the coming of Barthol and how he had utterly seduced Tandela. At last she spoke of her father and her deep concern for his soul, and she wept bitter tears for him.

They came to the pass in the Etsinn Mountains with winter creeping far down upon their shoulders. The treeless plain yielded to stony outcrops of rock and deep ravines filled with the resinous scent of spruce and pine. They ascended the Totmarin, for so the pass was named, by a thin trail, sometimes losing it in the growing and shifting drifts of snow. Finally, they came to a broad open space at the summit that commanded a view of the country beyond. The mountains thrust outward in long ridges that marched away to the northeast and southwest. Before them was yet another plain, vast and limitless, higher in elevation than the Plain of Dor they had left, and more arid. They had come to the Table of Vinsa, the immense triangle that divided the headwaters of the Lenai to the north from those of the Vinsatava, to the south. Winter storms swept unabated across its featureless sheet. From their high perch, it appeared wild, hostile and utterly uninhabitable.

Nonetheless, they rode on. The weather became bitter cold now. The snow, although not a burden by virtue of its depth, consisted of fine hard crystals, unlike the large, fluffy flakes that fell in the humid winters of Aestri. Here it was driven before the howling winds of the open steppes in fantastic forms that curled and writhed like white serpents. Mataforas found little forage and began to feel the bite of winter in his flesh. Ravennetus saw the effects in his thinning face. Ribs, each the width of his

312

master's hand, began to show through the skin of his flanks. Wolf moon had come and the wolf of deprivation began to slink about their small tent. Far-off howling came to their ears at night.

Then the weather eased. Ravennetus decided they should travel south for a time. A few warm, almost pleasant, days followed. They rode out of the swirling snow and biting wind and in a week's time came to a substantial river that issued from the Etsinn and flowed away to the southeast. In the quiet slackwater eddies the river was icebound but in the mainstream it flowed freely to warmer climes. They decided to follow it. By its banks they would find trees for shelter, game for subsistence, and water in abundance. They rode alongside it for several days, finally coming to its confluence with another, yet larger river. They gazed upon it in wonder, for neither of them had ever seen a body of water so broad, except for the great sea itself. Here surely, Allisyn said, must be the river Utmos, spoken of old, that was thought to encircle the world. But Randor spoke to them, saying it was not so; that this river, the Vinsa, came out of the Utlai still far to the east, and that in time, if they meant to go on, they must cross that frostbound range. Then he could not help them, for though he had roamed far and wide and taken in a large measure of the world, he had never crossed those mountains.

Daunted by his words and weary of travel, Allisyn and Ravennetus decided to stop and set up a more permanent camp. The weather was still very cold so they built a shelter of evergreens. Ravennetus cut a few trees in the midst of a thicket of young pines, clearing a circle. Those remaining on the edge he bent over, tying their tops to the ground at the other edge of the circle, forming a series of living arches. This done, the trees formed a dome tall enough to stand erect inside. Then with the boughs of trees he had cut down, he thatched the dome, making it nearly water repellent. In the center they built a fire to keep them warm. Mataforas grazed in the tall grasses by the river and soon his flesh filled out, his gaunt looks evaporated. Ravennetus hunted and trapped game. It was not many weeks before they were provisioned with food once again and outfitted with plush hides to turn the cold. Randor was happier too, having found a respite from the raging winds of the Table of Vinsa in the shelter of the trees.

Comfortable though their camp might be, Ravennetus felt

313

keenly Allisyn's desire to move on, to find Magor, to capture the Horn and return to her father. So on a mild morning with the pale crescent of the Eagle Moon lingering above the western horizon, they set out once again, this time traveling up the west bank of the Vinsa. The western bank, Randor had told them, would prove easier than the eastern. Here on the margin of the Table, the ground was more level for better riding. On the opposite shore, the ground was broken and the forests thick.

After further weeks of riding they faced yet another decision. Standing where the Vinsa plunged into the mountains, they could see the jagged teeth of the Utlai not many miles distant. But the way up to the divide was steep and narrow, and the snows lay deep, many times their height. They could not pass it in winter. Besides, Randor said, beyond the divide the mountains stretched on interminably, a sea of teeth more endless than the Table they had just crossed. How they might make that crossing he knew not. There was another way, he admitted. But to go that way they must continue on to the north where the winter would become bitter again and the storms that slashed inland off the Belgaran Sea more vicious. In either case, it seemed, they must pass the remainder of the winter here until the green shoots broke the ground and they might go forward under gentler skies.

Randor advised them to make their way up the Vale of the Vinsa. For there, high up in cliffs that formed the upper gorge were many caves, dry and safe. There they might spend the remainder of the winter in relative comfort. Game was plentiful on the high plateaus behind the cliffs and the Vale itself was a place of great tranquility and beauty.

They covered the distance to the upper valley in only a few days. Nearing the end of their journey, they climbed a rocky and tree-covered moraine, the infant Vinsa plummeting down a roaring white chute beside them. When they reached the top and looked upon the valley they were transfixed. At the level of their eyes a placid tarn spread out before them, filling the lower portion of the upper valley. Its waters were a glacial blue-green, deep and clear. Above it, climbing skyward and mirrored on its still surface, rose the vertical walls of the gorge, carved out in the time of creation by a leviathan of ice moving slowly among the mountains. To Ravennetus and Allisyn it seemed that the hand of Deus might easily have reached down and scooped it out. The walls of the gorge were pocked with innumerable

314

recesses, mere dots from where they stood, but in reality caves of mammoth proportion. The tops of the cliffs were plumed by a forest of dark firs. Immediately before them, at the end of the elongated bowl of the valley, rose the snow-encrusted, granite peaks of the Utlai, implacable, remote, aloof, untouchable, impassable. Randor flew away across the tarn. Ravennetus and Allisyn continued along the northern shore. Allisyn spied a path, broader than that made by deer, and she pointed it out to Ravennetus as they ambled along.

Further on, they found Randor perched in a great spruce just off the trail. With him sat another raven, slightly smaller, but with dazzling plumage. Whereas Randor's coloring was purple above, with a crimson neck and emerald green underbelly, in this new raven those same colors were thrown together like a confused rainbow. She seemed to be no one color in particular, becoming in aspect an iridescent purple, crimson, or teal-green as she moved her delicate head, shoulders or supple wings. The lovers watched the two of them from below.

"How exquisite!" remarked Allisyn.

"Randor, who is that with you?" called Ravennetus.

"This is Cora," Randor called back. "She is the daughter of the raven-king of this valley. Nimbror is his name and he bids us welcome!"

"Then may the blessing of Deus fall richly upon her and all her people!" Allisyn replied.

The ravens leaped from the branches and flew up the valley. There others joined them and soon the spruces adorning the feet of the cliffs were filled with them, singing a chorus of greeting. In that moment, Ravennetus was aware that many eyes were watching them, furtively, from hidden places, from behind boulders and trees and the dark mouths of caves. He lifted his arms and the voices of the raven-choir were stilled but still the singing continued. Now he realized that the song was being sung in the same bird-language by people whose throats belonged to the eyes that watched. He spoke to Randor, urging him to summon forth the singers.

Randor spoke and the other voices were suddenly hushed. He spoke again and a man came forward out of the shadow of the trees. He was short and bent with coarse black hair that almost entirely covered his body. Except for that covering, he was naked. He carried a sharpened stave, more like a stick for digging than a weapon, and leaned upon it as he walked. He

315

looked at the tall light-skinned people and at the white horse before him with wonder in his intelligent eyes. He spoke to Randor in a voice that contained the words of the raven language but was not uttered in the same pitch or with the same grace. Yet Randor understood him and passed his message along to Ravennetus.

"Iti-Ut is the chief of his people and he bids you welcome. He believes you have been sent by the gods. And so you have been, I have announced," said Randor. Then Ravennetus dismounted and helped Allisyn down. The raven-people gasped because they thought the creature had been all one, a titan with four arms and three heads. Now it had broken apart right before their eyes. They fell to the ground, covering their heads, and would not stand up again until Randor assured them that there was no danger.

Throughout the cycle of the Otter Moon, Ravennetus and Allisyn stayed with the raven-people of the cliffs. But the days were too short and propelled the lovers all too certainly to their appointment with fate. The Raven Moon rose one night as Allisyn stood, uncovered, at the door of the cave she and Ravennetus occupied. Its light fell upon her hair, her shoulders and breasts, and spilled about her feet in a sparkling pool of silver. She saw its crescent reflected starkly on the lucid waters of the tarn. A warm caressing wind wafted through the valley and she knew that their time here was at an end, the time given them by Deus to prepare for their trial, the time, perhaps, that would be their last time of joy upon the earth together. Silver tears fled down her cheeks, lingered there for a moment, then spattered the rocky shelf at her feet.

Ravennetus awakened from his sleep, and noticed Allisyn was gone. He saw her standing now, silhouetted against the stars at the mouth of the cave. Arising from the warmth of his bed of pelts he walked up behind her, touched her arms and kissed the back of her neck. She turned toward him and enfolded him in a tender embrace. When she finally pushed herself away, Ravennetus saw the solemn look in her eyes.

"What troubles you?" he asked tenderly.

"Our time of lingering is over, my love. Tomorrow we must leave to fulfill our destiny. We will need all the resources we

316

can muster, such things as we may carry, in our hands and in our hearts. Therefore, the time has come to give you a gift. Just as Hannys, the breathless stone, takes the fire of Hanthol and reflects it back to him, showing him the path through the heavens before they make their transit of the waters, just as she softens its brilliance so that it can be viewed, just as she creates love from power in the joyous union of opposites, so I take the pearls of Deus and give them to you, so that you may understand and know the way, so that you may endure the transit of the wasteland, so that you may know the true secret of conquest. For we must wage our war not with the weapons of this world, but with those of the Otherworld. These pearls are the battle dress of Deus, given us to fight his fight in the Now.

"The time has come for you to receive the four, the first quartet, the foundation upon which the wisdom of the remaining eight will be made manifest." She took a step back toward the mouth of the cave and away from Ravennetus. The crescent moon was above her head, and reflected in the pool of tears at her feet. Slowly its image began to revolve upon the floor, now an annulus of light, a halo that moved from her feet to a point above her head and back downward again, eventually coming to rest about her neck. She reached up and plucked the first pearl from the strand. She reached toward Ravennetus. With one hand, she gently opened his mouth and with the other she placed the pearl upon his tongue.

"This is *Fides*, the pearl of Faith, the pearl of belief in the unseen, in that which cannot be touched or reduced to reason. It is the essence of your belief in the existence and the power of Deus, of your belief in the power of love to heal the world and mend all things. It is your belief in the inherent good in all of humankind, of your ability to promise and to hold to the promise of another in trust." With those words, she released Fides and he swallowed it, but its light was not extinguished. It became a living, corporal part of his very being and it shone through his skin as if he were made of alabaster. Allisyn reached to her neck again and plucked another pearl.

"This is *Humus*, the pearl of Humility. Only when you have faith is humility to be grasped. It is the offspring of belief in Deus, the child whose message is that there is One stronger, wiser, more powerful, more loving that directs your path. It is the thought of the Wise Child, whose hand reaches up to grasp the hand of Deus, who knows that control of his own destiny is

317

but an illusion, that his feet are guided by One who sees all, who knows all ends, and has all means at His disposal. It admits of one's weaknesses as well as one's strengths, admits of mistakes and asks for forgiveness. It serves without expecting anything in return, it sees and respects the light of Deus that shines in every man. It is the bane of the pride of Thol-nys, whose emblem is 'I Am My Own' and which foolishly believes it needs no other. It has and gives rather than needs and takes. It is the pearl of the earth and of feet firmly planted there." With this she let go the pearl and it fell, shining, into his throat, adding its light to that of *Fides.* She reached up and took the third pearl from the strand.

"This is *Speras*, the pearl of Hope. Hope is the bread of the spirit, that which sustains us as a light in dark places. It is the knowledge that the path of Deus, laid out before us, is the true path, and no other." She opened her fingers and the pearl fell into Ravennetus' waiting mouth and throat, intensifying the glow that came from within him. Now Allisyn plucked the fourth pearl from the necklace. She pushed it in between his trembling lips and teeth and rested it upon his tongue.

"This is *Comitares*, the pearl of Commitment. It is your promise, your will and your determination. It is that from which you may not turn aside. It is your promise to love, which you alone can make." With this she withdrew her hand and the fourth pearl fell into him. She stepped away once again and beheld him as an object of veneration.

Light spilled from his shoulders, his arms, his brow, like snow shedding itself from the boughs of trees in winter, like water flowing over stones. And she was a mirror to him, and his light was her light, his wisdom her wisdom, his understanding her understanding. And it seemed to the squat bird-man who watched from below that a new sun and moon had risen in the heavens, rivaling the beauty and brightness of they who traveled there already. He fell to his knees and worshipped the light.

Randor flew into the mouth of the cave the next morning and found Ravennetus and Allisyn preparing for their journey. He perceived a change in Ravennetus. Randor sang a song of love and Cora alighted upon the shelf beside him that formed the floor and entrance to the cavern.

"I see that you are going," Randor spoke, gently placing the words into their minds, like seeds into furrowed earth.

"So we are," Ravennetus replied. "It is time."

"I have come to wish you well, then," Randor continued, "for I will not be going on with you. I have led you as far as my knowledge will allow. From now on, there will be no mortal guide for the paths that you tread. You will be on your own, together. Where you are going no one yet has ever gone."

"You have been a good guide and a mentor, Randor," Ravennetus replied. "All your instruction, I deem, has prepared me for this moment, as well as I could be prepared. Now there is to be no more teaching, no more learning, no more knowledge. It is a proud and a sad moment, here, upon the edge of the chasm."

"Yet I do not despair for you, good Ravennetus, gentle Allisyn. For I know that I will see you again, although I cannot foresee if our reunion will come in this world or in the Otherworld. But two measures of wisdom I would give you before you go. First, do not forget that your strength is in unity, and that only together will you overcome. Second, that you will come upon many gateways along your journey. You must go through these gates, yet, in order to pass, you must leave something behind, some facet of yourself, a thing that defines you, or is precious to you in the Now, something which you will think you cannot possibly do without. Only then, when you are finally and completely exposed, stripped clean of everything that binds you to the Now, will you become one with Deus, finding the thing you require to complete your journey and be reborn. The door of this cave is the first gateway, and here you must leave me behind.

"I have found love and completion here, as you have. I have taken Cora for my mate. When you return, you will celebrate our joy with us." He bowed low to the beloved humans that stood before him, then ran to the ledge beside Cora. Together they leaped over the precipice, spread their wings, and soared into the long valley.

Chapter 30
The Horn of Magor

Ravennetus and Allisyn traveled north from the Vale of the Vinsa, watching spring unfold like a gentle green wave beneath them as they rode upon its crest. They came to the broad Lenai, found a ford and crossed it, and thence followed its northern bank to where it plunged, as the Vinsa had, into the high mountains. They were far to the north now and the sun barely showed itself above the southern horizon, managing only a languid shallow arc between its late rising and early setting. They followed the curve of the mountains into the eastern mists. Further along, a river flung itself across their path. To the north was a great expanse of marsh, to the south the mountains loomed abruptly. There was no way around, and the river must be crossed. They found no ford.

After a time of doubt, they plunged into the icy flood of the Fila, swimming beside the strong Mataforas, holding onto his mane. The current was swifter than it had seemed from the bank and they were swept far down stream. Battling the frigid waters, they tired quickly. Ravennetus found himself slipping slowly beneath the waves, first his shoulders, then his neck. Soon he struggled to keep his lips above the torrent. The weight of his weapons was dragging him under and he knew it, but he was reluctant to part with them, to let them sink into the flood and be washed out to sea. But he must, or die. He let go of Mataforas' mane with one hand. His head dipped below the surface and he struggled with benumbed fingers to unbuckle the stiff leather belt that held his sword and scabbard. When he thought his lungs would burst, the buckle gave way and he let his weapons fall. Relieved of their weight, his head broke the surface and he gasped for air. He cut his bowstring and the sling that held his quiver of arrows, letting them swirl away. He struggled on.

When he stood upon the far shore and the cold had retreated from his limbs, he realized the gravity of what he had done. Without a bow, how would he slay the monster Magor? With no sword, how would he cut the horn from her head? Long he sat upon the bank and gazed into the water. Allisyn, exhausted and shivering from the crossing, held him in her arms, whispering warms words of encouragement and consolation. Mataforas nuzzled his master with his velvety nose as if to say "I am here and I will always be with you".

When they had rested, they went on. In another day they came to yet another river. The Nina was narrower but more swift than the Fila. They stood upon a narrow shelf of land beneath a frowning cliff, surveying the river in the hope of finding a place to cross, but none was revealed.

"Let us go north," Ravennetus shouted over the roar of the waters. "Perhaps we will find a ford farther along!" So they mounted Mataforas and rode. The river emptied itself into a marshy plain. The ground became pulpy and they picked their way through soft muds, testing hummocks of grass to find firm footing. Suddenly Mataforas twisted sickeningly beneath them and sank to his chest in the yielding mud. Ravennetus and Allisyn jumped free to see their old friend mired in a sucking bog. The more he struggled the faster he sank. Ravennetus grabbed his bridle and held it firmly. Mataforas sank lower, the mud oozing up his back. Ravennetus pulled all the harder. Soon only the white neck and noble head remained above the sticky surface. Ravennetus wound the bridle around his arm so that it would not slip. He began to slide along the ground, drawn closer each moment to the unrelenting bog as the great white horse sank lower and lower. Allisyn screamed.

"Let go, Ravennetus, let go or you will be drawn in too!"

"Mataforas, Mataforas, not this, no, not this!" cried Ravennetus. Now only the white head remained above the bulging surface of the muck.

With Ravennetus on the verge of the bog, the bridle snapped. A great muddy hand seemed to emerge from the quicksand, slapped at the muzzle of the horse, and jerked his face under at last. A muffled whinny, a belching grunt as the mud closed over him, and Mataforas was gone.

Ravennetus sat at the edge of the bog in disbelief. Tears streamed down his face and his whole frame shook with weeping. Allisyn kneeled behind him, wrapped her arms about his quivering shoulders, and joined in the wake for their lost companion.

Ravennetus and Allisyn sat by the bog all night. Cold mists crept about them and the winds howled mournfully over the marshes. It seemed to Ravennetus that the voices in the air mocked his sorrow and he cursed them. Allisyn was the first to realize, in the thin fog-bound dawn, that all their provisions, both food and shelter, had sunk into the mire with the horse. When she felt she could break the news to Ravennetus, she told him. He was unmoved. He simply sat, gazing at the bog upon which no sign of struggle appeared, in utter disbelief that his friend, the gift of Brahan, the horse that had come to him out of the sea, the horse whose taming had become the gift of consciousness, of authority, of power and freedom, to him and to others, was gone. His misery was complete.

With loving hands, Allisyn lifted his head from his chest and turned it toward her face. She searched his vacant eyes.

"Come, we must go on."

"Go on? What hope have we to go on? We have no weapons, no food, no shelter and no horse. All my decisions have gone awry, ever since Randor left me on my own. Why did he leave me? Why?"

Ravennetus pondered the failings of his troubled life and thought with shame and dismay of the brothers whose lives had been lost because of his errant decisions. And now he had led the innocent, faithful Mataforas to his death. He found new tears in eyes he thought had been cried dry.

"I cannot go on. You, ...you go on if you must, if you can. I will die here by the side of my friend!"

Allisyn raised her head and looked involuntarily toward the southern sky. As she did the mist parted momentarily and she saw the bright yellow ball of the sun with the crescent moon sailing improbably above it. Suddenly she found words to say.

"Do you remember what Randor said? Only in unity, Ravennetus. We must go on together. Do you remember what he said about the gateways, Ravennetus, and what we must leave behind? Now is not the time to give up. The prize is before us! Come!"

Reluctantly, as the light of understanding dawned upon him, Ravennetus stood. He stumbled forward as one blind, with Allisyn leading him out of the swamp-mist, picking a way for them among the quicksands. So she led them out of danger and back to the narrow shelf beneath the cliff where they spent a restless night under frigid stars and a clear black sky.

The next day they climbed until they stood atop the wall of rock. They clambered deeper into the Utlai until they found a place where boulders had been strewn across the river like stepping stones for giants. Downriver, the water churned through gorges and over falls, certain death if they were swept away. Before them the water roared incessantly, swirling around the immense stones. There was nothing to be done but let go of their fear and leap. Ravennetus went first, encouraging Allisyn from stone to stone.

In this way they came to the eastern shore of the deadly Nina. Scrambling down through the broken wasteland, hungry now and very tired, they once again found the plain. With heavy hearts they walked on, their hope sinking with each step.

Another day found them on the banks of a third river, the lifeless Ultana. Nothing grew upon its banks and nothing swam in it. The pallid surface seemed to arrest the very light that fell upon it. It was neither deep nor wide. Ravennetus spoke.

"We may as well cross this river too, Allisyn. But alas, if more is required, we have nothing left to give. Come, it does not look overly difficult." He took her hand and together they waded into the leaden stream. The water was surprisingly warm and shallow. Halfway across, it came only to their thighs. But a great weariness overtook them as they walked, and before they were upon the opposite bank, they could barely hold open their sleepy eyes. When they finally collapsed upon further shore, they fell into deep sleep and began to dream.

They had the same vision and the vision they shared was this. They stood before an imposing gate. 'Death' was written upon it in fiery letters. Before the gate sat a monster with four gaping mouths. Over each mouth a word was inscribed. Above the first was 'Fides', above the second, 'Humus', above the third, 'Speras', and above the fourth, 'Comitares'.

"Welcome to the Pit," said the monster, all of her mouths speaking at once, uttering the same words in unison. "This is the gateway of death. You may choose to enter if you wish, although you have no choice in the matter. For those who cross the last river may not return to the Now except by the road that leads through the Land of Death. There you will find Magor, who will give you all the death you can endure! You have brought your faith, humility, hope and commitment with you, I see. But you will not need them in the Pit. Toss them into the four mouths that you see here. Then when Magor stomps out the flame of your puny lives, the mouths will not gnaw your eternal souls." A rumbling laugh erupted from the mouths and burning spittle drooled from their corners like lava seething from restless fissures in the earth.

"We will keep them!" Allisyn cried aloud. Her voice, she thought, might well die before it reached the monster's ears. But the gatekeeper was not deaf.

"Ho, my pretty one. I can't wait to gnaw your beautiful bones! Keep them will you? Take a chance, will you? Then all bets are off. Don't try to feed me your precious pearls when I'm peeling off your skin. It will be too late then!"

"As for you, Crow boy, son of a fool, you can still save her, you know," the monster said, pointing at Allisyn. "Just step inside and shake hands with Magor. You're the one we really want down here. She's only a woman, after all, not good for much more than a few squalid nights of pleasure, but she'll soon give you little of that. Come in alone and I'll send the pretty one here back across the river. She'll be none the worse for the experience. Might even see her precious father again, she might. It would bring her a little of what you call 'joy' no doubt before she withers and dies."

Ravennetus turned to Allisyn. "She's right you know. This is a hopeless journey, my love. How could I have brought you here? What was I thinking? I will go to Magor and die. But you need not go. Go back while you can. Go back to your father. This is no place for you, this is no fitting death for you. Go and brighten the world while you may!"

The gates swung open and a foul vapor spilled out.

"I must go with you, Ravennetus. I belong at your side, no matter how sore the trial, no matter how loathsome or dangerous the wasteland we must cross! Only together, my love!"

"No!" he shouted. "Go back! I would not lead you to your death!"

Allisyn clung to him and would not let him go through the Gate alone. They struggled. Finally he pushed her into the outstretched claws of the beast who held her as Ravennetus ran through the creaking, closing gates. But the beast could not hold her. Allisyn broke free and scurried through the gate just as it slammed shut with a boom behind her.

"If you won't leave behind your precious jewels, my love, then you must leave something else. Those are the rules!" the beast shouted mockingly. "All right then, I'll decide for you!"

For a moment after the gates slammed shut there was only darkness and a horrible stench, as if the vapors from all the tombs of the world, the smoke of all the burning flesh, and the breath of all the feverish dying souls had been collected there. Their eyes grew accustomed to the light by degrees but the abominable smell did not abate. When Ravennetus' eyes had adjusted to the darkness, he turned to look at the figure beside him, a wretched bent and bedraggled hag. With disgust he realized that the stench came from her. He recoiled.

"Who are you?" he asked instinctively, already knowing and dreading the answer.

"It is I, Allisyn, my love," she said in a rasping voice. "The beast of the gates has taken the last thing I possessed. She has robbed me of my beauty forever."

Now Allisyn bent her crooked neck and looked toward her lover. To her horror she realized that he was a decrepit old lion, shorn of his mane, whose teeth and claws had all fallen away. He was a broken king, bereft of might and nobility, who would have to be fed and cared for until his miserable hide rotted off his bones.

"So," cackled Allisyn, flapping her toothless gums, "there was nothing left to give?"

"I was wrong," Ravennetus admitted. "There was much left to give. But now, truly there is nothing. She has taken everything."

"No, Ravennetus, we still have the Pearls. Look at us. Here we stand, at the end of our days, me a ugly hag, you a decrepit lion, with the chance to look back and reflect on what was truly important in our lives. The Pearls. We did not throw them to the beast. We have made our choice, and we have decided what is important. We have delivered up everything else but the Pearls, and those the beast will never get. Do you not realize, my love, we have won!"

The dream ended and Ravennetus awoke. Allisyn stretched and yawned beside him. She looked at her hands, young and strong and bronzed by the sun. She sat up suddenly, expecting to see the toothless lion lying beside her in an impotent heap. But it was not so. Ravennetus was there, just as he had been when they fell asleep, a strong young lion in the prime of his life. He turned toward the hag and was amazed to see the beautiful Allisyn still beside him.

"I had the strangest dream," they said simultaneously, then laughed for joy that they were still young, and strong, and full of life.

"So real it seemed!" she cried, "I bethought you..."

"It was real," Ravennetus explained, "for there is another world where Deus strives for mastery over the Darkness, a place where the Now is but an illusion."

For a moment his words hung in the air, then Allisyn breathed them in and understood.

"We have gone to the Otherworld, Ravennetus. We have spoken with Thol-nys!" Allisyn said, realizing what had happened. "We have passed the test!"

"Truly," Ravennetus said. "for the beast at the gates was she, not merely a slave or a minion, but the Great Calamity herself. We have passed the Gates of Death and she can no longer bind us in the Otherworld. But she may make us pay a price in the Now for her defeat among the shadows. No matter what happens from this day forward, Allisyn, I can say with surety that I love you, with body, mind and soul, beyond all measure of time and space, and though we may meet with sorrow in this life, we will find only joy in that which comes after."

They walked on now among the rolling skirts of the mountains, whose heights reared abruptly to the west and south. For in crossing the Ultana they had come at last behind the fence of the Utlai and to the country of the daughters of Thol-nys' blood, spawned in the very birth-throes of the world. They reached a point where the Utlai thrust out its easternmost spur. Undecided on which direction to take, Ravennetus suggested they climb the last mountain to gain a view of the land. For hours they climbed while the sun sped from the eastern horizon to the zenith.   When they stood at last, sweating and spent, at the summit, the valley below them lay desolate and vast in a tremulous spasm of heat.   The earth itself seemed to gasp for breath.

Looking out over the endless desert, Allisyn despaired of their cause. Perhaps Ravennetus had been right, perhaps they should have turned back long ago. Where in this forsaken land would they find Magor? How would they ever defeat her and wrest the Horn from her head? Even if that were accomplished, how would they take it back to Aestri? She thought of the long miles they had traveled from her home and her heart sank. At her side, Ravennetus turned to the east, cupped his hands to his mouth, and shouted,

"Magor, Magor,
Come forth from your den,
The Deathless Ones here,
Your time at its end!"

He turned to the south and shouted his challenge once again, the sound of his voice falling dead upon a dead land. He sat down with Allisyn at his side and waited in the baking heat. Here, in this desert, Hanthol himself seemed a tyrant rather than a benevolent father.

Far away in a sulfurous, pock-ridden vale, in a hole larger and more despicable than the others, Magor twisted in her sleep. She was troubled by a dream, an unsettling dream of pain. Some vermin had crawled into her ear and bitten her, she thought, waking abruptly. She writhed and slapped at the side of her head with her dreadful claw and the earth trembled. She shook her head and poked it out of the filthy cavern, as if to get her bearings. The great horn came forth, followed by the shaggy green head and yellow eye. Then the pain returned, but now she knew it was not a rodent or biting thing that had invaded her ear, it was the proud words of a worthless human. Worthless, she thought, except as a meal. How long had it been since she had tasted human flesh! Someone was abroad in her land, claiming to be Deathless. The very audacity of it! *She* was the Arbiter of Death. No one could walk deathless in her

327

realm except by her consent, and she had never given it. The stinging challenge propelled her into action. She heaved her ponderous body from the hole, stood and stretched her malignant frame.

The great horn upon her head, large as a tree, was a weapon of ancient renown. It had impaled enemies both larger and stronger than the little humans that had come within her reach, but none whose flesh was more tender or whose meat was more sweet. Besides its use as a weapon, it was also her primary organ of sensing. But in this aspect it was flawed, for it sensed only what its filter of hatred and fear would allow to pass. So Magor sensed only the evil, the vulgar, the fallen things in the world, and therefore perceived that evil only existed, as her Terrible Mother had told her. She believed, she had always believed. Eyes and ears and nose she had as well, but they brought her only vague report of what transpired in the Now.

She had been a favorite of Thol-nys, this odious daughter. She had wrought havoc and had been a stinging thorn in the side of Deus and his brood. But since Deus had fenced her and her sisters behind the Utlai their opportunities to torture and cause pain were much diminished. As the creations of Deus, which they loved to rend and eat, had become scarce, they had taken to preying upon one another. Magor had grown to be the strongest, most dominant of the demons and had killed and eaten all the rest. All except for Ghrunth, who had run away. Now she alone remained and an endless hunger gnawed voraciously at her belly.

Her last great task, Thol-nys had told her, would be to murder these children of Deus, these proud ones with their fragile and infantile consciousness, and defeat His bid to conquer darkness and death in the Now. The Now was to be her's and her's alone. Her great delight would be to extinguish the sun and watch the children of Deus grow pallid and weak and finally expire, begging her for mercy, for sweet death to enfold them. Then as each of them died, the stars would go out one by one, and the darkness would be complete.

Magor thrust her horn into the ground and ripped up the earth for her pleasure. Then she thrust it high into the befouled air of her valley, bellowed, and set off to find the interlopers.

Ravennetus, first heard, then saw her coming, walking with earthshaking strides across the wasteland. The impact of her feet left craters in the ruined earth where she stepped. Still far away, she stopped and lifted her horn into the air, trying to sense the fear and hate of those she sought. But the signals she received were confused and weak and she could obtain no clear sense of their whereabouts. Maddened, she stomped the ground. Great fissures opened and fire belched upward. Again she ripped the earth with her horn, flinging boulders and great chucks of its crusty mantle into the air. She roared and the mountains echoed her malice. So frightening was she in her fit of rage, that Ravennetus and Allisyn drew back from the summit of the mountain and hid themselves in a hollow. Aha! There, there they were, the frightened ones! Now she would make them hate her. That would be their undoing. They had not changed, these puny ones, they had never been able to conquer fear and hate, and they never would. Now she would have them, just as Mother had promised!

In the dell behind the mountaintop, Ravennetus and Allisyn cowered. Never had they seen any creature so fearsome, never had they been more at a loss for what to do. Ravennetus sat dazed, wondering what had come over him. Why had he shouted the challenge before he had a plan to deal with the monster? Weaponless, he felt the finality of their lot and fell completely within her power. The frailness of his mortality settled all about him as fallen leaves settle in the brooding, still air before the onslaught of a storm.

Without knowing why, Allisyn touched the base of her neck and the eight remaining pearls began to glow. She felt their presence and their heat. She reached up and plucked the fifth pearl from the strand. Then without a shred of fear, she stood and spoke in a loud, clear voice.

"This is *Coras*, the pearl of Courage. Thus courage is ours, but not the courage we have known, not the courage that comes from strength of mortal arms or power of intellect, not the ordinary courage of man, but the courage that comes from Deus. This is courage born of faith, of humility, a courage that comes from the certainty that Deus stands with us and that in the end, His outcome is sure. This is courage of the uncommon variety, courage born of weakness, not of strength, born of love and not of power. With such courage, we may indeed conquer death!"

The light of Coras enveloped them and they ran to the top of the mountain, shining, magnificent, free of fear, filled with the courage of love, unencumbered by hate.

Magor was again confused, having lost the sense of her

prey. She had thought they were there behind the mountain. But now the mountain was cloaked in a white mist and out of the mist came a blinding bright light. Within it, she could sense nothing. The fear was gone. She smashed at the mist on the summit with a knotted claw. She whirled about, tossing her head, slashing at the white vapor with her horn, but in futility. She was truly enraged now. With boiling anger she lashed out, searching, sensing, feeling with her onerous appendage, sniffing for the odor of fear, listening for cries of misery, watching for signs of retaliation and hate, but found none.

Then as Magor breathed, the white vapor entered her lungs. It clutched at her heart with freezing fingers, eating away at her brain, penetrating its dark recesses and bringing light to an abyss that had never before known light. She swooned and stumbled. She roared but not with the searing malice that had always sustained her. It was more a call than a roar, a cry of uncertainty, of desertion, of forsakeness. She lurched forward and stumbled. Her head went down and the tip of the horn struck the ground. It broke free from her head and tumbled, end over end. She fell after it and upon it. The horn ripped upward through her belly, pierced her heart and emerged out her back. Her dying scream filled all the land. It echoed from the mountains. Hillsides slid and boulders tumbled. Trees fell. Smoking rents opened in the earth and poured forth choking vapors. The skies opened and a black rain fell. Dark clouds rolled past the sun, blotting out its light and the blackness of night fell upon the landscape.

Ravennetus and Allisyn felt the nauseating lurch of the earth beneath their feet and fell to the ground. All about them the ground heaved and rolled. The mountain they lay upon convulsed. Then the heavens reeled and went black, leaving them adrift on a dark sea.

They awoke to a land altered. The earth was a sea of boulders and rubble. Strewn here and there were the charred remains of gigantic trees as if a scorching tongue of flame had passed over the earth, violating everything it touched. The mountain they had stood upon was gone. They picked themselves up and walked toward the point they had last seen Magor. Sudden rents and caverns loomed before them, dark holes having no discernible bottoms, ridges of slag and the broken bones of the earth reared precipitously across their path. In the hollows, poisonous vapors lurked and reached out for them, wraith-like, as they moved past. Stumbling forward on trembling, aching legs, bruised and scraped raw by the sharp stones, they at last came to the grave of Magor.

She lay in a bowl of crushed stone created of her own fall, twisted and ugly, in death as in life. Then, even as they looked, the flesh melted away until only her bones remained. Her spike rose from the bottom of the hollow through the mist and the arches of her ribcage, past her splintered spine, and jutted menacingly into the sky, towering above the heads of the onlookers. They felt as though they stood at the door of some ancient temple, awesome in its profanity.

Together they crawled down the slope, slipping on loose stones, until they came to the level bottom. From there they walked forward toward the Horn, through the gates formed by the immense ribs of Magor. The sun's rays seemed pale and cold here. Allisyn paused and caught Ravennetus by the arm. Her eyes pleaded with him not to go on; she knew not why. He stopped for a moment, questioning, then turned back to the Horn. He seemed to be drawn irresistibly forward. He walked on alone until he stood beside it. Its surface was smooth and gray-white in color, its arching tip pierced the sky, many times Ravennetus' own height above his head. Its was rooted firmly in the rubble at his feet, its girth such that he could not reach around it with his arms.

He pondered their dilemma. How would they remove it? How would they get it back to Aestri? He reached out to touch it but hesitated, a voice within seeming to caution against it. Finally, conquering all apprehension, he bent his knees, wrapped his arms about the Horn and placed his shoulder against it. He pulled upward with all his strength but the Horn did not move. He pushed against it with all his mien but the Horn remained implacably rooted in the ground. There was no sound. He turned to face Allisyn, placing his back against the Horn, and closed his eyes to think.

Allisyn watched Ravennetus' face. She knew what was going through his mind and she pitied him. She pitied herself. She closed her own eyes for a moment. The silence was palpable. She remembered how she had felt as a little girl when she hid from her mother behind a tapestry. It was dark and the tapestry deadened every sound. She could hear only the beating of her heart. Voices seemed far away and muffled, as though she had been lowered into a grave. Frightened, she had tried to escape but the weight of the shroud had pinned her to the wall. She screamed but the sound of it died around her. Her breath had seemed cut off as though suddenly all the air was gone. She had panicked.

Frightened by her recollection, Allisyn opened her eyes to see a that black mist had seeped from the ground. At the distance of a few paces she could barely see Ravennetus. She called out to him but the sound fell impotently about her. She tried to run forward to him but every step seemed to require an expenditure of energy too great. She forced her legs to move. She forced the air from her lungs to shout. She gained her lover's side. At her touch he opened his eyes. She dragged him away from the Horn, step by weighty step.

The mist began to swirl, slowly at first, now gaining momentum, now rushing at whirlwind force around the saucer in which the bones of the terrible Magor lay. Guessing their peril, Ravennetus and Allisyn started to run. A vortex opened around the base of the Horn. First ashes, then dust, stones, and boulders were sucked into the black gullet. The Horn began slowly to sink downward, the bones of the ribs toppled and began to revolve in the black hurricane. Soon the whole skeleton was moving, wheeling, sinking, passing out of the Now. The wind tugged at the clothes of Allisyn and Ravennetus. It blew inward toward the vortex from all directions with the force of a gale, threatening to pull them in. They struggled against it, pelted by a rain of stinging dust and stones. Allisyn lost her balance and was swept from her feet, tumbling toward the gaping pit, clutching in vain at sliding stones. Ravennetus caught her and pulled her back to her feet. They ran again. Impossibly, the wind increased. Now they could no longer stand. They dropped to the ground and crawled along the serrated surface, reptile-like, away from the sucking, grinding hole. The wind, the echo of Magor's death scream, was dragged howling back to be with her in everlasting night. The lovers scratched and clawed their way to a low ridge where they tumbled, battered and bleeding, down the other side.

Almost immediately, the wind dropped. Catching their breath, they peered over the ridge and back into the pit. Nothing remained. A few stones tumbled down the steep sides into what

332

had been the whirling vortex at the center.

"The Horn is gone," Ravennetus said finally. "Now all we have struggled to obtain, all for which we labored, has disappeared in but a moment. What shall we do?"

Chapter 31
Return to Aestri

In the end there was nothing to do but return, unfulfilled and empty-handed. Reality had turned out very differently for Ravennetus than his dream, for he had thought to return in triumph, bearing the Horn of Magor, claiming the beautiful Allisyn as his own, banishing the evil Barthol from Aestri and reestablishing peace in the house of her father. Now he must return defeated in the eyes of men, an object of their scorn rather than of their veneration, to an uncertain fate.

Allisyn and Ravennetus walked westward through the mountains, skirting to the south the headwaters of the dread Ultana, the River of Dark Dreams. They gazed across the swampy mouth of the Nina and mourned the death of the faithful Mataforas. They crossed the cold Fila and with weary steps came at last to the pristine headwaters of the Lenai. There, with yielding, slender boughs of willow, Ravennetus lashed together fallen trees to make a raft. With failing strength they floated downriver amid falling leaves under powder-blue autumn skies. At the eastern edge of the table of Vinsa, under the compassionate eye of the Stag Moon, the raft swirled in an eddy and drifted to the south shore where it went aground in the shallows. In the cold hours before dawn, Allisyn awoke shivering to the rhythmic lapping of the waters against their vessel. She jostled her companion awake and they pulled themselves from the water, gaunt and worn. Ravennetus tugged on the raft and beached it a handsbreadth higher on the sandy bar. In the night as they slept again, the river rose, eased it from the shore, and floated it out of sight and reckoning.

The next morning the couple awoke to the musical song of ravens. Randor sat nearby in a tall cedar. When the travelers had refreshed themselves in the sympathetic waters of the Lenai, the venerable bird led them back to the peaceful valley among the bird-people, where they once again passed the long winter.

In that time Ravennetus and Allisyn tended to their physical needs for the long days of walking and privation had taken their toll. When they were strong once more they undertook the mending of their spirits. They spent the endless winter nights in the high caves by a blazing fire, talking about what had been and dreaming about what might be. In the depths of winter, Allisyn discovered she was carrying their child. She and Ravennetus watched in patient wonder as the baby grew inside her. In the spring, Randor and Cora hatched out two fine sons. Corvus and Corax they called them. Allisyn gave birth to a daughter and they called her Daena.

It was a time of immense inner struggle and reflection for Ravennetus. There was much to consider. He now had a family to nurture and it seemed fitting that his first allegiance should be to them. But he was troubled by the nature of his yet unrevealed duty to Deus and the path that he should take to discover and fulfill it. To further muddle his thoughts, he felt the tug of his oath to Aefalas and the unfinished business in Aestri. He had taken the king's daughter, had traveled to the limits of the earth and had a child with her, all without fulfilling his oath. Aefalas' wrath would be great, yet he felt he must go back, as Allisyn herself had desired, and face the consequences, no matter that they were undeserved; otherwise he would be forever banned from Aestri.

When Allisyn felt in her soul that the time had come, she gave Ravennetus the three remaining pearls of the second quartet, *Respiceres*, the pearl of Respect, *Carus*, the pearl of Caring, and *Responsus*, the pearl of Responsibility.

"With the pearl of Respect, Ravennetus, you are called upon to respect not only the life of your daughter as the sacred gift of Deus, but the sanctity of all life and the inherent value of the every man, woman, and child. Each of us comes into the Now with the rank of a child, a child of Deus, and we take nothing more when we leave. Respect means to look to the inner value of each person and treat them accordingly.

"With the pearl of Caring, you are called to reach out to those who need your strength and wisdom, just as you will

335

reach out to take the hand of your daughter, helping her to take her first steps. The pearl of Caring calls you to attend to the needs of humanity with the same sense of purpose that you care for your own, or mine, or little Daena's.

"With the pearl of Responsibility, you are called to love and care for yourself. But as the bearer of the wisdom of Deus to humankind, you are called to love and care for others; meaning that you should share this wisdom, caring for them, leading them, nurturing them, protecting them, sheltering them, as the hen takes her chicks under her wing at the approach of the fox. Because you are the first, you must light the way for the rest. You have been given great gifts and you are not to abuse them, nor keep them to yourself for your sole benefit. Indeed, the Pearls have no value unless their gifts are given to others. You are called to bring the people together in Deus, and bind them with the love of Deus, that the children may know their Father and Mother."

In the summer when Daena was old enough to travel, Ravennetus and Allisyn, accompanied by Randor, Cora and the youthful Corvus and Corax, set off westward once again. Ravennetus had resolved to take his family to Horen where Bronwyn would be waiting for them. There they would remain in safety while he went to Aestri to stand before Aefalas, to explain the disappearance of his daughter, to tell him the story of the Horn, and to claim Allisyn by right of his fealty to Aefalas and to the task, though he had come back empty-handed.

Bronwyn was overcome with joy to see them. It gathered in blissful tears behind her eyelids and rolled down her cheeks when she tried to speak.

"Oooh, Allisyn... may I?" she asked, quivering with excitement when the words would come, reaching out for the child. She took the warm bundle and gently pressed it to her neck. The baby smiled and reached up to touch Bronwyn's cheek. Thereafter, when not in her own mother's arms, Daena was happiest being coddled by Bronwyn.

When the tale of their ordeal was told and they had taken a much needed rest, Ravennetus announced his intention to go to Aestri, making known his desire that Allisyn should stay behind with Daena and Bronwyn in Horen, beyond the reach of Barthol and Tandela. But Allisyn had determined to go with him and would not be gainsaid.

"I cannot let you go, my love," Ravennetus insisted. "It is too dangerous. Deus knows what has transpired there and what the outcome will be. Stay here in safety. We have Daena to consider now. Stay with her."

"I have thought through all of that. It breaks my heart to leave her but I know that she will be safe with Bronwyn. I have trusted my handmaid often with my own life, and I will trust her now with the life of my daughter."

"But why must you go back?" he required. "Your future is not there."

"No, husband, but the unfinished business of the past is there. Father is there and he needs me. I cannot forsake him, not if there is a chance to save him.

"He has not loved you well."

"Perhaps not, but is that any reason for me not to love him now? We have been given a great gift, Ravennetus, and a charge. The work we must do concerns Barthol and Tandela. The work of Deus is in Faenwys, not here in Horen. Do you deny that this burden is laid on me as well as you? I want to be be with my child, Ravennetus, but I want to be with you as well. I cannot do both and I have made my choice. Only in unity," she repeated, reminding him of the words of Randor.

And so they set off afoot, walking over the plains and hills and up the long Valley Droemen, coming at last to the high Bridge of Vapors over the Mergruen, the River of Long Memory, and so to the gates of Faenwys.

The gates were closed against them, but Allisyn made herself known to the surprised gate wardens and they were admitted. A runner was immediately dispatched to Aefalas, another to Tandela. The rumor of their coming fanned out like waves in all directions. Walking through the City, they attracted a group of chattering followers that swelled in number as they went. The people whispered at the changes in their own Allisyn and at the stolid courage and self-assurance that marked the young man at her side. By the time they had passed through the inner wall the crowd of curious citizenry had swelled to a throng.

"Look how tall she has grown!" someone said.

337

"Aye, a match for the queen, I'll warrant," said another. "Look at her eyes!"

"Are you daft? She won't last a minute against that witch."

"Too true," added someone else, "they'll rue the day they returned."

"Long live the Princess Allisyn! Here she comes! And look there, at her side, the bright one who stole her away! Or so they say. He looks grand. Perhaps he will set things right in the palace!"

Ravennetus hailed the door wardens of the Great Hall of Aestri, stated their business, and the two of them were admitted to the vast, reverberant chamber. At the far end sat Aefalas, just as when they had departed. His head was erect, his jaw set, but his mind, having been held so long in the clutches of Tandela and Barthol, had shriveled. His cape was swept back over his shoulders revealing the gleam of his breastplate. Watching his daughter approach Aefalas' thoughts inexplicably drifted from his purpose. For a moment he forgot where he was and why he was there.

Seated beside the king was Tandela, outwardly indifferent, inwardly seething. Behind her and to her right stood Barthol, his quick eyes sizing up the approaching pair. The aura that shimmered about them as they walked and their proud demeanor galled him. He thrust his malice forward, resisting their every step. Bors stood impassively by at the foot of the steps.

Ravennetus and Allisyn strode forward undaunted. The crowd spilled into the hall behind them, squeezing themselves into the boxes between the central pillars and the outer walls, eager to hear the report of the young man who had been gone now these two years and to find out the truth about the disappearance of their princess. The roar of their debate rose to the vaulted roof. Aefalas' brow was dark and furrowed. Ravennetus raised his hand in greeting. The clamor trailed off to a low, expectant buzz. The young man spoke.

"Hail Aefalas, King of Aestri. I have returned to claim the hand of your daughter Allisyn!" he said so that all might hear.

"Why would the criminal return to the scene of the crime, and with the victim?" Barthol interjected, glowering at the shining ones before him.

"I did not abduct her, Aefalas," Ravennetus answered, not deigning to speak to Barthol directly.

"It this true?" Aefalas asked his daughter.

338

"It is true, Father," she replied. "When he left I followed him. He was unaware of my going."

"But why?" Aefalas asked his daughter stridently.

"I needed to be with him, to aid him in his quest!"

Barthol, amused by Allisyn's answer, as was her cousin, the queen, laughed aloud. A nervous but subdued titter wafted through the crowd. Aefalas' face remained stern.

"What sort of man is this, Aefalas, that he requires the assistance of a woman to fight his battles?" Barthol sneered. Then he turned once more to Ravennetus. "I do not doubt that you have failed in your quest, if indeed you ever attempted it. For I see that you do not bring the Horn of Magor with you, the prize that Aefalas requested in exchange for his daughter's hand."

"Where is the Horn?" asked Aefalas.

"I do not have it," Ravennetus replied.

"So I thought!" interjected Barthol.

"Silence!" cried Aefalas. Barthol glared at the king. "Then why have you returned?"

"So as not to dishonor myself, Lord."

"Honor," Aefalas said vacantly, mechanically. *He had heard that word before but could not recall where; he must ask Vaalta about it when he saw her next.* Barthol took a step toward him and Aefalas came back to his senses suddenly. "Speak then!" the king growled.

"Lord Aefalas, we quested for the horn and came to the land that lies east of the Utlai, a realm of dread, to the lair of Magor. We did battle with her and she died, impaling herself upon the very Horn we sought. But, alas, a black mist formed about her in her death, the ground opened and a whirlwind came, dragging her remains, along with the prized Horn, into the earth."

"Impaled herself? Sucked into the ground?" roared Barthol with a laugh so incredulous and infectious that soon the entire company had joined in his derision.

"Do you think this is some great jest, boy?" Aefalas asked uncomfortably. "Do you take me for a fool? Answer true, for your life may depend upon it!"

"I swear that it is true, with Deus and your daughter Allisyn as my witnesses."

"Poor witnesses, imbecile, one the figment of a deluded imagination and the other your accomplice!" Tandela barked. "We do not believe in this false god here, or have you not seen

339

the altar to Thol-nys, the goddess of this City. If you swear, then you must swear by her. Then for my part, I will believe you."

"He will not swear by Thol-nys, Tandela," Barthol announced.

"For once you are right Barthol, for to swear by her would be to recognize her authority, and I do not. There is only one true God and his name is Deus," Ravennetus challenged.

"Blasphemer!" Tandela shouted. "Now you have outwitted yourself, boy. For things have changed in this City since you have been away. There is a penalty for blasphemy of the goddess and that penalty is death! Are you prepared then to die? Or will you recant?"

"He will not recant!" Allisyn answered for him. "And I shall add my voice to his, for what he says is true. There is no God but Deus, and the fact that we passed the Gates of Death and returned to the Now is proof of it!"

"Stop! Stop!" shouted Aefalas, standing, realizing where Tandela was headed with her threats. *He did not wish his daughter to die. He could not remember why. Had he remembered to tell the Master of Hounds to feed the dogs? The bothersome boy was another matter.* Out of the corner of his eye he saw his detestable bride, leaning forward, leering at Allisyn. *Oh, to be rid of her for good!* Looming behind her, a black blight on the periphery of his vision, was Barthol. *He had promised him his own daughter, had he not? Was freedom from Tandela worth that price? Could Barthol be trusted? Would he make good his word?*

"This is no religious debate," Aefalas said with sudden clarity and authority. "We are met for one purpose only, to determine whether the boy shall have the hand of Allisyn." He turned to Ravennetus.

"You promised to bring back the Horn of Magor. You have not done so. Whether you abducted her, or whether she followed you, you have lived with my daughter without my permission. Explain yourself!"

"We have told you the truth of it, Aefalas. Allisyn came to aid me of her own will. We have no further explanations to make. But I would ask a question of you, Aefalas. Why did you send me on an impossible quest to meet my death? Why did you desire it? Explain this to me!"

"Do not be impertinent, boy!" Tandela warned.

"Silence Tandela!" Allisyn flashed back. The light that had gently glowed about her suddenly flared. "Do not speak to us of impertinence. You, who had the impertinence to seize the reins of the Council when my mother was killed, to coil yourself about my father, to carve the tongue of the prophetess of the One God, to bring this black-hearted dog to Aestri as your counselor, to establish the worship of evil in the city of our mothers. Bow down before Deus, repent of your evil in the presence of the light of truth."

Tandela rose to her feet.

"You have gone too far this time, cousin!" she spat, advancing down the steps toward Allisyn. "You have been a thorn in my side too long. I should have dealt with you long ago. I *will* deal with you now!"

"Stand back, Tandela," Barthol intervened, his eyes darting toward Aefalas, then to Bors. He advanced to the king's side and placed his hand on Aefalas' shoulder. The king slumped back onto his throne with a sigh, as if the strain of the proceedings had been too much for him. Meanwhile Bors crossed in front of the dais and placed himself between Tandela and Allisyn.

Seeing how Barthol had moved his players upon the board, Ravennetus spoke.

"You seem to have situated yourself well here, Barthol," Ravennetus said. Barthol nodded and a thin smile crossed his lips, accepting his adversary's sarcasm as a compliment. "You have extended your influence over Aefalas as well as Tandela."

"You perceive well, brother. The weight of rule sits too gravely upon our good Aefalas at times. And in those times he has come to lean most heavily upon me for counsel. You have kept our Allisyn from us and it has contributed greatly to our suffering," Barthol said, laying his hand upon Aefalas' head with feigned gentleness.

Tandela whirled around and returned to her throne. She sat down in obvious disgust and glared at Barthol, then turned back to Ravennetus and Allisyn. "You have committed treason and in Aestri the penalty for treason is death."

"No! Allisyn shouted. "He has committed no treason! For your own sake, Barthol, if that is all you care about, do not add murder to your list of sins."

Barthol chuckled at her naivete. From an unidentifiable quarter, a whisper began to drift through the crowd. It rose to a

341

dull rumble, punctuated by occasional cries, as lightning crashes over the report of distant thunder.

"Free them!" a voice shouted.

"Yes, let them go. They have done nothing!"

Barthol whipped his head around to silence the assembly.

"Allisyn, Allisyn, Aestri for the Princess Allisyn!"

"Yes, yes, Allisyn!"

Now Tandela too, stood, angered by the rabble. On a signal from Bors, guards ran throughout the length of the hall, positioning themselves to control the increasingly restless mob. Incensed by the haughtiness of the soldiers, the crowd began to surge inward toward Ravennetus and Allisyn, pushing the line of guards before them. Distracted by the fray, neither Tandela nor Barthol noticed that Aefalas had risen from his seat. When he raised his arms, the mob stopped moving and quieted.

"The rule of law is the mark of a great people and has long been valued by both the monarchs and the subjects of Aestri," Aefalas proclaimed. "The people have discerned the truth in this matter and they have spoken. Therefore I will pronounce the joint will of the people and their monarch. My daughter Allisyn... is to be held blameless... and will be reinstated to her rightful place in my house." He paused for a moment to collect his wits. Barthol took the chance to draw close to the king's side and latch onto his will, stifling whatever independent thought the foundering man might have mustered.

"The young man, Ravennetus... is... to be... banished... from Aestri. He is hereby... dispossessed... of my daughter. From this time forward she will be under the guardianship... of Barthol and she will never see the man Ravennetus again, so long as she shall live!"

"What?!" Tandela screeched.

"No, Father, not this, no!!!" Allisyn screamed, reaching out instinctively for her lover. Ravennetus thrust out his hand and grabbed hers, but Aefalas' guards, many and strong, held him fast and dragged him inevitably away. Others pinioned Allisyn, pulling her in the opposite direction.

"Do not let go, Allisyn. Hold on to me, always!" Ravennetus cried.

"I am trying... Oh Deus, I shall!" Allisyn called to him between gasps for air. They held hands as long as they could, until the powers that sought to sunder all humankind had separated them finally.

342

Ravennetus was bound and led by armed guards through the City. The curious citizenry followed. They had secured the freedom of their beloved princess. The banishment of the young interloper seemed a fair trade for it. Perhaps it was only natural that the little steam that remained in their kettle was finally vented on him.

"Got the Horn he did, but it was sucked down into a great hole!" someone prated.

"Tripped and fell on her own horn!" cackled another, mimicking the sarcasm of Barthol.

He was taken to the ironsmith, pushed to his knees before the forge, and forced to watch as the smith fanned the coals with his bellows until they were red-hot. He saw the branding iron placed in the midst of the coals. The smith turned it until it had absorbed the heat of the embers and glowed bright orange. With deliberate movements, a soldier removed it from the fire and brought it to within an inch of Ravennetus' forehead. Sweat beaded and the oils of his skin surfaced and sizzled. He closed his eyes and asked Deus for strength. The soldier set the brand to Ravennetus' brow. His body quaked but he did not cry out. When the soldier pulled the iron away from the sticky flesh, Ravennetus bore the mark of banishment from Aestri. In the castle, Barthol sensed his brother's agony and gloated.

The taunting and jeering accompanied Ravennetus through the outer walls and onto the Droemenvale Roed, but it was now only a dissonant shell around the core of pain that burned between his eyes. When the entourage arrived at the Bridge of Vapors only a few boys remained, but they hurled insults no less painful. Ravennetus did not hear them.

The guards marched him back up the Droemen to the frontier where they read the order of banishment. They threw him forward into the dust, then turned and marched back to the City, leaving him utterly alone. Long he lay in the road, until the shadows of the trees had crossed it, until night fell and the stars winked open, until the morning dews had soaked his clothes and evaporated. But the pain, neither the burning spike in his forehead, nor the prospect of life-long separation from his beloved, would leave him.

For days he wandered aimlessly, trying to forget, trying to banish the pain, purge it, starve it out. He found himself by the ocean, but the surge of the tide, the white caps and the spray only reminded him of Mataforas and another, older pain. He

343

walked on without destination for many weeks, often in circles, his mind a wasteland and his body wracked with hunger.

Patrolling the borders of Aestri from the sky, Corvus and Corax, who loved to fly far and high, discovered him and rushed back on tireless wings to tell their father. Randor came and found his son near death, lying upon a stone, his face burned red by the sun, his brow infected and swollen. He fed Ravennetus from his own mouth and tried to comfort him with gentle words.

"Do you remember what I told you from the beginning?" asked the great bird. "That your joining with Allisyn would be the end of your search but not the end of your sorrow? It is the fate of man to suffer, Ravennetus. But all suffering has a purpose. For out of it comes change, out of death comes new life. Take heart, for it may be that you will see your beloved yet again. But do not look back for her. She is not there, not as she was, not as you knew her before, for things will never be as they were. There is another. Think of your daughter. She needs you now, more than ever, for I fear that she may never know her true mother. You must give her what she needs to grow and thrive. She is your responsibility, she needs your love and your care. But you cannot love her as a father if you do not love yourself, nor care for her if you do not care for yourself."

The words of Allisyn as she bestowed the last three pearls came back to Ravennetus now and he lifted his head. Randor saw once again the glimmer of life and hope in his eyes.

"Come," the raven said. "Let us go to her."

Chapter 32
The World Dream

Ravennetus traveled to Horen by a slow and deliberate road. Although the summer was full about him, his eyes and his heart perceived only a ravaged waste. Ravennetus had suffered far beyond his years and pain lay on him like a shadow that would not lift. Randor was deeply concerned, for his son had the look of one whose heart, mind and spirit were broken beyond the skill of any to heal, save Deus. They walked slowly through the forest, Randor sitting upon Ravennetus' shoulders, counseling, teaching. Long he sat. To Ravennetus, the bird's weight seemed to grow and the talons to dig into his flesh. The bereaved one felt this new pain dawn within him, but it did not matter any more, there were so many pains he had already endured. Patiently he bore the bird. In time, he sang as he walked. He sang a song to take his mind from his grief, the song of his life, the song of his years, a song of things dark and bitter, of despair, of suffering and of understanding.

Still Randor sat upon his shoulders and the talons dug further into his flesh, biting Ravennetus' bones, gripping him like claws of iron. Under the influence of this new and exquisite pain he forgot the brand-wound in his forehead. The burden of the raven bowed his back. The pain crept throughout his body, and his steps slowed. His singing ceased. The trees became as shadows, the world about him seemed to fade, becoming misty, ethereal. The only thing that remained in his consciousness was this new pain. He bent until he could bend no further. At last he crumpled to the ground and cried out, "Father, why do you torture me? Why this suffering? Why always grief and sadness

345

in this life? Please go, go Father, leave me and let me die. Better to die than to suffer and to make others suffer. Better not to live than to ruin and misdirect the lives of those I love because of my ignorance, my pride, my honor, of all things most worthless now."

A bright light suddenly shone upon them both. It filled the dark forest of his wandering grief, vibrating, scorching out all other light, sound and reality. Ravennetus groped along the ground, blinded by its intensity. A voice came out of the light, or out of the mouth of Randor, he was not sure. "Behold," it said, "I will show you a mystery."

Then still clutching the man, Randor lifted them both skyward, beating his purple wings, feeling the tension in his bones and ligaments, the wind among his feathers, the enormous weight of the man beneath him. Slowly he pulled away from the earth, bearing the burden of the man and his pain aloft, up through the green fingers of the trees, through the mists that lay close to the earth, through a region of screaming winds, through zones of numbing cold and searing heat. Higher and higher he flew until the sky lost its color and the earth below faded into a formless gray.

And still Randor flew on. When Ravennetus awoke he lay on a rocky ledge of a high mountain. Above him was a deep blue void, below him the shoulders of the mountain faded into mist, the vapors of the great river that enfolded the world. He was upon the other side. The effect of the intense light, brighter than the sun, had passed and he could see again, though not with his mortal eyes, not with eyes that looked at all through the veil of sorrow and suffering; but with new eyes. For the illusions of life had been stripped away and he saw things as they truly were, and are, and would be.

Randor spoke.

"Ravennetus, wisest of mortal men, chosen of Deus. He will teach you much that you do not know and show you much that you have not seen. Wisdom is a heavy burden and vision multiplies its weight. Wisdom and vision will sit upon your shoulders as a great bird that will not depart. But they cannot be escaped or put aside once you have been shown. Do you desire the wisdom of Deus? Do you desire his vision? Then look!"

Ravennetus looked to where Randor stretched out his wing. The mists below them began to swirl, the winds to speak. The icy vortex pulled at him as though it yearned to strip the very

346

flesh from his bones. With the look of one who has lost all, he let go the ledge and was blown off into the swirling funnel, spinning, tumbling, falling out of control, the metaphor of his life. As he fell he began to see visions.

The visions were first of his own time in the Now. He recognized the music of the song of his life, so recently sung. But he also saw other versions of his life, heard other music, as if viewed by someone else from another perspective. In some he was venerated and loved. In some his was cursed and reviled. Then he realized that none of the visions, least of all that which he saw through his own eyes, were true. He saw a final version and realized this was his life as seen through the eyes of Deus, and that it was true. He saw the true significance of his failures and successes. Some things he had thought to be of the least importance, a kind word, an act of unselfish giving, were elevated among his great deeds. And those he bethought far-reaching and of great import were counted among the least. For these had been born of arrogance, the selfish taking of that which was not truly his.

Then he saw, from beginning to end, the whole of the existence of his spirit. That portion which he spent in the Now and the flesh was but an instant. He saw the infancy of his consciousness, the growth, the change, the dependency on the Mother, the breaking away, the fearful hiding, the swelling pride and independence, the gathering together of kindred spirits in defiance of the old ways, the challenge, the harsh words, the fighting, the killing, the mountaintop upon which he stood when he declared "I am I".

He saw the fallen pride, the questioning, the searching for his Mother; he felt the joy of finding her and the sadness when he realized she could no longer hold him in her arms, the search for his Father, the cognition of the meaning of life. He saw the long road which led back to Deus, the mother / father, the light and the dark pitted against one another, and finally, at the end of all things, the light accepting, embracing the darkness. He fled blissfully into the light.

In the midst of this vision he beheld his beloved Allisyn. He recalled their first meeting, the blissful years of their freedom, their search for the Horn of Magor and their last parting in the Great Hall of Aefalas. But he saw more, scenes from their life yet to come. He saw her death, the moment of her passing to the Otherworld. She stood upon a high bridge over a dark and

347

perilous chasm, like a beam of moonlight on a dark sea. Daena was in danger nearby. He must choose between them, save the one and the let the other go. He witnessed the choice that he made and the consequence of his choice.

He beheld the beginning of all things. He saw the mother / father, Osinniso, turn herself inside out, witnessed the birth of the twins Osyn and Nyso, and the creation of the universe. He watched as Nyso divided into darkness and light, saw Han-nys nurse the infant Osyn and saw Osyn become strong and beautiful as Han-nys faded. He watched as the battle raged between Osyn and Thol-nys, witnessed their wrestling and their falling into the Great Sea, their strangling, clutching, tearing fight in the depths. He saw Deus rise from the blackness, saw the sun burst into the skies of the first dawn, saw the moon running before Hanthol, urging him on, encouraging him, consoling him, mirroring Hanthol to himself, showing him the way across the trackless heavens. And he saw more. He saw the last battle of Deus and Thol-nys and the final outcome, the end of all things.

Then in a divine epiphany, he realized that the history of God and the history of man were one in the same, happening at the same time, one the mirror of the other, a beautiful, hopeful dance through the known and the unknown, preconceived by the divine partner and discovered by the mortal one as it unfolded. He watched it as a play upon a stage. There was a moment when the man deigned to dance way on his own, even to dance with the Dark One. Then there was great danger. But Deus gently bound the man with a girdle of Pearls and drew him back into the dance. And Ravennetus realized that moment had come to him, now.

Then the vision changed and he saw that he stood first in a long line of souls. Now he was in the play, on the stage itself. Some souls were near him and some were far behind in a long queue that stretched back into the darkness. His burden and joy was to teach the dance, show and pattern and illuminate the path with the Pearls that he held. But there were many souls and he could not help them all. So he must teach others to become teachers, and each of the teachers must make teachers of others, thus bringing all out of the darkness to the light and binding them with the Pearls.

The vision changed yet again and he saw his own life woven into the web of all things, of the Now and the Otherworld, of the seen and the unseen. He saw the times and places where the veil was pierced and those who passed between. He saw the times he himself had passed and would pass between. He stood upon a hill in a thunderbolt with his father Brahan, with Allisyn at the Gates of Death, upon a mountain speaking with a man who lay upon a rock, giving a treasure box to a boy, embracing his beloved in a flash of dazzling light.

The visions came and went, faster and faster they swirled until color bled upon color, form melted upon form, and in the end, there was no color, no form, nothing but the light of Deus. Then he was grounded once again on the forest floor. Randor revealed his thought to his son, mind to mind.

"Deus has given you the greatest of gifts, and the greatest of opportunities, Ravennetus. To you he has shown the World Dream, the revelation of the Now, the way things have been, and are, and will be. You are the first, and within the lifetime of your spirit, you will experience the total evolution of man, his body and soul. Your life will span that evolution from the beginning to the end. In you, Ravennetus, Deus has planned and perfected the evolution of man, from creation, to separation, to reunion. He has shown you the history and future of Himself, which is the history and future of humankind. Deus has chosen to play the divine music, to dance the divine dance, with you. You must show it to others so that they may come at last into the light. This is your duty and your obligation, yet it is your choice. For Deus does not force it upon you. He desires, above all, that you choose it freely of your own will."

Ravennetus walked on now with Randor, realizing his life had changed yet again. The pain was gone, the suffering was behind him. The searching was past. Now he saw before him the true path. There was but one divergence in that path and he stood at the parting of the ways. The one way was marked by a sign that read 'To Serve Deus' and the other had a sign that read 'To Serve Death'. He must go one way or the other, for the paths diverged forever and once embarked, there was no turning back. On the surface it seemed any easy choice but he found he was not yet ready.

He reached the village of Horen and knocked upon the door of the house where Bronwyn rocked his infant daughter. She opened it and gasped. Before her stood the man she knew as Ravennetus, yet he looked older, far older. He leaned upon a staff and smiled at her. She took his arm and led him to a chair by the fire where he sat long, saying nothing. She brought him soup and a small loaf. When he had eaten, he looked at Bronwyn and spoke.

"Where is she?"

Bronwyn brought the sleeping Daena from her cradle and placed her in her father's arms. He rocked her gently and fell asleep before the fire. It was evening when the restless cries and the shaking of Daena's tiny fists woke him. Ravennetus handed her back to Bronwyn. A wet nurse came and fed her. Then Daena calmed down, her little belly taut and warm, and she yielded once again to sleep. As they sat before the fire, Ravennetus told Bronwyn the sorrowful story, of his arrival with Allisyn in Aestri, of the tribunal of Aefalas, of the curse of his banishment from Aestri forever, and of the dreadful fate of Allisyn, to be placed under the suffocating guardianship of Barthol. They wept together as the tale unfolded to its pitiful end. He told her everything except for the passage to the Otherworld and the unveiling of the World Dream. For he had not yet chosen the path he would take.

When the tale was ended, Bronwyn rose and went into the spartan bedroom. She returned carrying an unadorned leather pouch. Sitting back down she looked deeply into Ravennetus' eyes.

"Allisyn asked me to keep this for her. She said that if you returned from Aestri and she did not, I should give it to you."

She took Ravennetus' hand, turned it upward, then gently opened it. Untying the leather thong that held the pouch closed she poured its contents into her visitor's waiting palm; four pearls, the last quartet. They were large and round and appeared in the firelight to be four infant moons, but they shone not. He looked questioningly into Bronwyn's blank, colorless eyes. Feeling his stare, she continued.

"My lady said that when you, and only you, had discovered their names, then their light would return. She feared they would fall into the hands of Barthol. She said that you must go on, without... without her... if need be," Bronwyn stammered with difficulty, then was quiet.

Ravennetus looked at the pearls and rolled them about in his hand, feeling their roundness, their coolness, their perfection.

And his difficult choice was made.

"Bronwyn, you must be mother and father to Daena, for she may know no other. You know that I must go. I do not wish to leave her but I must. Allisyn made such a choice and I must make it now. There may come a time when Allisyn, when I, will come once again to this door, and knock upon it, and enfold her in our arms. Yet..."

He did not finish. Taking a candle from the low mantle he walked into Daena's room and spoke with her for a long time while she slept. Then he placed the candle at the head of her bed and watched her sleep for a beautiful, sad and protracted moment in its flickering glow. Returning quietly into the next room, he kissed Bronwyn on the forehead and slipped away into the night.

Part IV

Chapter 33
The Miracle

"It is good for you to be here, my son, if you intend to dedicate your life to Deus," Randor said approvingly.

"I have thought it over much, Randor, as we have wandered. I feel led to this place near your holy mountain, Braemara, my first home, where I was raised by the lioness. It is near my second home, the village of the Cyryn. It is near the source of the Vahlen, that flows to the sea through the Dacon, the land of my brothers. But most importantly, it is here, atop this summit, that I feel very close to Deus. I feel His presence in the stones and the earth, His breath in the breeze. I hear His voice in the music of the springs on the mountainside," Ravennetus mused. "I believe with all my heart I have chosen the true way and I will wait for a sign that will affirm me."

"Then let it be so," Randor announced. "Here you will build the House of Deus. Here you will gather his people, the people of the Light. I will make the cedar forests which surround the summit the home of my own people. Hethraven we will call it."

"But how will you begin? You are only one. To build a temple to Deus and a center of wisdom and worship will take many strong hands. It will take the work of stonewrights and smiths, of laborers and artisans. Where will you find them? How will you compensate them?"

"Wisdom tells me that in this undertaking, Randor, to *be* is more important than to *do*. So many of my plans, so much of my *doing*, I fear, has gone awry. So I will begin by *being*. You are forgetting that I have seen the unfolding of the future in the World Dream. It is both a tremendous advantage and a weighty burden to know all that will happen *before* it happens. There is much I would change. But life holds both joy and sorrow and I realize that one cannot always have joy. Sorrow is the measure of joy, for without it we would not know what joy is. The Dream will unfold of its own accord. All I must *do*, then, is to live my life in harmony with the lessons of the Pearls and the Dream will unfold according to Deus' plan for his children. Such is His prophecy for me."

"That may be more difficult than you deem. There are four Pearls that you do not yet know, four lessons that have yet to be revealed. How can you live in accord with principles you do not understand?"

"Would Deus let me go astray from the true path?"

"He gives you choices."

"Then I will make the right choices, Father. I will discover the lessons of the Twelve. I will be the light of Deus on the mountaintop. I will send out His call, and those who may come will come. For in this effort I deem that hearts will be as important as hands," Ravennetus answered.

"But you may do much to abet me, Randor. Send your sons, Corvus and Corax, to find my brothers upon the plains. Send this message to Ulf. Tell him that Ravennetus waits for him upon Hethraven, the home of the *Sodalitas Ravenites*, the Brotherhood of Ravens, and ask him to come."

So it was that Ravennetus, banished from Aestri, the woman he loved and the child born to them, made his home atop the mountain called Hethraven. To the forest of tall cedars that ringed its summit, Randor called his people. Corvus and Corax took wives to themselves and the ravens multiplied there. And when the time had come, Randor sent his sons flying far and wide to find the brothers, and take Ravennetus' message to Ulf.

Ravennetus took up residence in a shallow cave on the mountainside, near the springs that flowed from gurgling mouths over mossy stones to join the headwaters of the Vahlen. He enlarged the mouths of the springs and made a basin where he might draw water and bathe, calling it Lympha Placida, the Spring of Tranquility. Nearby was an immense stone, as flat as a table and tilted toward the east. There, at sunrise, Ravennetus would sit, watch Hanthol leap into the sky, and talk with Deus.

Ravennetus loved to walk the summit of the mountain and explore his new home, learning every facet of its character. One day as he roamed among the broom and heather on the eastern slope, near the eaves of the forest, he came upon a cedar that had fallen. Through some peculiarity of sun and wind and rain it had become hollow but had retained a shell both thick and sound. He took his walking stick and tapped it, whereupon it replied in a lingering, humming voice. With some difficulty, he moved it to a dell further up the mountainside. There with primitive tools and patience, he sized and trimmed it, and hung it vertically from a wooden frame. Then he mounted another, shorter log upon the frame, free to be swung and to strike the hollow log.

The resulting sound was the voice of all nature singing in chorus, the dull ring of a large stone when it is thrown into water, the voice of thunder in the heavens, the surf upon a rocky shore, the throaty growl of a lion, loud, resonant and magnificent, the consuming roar of the Fire of Han-Thol, the manifest voice of Deus.

From the first time Ravennetus heard the sound he could not get it out of his mind. After rising at dawn each day, and before retiring to his cave each night, he would go to the drum and summon its voice. The striker log was massive and heavy. He would push it with all his strength, moving it at first only a handsbreadth. The next swing would take it further, the next further, bringing it closer and closer to the drum. At last it would strike the hollow cedar log. Then the slow, majestic drumming would leap up from the hollow, roll down the mountainside, spill into the river valley and echo back from the forest. The animals who lived there would hear and come quietly from their woodland homes to sit listening, mesmerized, for they too found comfort in its measured voice. All of creation lived in harmony upon Hethraven.

Upon a certain morning, a silver droplet clinging to the tip of each leaf, Ravennetus rose and walked through the dewy broom to the drum. He heaved against the massive striker with all his weight as Hanthol rose out of the gray-white eastern mists. The voice of the drum boomed. Out of the flame of the sun, Corvus and Corax came looping overhead, joyously cavorting in the air, diving, rising, falling, then soaring heavenward on ecstatic wings with loud singing cries. Ravennetus heard their exhortations and squinted to see them against the brilliant orange light. They turned and raced down the mountainside and were lost behind the trees, then came suddenly back, landing upon Ravennetus' shoulders. Ravennetus smiled at his excited companions. "Look!" they cried. "See who has come!"

Ravennetus turned his head where Corvus pointed his sleek wing. At first he saw nothing, then a head, followed by familiar shoulders appeared, rising above the crest of the hill.

It was Ulf and behind him were forty of the brothers, the tips of their spears glinting in the sunfire. Memories, both sweet and painful, came flooding back to Ravennetus and he ran to embrace his old friend. Ulf was just as Ravennetus had remembered him, jet-black hair and beard, jaw firmly set, sea-gray eyes, bronze breastplate over leather jerkin, short sword at his side, leather sandals that laced up high on his calf. Ulf gave his spear to Boran and slid from his horse, Laeticia, wrapping his arms around Ravennetus.

"My brother," Ulf said at last. "It has been too long. Are you well?" he asked, noting with concern how heavily the years seemed to sit upon Ravennetus. He had changed much in Ulf's eyes. Gone were the weapons of war and outer ornamentation, replaced by a simple, heather-brown homespun cloak and an inner light that seemed to leap from his eyes when he spoke, bathing the listener in the surety of his words.

"I am well," Ravennetus replied. "And overjoyed that you have come. I have been calling you."

"Yes, the ravens came and bade us follow. They sang a song of Ravennetus, sitting high upon his mountain, playing the music of the earth and sky, the Now and the Otherworld. We followed them up the river valley. Then we heard the sound of your drum for ourselves and knew we had arrived."

Ravennetus greeted each of the brothers with an enthusiastic smile and his tears flowed unrestrained. Many of the faces he had known from the beginning and some, youthful and untroubled by care, he had never seen. He asked them to sit and they gathered in a circle around him to listen. He told them the tale of the years since they had parted, of Allisyn, of the quest for the Horn of Magor, of his banishment and wandering. Then he told them of the World Dream of Deus, the tale of the future, and how he had pledged himself to bring that vision to its fruition in the Now. When he had finished it was past noon, and the shadows of the circled men had revolved from the west back to the east. Ulf spoke.

"Ever your life spirals toward the light, Ravennetus. To be the chosen of the gods is a great thing. We honor you. But what can we do? We are made of clay, not of sun and moon as you are. Why have you called us here?" he asked.

"No Ulf, I have called you because we *are* of the same stock. You *are* my brothers," he answered. "Many years ago I called you out of the darkness and told you my purpose; to shake up the order of things, to bring the light of Brahan, my Father, the Fire of Han-Thol, into the world. I have traveled many roads and gained many insights since I dreamed of the young lion who leaped across the page to devour the goddess. But I am still upon the path set before me then, and it has led me here, to this mountain, to this moment.

"You followed me down the first steps of that path. We tamed the horses, we challenged the ways of the goddess, we rode the plains and we developed a new intellect, a new way of perceiving and living life. Then our paths were sundered, for I had a new way to go, different from yours. Now we have the chance to be joined again. Deus has brought us back together."

"Will you come with us, then, back to the Dacon, where we can live as free men?" asked Ulf.

Ravennetus lowered his head and his voice.

"Alas, I cannot, for I am no longer free, not in the sense that you perceive freedom. I have become a *servant* Ulf, the servant of Deus, but therein lies a new freedom. I offer that to you if you will join me, here, on Hethraven," Ravennetus answered.

Ulf looked puzzled.

"What is this new freedom? How can the servant be free? We know the freedom of the wind in our hair, of new horizons, of independent thought. That is the freedom you taught us. What other freedom can there be?"

"What I offered you before was the freedom of the body, of the senses, and of the mind. The freedom I offer you now is the freedom of the spirit, the freedom from doubt, from pain, from fear. The freedom that comes with knowing that evil cannot touch you, that death is no longer your master."

"But all men must die, Ravennetus, even you," Ulf protested.

"It is true that all must die, but all need not fear death and thus become its slave. Name that which enslaves you, Ulf, and I will show you how to be free of it."

Ulf thought for a moment.

359

"There is nothing that enslaves me save my flesh, for I must feed it and cloth it. I am slave to those needs. But so are you. You must eat and be clothed, the same as I. How can I be free of these except to die? And if I thus escape slavery to life, am I not then a slave to death?"

"I can show you a way to transcend both life and death."

"How Ravennetus?" the intrigued Ulf leaned closer and asked.

"To make them not matter. Life and death exist, there is no question of that. The secret is to get beyond life, in life, and beyond death, in death."

"I do not understand, but then, understanding has never been my strength," he said, smiling at Ravennetus.

"Your faith has been your strength, Ulf. And it is far better to have faith than understanding. For if you have faith, then understanding will follow."

"Your head is still like the overripe melon, Ravennetus, bursting with ideas. Still, I am curious. Tell me about life transcending life, and death transcending death. It seems not possible. How can life be more than life, or death more than death?"

"Ah, Ulf, there you hit upon the key question. Since the beginning, you have always asked the right questions. Life is what you perceive life to be, is it not? The lion perceives of life as only consisting of killing and eating, sleeping and mating. You may think of life as only a struggle to keep fed and stay warm. Yet that existence, or your perception of that existence, can be transcended. Once you only knew the life you lived in the village, where men were slaughtered and their blood spread upon the fields to insure the fertility of the soil and the harvest, where the only thought was the collective thought of the group. You knew nothing of freedom; the idea was foreign to you. But you transcended that. You live life now on a higher plane. You have your freedom, your independence, and the will to do as you please. But I tell you there is yet a higher plane. There is a freedom that goes beyond the independence of will; it is the freedom that comes from merging your will with the will of Deus. I can show you that freedom. Do you believe me?"

"I believe you, Ravennetus, though I do not understand. Yet, as you say, when I was in the village, I could not comprehend the freedom that you offered me. So it will be with this new way of life, this new consciousness, this new freedom.

I will put my faith in you, and follow you."

"Do not place your faith in me, Ulf, but in Deus, for that is the beginning of new life. And with your new life, you shall bear a new name. Fidelis Sampras I name you, Ever Faithful."

Fidelis kneeled down and offered Ravennetus his sword.

"This I will take because it is a great gift, a symbol of yourself and all that you have become," Ravennetus said. "But much more than these, more than your sword or your intellect, I will need your heart."

"Alas," Fidelis answered, "I gave that to you long ago."

Ravennetus and Fidelis spent many days talking to the brotherhood. Each day, Ravennetus would tell them of the future, of his vision, and of their role in that vision. He tried to convince them, as he had convinced Fidelis, that there would be a new way and new life for them here, on Hethraven. Here the brotherhood would become a force in the master plan, the World Dream of Deus. Some of them, either out of loyalty to Ravennetus or to their brother Fidelis, made the decision to stay. But most could not comprehend life upon the mountain. They could not understand the higher purpose of which Ravennetus spoke. They cared only for the freedom of the plains and that life they had already known and savored. So they chose a new leader and turned their faces toward the Dacon. Altogether, thirteen remained on Hethraven, including Ravennetus and Fidelis, when the brothers departed.

But thirteen were enough. Ravennetus revealed his plan to build a temple upon the mountain. He dreamed a dream that had revealed the form and dimensions of the buildings to be erected. He laid it out upon the ground in the exact location the dream had instructed. Thus they began to build the Temple of Deus. The first task was to lay a stone foundation and the brothers went to work with surprising fervor. Their faith was indeed great, for they had only crude tools with which to work. Inwardly some may have asked, "How are we to build a temple with only sticks for tools and no knowledge of the craft of stone cutting?" But no one asked that question aloud and they dug the foundation on the pattern Ravennetus had shown them.

Each morning at the rising of the sun, Ravennetus made the music of the drum and the brothers prayed, asking Deus to increase their faith, and for the humility to submit to His will.

361

They besought Him to sustain their commitment to the building of His temple and the hope that He would show them the way to proceed. Sometimes, as the song of the drum drifted over the forest and the vales beyond, curious strangers would hear it and follow its sound. Then the brothers would tell them of their work. Some were unable to comprehend, and some simply laughed and walked away, shaking their heads at the folly. But some stayed and joined in the work, and the numbers of the brothers grew. And still Ravennetus waited for a sign.

Every evening, Lyricus the musician, the gentle Fremd, played upon the pipes as he circumambulated the mountain top. Then the prayers of the brothers rose. They thanked Deus for life and for the opportunity to serve Him. And they were at peace.

Ravennetus served Deus by serving the brotherhood. One wilting afternoon, as he drew water for the brothers while they worked, Fidelis came running, breathless with exertion and excitement.

"Ravennetus! Ravennetus!" he called. "Come and see the miracle! Our prayers have been answered! It is true, I tell you... come and see!"

Ravennetus followed Ulf to the summit where they mounted a rock in the center of the excavation.

"Look! See, along the lines that we laid out. See! See the stones in the ground, already laid out square and true? Now come with me again." He grabbed Ravennetus' arm, dragging him along as he talked. "Here, look at what Brother Boran has unearthed!"

Ravennetus studied the carved rock, still half-buried in the mountain.

"It looks like the the capital of a column, Fidelis."

"Yes, Ravennetus, yes, it is! It is! The temple, Ravennetus, the temple is already here, carved from the bones of the earth, waiting to be dug up! Our prayers are answered! Thus, we build the temple with simple digging tools! It is a miracle, truly a miracle!"

It *was* a miracle and the sign from Deus that Ravennetus had awaited. The brothers bent their backs and worked eagerly, digging upon the eastern side where the main entrance of the temple was to be. With each passing sun, more and more of the portico was uncovered and columns, one by one, were revealed. There were twelve of them, and the capital of each column was

362

the likeness of one of the twelve brothers who had begun the work with Ravennetus. Day after day, the excavation never ceased to yield up some amazing revelation.

When the temple was unearthed at last, the Sodalitas Ravenites worshiped there. News of the miracle upon the mountain spread throughout the surrounding lands and people came to marvel at the white stone building, the like of which they had never seen. Ravennetus taught them the lessons of the Pearls and the Will of Deus. Some believed and stayed on and the brotherhood grew.

It was not many years until the temple, the dormitory for the brothers, the kitchens, and the quarters for pilgrims were completely excavated. When this was accomplished, the summit of the mountain had been wholly removed and in its place stood the marvelous monastery.

The porch of the temple faced eastward, and the brothers discovered, to their amazement, that when the sun rose on the morning of the summer solstice, its light shone through the entrance and down its central hallway, striking a jewel in the altar, breaking into a thousand colorful shards, and illuminating the interior of the House of Deus. The jewel was called Boreastrum, the Star of the North, and it had twelve facets. On the front of the temple, as well as on each side, were twelve columns, for its footprint was a perfect square. Atop each wall, at the center of the span, was the stone image of a raven. The interior columns were carved in the shape and texture of great cedar trees, their stately boles rising up through the floor and branching into thick limbs with many-fingered boughs, interlacing in an intricate web of delicate arches to support the roof. In the southwest corner near the altar was a fountain, the Well of Deus, Puteus Aeternus Lux, the Well of Knowledge, the Well of Eternal Life. From its depths a light shone and cool waters flowed into a shallow basin. And it was said that whoever drank from this well would thereafter be filled with wisdom and a source of light to everyone they might meet.

The house of the brothers was lower in height than the temple and further down the mountainside. It was filled with many comfortable small rooms, warm in the winter and cool in the summer, each neatly laid out with an altar and a modest sleeping area. Adjacent to this were kitchens where simple, wholesome food was prepared. Great stone ovens had been unearthed there and the baking skills attained by the brothers were deemed as great a miracle as the ovens themselves.

During this time of abundance the brothers planted gardens, vineyards, and orchards so that there was ample food, not only for the brotherhood, but for the exhausted pilgrims who came to see and hear and worship. Trees were planted by the Lympha Placida to make a shade and there, on frequent occasions, Ravennetus would sit and write, or teach the brothers and the strangers who had come to hear the lessons of the Pearls. And the strangers would listen and go on their way to tell others about the miracle on the mountain and the fountain that flowed there.

Thus the brotherhood grew and prospered. Rumor of the monastery at Hethraven spread and it was known far and wide as a place both holy and peaceful, the place in which Deus, the Father-god, had come into the Now, and from which his ways were taught to humankind.

Inevitably, the news reached into the furthest corners of the land, even unto the hungry and ever-listening ears of the ravishing Tandela, High Priestess of Thol-nys, Queen of Aestri.

Chapter 34
A Secret Revealed

"But we have given all we own! There is no more to give!" the peasant woman pleaded with the soldier who had come to collect the tax.

"No excuses!" the soldier shouted. "Everyone must pay. And you know the consequences if you do not. Now where is your payment?"

"Sir, please we do not have it. Can you give us some more time, a few days? Please, I beg of you. Only a few more days!"

"No! No more time. You must pay now!"

"We haven't anything left, I swear to you. Please!"

"All right woman. Enough of your sniveling. Where is your oldest? If the payment cannot be made, the law says you must pay with your eldest child. Where is he?"

"No!" the woman cried as tears erupted from her eyes. "You cannot have him!" She ran to the back room of the cottage and shouted out the window to her son, who was in the barnyard pitching fodder to the kine. "Run, Danur! Run!"

Two younger children, a younger boy and girl followed their mother and clung to her skirts. With her older son running into the woods, the woman turned to face the soldier. There was madness in his eyes and he drew his sword.

"Do you think you can make a fool of me, woman? That one," he said pointing to her small son who had wrapped himself around her leg. "That one will do. Hand him over!"

A sudden fear rounded the woman's eyes as she watched her husband creep up behind the soldier. From the adjacent byre where he had been delivering a lamb, he had heard the harsh voice of the soldier, the pleas of this wife, and had come to investigate, a wooden pitchfork in his hand. As the soldier reached for the boy, the farmer jammed it into the soldier's back. But the copper armor beneath his cloak turned the tines and they stuck into his hip instead. The enraged soldier whirled about with deadly surprise and stabbed the farmer with his sword. The woman screamed as her husband crumpled to the ground. The soldier winced, grabbed for the young boy and took him roughly by the arm. The boy screamed. His mother reached for him, but stopped short when she saw the sword raised against her, red with her own husband's blood. She swooned as the soldier grabbed up the struggling, wailing boy and limped cursing from the house.

Everywhere in Aestri, the people were in misery. The tax upon them had increased year by year. Now their larders were nearly empty with winter coming on. It would be a cruel one, with scant provisions and little money left to purchase any. Given the scarcity of goods, prices for staples had become exorbitant.

The reaction of the people as the noose tightened was as Barthol had predicted. Some had become bellicose, openly defying the taxes and those who came to collect them. One by one these dissidents were dealt with. Some had run, it was true, forming bands of outlaws in the forest. But the majority had simply given up. Now they were to be seen at the gates of the City each morning, begging for morsels with which to feed their starving families, begging the very ones who had taken everything from them.

There was confusion concerning their impoverishment. How could such a thing happen in this land of plenty? Destitution had never been known in the Chent of Aestri, the bountiful heart of the kingdom. Some pointed to the coming of Barthol as the beginning of their misery. But those who spread this rumor were silenced, quickly and severely, and soon, though it may have been privately believed, the thought was never openly spoken. More and more, rumors began to circulate that Aefalas was responsible. Was he not the King? Was not his seal on all these terrible new laws that had been forced upon

366

them? Was he not answerable for the welfare of the people? Was not their fealty pledged in exchange for his protection? Although some believed that Tandela had bewitched Aefalas, still he, in their eyes, was to blame. Treasonous talk was spread. Barthol's spies fanned the flames of unrest wherever they went. In exchange, they lived and ate well. From these chosen few, Barthol seemingly withheld nothing.

Barthol continued to weave his web of deception. Whenever Aefalas protested the treatment of the people, Barthol would console him with the promise that they would only suffer a little longer. Soon they would be convinced that Tandela, the enchantress, was responsible for their plight. Soon they would rise up and demand that she be put in her place. Soon Aefalas would be rid of her once and for all time. Then the king would return the harvest and money Tandela had stolen from the people and have their undying loyalty. Then his place in their hearts and minds would be firmly established. He would be like a god to them, venerated forever. With Tandela out of the way, he, Barthol, would wed Allisyn and provide heirs of Aefalas' blood for the throne. And all would be as he desired it to be.

To Tandela, Barthol told a different tale. With her he plotted Aefalas' downfall by spreading the rumor that Aefalas was to blame for the demise of the kingdom. Soon, he guaranteed her, the people would rise to rid themselves of this weak and vile king, whose chafing and burdensome yoke they wore every day. Even now, food and relief for the downtrodden were being distributed secretly in her name. Slowly but certainly, he assured, he was building her a foundation of support. Soon her waiting would be over. Soon she would be the uncontested sovereign and enjoy the unwavering loyalty of her grateful subjects. If she could wait a little longer, then all these things would be hers, just as he had promised.

Barthol continued to bend the ear of Bors, the chief of Aefalas' army, playing upon his honor. He was quick to point out the suffering of the people but kept him in a quandary as to who was responsible. Was it the malignant Tandela who had enchanted the mind of the witless king, or Aefalas to whom all were pawns, including the redoubtable Bors? The chieftain's unrest grew. Barthol could feel it turning to anger, seething in Bors heart, and knew it was only a matter of time until it would brim over. Then he would direct it in the manner, and at the target, he chose. His plans were nearly complete.

Only Allisyn continued to rankle him. She alone seemed to evade his snare, she alone continued to elude. He had not yet found her weakness, the chink in the armor of her soul. But he would, oh yes, he would. And when he did his victory would be complete. He would possess her, the beautiful one, the proud one; he would strip the Pearls from her and give them to Thol-nys. Then he would be master of the Now, with complete control, complete power. That the Great Calamity had promised him.

With an angry resolve to break her will, Barthol made his way to Allisyn's apartments. Aefalas was away to the north, hunting wild boars in the swamp forests of Wyeth, a favorite diversion. Bors was with him, along with other high ranking officers of the army. With them gone, there would be no prying eyes or ears, no one to come to Allisyn's aid if he had to get rough. He placed his hand upon the cold iron handle of her door, retrieved the key from his pocket and placed it in the lock. He turned it, feeling the familiar mechanical click as it opened, and swung the massive wooden door.

Allisyn was seated by the window overlooking the gorge. She heard the lock turn and saw the door swing. Then Barthol stood before her.

"I will assume you have come to release me Barthol."

"That I have, but not in the way you might think. I have come to release you from the chains that bind you, from your little secrets, Ma'am. Secrets, Allisyn, are like poison. Only when they are told can you be free of them. Only then will they release you and allow you to live your life unencumbered."

"I have no secrets, Barthol, only memories, sweet and pleasant."

"You will never see him again, Allisyn," Barthol spat. "He is gone forever, banished for good. He has forgotten about you. He is chasing some other dream now. Forget him and forget whatever you had with him. It will never return. Things will never be again as they were before." Even as he spoke these words, he felt the hatred for his brother burn in his heart. Controlling it, he softened his voice.

"I want to share something with you, Allisyn. I want to confirm something you have long suspected and dreaded." He paused to let the gravity of his words settle upon her.

"Aefalas, your father, has promised you to me in marriage. Very soon I intend to lay claim to what is mine. I have come to discuss the particulars with you."

Allisyn stood in defiance but she trembled.

"No, it is not true! He would not do that to me!" she exclaimed with quivering lips. "You cannot have twisted him so!"

"You may deny that it is so, Allisyn, but in your heart you know it to be true. Do you deny that your father has many weaknesses? And do you further deny that there is no one as capable of finding weaknesses and exploiting them as I?" Barthol laughed as he saw the brightness dim in her eyes. Oh yes, she knew.

"Of course, I might be persuaded to forego the marriage, if you would give me the Pearls," he lied.

Allisyn instinctively touched her hand to the base of her neck, where the Pearls had graced her for so long. *As long as he thinks I still have them, I am safe,"* she mused.

"I will never give them to you," she said adamantly. "I am the guardian of their secret, and nothing of this world can induce me give to them up to you!"

"You are too certain, Allisyn. I know enough about human nature to know that such outward displays of bravado are only the foils of inner weakness. I do not doubt there is something, some weakness, some soft spot, that I might penetrate." His dark eyes bored into hers as if he might see into her very soul. She shut her eyelids and turned her head away, breaking their malevolent spell.

"Everything you do reveals your fear Allisyn. What do you fear, my pretty one? Do not think, it, Allisyn, I warn you. For I will read your thoughts. Hide it deeply if you want to keep it from me." He paused for a moment, then walked around behind her. Placing his hands on her neck, he pressed her down into her chair. She shuddered and he felt the tremor pass through her, like a ripple on a dark pond into which a tear has dropped. She felt the chill of his hands against her warm skin.

"This little secret of yours, no doubt it has to do with that bird-boy, my brother. That was quite a little shock when you found out about our 'relationship', wasn't it? Yes, you may discover many shocking things before I am finished with you, Allisyn.

369

"This secret... I fancy it has to do with the little journey you undertook with him, the little quest. Why did you run off after him I wonder? What would possess a rational girl to do something so rash? Perhaps, ...perhaps your little secret has to do with why you came back. So foolish to come back. You were free. You could have been with him forever if you had chosen it, if you had only stayed away. But no, you came back. Why? For him? Because he wanted to? Or for yourself? Perhaps you wanted poor Barthol after all. No, no. I could not be so fortunate. Have you ever thought that perhaps... perhaps he had got what he wanted from you, that he had no further use for you, that he came back only to return you, to dump you off, to be rid of you?

"All that talk about love. You know, there is no such thing as love, Allisyn. It is only an illusion. Love is a lie people tell to get what they want." As he spoke, he continued to press his hands against her neck, feeling for any change in the tension in her muscles as he talked, anything flinching or tightening that would betray her emotions. Like a green leaf touched by frost, Allisyn withered in his grip.

"Or perhaps your little secret has to do with something that happened while you were gone, something you wanted to run away from, something that you wanted to forget. Something was not right, else the two of you would have stayed away. Perhaps there was something of which you were ashamed. Yes that's it, is it not, shame? One feels shame when there is hidden guilt. What are you guilty of, Allisyn, that coming back to Faenwys would erase? What possibly would a spotless woman like yourself be guilty of? Running away? Feeling that you had betrayed your father? Feeling that you had left that poor sheep among so many wolves?" Allisyn tried hard not to reveal herself to him. She began to pray to Deus for the strength to resist his probing.

"Perhaps this all has to do with that little white-eyed imp, Bronwyn, that went away with you but did not return."

Allisyn felt a shock go through her.

"Ah! So it is! So it is! Your little secret has to do with her! Do you not see, Allisyn? I *will* find out. It is futile to resist me. Why did she not return with you? I strike closer to the mark, do I not?"

Allisyn gave a little cry and tried to get up but Barthol's strong hands shoved her forcefully back down into the chair.

He sensed the panic within her now. He was on the trail.

"Why did she not come back with you, Allisyn? There is some shame there. She is dead? She died for you? You sacrificed her to save yourself from something, something terrible. No, no, that's not it. She's hiding. Why is she hiding. You are hiding her? She is hiding something for you!"

Allisyn tensed. A lump came to her throat and tears to her eyes. She tried to pull Barthol's hands from her neck. She squirmed in his grip and tried to wrest herself free but he held her fast. She knew she could not resist him much longer.

"Leave me alone!" Allisyn cried frantically.

"Leave me alone! Leave me alone!" Barthol squeaked in mimicry. "Is that all the resistance you can offer up, my beauty? Oh no, Allisyn. I'm not going to leave you alone," he whispered, his lips close to her ear, so that she could feel his breath, hot and damp, against her skin. "I'm going to stay with you. I going to find out everything about you. I will never leave you alone; not until you tell me everything. Not until I have opened up your 'immaculate' little soul and stepped inside and rummaged about and found all your dirty little secrets. Then I will leave you alone. Then I will give you peace, Allisyn. But until then you will have no peace. I shall be like a rat that gnaws at you, that will not stop its biting and grinding. I will be like the serpent that coils itself about you, squeezing harder and harder until all the little secrets pop out," he menaced, his hands tightening about her throat, as his emotions boiled. Suddenly he relaxed his grip, but kept his icy hands on her shoulders.

"Let's get back to your secret, shall we? She's hiding something for you, something precious. What is so precious to you Allisyn, what could be so precious? What would be so precious that you would want to hide it from me, from Tandela, from your own father? You took nothing with you. Perhaps it is something that you found along the way. That's it. Something precious you found along the way. Let us see. A ring? A stone? No, not a bauble. Let us think. What do women prize above all else? Love? Relationships? Yes, those are their treasures, to be sure. To feel wanted, to feel affirmed. That's it. You have hidden something from us that you love, something that you have a loving relationship with, something that affirms you and gives meaning to your life. Ha! I have it, how could I have been so blind! A child, a child! You have a child! You have had a child with the bird-boy!"

371

"No!" Allisyn screamed, the tears shooting from her eyes into her lap. "It is not true!"

"Aha!" Barthol exclaimed. He felt her squirming again now, as if she were an insect he had pinned on the end of a needle. "Now you *will* tell me where it is. Where is Bronwyn hiding your imp? TELL ME!!" he screamed.

Allisyn fell from the chair and onto the floor in a swoon beneath the weight of Barthol's hatred. She twisted about involuntarily holding up her hands to ward him off.

"Tell me everything Allisyn!" Barthol shouted. "You can hide nothing from me, nothing! Is that not apparent to you now? I will know it all, sooner or later. Don't make me squeeze you, Allisyn!"

"It is not true!" she maintained. "I have no child!"

"Stop your lying, Allisyn! I know it is true! Do you think the Master of Lies could be so easily deceived? I tell you truly Allisyn. I *am* the Son of the Great Calamity, the Prince of Darkness, the very offspring of Deception. Do you think I cannot tell a lie when I hear one? You *do* have child and I will find it! And when I do, Allisyn, I will make you give me the Pearls. For no mother can stand to see her child tortured before her very eyes, to hear its little screams and know that she has the power to make the pain stop. You cannot resist it Allisyn; your little light cannot overcome the power of the Darkness, god or no god to help you! But you can save her now, Allisyn, save her and yourself anguish and pain and torment. Give me the Pearls now and I will forget her. Give them to me now!"

"Please, Barthol, please," Allisyn wept agonizingly. "Do not hurt her, do not hurt my baby! Ravennetus has them. He has the Pearls. They have passed on from me, I have given them to him. Bronwyn does not know. Please, do not hurt my baby, Barthol! Oh Deus, I have failed you! I have failed you! Have mercy on me!"

Barthol left the pitiful Allisyn lying upon the floor and went to his rooms. Knowing that Allisyn no longer possessed the Pearls changed his plans. He must leave Aestri to seek out his brother. Behind him, he would leave no possibility of mishap. Now he would fulfill his promise to Tandela and put her on the throne of Aestri. Aefalas must die.

He took a knife and sat down upon the floor. He cleared his mind until it became a black void, and conjured up the image of Aefalas walking in the swamp-forests of Wyeth, stalking the boar. He saw Aefalas kneel behind a tree, spear in hand.

In the steamy semi-darkness of the forest, Aefalas heard grunting, the tearing and snapping of roots, as the boar plowed the earth with his tusks. Suddenly the pig stopped and lifted his head, snorting, sniffing the air. Now there was silence, broken only by the buzzing of flies. Then from the side, as if by magic, the great boar appeared. Bristling, black as coal it was, its eyes rimmed in red, its curving tusks bone-hard and razor sharp. It stared at Aefalas. Then Aefalas knew. He remembered his dream of long ago. His stomach twisted. The boar charged and Aefalas turned to face it.

In his chamber, Barthol drew the knife symbolically across his abdomen. Aefalas lunged at the boar with his spear, but off balance, and his thrust went wide. The boar lunged into Aefalas' stomach, slashing with his tusks, rending and ripping. Blood and viscera flew, spattering the tree and forest floor.

Up trotted Bors as the pig bounded away through the undergrowth. Aefalas relived the dream now, the frightening vision of himself in the forest, gored and alone, trying to replace his insides, bleeding, dying. He fell back against the tree. The light of the world was dimming. He held out his hand thinking he saw Allisyn approaching through the wispy gray fog. "I am sorry," he moaned through blood moistened lips, "sorry... for all... the e... vil..."

Bors took the Aefalas' words to be a confession, that he was responsible for the misery of the people of Aestri. But he was not sure if a sense of pity or of justice compelled him to place his spear against the dying monarch's chest and end him with a quick thrust.

Chapter 35
Dark Brother

With Tandela upon the throne and the knowledge that the Pearls were in the care of Ravennetus, Barthol undertook a journey to the south. He was not sure of the location of the monastery but it was easy to find. He had kept his ears open in Aestri and had learned many things. The pilgrims who had made their way to Hethraven, who had seen the miracle and had heard the teachings of Ravennetus, were only too eager to share the news with any whom they met. In this way, Barthol learned that the mountain lay beyond the Iechryn between the headwaters of the Cyryn and the Vahlen.

After weeks of travel, he stood watching the flanks of Hethraven glow in the sunset. He made his way up the hill and arrived at dusk. In the twilight under his large hooded cowl he went about unknown and unrecognized. He was shown to the pilgrim's quarters by one of the brothers where he passed the night. The next morning he made his way slowly around the grounds, although he did not venture inside the temple. After the noon meal he asked one of the brothers to show him where he might find Ravennetus. He was led to the spring by the Lympha Placida. There the venerable one sat, gazing at a still pool of water drawn from the spring that he held cupped in his hands. He felt the weight of the pouch around his neck that contained the four as yet unnamed Pearls and meditated upon them. Ravennetus felt a presence behind him and spoke before turning.

"One may see much by gazing into a still pool," he said in a gentle voice.

374

"Here is one desiring an audience, Master."

Ravennetus saw the reflection of the two figures in the basin. He studied the one, the darker one, for a moment. When he recognized Barthol he was suddenly filled with emotions, surging back over the timescape of the Now. His first thought was for Allisyn. What had Barthol done with her? Where might she be? Was she safe? His concern deepened to sadness. He thought of the quest for the Horn and those who had been responsible for sending him in pursuit of the impossible. He felt a sudden anger for Aefalas and Barthol. It increased as he remembered the deception of Reyk and the treachery that had nearly cost him his life, that *had* cost the lives of so many of the brothers. The anger and sadness filled his heart to overflowing. He mastered them only with great difficulty. "Why must he come here?" Ravennetus wondered. "Has he not caused me enough misery? Why does he hate me so? Can he be unaware of my feelings toward him?"

He spilled the water from his hands back into the pool, wiped them upon his robe and turned around to meet his brother. Barthol had thrown back his hood and stood revealed in the shade of the trees. Ravennetus could think of nothing to say, so he remained silent. Barthol crossed the small space between them, kneeled and kissed his brother's hand. Ravennetus showed his surprise.

"My brother," Barthol began in a well-rehearsed speech. "I have come to tell you I am sorry for the wrong I have done you. I have spoken with Allisyn and she has shown me the true way. I have come to join the brotherhood."

Ravennetus was shocked. He closed his eyes to gather his wits. Had he truly heard the words that Barthol spoke? Had they really come from his mouth? Then what should his response be? *Carus*, he thought to himself. *Am I to care for even this one, Deus, this one who has been so wicked toward me, who has reviled me and sought my death? Humus, am I to humble myself before one who has never had a humble thought, who has sought to extend his lordship over the world? Respices, how can I respect this one who has been so disrespectful of human life and souls? Responsis, am I to be responsible for the teaching of him who I have looked upon for so long as my enemy? Am I to assume the role of his mentor and protector? How can I respond to this one with caring and respect and humility? What if he is lying? What if, even as he*

375

*stands here, he plots my demise, even plans my death? I am too
vulnerable. I should throw up my defenses. I should throw
him out. But can I treat him the way he has treated me and still
do what I know is right in my heart? Can I? What will I tell the
others? What sort of example will I make for them? Do the
teachings of Deus only apply to a few? Are some to be
excluded? Am I to be the judge of that? And what of Fides?
What sort of faith can I claim if I do not have the faith to accept
him, if I do not take him in, trusting in the good in him, trusting
that even he can be turned to the light?*

In that moment it seemed to Ravennetus that he stood upon
the verge of a yawning chasm and a choice loomed before him.
If he stepped off the edge, into the thin air, into the uncertain
void, if he committed everything to faith, he would accomplish
all he had dreamed. If he turned and walked away to safety, all
he had worked for, indeed his whole life, would come to
naught. He swayed for a moment on the edge with closed eyes.
Then, in the most courageous action he had ever taken, he
smiled and embraced his brother Barthol, and placed a holy kiss
upon his cheek.

"Welcome, brother," Ravennetus said softly. A cold pain
shot through his heart and he stumbled. Barthol caught him.

The days turned into weeks, weeks into months, and the
seasons unfurled their splendor. To all, including Ravennetus,
Barthol seemed a model novice. He accepted the teachings of
Deus and became as a servant to the brothers. He was kind to
everyone and seemed completely reformed. When Ravennetus
was convinced that Barthol had truly been changed, he ventured
to ask the question so dear to his heart.

"Tell me something I have desired to hear, Barthol. Tell me
of Allisyn. How did you leave her? Is she all right?" Barthol
looked him straight in the eye. Ravennetus returned his gaze,
ashamed that he searched for traces of falsehood, but Barthol's
mind was doubly veiled.

"When I left Faenwys, Tandela was on the throne of Aestri.
Aefalas had been killed in a hunting accident. Thus she finally
got her wish. There is no love lost between her and Allisyn; I
need not tell you that. Allisyn started me upon a new path, a
path I thought I would never walk. She showed me the error of

376

the worship of the Great Calamity and she bade me come here, to you, to learn all that I could, ere I go back to help her in the struggle against the Darkness. She knows you can never return, for the order of banishment is still upon you. Tandela has not rescinded it and I doubt that she will. For she despises anything that would give Allisyn any pleasure and would never let her leave. Yet Allisyn is safe, I deem, for a while. The people still love her and secretly wish her upon the throne. Their misgivings for Tandela run deep."

"Thank you brother, for those words of comfort. Yet I still hunger for... for aught she might have said to me, for any message she might have passed along to give to me."

"She bids you to be at peace and not to worry about her, and to trust Deus that some day you will be reunited. She misses you deeply. Not a day goes by that she does not speak of you."

Ravennetus placed his arm around Barthol and smiled. "Thank you, brother." And he left.

Barthol hid his disgust until Ravennetus was out of sight.

It had long been the custom of Ravennetus to take some time to himself in the late summer months. The brothers would lovingly pack provisions for him. He would take a horse from the stable and set off. No one knew where he went, and no one asked. Some said he went to Braemara, the holy mountain of Randor, spending the days in conversation there with his father and with Deus. Some said that he went further afield, to the north and to the east, but to where they knew not. Ravennetus had been careful about this midsummer sojourn, always keeping it his secret. Never had he revealed his destination to anyone, not even to Fidelis Sampras. But when one of the brothers casually mentioned Ravennetus' curious habit to Barthol, the latter was mightily intrigued. Here, perhaps, was the chink in *his* armor, *his* little secret. He sensed it as a viper senses the heat of its approaching victim in the pits below its eyes. Barthol began to furtively inquire among the brothers, that is, among those in whom his questioning would arouse no suspicion.

For none of the brothers, not even Fidelis, had the faith that Ravennetus had. None had stepped in the chasm as he had and Barthol knew it. He read it in their faces, in their gestures and in their conversations. Their lack of faith manifested itself in

377

various ways. In some, in those who knew something of Barthol's history, suspicion was aroused. Fidelis was one of these. He did not, he could not, trust Barthol and he watched him carefully for any signs of misbehavior or treachery. To him, Barthol seemed too good, his manner too self-effacing.

But not all suspected or were repelled by Barthol. Some gravitated to him, attracted by his mystery, his wisdom borne of insights into the thoughts of men, and the sense of the divine power that dwelled behind his veil of deception. Thus the brotherhood was divided by him and they knew it not. And it was his great pleasure.

To this latter group Barthol paid careful attention and showed particular interest. Often a small group of them would be gathered with Barthol at their center. It was to one of these adherents that Barthol went, when he found that Ravennetus was leaving, to ask the smallest of favors. Would he follow the Master, to see whither he journeyed, to come back and tell his concerned brother Barthol? For brother feared for brother's safety and it would relieve him to know that Ravennetus was safe from danger. Thus Barthol ensnared his first fool in his scheme to bring Hethraven down.

This year as he prepared to leave, Ravennetus had been working on a curious project. The Master had what appeared to be a stone, about the size of his palm, that he kept with him always. In his times of leisure and solitude, he would pull it out and a smile would brighten his face. The stone, if a stone it was, was of a strange composition. It had a bright watery sheen and was very hard. Deep purple was its color with varves of emerald green and crimson running through it. He shaped and ground it until it assumed the shape of a raven in flight. There was a hole where the bird's eye would have been and when he had finished shaping and polishing the piece, he set a pearl there and hung it from a leather thong. He told no one the reason behind his intense interest in it. As always, Barthol was attracted to the mystery.

The day came, just prior to Ravennetus' departure, when the new initiates would be inducted into the brotherhood. Barthol was among the aspiring novices. Before dawn on the morning of the summer solstice, the brothers filed into the temple and

378

stood behind the columns of stone cedars making a pathway for the light. Morning broke clear and bright in the east and the sun fired the haze that lingered there with an intense red-orange light. Hanthol peeked above the hills and threw a shaft of sunfire into the central hall of the temple. Boreastrum, the gem in the altar, swelled with the light and broke it into multicolored beams, casting them all about, illuminating the darkened space. The brothers burst into a sonorous chant. The light receded from the altarstone back toward the door as the sun rose but the light of the gem shone still. The twelve initiates came forward and knelt at the altar. Ravennetus filled twelve cups from the well, whose water was itself alive with light and the light of the water in each cup was like a lamp. He blessed each of the initiates and they drank of the Well of Deus. Upon every one of them appeared a sign, the Ravenmark, the image of a raven in flight, that marked them forever as a brother of the Sodalitas Ravenites and a man of Deus. Ravennetus gave them all new names, new names for a new life. And he pronounced that Barthol should henceforth be called Bartolemus.

Suddenly the light of the sun dimmed and the sky grew dark, boiling with unexpected clouds. Deep within the earth was a rumbling that drew closer as the brothers listened. The earth began to shake. The rumbling became a ripping sound that seemed to tear the very ground apart. The shaking grew worse. The light of the Well went out and its waters ceased to flow. The temple shook violently and the brothers fell upon their faces, all save Ravennetus and Bartolemus. Ravennetus remained standing by the altar, unperturbed, and Bartolemus continued to kneel before him. When the earthquake was over they were still there.

Some said that the initiation had been cursed by Deus because Barthol should never have been admitted to the brotherhood. Others argued that the sun was dimmed so that Bartolemus' light might have shined more brightly on that day, and that he was destined to become great among them. Afterward, the stone raven that surmounted the north wall was discovered to have been ripped from its pedestal during the earthquake and cast down. Some suggested the fall of the raven was an omen and there was much whispered speculation as to its meaning.

A few days later, Ravennetus left Hethraven. Fidelis, as always, was asked to lead the brotherhood in his absence. There was still much talk of the initiation, for much besides the ground had been shaken. Still Ravennetus left to an outpouring of sentiment and good will. Had he known to what grief his departure would lead, perhaps he would not have gone. But he did not yet know Barthol's true intentions and held blindly to his faith that he might redeem his Dark Brother with love.

Ravennetus' journey was shadowed by Barthol's spy. Since he was traveling far to the north and still under banishment in Aestri, he loped first down the rock strewn gorge of the Vahlen, then eastward among the broken hills and the broad sweep of the Sothmont, the river that formed the boundary between the mountains and the Dacon Plain. Thence he crossed the river and swung north. For many days he traveled, enjoying the simple pleasure of riding, unburdened by his responsibility to the Sodalitas Ravenites. Then abruptly, a river hove across his path from the hills to the west. There he stopped and camped, lulled to sleep by the rush of the blue-green waters. Not many more days had passed until he saw the pinnacle of the Graf thrusting up before him, a purple mass on the northern horizon. He forded the river at its feet and turned west to cross the Plain of Dor. At last, he turned his face toward the village of Horen. For he traveled now, as he had each year since his exile began, to see Daena, his bright-eyed daughter, the image of her mother, his greatest joy and hope.

Had he been able to travel through Aestri the journey would have taken but a few days. With that way barred, it was nearly two weeks before he knocked with suppressed excitement upon the door of the house where Bronwyn kept his daughter. A young woman answered, but it was not Bronwyn. She stepped outside and into the light to study the man standing before her more closely. Following her questions, which Ravennetus patiently answered, she invited him in. When she spoke next it was in a whisper.

"Please sir, excuse my caution. I had to make sure it were you. Bronwyn told me, 'You will know him by the brand on his forehead'. And so I do, beggin' yer pardon. There have been strangers pryin' about, askin' questions mind you, about a child, the child of Allisyn. So Bronwyn thought it best to move her. She has tak'n the child to the hamlet of Brega, not far from here. When it's night, I'll take you to there my own self!"

Ravennetus was fearful for the child and he fretted away the afternoon and evening. "Eat, eat!" the girl reprimanded him. "They're safe. You'll see. You've had a long journey and you're weary. I see it in your face. Eat!"

When the night was deep, the peasant girl led him from Horen. She was intimidated by the horse and would not climb onto its back. So they walked, and their talk filled a little space around them in the vastness of the open plain. In a few hours they topped a rise and the meager lights of Brega came into view. They approached a poor little house where the young woman knocked, in a somewhat intricate pattern, then waited. The door was opened by a black shape that revealed itself darker than the unlighted room behind it. From the shadow peeked the light of two pale eyes. Ravennetus knew Bronwyn immediately and threw his arms around her.

"Is she alright?" he asked anxiously.

"She is asleep," Bronwyn whispered. "Come in!" She lit a candle and led Ravennetus into the room where the sleeping Daena lay. He watched his daughter for a long while in its feathery glow. Then he placed the candle at the head of her bed and lay down on the floor beside her. Outside, a shadow watched from the shadow of a nearby house. Then it crept away, far out onto the plain where it had tethered its horse, mounted and rode back to the south on the now familiar path.

Ravennetus awoke the next morning, pinned to the ground by a vivacious, blond-haired, green-eyed sprite. She sat upon his chest and contemplated his face, letting her silky hair tickle it. He played with her, snoring and feigning sleep until he could resist no longer. He opened his eyes abruptly and a huge smile parted his brown lips.

"Papa!" Daena cried.

"Oh, Daena, my sweetheart!" Ravennetus answered merrily. "I have missed you so!" He gave her a huge hug. Daena hugged him back, wishing it would never end.

Ravennetus spent a few idyllic days with his daughter. Then, too soon as always, it was time to depart. But things were different now. Daena had grown; she was six years old and she had questions. She posed them on their last day together as they walked through a grove of birches by a dancing stream.

"Papa," she asked, "why won't you tell me your name? Don't you like it?"

Ravennetus smiled, holding her chubby hand in his. He was thinking of an answer when she posed another question, and another, and another, hard on the heels of the first.

"Why can't I see my mama? Who is she? Where is she? Why doesn't she come to see me like you do? Why can't I go with you this time? Why do you always have to leave me?"

Before he could answer, tears came to her eyes. She rubbed them on the back of her father's thick-veined hand as they walked. He thought of the long and lonely hours spent when he was a boy upon discovering that the lioness was not his real mother, asking the same questions. *Where was she? How could she have left me alone? Would she ever come back for me?* Presently, Ravennetus stopped. He sat down on the ground and invited Daena to sit in his lap. Holding her close, he told her a story.

"Daena, your mother... your mother is a beautiful princess."

"She is?" the little girl asked in amazement.

"Yes, she is. When I saw her the very first time I knew that she was the perfect one for me. Her father, the king, had some wicked friends, and they convinced him to keep us apart. But your mother ran away and became my wife anyway. That made her father very angry. After you were born, we went back to her father's house..."

"Does Mama live in a castle?" Daena interrupted.

"Oh yes, a big one. We went back to her father to try to explain what had happened. He was very angry."

"Like Bronwyn was when I broke the eggs?"

"Even angrier than that! He made her stay with him in his house and sent me far away. He put this mark on my forehead, so that everyone would know I was not supposed to come there anymore. That's why your mother and I don't live together. That's why she doesn't come to see you, because he makes her stay in his house all the time." Daena reached up and touched the disfigured flesh on her father's brow with her innocent little finger.

"Oh," she sighed. "Why can't I go see *her* then? I think I would love her very much, if she is as beautiful as you say, and I would want to live with her. Why can't I, Papa?"

"Well, Daena, the wicked friends of your mother's father don't like her, or me, very much. In fact, they dislike us so

382

much that they might try to hurt you if they knew that you were alive and where you were. That's why we have kept you a secret. That's why I haven't told you my name, or your mother's name. We want to keep you very safe, because we love you so much."

"Well couldn't *you* keep me safe? Couldn't I go with *you*?"

"No, Daena, I'm afraid not."

"Why?"

"Because you will be safer if you stay here with Bronwyn. You have to trust me."

"What does trust mean?"

"It means... it means that if I tell you something, you must believe it is true."

"You mean, if you tell me birds don't fly, I have to believe you?"

"No, it's not like that. It is like, well... if I tell you that Deus made the sky blue you would either believe it or you would not, just because you feel in your heart that it is true, not because I could prove it to you. You would just have to trust that I am telling you something you should believe."

"So when you tell me to stay with Bronwyn, I just have to believe that is the best thing for me?"

"Yes, that is right."

"I do trust you Papa."

"I'm glad, Daena. That makes me feel very good. Do you know why?"

"'Cause you know I love you?"

"That is right, and you know I love you too!"

There was a long space in their conversation. Daena watched the grasses bend in the wind and listened to their whistling voices. Finally, feeling secure in her father's arms, she spoke again.

"Tell me about love, Papa. What is it, really?"

"Ah, my child, love is a long story."

"Tell me, please!"

"Love... true love comes from Deus. To really love, you have to believe that Deus created love, that He is love, and love is Him. To know love is to know joy, just as to know Deus is to know joy. So the thing you must have to love is faith, which is believing in something you cannot see or feel or touch. It is trust, just like we were talking about.

"Love is also about caring. To love someone means that you

383

care for them deeply, from your heart, like I care about you. I come to see you and talk to you and listen to you because I care about you.

"Sometimes it takes courage to love. Because if you truly... love someone, you love them even in the face of danger, like I love... your mother. And you keep on loving, no matter what, even if you are apart from the one you love, because you have promised to love that person. You have promised them... that your love... will never fail them, it will always be there to support and comfort them, especially when they are sad or hurt or angry.

"You always treat the people you love with respect and you never do anything to hurt them. You always hope that Deus will continue to bless your love and show you how to love more deeply and more perfectly. The purpose for living, Daena, is to undertake the quest to perfect your love so that you may love everyone, ...everyone, as Deus loves everyone."

As Ravennetus spoke these words, his soul was riddled with pangs of guilt. Had he been there for Allisyn? Did he truly love and care for her? Did he have the courage to love her? Was he failing in his love for her? Why had he not made every effort to go to her, to see her, to take her away so that they might make a life together? Was he afraid, or did the task simply seem impossible? If he truly believed in Deus, then he must believe that all things are possible, being with Allisyn once more, the three of them living together as a family once more. Suddenly he knew he was hiding behind the brotherhood and his avowed obligation to Deus. Was he still on the true path? His painful reverie was interrupted by Daena's next question.

"Do you even have to love people who are mean to you?"

"Especially those," and he thought of Bartolemus as he spoke. Suddenly he realized that the struggle with Barthol was not the struggle to overthrow him, but to find a way to love him; the battle against evil was not to defeat evil, but to love it out of existence.

"Is that all?" Daena asked innocently.

"You are a bright little girl. What do you think?"

"I think you have to tell the truth. 'Cause if you tell a lie to somebody, it means you don't love them. And you have to wait sometimes, 'cause sometimes people don't understand. And if you have lots of love, when your heart is so full of love, you want to give it to everybody!"

384

"That is very true, Daena. And there is one more thing about love. It does not just happen to you. Loving is hard work, something you have to work on your whole life, to get better and better at it. All of that is love."

"That's a lot to remember, Papa."

"Perhaps, but if you just remember that you make love grow by giving it to everybody else, that is all you need to know. Because love is not selfish."

"Being selfish is like having a hole inside your heart you are trying to fill up by taking things away from others, that's what Bronwyn says."

"She's right. To love means to give, not to take."

"I'll always love you, Papa. And Mama too. But one day I wish we could all be together."

"I wish that too. But until then I have a present for you."

He reached into his pocket and pulled out the amulet.

"What is it? It's beauuuutiful!"

"It is a necklace I made for you." He placed it around her slender neck with his rough brown hands. "There, as long as you wear this necklace, you will always be safe. If danger comes near, the little stone in the eye of the raven will shine, and the raven will sing, just like real ravens do when danger is near. Then remember me, my little one, and remember how much I love you and want to keep you safe."

"Thank you Papa. I will always wear it, always."

Chapter 36
Frater Transfugas

Ravennetus returned to strife among the brothers and it drove all else from his mind. One of the faithful spotted him as he walked up the mountainside, leading his horse up the last ascent. He ran to tell Fidelis, who came quickly, and turned Ravennetus aside before he came to the monastery.

"Ravennetus," Fidelis said in a state of great agitation, "I must speak with you before you come to the temple. There is unrest upon the mountain. Brother has turned against brother in their hearts."

"What is the problem?" Ravennetus asked calmly.

"Some of the brothers have turned from the truth. I fear they have been listening to Bartolemus, who is telling them that their faith in Deus is insufficient. He teaches that only by acquiring power can we defeat the darkness. He proclaims that the way of humility, the way of the servant, the submission of the will of man to the will of Deus is the path to powerlessness. He claims there is no higher will than the will of man."

Ravennetus' brow wrinkled.

"Bless you Fidelis Sampras for seeing clearly. For I perceive that this poison has not infected you. On my journey I had a revelation. And it is this, that love is the only force that can overcome the darkness. Our battle is to love with fervent love, most of all those who misuse us, or oppose us. I must speak with Brother Bartolemus."

"Be careful, Ravennetus, for I fear him."

"Then be careful of yourself, Fidelis, for if you fear him, then you do not love him."

Ravennetus found Bartolemus in the temple. With the light of the well extinguished, it was dark inside. The fountain, which no longer flowed, had become stagnant and an unpleasant odor issued from its depths. Barthol was peering into the well. The approach of Ravennetus was like the dawning of the day in that unlit corner, and Barthol winced as one who is wakened by a sudden bright light.

"My brother," Ravennetus said in a soothing voice. "I must speak with you. Our brother Fidelis has told me that you have engaged in certain false teachings."

"I?" Barthol asked with surprise.

"He said that you were teaching a doctrine of power, that we should gain power so that we might assert our will in our battle against the darkness."

"Certain of the brothers came to me for advice in your absence. I only tried to answer their questions according to my interpretation of your teachings," Bartolemus lied.

"Your interpretations? My teachings? I fear that you have missed the point, Bartolemus. The teachings come from Deus, not from me. When a brother asks you a question, it is not your interpretation you should give; rather you should seek the wisdom that Deus imparts through you. You give yourself, and me, too much credit. We are only the instruments upon which Deus plays the divine music. But the music is his, not ours."

"Ah! Then answer me this. If Deus is omnipotent, as you claim, why then has he not already defeated the darkness? Why does he need us?"

"The battle against the darkness is fought here, in the Now. We are of the Now and He is not. We are his soldiers but He directs the battle."

"Then it makes sense that his soldiers should be strong, that we should be masters and not slaves. An army of slaves is no army at all!"

"Not slaves, Bartolemus, servants. There is a difference. The servant undertakes service willingly, the slave unwillingly."

"But both are trodden under, good brother. What difference does it make if a man is shackled by love or by fear? In either case he is a captive. In either case he has lost his freedom. In either case his will is not his own. To fight, a man must *will* to fight. To win, he must *will* to overcome. Otherwise he can do nothing. Without his will, man is an impotent and useless creature."

387

"That is where you err, Bartolemus. Man's will is nothing; it does not matter. He is only impotent and useless if he lacks the knowledge of the Will of Deus. The importance you assign to your own will is overly inflated."

"*My* will inflated? What about *your* will? You seek to impose your teachings upon these men; to use them for your own purposes. You seek to control them. How can you accuse me of having an inflated will?"

"With every word you speak, Bartolemus, you show me more and more that you lack understanding. I must ask Deus for guidance in this matter. But for now I insist that you cease to spread your teachings among the brothers."

"*You* insist? You deceive yourself, Ravennetus, if you think you do not wish to control me! You make a mockery of your own teachings!"

Ravennetus felt frustration and anger rise within him.

"Thank you, Bartolemus, for the gift of this test," he said when he had controlled his emotions. "I must learn to love you the more for it." Ravennetus turned and walked away. Bartolemus heard his last words but did not understand their meaning.

The division within the brotherhood deepened with each passing day. Ravennetus continued to urge the faithful to treat Bartolemus and his adherents with respect and love, while they struggled to mend their differences. It was not difficult to agree to this, but to actually do it was another matter. As the faithful found themselves failing more and more, they unwittingly and increasingly turned to vengeful solutions. They urged Ravennetus to dismiss Bartolemus from the order. That would solve the problem. He was the cause of the rift and banishing him would restore things to the way they were before he came. The more Ravennetus protested, the more even the faithful began to doubt his credibility. They began to make their own plans for dealing with Bartolemus. In the end, as had so often happened before, Ravennetus stood alone.

The faithful brothers, if they could any longer be called that, came to him one evening. Fidelis was among them, leaning against the wall at the back of the company and hanging his head. Ravennetus sat holding four small round stones in the palm of his hand. He looked very tired.

"Ravennetus, we have come to demand that you rid us of Bartolemus. It is the only way. Every day his power and influence grows among the brothers. If you keep to your path, you will soon have no support."

"It seems that I have none now," Ravennetus said. "I have told you how to deal with this problem."

"But it has not worked."

"It has not worked because your faith is not strong enough. Your faith has died and so has your love. How can you love without faith?"

"So you have said. Yet we have only such faith and only such love as we possess, no more. If what we have is insufficient, so be it. We must try another way."

"But in seeking another way you only deceive yourselves. You are only led further and further away from the truth."

"The truth, Ravennetus, is that Bartolemus is tearing the brotherhood apart! Perhaps what we suggest is not the *best* way, but if can keep the brotherhood together might it not serve the greater good?"

"For what purpose would you keep the brotherhood together, if in doing so, you deny its very principles? Better that it not exist than it exist in hypocrisy."

"Do you mean to tear it apart yourself, then, with your stubbornness? It was worth beginning. Is it not worth saving? The brotherhood is like a man, Master. It is not perfect, because the men of whom it consists are not perfect. Just as a man must struggle toward the perfection of Deus, so must the brotherhood. Ravennetus, should our eyes be so fixed upon the sky that we fall into holes in the road?"

Ravennetus sighed and he closed his eyes. For a long time no one spoke.

"I am weary, my brothers, and my heart is cold. I have tried to show you the way. When that has failed I have asked Deus to show you the way. I have asked Him to strengthen you, to enlighten you. But I see that my prayers have gone unanswered. Do what you must, do what you think is best. I will have no part in it."

"You must convene the brotherhood. You must speak for us."

"I cannot, I will not, speak for you. I am dead in you, Deus is dead in you. Seek your own path."

"We must have a spokesman," someone said.

"What about Brother Fidelis?" suggested another.

"Yes!" the brothers cried. "Fidelis! He will do it. He will speak for us!" All turned to look at him. Throughout the debate, he had remained silent with his eyes cast down. Now as he looked up, he saw the light of Ravennetus' eyes burning into him. He felt a pain in his chest and he labored to breathe. He wanted to be somewhere else, anywhere that those eyes, the eyes of Deus, could not find him.

"I only do this for them, Ravennetus, because I love you. And I would not see all you have worked for come to nothing," Fidelis said finally.

Ravennetus turned away and left them all together. That night, he took the pouch from around his neck that contained the four unnamed Pearls. Loosening the leather thong that held it closed he opened it and dropped them into his upturned hand. The candlelight shone on them, revealing their roundness, but the Pearls did not respond. The light fell dead upon their lifeless surface. He sighed and placed them back into the pouch. Crossing the room he opened a trunk that held some of his things. Then he placed the Pearls inside and closed the lid.

The next morning Fidelis assembled the brotherhood. Ravennetus was not among them.

"I have called you here this morning on a matter that is most difficult for us all," he spoke. "The matter is that of our brother, Bartolemus. He has believed and taught contrary to the beliefs and teachings of the brotherhood. Therefore it is our desire that he separate himself from the brotherhood and go his own way."

Barthol stood.

"Who makes this claim?" he asked angrily.

Fidelis had no ready answer.

"We do," he replied at last.

"And just who constitutes this 'we'?" Barthol probed.

Fidelis cleared his throat, feeling his uneasiness rise and lodge there.

"We, the brothers."

"Well I am a brother, and I do not agree," Barthol argued. "Are there others who do not agree that I should be severed from the brotherhood?" Several stood with Barthol. "So, Brother

Fidelis, you see there are those who support me, who feel as I do. Who, then, are those who oppose me?"

Now several of the brothers stood with Fidelis, but most remained seated.

"What about the rest of you? What do you think?" Barthol queried. The seated mass were silent. "Well, Fidelis, it seems there are only a few of the brothers who agree with you. The rest of these sheep are too mindless to answer."

"Where is Ravennetus?" asked one who had remained seated. What is his judgment in this matter?"

"He would not agree to dismiss Bartolemus," answered Fidelis. "He wants no part of this proceeding. He wishes only that this division be healed."

"What kind of shepherd deserts his flock when the wolf comes stalking?" Barthol asked cynically. "Better to have a poor shepherd than none at all. Better to have someone who has faith in himself than one who has lost his faith entirely. Who will join me then? At least I am no coward." Several more rose and stood now with Barthol.

"See here, Barthol," Fidelis asserted. We do not seek to make this a contest for the loyalty of the brothers. We want only that you leave peacefully."

"You may seek what you wish to seek. I choose otherwise. And I *do* seek to make this a contest for the loyalty of the brothers. If I am to be dismissed, I will not leave those behind whose would go with me."

"No!" Fidelis shouted. "They will stay and you will depart. You must do as we say."

"I will not!" Barthol said defiantly, theatrically stomping his foot for emphasis. "I will do that which *I* wish to do. You *shall not* impose *your* will upon me. You say that the teaching of the brotherhood is to submit to the Will of Deus. Yet you seek to impose your own will upon me. Ha! You hypocrites! I see that my work here is through. I have proven my premise. No man can live up to the standard that Ravennetus has required. Not you, not even he himself. It is not possible, therefore man is doomed. I have no need to stay further, for you have sown the seeds of your own undoing. I will go... I will go and prepare for the time when the brotherhood falls under the weight of its own guilt. I will go and prepare for the coming of the darkness. For surely now it will come."

Everyone started talking at once. In the confusion, one of

the angered brothers standing near Fidelis picked up a stone and hurled it at Barthol, striking him in the chest. The thudding sound of it brought down a shocked silence on the group. Those in attendance of the Dark One reached down to pick up stones.

"Stop!" Barthol called to them. "Let Ravennetus know that one of his own precious brothers, a brother that stands for him and all his high principles, cast a stone at me. And that I... I, Bartolemus, his 'wicked' brother, chose not to meet that evil with evil. Let Ravennetus know that the tables are turned; that the good have fallen, that even the wicked are more righteous than they. Let him drink from that cup!"

With that he turned and walked off the mountain and many of the brothers followed him.

When Barthol and the renegade brothers had gone the rest sought out Ravennetus and told him of the events of the morning.

"What is done is done, my friends," he comforted them. "Barthol came here to work his evil among us and he has accomplished what he set out to do. Now he is gone. He has divided us and has planted the seeds of dissension among us. But something good has happened. Something has passed from us. Something has died. And for everything that dies we must trust that something better will be born. Barthol has shown us our weakness. That weakness, brothers, is that we are only men. And it is the lot of men to fail at what they would do if what they would do lies outside the will of Deus. But he has also shown us our strength, and our strength is that Deus is always there when we fall, to pick us up and place us back upon our feet, to set us back on the true way. He extends that opportunity to us now."

"But we are not worthy, Ravennetus. We have fallen short. How can such hypocrites as we seek His blessing?"

Ravennetus smiled.

"You have heard the Great Calamity speaking. Close your ears to her and forget what she has said. If Deus chose only to walk with perfect men then he would walk alone. No, he desires the company of 'hypocrites' such as we. He loves most those who can admit their mistakes, humble themselves, and

392

seek his favor again. Those are the most blessed among his children."

Thus Ravennetus spoke to his brothers. But deep inside he was troubled. He had done all that he could do and yet he himself had fallen short. He had loved Barthol with a pure love, trusting him completely, and he had been betrayed. He had hoped beyond all hope that his love could turn Barthol from the Darkness, but it had not been sufficient. To love Barthol had been the great challenge, and the great opportunity, of his life. To take on that challenge he had forsaken everything, even the woman that he loved. He had put the brotherhood at risk. He had loved Barthol, but his love had failed to change him. And thus beyond the void of despair caused by the betrayal of Barthol loomed a darker and deeper and blacker pit. And out of that pit came words he struggled to deny. "Fool," they said, "Deus has lied to you. Love is powerless. There is no hope after all."

Another five years went by and it was high summer again. The brothers, though reduced in number, had rededicated themselves to the cause and worked for the edification of their souls, and the souls of others, with greater zeal than ever before. Ravennetus was not least among them in his fervency. He put his all into repairing the damage Barthol had done. He buried his thoughts for Allisyn deeply and the shame he felt over deserting her. He did not go to see his daughter in those critical years, for he feared to leave the brothers again, or so he told himself.

Over time, the brothers noticed a change in those who approached the mountain. Fewer came in earnest to receive their teachings. The Holy Well, once a source of light and healing, became a putrid source of embarrassment to the Ravenites. They no longer allowed pilgrims into the temple. Many more came to jeer and some to hurl insults at the holy men. "Look at them," they prated, "living up here in isolation. What can they know of life? What can they teach us?"

Even nature seemed to conspire against their faith. The orchards and vineyards on the mountainside no longer produced as they once had. All seemed blighted. But in the face of these difficulties the remaining brothers drew together in a more firm solidarity and their resolve grew ever stronger.

Randor's family had grown to great numbers. While he himself had withdrawn to Braemara, dwelling there alone with Cora, his sons, Corvus and Corax, and their families populated the towering cedar groves that rimmed Hethraven. The ravens were loved by the brothers, and the brothers by the birds. Nothing happened, on hill or in vale, that Ravennetus did not know about through the efforts of the vigilant avians.

And so it was, late one bitter autumn day, that Corax came flying with all speed to the mountaintop. He sought out the Master and spoke to him excitedly.

"There is a large press of men, with weapons and fire, ascending the mountain. Quickly, we must act!"

Ravennetus reacted immediately, hurriedly calling the brothers together. As he told them this news, Corvus flew in with more grim tidings.

"They are setting the orchards afire. They are killing our people, knocking them from the trees with stones shot from slings and arrows from the bowstring, even the young ones! There are large birds, black and vile with detestable scaly heads. Whenever a raven goes down, these creatures pounce upon it and tear it apart. They are hideous!"

Thus Barthol came back to Hethraven leading an army of the renegade brothers, the Frater Transfugas, swollen in number and burning with an enmity that Barthol had fanned into hate. With them were vultures, immense, revolting birds that Barthol had bred in mockery of the ravens. They were black and ate the flesh of the dead and dying. The stench of death was emitted when they flapped their wings.

"What shall we do?" the brothers asked helplessly. "We have few weapons and it is long since we wielded them! They will burn us out. They will slaughter us and the birds of death will eat our flesh!"

"Do not fret yourselves, brothers, for Deus will not forsake us. Stand firm. I will go out to them."

Some of the brothers went with Ravennetus as he strode from the crest of the hill to face the threat of death. As they walked, the sun failed in the west and the long shadows faded. Evening came on quickly. Ravennetus stopped before the oncoming army.

"Peace! Peace!" He cried at the top of his voice. "Why do you come thus, to the Holy Mountain of Deus, armed and bent

394

upon destruction? We have nothing of value here, unless you come for enlightenment. Speak!" As he looked at the crowd, he began to recognize faces, faces of those who had followed Barthol off the mountain long ago.

"We come to claim what is ours!" cried a voice. "In the name of Barthol we come! Years ago you ridiculed us, disowned us and threw us aside. We come to reclaim our dignity." As the voice spoke Ravennetus' eyes were drawn upward. High above, vultures soared in the blackening sky.

"If you would reclaim your dignity then throw down your weapons and come to the temple. Repent of your pride. Seek not to humble us, but humble yourselves before Deus! Then will you reclaim your birthright as his sons!" Ravennetus shouted.

"Out of the way, Ravennetus," a voice commanded. Ravennetus recognized it as Barthol's. Now he rode forward, cloaked in deepest black upon a black horse. "Your time has come and gone. The time of darkness is here. I have shown you that the Will of Deus cannot prevail over the Great Calamity. You know that in your heart. Why continue to deceive these men? Go and leave them to me, or I will destroy them."

"You shall not have your way here, Barthol!" Ravennetus protested. "Go back. Leave us in peace!"

"Peace?" Barthol sneered. "There is no peace, and there will *be* no peace until the Light is forever snuffed out! Let vengeance be ours!"

Turning to his men he signaled them to fall upon the monastery. The renegades rode by either side of Ravennetus. The Master motioned and shouted for them to stop but they did not heed him. But neither did they harm him, for such were Barthol's instructions. "Let no man raise his hand against Ravennetus. His time has not yet come. There is something still I need from him. For now, I only want him to learn to hate me."

Ravennetus stood dumbly with the dust of the attack enveloping him. For a moment, the world turned a choking, dust-brown cocoon and he stood cut off, as if he had lost his senses and could neither hear nor see nor feel. His head was empty and his hands were useless. Time passed, or did it? Finally an unbidden thought invaded the void behind his eyes. He was dead and was standing on the threshold of the Otherworld... yes, that was it. In his weakest moments he had thought that to set aside the burden of consciousness would be painlessly sweet. How easy the passage had been...

But no... it was not so. One by one, his senses returned. He was first aware of the pounding of his heart, the throbbing in his temples and the earth trembling in the soles of his feet. Then the chaotic sounds of running feet and neighing of horses, mixed with the ringing of swords, the whistle of flying arrows, the curses of the attackers and the screams of the brothers, penetrated the chalky walls of his tomb. Something fell against his thigh, something material that jolted him and crumpled at his feet, a dark blur that groaned and then was still. Ravennetus' eyes slowly focused on the object, a man with a gaping wound from which his life drained away and soaked into the earth. *Khol... Khol... I am sorry, I wanted to save you, but I have come too late...* Khol, no, not Khol... a brother, a friend. *Deus, no, not this!*

In that instant Ravennetus knew his brother and his heart broke. He reached down and touched the shoulder of his fallen companion, feeling the fabric of the coarse brown homespun swimming in the warm, slick sap of his blood. He placed his hand upon the dying brow and felt the final spasm of death pass through the body, releasing the soul it had bound to the Now. He bowed his head and uttered a prayer of hope, a guardian to accompany his brother's spirit on its journey to the Otherworld, but the words suddenly seemed hollow. Tears came and the weight of his despair forced him earthward. He lay draped over the corpse and could not rise. But the tears were not for the dead man, and he knew it. They were for himself and his failure, the specter that had haunted him relentlessly, for the whole of his life.

The smell of burning brought him to his senses once again. Ravennetus rose and looked around. Slaughter raged rampant on the mountaintop. Everywhere there was fighting and the bodies of the slain. The murderous Frater Transfugas chased the faithful brothers on horseback and slew them. The valiant ravens flew among the horsemen, raking with their talons and pecking with their strong beaks. The Ravenites stood their ground and fought back with rocks and sticks. Above the mayhem the vultures soared. When anyone went down, man or bird, they fell from the skies and began their murderous ritual.

Ravennetus heard the defiant voice of Ulf amid the flames and the mayhem. He was carried suddenly back to the attack of the brotherhood on the City of Women. They had resisted. They had fought with every last shred of sinew. Now the tables were turned, now the brothers were defenseless in the face of their tormenters. Ravennetus was once again confronted by his failure and his guilt, the twin demons that stalked him, that met him at every corner, that ate away at him, that would not let him rest, that mocked his every thought and shadowed his every step.

He began to run, but to where? His demons pursued him. He ran to the summit of the mountain through the battle and the gray smoke. Hard on his heels, the demons howled with delight. Ravennetus stumbled into the house of the brothers and found his rooms. Quickly he slammed and barred the door. Outside the demons scratched at the wooden barrier and shouted their curses.

"Come deal with us, Ravennetus! There is only one way to do it and you know what it is! You must fight us. You must slay us! You have the weapon. The only thing that can kill us forever. Unleash it and be free!" the voices called from the other side. Or were they inside, inside the room with him, inside his head, clawing away at the inside of his skull?

Frantically and with trembling fingers he knelt beside a trunk that held the relics of his past and threw it open. He groped among the garments until his fumbling hands came across the object of his search, the cold, sharp sword of bronze that had hung at Ulf's side when he had ridden to Hethraven. Ravennetus had hidden it deep among the other memories, things he wanted to forget but could not. Now his hand closed around its hilt and he drew it forth.

It felt good to hold a sword once again. He delighted in the strength of his grip and the firmness of the muscles of his arm as his lifted it. It had been a long time...

The demons bumped at the door. He turned sharply towards it with a sudden violent urge. A vision erupted into his brain. It was not his thought, not his memory. Or was it? He was in the City of Women searching for Barthol in his rooms. How he had hated him then and wanted to kill him. But he had conquered that emotion. Now he loved his brother, his evil twin. He felt the sword in his hand, the symbol of his failure. He had opened the trunk and there was no turning back. Emotions long repressed were spilling from it. He had failed to love him, failed to kill him. He would not fail this time. Either he would kill

Barthol or kill himself. It was the only way to be free...

Ravennetus placed his hand on the edge of the trunk, pushing himself to his feet. When he did, his fingers brushed the leather pouch that held the four Pearls. These too he had nearly forgotten in the intervening years since he had put them aside. Outside, a tree crashed to the ground in flames. He started. His attention was drawn back to the yammering demons at the door. Mindlessly, he took the pouch, placed it around his neck and tucked it into his cloak. He crossed the room in a few quick steps. The moment he touched the door it became strangely quiet on the other side. He grasped the bolt and threw it back. Gritting his teeth, he took the latch in his hand and flung the door open. The fiends were gone. But there, standing in the hallway with a demonic smile on his face, was Barthol.

Chapter 37
Commutatus Secundus

Barthol's sword was drawn and he threw his jet-black cape aside with his free hand. His eyes were drawn to Ravennetus' blade.

"I see you are prepared at last to fight," Barthol smirked. "Good. As much as you would deny it, you have always wished for this, the chance to meet me face to face, sword to sword. You have wanted my death as much as I have wanted yours. You have a sword now... use it!"

Ravennetus advanced a step forward. The smell of smoke filled his nostrils and the voices of the dying came to his ears from without. "I should have used it long ago, Barthol, before you had the chance to destroy everything. All I have sought to build you have sought to tear down."

"You don't know the half of it!" Barthol taunted.

"I should have hunted you down and ended you. It would have saved the world much grief."

"Would it? The grief is of your own making, not mine dear brother. Your fight against the Darkness is folly. That is the source of your misery. Had you sought me out sooner, you could have saved *yourself* much grief. But let's not be overly philosophical. This is not the time for it. You have put off dying long enough, so get on with it. Slay me if you can! You will never amount to anything as long as I am alive! Your only chance is to kill me now, here."

"So be it!" Ravennetus lunged at Barthol, but the Dark One retreated and the blow rang off the stone wall of the passageway.

"You're out of practice!" Barthol chided. Ravennetus swung at him, again and again Barthol evaded the stroke, stepping backwards down the hallway.

"I fear this is not going to work out the way you have planned, brother," Barthol mocked.

Ravennetus grabbed a candle from the wall and flung it at Barthol's head, then moved once again to the attack. This time the Dark One stood his ground in the dim corridor and parried Ravennetus' stroke. Metal rang against metal. Ravennetus attacked again and again until his arm ached and his breath came in shallow pants.

"Ha!" laughed Barthol, who hardly seemed winded. "Surely you can do better than that!" Ravennetus leaned against the wall, his forearm cramping, sweat beading on his brow.

"I am your nemesis, brother, your undoing. It was I who sent Reyk to you, I who used his mouth to persuade you to attack the village where we were born. Think back, think about all your brothers with their gaping throats. Think about how much you despise me!" he spat, springing to the attack.

Ravennetus barely raised his arm in time to parry the stroke. Barthol rained down one after another in swift succession. Ravennetus, unused to wielding a sword and tiring rapidly, gave way before the onslaught. An unlit side-passage appeared to his left. Thinking quickly, he dodged out of sight down its length. Barthol turned the corner to stare into the blackness and hear the retreating footfalls. Running back down the main hallway, he took a candle from a lamp and returned to the portal of the darkened corridor. He took a cautious step forward. The blackness receded grudgingly before the flickering candlelight. Barthol took a few more halting steps, trying to remember the layout of the passages.

"It was I who dreamed up the little quest for Magor's Horn, not Aefalas. He was an idiot, too stupid to think of anything so clever. You were supposed to die then, you know, a meal for one of Mother's nasty little offspring."

Pressed into an alcove further down the corridor, Ravennetus listened, catching his breath and massaging his cramping sword arm. Barthol's steps drew nearer.

"Aefalas had already promised her to me, you know. I made a bargain with him. His part was to give me Allisyn for my bride. The quest for the Horn was a scheme to get you out of the way. Allisyn and I became very close after your departure."

400

Ravennetus seethed as Barthol's taunting echoes trailed off down the passageway.

"I was surprised that you never came back for her. For all your expressions of love, in the end you didn't seem too concerned for her well-being. But then again, she did seem rather... used. I tired of her myself after a time..."

Ravennetus leaped from the alcove and swung at Barthol, slashing the hand that held the candle, just above the wrist, and shattering his forearm. Barthol cried out and dropped the candle, plunging the corridor into darkness once again. As he fell to the floor he rolled away. The sword of his adversary whistled through the air above him, narrowly missing his head. Ravennetus could hear Barthol's labored breathing but could not find him in the utter darkness.

Recovering from the initial shock of his wound, Barthol drew a small dagger from his belt and threw it down the hallway. It clattered on the stones. In the blackness, Ravennetus followed the sound. Barthol got up and ran in the opposite direction, pinning his broken and bleeding arm against his chest with his sword arm. Ravennetus turned and pursued the sound of Barthol's retreating footfalls.

Barthol turned a corner and hurried up the flight of stairs that led to the temple, where he ducked behind one of the great stone cedar columns. Making a cut near the bottom of his cape he ripped off a strip of cloth and sheathed his sword. Ravennetus came up the stairs just in time to hear the ripping sound but Barthol was nowhere to be seen. In the cavernous, echoing temple it was impossible to locate the source of the sound. Through clenched teeth, Barthol stifled a cry as he wrapped the cloth around his mangled wrist. He secured it to his body by looping the strip around his waist and tying it off.

When he peered around the column Ravennetus had disappeared. Now it was Barthol's turn to wonder where his adversary was lurking. Once again he drew his sword and slid around the column, keeping his back to its rough-veined surface. Seeing nothing he bolted for the main door.

From out of nowhere Ravennetus cut him off, diving at his legs. Barthol went down on top of his injured arm and screamed in pain. His sword went flying across the floor. Ravennetus was atop him before he could crawl away to retrieve it, the pugnacious bronze sword of Ulf sticking uncomfortably in the Dark One's ribcage.

"So, Ravennetus, this is the moment you have waited for, is it not?" the Prince of Lies panted. "Go ahead, Ravennetus. Murder me."

"I may yet do it, Barthol. Do not be so hasty to throw away your life. I want to speak with you first. Since you are going to die, you may as well tell the truth. Why did you come to Hethraven?"

"Because I hate you. I hate everything you do and everything you stand for. I hate the brotherhood. It was my joy to destroy it."

"There is something else, Barthol. You could have brought an army against me in the beginning. But you did not. You deceived me. You crept into our midst and worked your evil. You could have killed me at almost any time. But you did not choose to do so. Why?"

"Because I know what you are about. I wanted you to fail more than I wanted you to die."

"You are lying Barthol. Tell me why you came!" Ravennetus asked, pressing the sword into Barthol's side. The fallen man caught his breath. For the first time in his life, the shadow fear crept into his heart and his lies gave way.

"The Pearls. Allisyn told me that you have them. Mother wants them. That's why I came. To learn their secret. To steal them from you and give them to her!"

"You will never get them Barthol. Never! Their secret is safe with me."

"So you believe! I have a way with secrets, dearest brother. Ask your wife. I found out Allisyn's secrets... all of them. And I will find out yours, no matter how deeply you conceal them."

Ravennetus pulled the tip of the sword away from Barthol's heart.

"That's right, *brother*. I know about the child. You were too careless with your summer journeys to the north. I sent a spy on your trail and he followed you to her. I know where she is. Tandela knows where she is. If I die, she dies, and Allisyn with her. So why don't you tell me about the Pearls. You can have your precious wife and daughter back and we'll call it even."

A pang of dread smote Ravennetus' heart.

"Your soul is black, Barthol..."

"Why thank you, brother. I had never hoped for such a

402

compliment from you." He laughed maliciously.

"...but I will never give you the Pearls nor reveal their secret to you." Ravennetus got up carefully, keeping the serpent Barthol, at sword's length.

"So be it, brother. But I promise you, the only way you can keep me from getting them is to kill me now."

"I know the game, Barthol. Randor told me. I know what happens if I kill you. To kill you I must learn to hate you, and if I learn to hate you, *I* become the servant of Thol-nys, and she will own the Pearls. I will not murder you. I will not be tricked into it."

"Then ponder this question, brother. How can you claim to love your wife and daughter and protect them if you do not renounce love and murder me in this moment? For if you do not they will surely die. A pretty dilemma, is it not, and cunningly wrought?" Barthol laughed heartily and mockingly placed the point of Ravennetus' sword at the base of his neck, inviting his brother to end his life.

"Do not be too sure of yourself and your cunning, Barthol," Ravennetus replied. "There is a time and a place for all things." And he ran from the temple.

Some of the brothers escaped into the trees, Ravennetus among them. Those who were not killed, Barthol captured and locked up. Many ravens also he took captive and threw them into cages, for he had dark designs upon them.

So it was that Barthol came back to Hethraven, driving out what remained of light and goodness there. He ripped the jewel Boreastrum from the altar stone and set it in a crown that he wore thereafter. What the vultures did not eat of the slain and maimed were thrown into the holy well to rot and further profane its sanctity. Then the Puteus Aeternus Lux was sealed and Barthol cursed the spirits of those who slept there, that they should forever be bound to the decaying hole and have no peace for all eternity, until the Great Darkness should finally come.

The next day he led the captive brothers and ravens to the headwaters of the Vahlen. There he forced the brothers to break the legs of the noble birds, speaking the words "the love of Deus" as they broke each bone, and then to drown them. One hundred ravens he put to death in this way. Brave Corvus and

Corax were murdered along with many of their children. The Vahlen was thereafter known as the River of the Hundred Ravens, in honor of those who died there. And Barthol cursed the ravens that their offspring should be born black, that their gait should always be querulous to recall that their ancestors had been broken by him, that their beautiful song should become a rasping croak, and that they should forevermore eat the flesh of the dead, as the vultures they had come to detest. The news of this transgression was spread far and wide by the creatures of the forest. When Ravennetus heard it he wept. And he wondered how he could find a way, after all that had happened, after all the suffering Barthol had caused, to keep loving his brother.

Away to the north, walking in the cool shade of the white-barked birches that stood by the singing stream, Daena poured out her heart to the stones, the grasses and the water. For five years she had waited patiently in the weeks following midsummer for the father who had not come. Now it looked as though he would never come again. The next morning she awoke and beheld his treasured gift, the amulet about her neck. She wondered why the beautiful stone had turned black and why the white stone of the eye had become blood red. She feared that her father loved her no more. And Bronwyn feared, if it were possible, that something yet worse had befallen.

Ravennetus wandered through the woods, careful not to make a noise that might give him away. He did not know if the hounds of Barthol had given up the chase or if they still pursued. He had spent the night in the arms of a great oak tree and had forgotten his troubles for a few hours. Now he sat in its shade wondering what to do next. He knew that the brothers had been scattered, some killed, and some taken captive. How many more might be wandering in the forest he did not know, nor how or when he might find them. He had thought to wander until he could discover them. Then he realized he was being hunted, and thought only of escape.

He heard the call of a bird above him and the sound of its

voice lightened his heart. When he peered up in the branches to catch sight of it, he saw only circling vultures and slid back toward the trunk to hide himself. But the song of the bird had given him an idea. He would go to Braemara, the place that held his first memories of the living world, and seek out his father Randor. At least he might find a respite there from the fear and weariness of the chase.

He set off in that direction, his eyes and ears tuned to catch any sight or sound that might mean the difference between life and death. It was not long until he heard voices. He checked his stride and clung to a tree, hoping not to be seen or otherwise discovered. The voices came closer and he eased around the tree opposite the sound. Momentarily he saw three of the brothers coming toward him, Lyricus, Boran and Brynetus. He stepped out from behind the tree and greeted them with a relieved whisper. They were exchanging news when an arrow whistled through the trees, piercing the back of Boran with a dull thud. He fell with a cry, wounded beyond hope, and the others ran away together. Behind them they heard the screams of their brother mingled with the shrieks of the vultures as they fell upon their prey. The frightened, fleeing threesome came to a stream and stumbled up its slippery bed until it fell over a series of stony crags. They climbed and rested for a while where the stream had scoured out a little pool. They drank gratefully and began to talk again.

"Deus, when will this end?" sighed Ravennetus aloud. "How much more death? I pray that there are others left alive."

"I know there are others," said Brother Brynetus. "There were many that ran into the forest with me last night but we became separated in the dark. We must have been forty altogether."

"We should find a place to stay, a place were we can make a permanent camp, some secret place we can always come back to. It is no good wandering. Then when we find others, we can bring them there as well," said Lyricus.

"I know a valley," Ravennetus revealed, "on the shoulders of Braemara. It is a hidden place where people do not come for fear of the lions that dwell there."

"You would lead us to a lion's den? I would as soon get an arrow in my back than to be torn to pieces by lions."

"Do not worry, Brynetus," Ravennetus said. "I lived among the lions as a boy. They will not harm us."

"But it is far from Heth. Will we not want to return there? Will we not want to take it back, to go there once again to live, when the others have gone?" Brynetus asked.

"As for me," said Ravennetus, "I am content to leave Hethraven for now. Nothing but misery is there for me. Perhaps one day... one day we may return," he mused. "But I cannot see that day."

So the three of them set out for Garschglen, the Valley of Lions, there to begin a new life. Fidelis came. More than all the others, Ravennetus was glad to see him safe. One by one they found the remnants of the brotherhood and brought them to the Garschglen. There the Sodalitas Ravenites lived and worshiped in secret, not daring to leave the valley.

Over the years a legend grew up around the outlawed brotherhood of ravens. It was said that they developed the uncanny ability to appear and disappear at will in the forest, for they were hunted mercilessly by Barthol's soldiers. Some said that they came by the ability to change shape, to turn themselves into animals. Around the hearth on many a wild and rainy night, to generations of wide-eyed boys and girls, it was whispered that the brothers could change themselves into ravens and that they learned this trick from Randor, the raven-god. Others held that when the need was great, the brothers would change into a herd of elk and go scampering, swift as hawks, through the forest and over the hills. And the legend was true.

Indeed many of the brothers longed for the times when they were incorporated as animals and could set aside the burden of consciousness. So many came to choose that simple, unassuming life, becoming the fathers of flocks of ravens or the vast elk herds that roamed thereafter the mountains and plains west of the Utlai.

But Ravennetus was bound by his calling and sought the counsel of Deus. And Randor, who had become increasingly withdrawn following the loss of his raven sons, found encouragement to go on living in his mortal son. So their inseparable fate became entwined once again.

One day as they walked up the long slope of Braemara, Randor upon Ravennetus' shoulder, the bird motioned for him to stop. He pointed a long wing down the line of a path that wound its way through the boulders.

"There," he said, "that path leads to the den where I had you brought when you were but a baby. Did I ever tell you about Carthyn, the man who carried you here to live among the lions? He was a mighty man, that Carthyn, one of the raven clan in his tribe. Not much of a thinker, I'm afraid, but trustworthy. Didn't get a lot of ideas in his head and go off trying to figure things out."

"You are making fun of me, Randor, are you not? Was it not your idea that I wake up, that I become 'enlightened'?"

"There was, and still is, good reason for it. For without you, Ravennetus, the darkness will surely come. Everything hinges upon your decisions. Do you not remember that Deus has shown you the World Dream? Have you forgotten your promise to him? You cannot hide in the hills forever. You must go... perhaps not today... perhaps not tomorrow, but someday you must go back out into the world. You possess the light, Ravennetus, and that torch must be carried into the darkness."

Ravennetus thought long before he spoke.

"I have pondered your words, Randor. I have asked myself over and over again, what now... now that Hethraven is a charred ruin, now that I have failed to establish it as a place for teaching and worship of Deus. I saw it in a dream, Randor, his temple upon Hethraven. I tried with great faith to accomplish all that he desired of me. He gave me the sign. But it all came to nothing. It all fell and lies about me in ashes. I have failed Him. And now... now that I have failed to discover the meaning of the four remaining Pearls, now..." He stopped short.

Ravennetus took the leather pouch from around his neck and held it in his hand. He loosened the thong and emptied the last four Pearls into his palm.

"Look," he said, holding the hand out to Randor. "Allisyn said that when I understood, when I knew the names and the meaning of these four pearls, they would shine once again. Look, Randor! What do you see?"

The Pearls lay in his hand and indeed they did not shine. Not only had they no brilliance of their own, but light did not even reflect from their surface. They looked rather like gray stones from a river bottom, dead and tinged with black around their dull edges.

"I have thought, Randor, I have prayed to Deus, I have

407

poured my soul into discovering their names and their lessons, but I cannot."

"So you have given up?"

Ravennetus did not answer.

"You failed to establish the worship of Deus on the mountain and you have failed to discover the meaning of the Pearls. Now what about the other, the unnamed failure, the unnamed fear? Tell me about that."

Ravennetus looked at his father with surprise.

"What do you mean?"

"You know that of which I speak. You have no secrets from me Ravennetus. I am within you. Do you not remember?"

"If you know it already then I need not tell you."

"I do not ask you to name your fear for my sake, but for your own."

Ravennetus hesitated.

"I cannot say it."

"When you come to that which seems an impasse, Ravennetus, that is where you find the doorway. Have you not learned that? Speak it, speak your fear!"

It was long before Ravennetus spoke.

"My fear... my fear is a fear so deep that by even speaking it I may bring on the darkness."

"Yet if you do not, the darkness will come of its own accord. Name your fear! Do not be afraid that by speaking it Deus will find out, because he knows your heart, your fear, already, as I do. You are the only one that continues to deny it, son. But unless you name it, unless you drag it out in the open and wrestle with it, it will forever bind you."

"My fear, Randor... is... that Deus... that He lied... to me. That love is not strong enough to conquer the Darkness. That love is not strong enough to bring about the World Dream. I tried it. I tried it fully, without condition or reservation. I asked Deus for strength and courage to do it. I asked him for the love to love my brother Barthol, for the love to change him, the love to turn him from the darkness and into the light. And I failed. Love failed. Love is not enough."

Ravennetus wept when he had finished saying these words. He wept with the passion of a man who realizes that his life has come to nothing, with the passion of years of pent up emotion and frustration. Randor let him weep, let the tears flow, let the sorrow and the anger and the frustration and the self-pity all

408

dissolve and flow away. When Ravennetus' tears had dried, the raven spoke.

"And is it this fear that keeps you from trying again?"

"No, Randor, it is the fear of dying, of dying with that thought in my mind, of losing access to the life beyond life in the Otherworld. Of realizing the ultimate failure."

"Yours is not the only soul at stake here. There are others, Ravennetus. There is Allisyn, there is your daughter, Daena; they need you. There are uncounted generations that will be born and die outside the love of Deus if you do not bring it to them. What about them? Why have you not gone to your daughter?"

"I have told you, Randor. I have come to count on Barthol's lies. He told me he knew her whereabouts but I cannot be sure of it. By going to her I may lead Barthol there. I cannot take the risk!"

"But what of the risk of living your life without her, of denying her your love? Why have you not gone to Allisyn?"

"I am *afraid*, Randor. Do you hear me? *Afraid!*" he shouted, trembling with pent up emotion. "I fear what what will happen if I stay here. But I fear more what will happen if I go! When Deus showed me the World Dream... he showed me everything. I saw... I saw my death! I saw the death of Allisyn. I was going to her, to Daena, Randor, to save them. But I failed, as I have so often failed. If I never go, then perhaps it will never happen. I would rather remain here, never to see them again, if my going means they must meet their fate."

"There is only one certainty in this life, Ravennetus, the certainty that fate will catch up to you. It cannot be cheated. It cannot be denied. Running from your destiny is not a choice, for them or for you. Your only choice is whether to try again, to recover your faith that the way of Deus is the true way, or to give up and die unfulfilled. But to try again, you need the wisdom of the last four Pearls. They are the key. He who has the wisdom of the Pearls may influence the unfolding of the World Dream, aligning it with the will of Deus. But without the wisdom of the Twelve there is no hope."

"Why do you say this cruel thing to me, Randor? Why do you torture me? Have I not just told you that I have tried to discover their meaning to no avail? Must you season the pain of my failure with gall? Leave me, then, if bitterness is all you have to offer!"

409

"My son, how long will it take you to understand? Life is not a straight line; it is a spiral. You have been at this very point before, but further up, where the pain and the frustration were not so deep. And what did you do then? You went on. You cannot discover the meaning of the Pearls by thinking or wishing or hoping; only by doing, only by living, ...perhaps only by dying. Only by moving further along the curving path will you discover their meaning. Life is meant to be lived, not pondered. To succeed, you must do more than think about success. When you decide to live your life in the Now, not as a hermit on a mountain, not as a beast of the hills, with all the pain and sorrow and joy that goes along with it, will the road to discovering the last four Pearls be opened to you."

Ravennetus gathered himself and stood, the Pearls still lying inert in his hand. Just then, a raven came hurtling through the skies toward the summit of the mountain. Randor saw him first, then did Ravennetus, following his father's line of sight. The bird landed, exhausted, upon a branch of a gnarled pine nearby.

"Randor, my Prince," he sang, "I have news of great import. The girl, the one they call Daena, the daughter of our brother Ravennetus, has been captured by Tandela of Aestri! She is even now being taken to Faenwys!"

Ravennetus blanched as the blood drained from his face.

"My son," Randor warned, turning quickly to Ravennetus. "You can begin no journey without taking the first steps. So it is with this one. As much as you may want to run down the mountain and rescue your wife and daughter, you cannot begin *this* journey without the first four steps. Those four steps are discovering the secrets of the four Pearls in your hand. For you cannot save her alone. You will need the wisdom of all the Pearls to do it. If you go without first discovering their lessons and completing your understanding of the Twelve, then you will be lost and they along with you."

Ravennetus wavered.

"Both your head and your heart are needed to save her, Ravennetus! But use your head now, discover the meaning of the last four!"

Ravennetus looked at the four drab stones in his hand. His heart and mind were in turmoil, wanting to fly to his loved ones, knowing that Randor was right, that he was as yet unable to steer the World Dream, as yet powerless to save them. But the choice had been made. Daena had been found and he must go.

410

The World Dream was unfolding.

"Ravennetus, sometimes when you are closest to your goal it may seem the most unattainable. That is when you must make the last push, the effort that will take you the last uncertain, terrifying steps. But beware, that is also when the journey may be the most perilous. You must be willing to give everything, you may be asked to leave everything behind to attain it. Do you recall the Gates of Death?"

Ravennetus closed his eyes in a desperate prayer and one of the pearls began to change. Its surface brightened as it began to reflect light once again. It began to glow, then shine with the brilliance of the full moon. Ravennetus felt its light bathe his eyelids, opened them, and gazed at it in wonder as understanding dawned. He took another step and the second pearl began to glow. He laughed with relief and with joy as he discovered its name. With the third step, the third pearl glowed.

The raven who had come bearing the message suddenly flapped his wings and left his perch, flying away toward Aestri. He called back to Ravennetus as he flew.

"Come," he cried, "there is no time to lose!" Ravennetus saw him hurry away and his thoughts followed. He jerked his head toward Randor who implored him to discover the lesson of the last Pearl. But Ravennetus' thoughts were suddenly far away, on the sheer cliffs of the Mergruen, and it remained dull and lifeless in his hand. Ravennetus turned back toward the flying raven, his eyes riveted to the black silhouette retreating on the horizon.

"No!" Randor called to him. "Discover the lesson of the Twelfth Pearl now, before you take another step, or you will discover it too late!'

The World Dream! Ravennetus saw it once more, saw his beloved standing on the Bridge of Vapors. He could not let her die! Randor called again but Ravennetus was already on his way down the mountainside, leaping from boulder to boulder with the agility of a young lion, his thoughts trained on Allisyn and his daughter. With a sad sigh of resignation, Randor spread his wings and followed.

411

Chapter 38
Three Women

Barthol brooded upon the summit of Heth, nursing his wound while his vultures circled overhead. His futile efforts to find and eradicate the remainder of the faithful brothers had left him sullen. Around him, the monastery was abused by the Frater Transfugas and their brigand cohorts. The summit, once resplendent with the bloom of flower and thought, became a wasteland. Weeds grew in the razed gardens, vineyards and orchards. Vines grew up the walls of the temple and the buildings fell into disrepair. Barthol's only joy was to walk among the ruins gloating over the fall of his brother and the stultification of his plans.

When there was nothing left to pillage and the renegades tired of hunting their brothers down, they left, one by one. Their usefulness to Barthol had run its course and he released them, empty of pocket and bereft of soul, to find their fearsome way in the world. Barthol alone remained upon the summit. Even as Ravennetus was wandering the Garschglen looking for answers to his questions, Barthol was plotting his next move.

Moving among the ruins he came upon the cell that Ravennetus had once occupied. He had heard the brothers allude on many occasions to the writings of their master, he had even caught glimpses of the books themselves, but he had never actually touched them or read the words they contained. As he browsed about the room, he was filled with a desire to see them. Perhaps, he thought, Ravennetus had written the secrets of the Pearls in one of his journals. Perhaps he did not need Ravennetus at all, but simply to find his books. He began to

412

search, looking among the boxes and trunks, many of which had already been looted. There was one however that had not been opened. He took a fallen beam and beat upon the lock until it broke, greedily opened the box, and rummaged through it. Nothing... nothing but worthless old clothes! In anger he slammed shut the lid and banged his fist upon it.

He emerged from the cell and walked to the Lympha Placida to assuage his thirst. Bending down to wash his face and hands he saw the entrance to the cave reflected in the pool. The image of Ravennetus seated beside it, his manuscripts lying open in his lap, came suddenly to him. He stood and ran into the musty cavern. He looked hastily about, but found no shelf or hole in which such things might be stored. Frustrated again, he sat down heavily upon the stone bench. As he did, it rocked ever so slightly and made a scraping sound. Jumping up, he pulled the weighty stone lid aside and reached into its darkened recess. There! There they were! One by one he pulled them up, large, leather-bound books with inlaid writing. He could not read the words for they were written in a language foreign to him and in an archaic script not used by the brothers. Gathering them in his arms he ran back to his rooms. There, in the light of the sun by day and of candles by night, he began, with wicked intent, to translate them and discover their secrets.

Eventually he succeeded in understanding the language of the manuscripts and much was revealed to him from their pages. But much remained hidden and what was yet hidden, he mused, would take a lifetime to discover. As the months passed the mountain became inhospitable. Cold, late autumn winds blew, tossing the tops of the cedars and littering the ruins with fallen leaves, heralding the approach of winter.

It was then that Barthol resolved to go back to Faenwys. There he would find comforts, good food and a soft bed to lie in. He could take the manuscripts with him and continue the process of translating and understanding the guise of the metaphors in which some of the teachings were concealed. He bundled up the few possessions he had acquired in his life as a monk and packed them on the back of his horse. Ultimately, concerned that the writings might fall inauspiciously into Tandela's hands in Faenwys, he decided to leave them on Hethraven where they would be safe. So he returned the books to the stone seat in the cave by the Lympha Placida and deserted the Holy Mountain.

Meanwhile Tandela had been exerting all her efforts to find the child of Allisyn, ever since Barthol had sent word of her existence and whereabouts. Rumor had it that she was beautiful, even more beautiful than her mother, and that possibility vexed the queen.

With Aefalas and Barthol gone, Tandela was in sole possession of the throne and her lust for power, at least for a time, was sated. She doted more than ever upon her appearance. With the passing years she had despaired of the decline of her legendary beauty. She fancied that as it failed, so would her power to enchant the victims of her deception. She became obsessed with preserving both. So she studied to perfect the black art of making potions and channeled the power of her wicked mentor, Thol-nys, into them. As she wove these spells to make herself more beautiful her soul became utterly malformed and twisted.

Every opportunity to prove to herself and to others that she was the most beautiful, most powerful woman in the world, she seized. She set snares for unwary men of the city, old ones with some semblance of rival power whom she sought to subdue, young ones whose handsome looks appealed to her. Her appetite for them became unquenchable. But once her conquest for these unfortunate and ambitious lovers was completed, they would curiously disappear. No one knew their fate. It became known that to be favored by Tandela was to die. Still many came to her willingly, either to savor with her a brief time of unexpurgated pleasure, or under the delusion that they could bend her to their will and so usurp her power. But none could do so, for a power worked in her far beyond their puny abilities to countermand. And so she had her way with them all.

All except one, and that fact burned within her, almost as much as Allisyn's stubborn presence. That one was Bors, still the chief of the army and still a man of power. Always he was on her mind. The thought of his autonomy galled her. If he could be brought under control then she would fear no one. With the army behind her, she could enforce her rule with impunity. Often she would watch him from the walls and fantasize how she might entrap him, as she had ensnared Aefalas so long ago.

414

Allisyn was aware of Tandela's desires and her methods. So she worked secretly to thwart the queen's plans, being careful that Tandela did not know, for the least mishap would mean her death. Tandela's power had grown while she had kept Allisyn incarcerated. Few were those who gave a thought to Aefalas' daughter now, consumed as they were by their own desperate affairs, and their support for her had been all that kept her alive. Now her position had grown increasingly tenuous. Tandela's promise to Barthol to keep Allisyn alive until his return, which she bitterly rued, was all that held back the axe.

Allisyn understood the influence that Bors wielded and Tandela's intention to subvert him. So Allisyn worked diligently to win Bors over to her cause, to keep him free of Tandela's web. Each time Tandela threw a sticky strand about him, Allisyn would cut it loose. It was very dangerous, for the queen's spies were everywhere and no one was to be trusted. But Allisyn had come to realize that her very existence depended upon keeping Bors free, and she bent all her energies there, listening, doing, and undoing.

It came to pass that Allisyn heard her daughter had been found and that soldiers were bringing her to the City. In her distress she appointed a time and a place to secretly meet the tall and honorable captain. Their rendezvous occurred along the walls one night, in an outthrust shadow of the castle. The roaring of the nearby waters insured that no one would overhear their discourse.

"Bors," she said, "bless you for coming. I have news I must give you and not much time. Tandela has learned the whereabouts of my daughter, Daena, and even now she brings her to the City. She will murder her, Bors, and I must stop it."

"What do you want of me?" he asked.

"You can help her, if you will. See that she is not brought here. Take her and hide her again."

"I cannot openly oppose the queen. It would not benefit either of us to do so. You walk a fine line, Lady Allisyn."

"There must be a way to keep her safe! Bors, she is only twelve years old! She is a threat only in Tandela's twisted mind! You must help her. She is innocent!"

"I will do what I can for her."

Allisyn showed her disappointment in the lack of a stronger pledge of Bors' support, but more he would not promise.

"Thank you Bors," she said, her resignation apparent.

415

"There is one more thing. When Daena is brought here... Bronwyn, if she is alive, will come looking for her, for she will not willingly forsake my daughter. If there is any hope to save Daena, she will come. Tandela hates her, Bors. Say that you will assist her in any way that you can! Promise me, Bors."

"Please, Lady Allisyn, I told you. I will help if I can. And now I must go. Tandela has asked to see me this very hour."

"The blessing of Deus follow you Bors. Thank you," Allisyn ended, with tears of despair and hope commingling on her cheeks.

Bors looked on Allisyn with pity. He was less hopeful than she that something might be done to save her daughter. He wanted to promise more but feared to do so. There were so many ways that his efforts might go awry. And although his honor ran deep, he knew that he could do more good in Aestri alive than dead.

He knocked upon Tandela's door with misgivings. Never had she invited him to her apartments in the evening and he mistrusted her motives. The doors were opened by two chamberlains and he felt a semblance of comfort in their presence, that dissolved when the queen dismissed them. A fire burned upon the hearth and a table had been set for two near the fire. The blaze had taken the chill from the air that had made Bors shiver in the hallway.

The queen invited him to sit and poured him a glass of wine. She wore a thick robe with a collar of mink pulled tightly about her neck. Its red fabric flowed to her feet where it terminated in a hem of the same trim. In the side of the robe were slits where her arms emerged, bare, soft and white. Her chestnut hair was pulled up atop her head, revealing the delicate curve of her neck and the fine down that grew there. Bors thought to himself that he had never seen her look so alluring, and that thought concerned him. He was well aware of the enchantments of this unscrupulous woman and he braced himself to withstand her wiles.

"Why have you sent for me, Ma'am?" Bors asked, the slight flutter in his voice divulging a hint of nervousness. Tandela was pleased.

"There is a matter of some importance, Bors, that I wish to discuss with you," Tandela rejoined, sticking to business until the time had come to spring her trap. "For some time I have known that my cousin, Allisyn, gave birth to a daughter while she was away from Aestri. She has kept her in hiding until now but I have discovered her whereabouts. Even now she is on her way here, under an armed escort. I hope you do not mind that I appropriated soldiers from your command to retrieve her."

"That is your privilege, Ma'am," Bors answered bluntly. "What interest have you in her?" he continued, feigning ignorance of the situation.

"Come Bors, you cannot be that simple. You cannot be unaware that Allisyn is my rival, that she seeks to dethrone me. She works unceasingly to poison everyone against me. I fear that the knowledge of her daughter's existence might put ideas into the peoples' heads, strengthen her cause, so to speak. Drink some wine Bors."

Bors complied by lifting the goblet to his lips, taking a small sip, barely enough to moisten his lips. Tandela watched him carefully.

"What then, my queen, would you have me do?"

"Meet the escort on the frontier in the Droemenvael. Bring the daughter here in secret. I do not want it known that she is in Aestri."

"That seems a simple enough task."

"My requests are always simple Bors, always easy, always a pleasure to perform." She looked at him intently across the table and smiled seductively. Tandela drank deeply and Bors put the goblet to his lips again. He met her smile with his own. Tandela pursed her lips and her mood changed abruptly.

"Is something wrong, Ma'am?" Bors inquired.

"Oh, it is nothing," Tandela sighed. "I often think of children, you know. Aefalas was not able to give me any. Ever since I learned that Allisyn had a child, my own barrenness has plagued me. I have had lovers," she paused, letting this last word hover in the atmosphere over the table, "but none of them have succeeded either. I have nearly despaired of finding a man virile enough to do the job. I would do much for the man who could give me a child."

She drank again and looked hard at Bors. She saw that his eyes were slightly dilated and sensed that the potion she had poured in his wine was beginning to take effect.

"What would you give, Ma'am?" Bors asked.

"Why half the throne, half the realm. What is the good of it if I cannot pass it on to a heir of my blood?"

"I cannot imagine, Ma'am."

417

"What can you imagine, my good Bors, my stout love?" she asked, slightly parting the folds of her robe to reveal what lay beneath. Bors saw the glow of the firelight reflecting from her oiled skin. He sat transfixed. Tandela got up slowly and walked around the table to his chair. She lifted him up, her hand cupped under his chin, then took his arm and led him senseless to her bower.

The next morning Bors departed the castle. Passing over the high bridge that spanned the gorge, he sauntered down into the Droemenvael. His recollection of the previous night was hazy but his allegiance to Tandela had somehow grown stronger and utterly displaced the memory of his earlier promise to Allisyn. By noon he had come to the frontier and waited there for the troop escorting the royal captive. When they arrived he led them off the road and into the shelter of the trees. He threw back the hooded cloak of the diminutive prisoner.

Undaunted, Daena raised her eyes to meet his stare. She said nothing but her look was enough to convince Bors that she was proud, strong-willed, and ready to face any challenge. And she was beautiful, as Tandela had feared, the image of her mother. Now he could understand Tandela's concern. For here was a girl that men would follow, a girl to whom men would give their loyalty and their lives, a wildflower of a girl whose every word would be worshiped. He covered her head again, even as she stared into his eyes, and instructed the soldiers.

"No one is to see her or learn who she is. On pain of death," he added. And they took her away by hidden paths through the hills to the Bridge of Vapors. When night came, they brought her to the City and locked her in the dungeon beneath the castle.

It was scarcely a week later that Bors found himself once again on the border near the upper end of the Droemenvael. He had come on a routine matter, to inspect the guard that kept watch on the frontier from a tower recently constructed in the hills. Having finished his business, he was making his way back to the road when a peasant approached him.

418

"Sir Bors," the old man hailed the tall captain with a toothless grin, "Is it in your power to give sight to the blind?" The odd question intrigued Bors.

"Why do you ask?" he replied gruffly.

"It is said in the old stories that a truly honorable man might give sight to the blind," the peasant went on.

"You seek an honorable man, then, do you?" he inquired. Suddenly Allisyn's request reappeared, an island looming out of the mist on a dark ocean.

"Yes sir, I seek a man who might above all else value the truth."

"The truth?" Bors questioned with a note of cynicism. "I have heard of that before, but have found it rarely on the lips and in the hearts of men. But, verily, I understand the reason for your inquiry."

"Then follow me, sir, if you please. For I can show you that rare thing, someone who speaks the truth."

The peasant led the burly soldier through thicket and glen, winding his way through the low hills to the west. Presently, Bors smelled the smoke of a wood fire. Ahead of him was a clearing, and in it, a low house with walls of turf and a roof of thatch. He stooped low and followed the man inside. The light was dim. From the rear of the cottage came the plodding tread of an ox and the grinding rasp of the quern. To his right, among the sheep on the earthen floor, sat a young woman singing softly to herself.

"Here she is, Sir, the one I told you about."

At the sound of the peasant's voice, Bronwyn raised her head and turned her face toward it. She rose and approached Bors.

"Are *you* the honorable one?"

Bors hesitated and shifted his weight from one foot to another.

"Yes," he answered finally.

Bronwyn threw back her shawl and studied him with her blank, white eyes, ghost-like in her serious face. Bors looked back in amazement at the colorless orbs, endowed with a searching purpose, that sought to plumb the depths of his being.

"I am Bronwyn."

"Lady Allisyn told me you would come."

"The *girl* must live."

"I have promised Allisyn I would do what I could to save her," he said, skirting the truth.

419

"Promised?" Bronwyn queried, an edge of concern in her voice. "You said you promised?"

"It will not be easy to find a way," Bors said elusively.

"Will you take me to her?"

"To whom?"

"Why to Allisyn, Sir."

"It is impossible. She is confined to the castle, watched night and day."

Bronwyn's face fell.

"Then what can I do, Sir? I cannot sit idly by while my dear ones are in danger."

"You do not know the extent of the danger, not only to them, but to yourself as well."

"I would walk into the very jaws of death for them, Sir."

"I do not doubt it. But it would be foolish."

"A fool may succeed where the wise may fail. And the blind may see things that the seeing may not. There is a seed of treachery in you, Bors. I can feel it. But it has not yet taken root. Take care! Tandela serves the Darkness, Bors; she serves Thol-nys, the Great Calamity, the Unfathomable Blackness. And *that* is the truth. Whatever she has promised you is a lie. Whatever she has given you, she has taken yet more. Do not be deceived by her. Do not let her have your soul, Bors. Listen to one who speaks the truth and search your heart."

Torn between honor and self-preservation, Bors watched the featureless white orbs of Bronwyn's eyes for a moment, then turned quickly and left the cottage.

Chapter 39
The Sacrifice

Even as Bors spoke with Bronwyn, Barthol arrived unexpected at the City gates. He led his horse up through the winding streets and arrived unannounced at the castle. Unpacking his things, he sought his rooms and some refreshment. Then he went to find Tandela. She was seated in the Great Hall. She did not rise as he drew near.

"Tandela, you are more beautiful than ever. How could I have neglected you for so long? In the end, it was only the desire to see you that brought me back. What news?"

She watched him for a moment, as a cat might watch a serpent slither through the grass, before she answered.

"I have spent my time well."

"I do not doubt that, my love. Have you kept our sweet Allisyn safe?"

"She is not yet dead, if that is what you mean."

"Good, because I have need of her. Ravennetus is coming back to pay us a visit."

"Him?"

"Yes, and I fear he is very angry, especially with you love."

"And why is that?"

"He knows that you have his daughter and is determined to free her."

"How did you know?"

"Let's just say I have friends with keen eyes and tireless wings."

"I was going to surprise you with the good news myself," Tandela cooed malevolently.

"You are too kind, Tandela."

"I plan to sacrifice her tonight. She will be the first child to serve as a blood sacrifice to Thol-nys. You may think of it as a 'welcome home' gift, ...from me to you."

"You think of everything, my dear," Barthol joked. Then he grew serious. "All the universe appears to be converging here, to this place, on this night. It will be a fateful and infamous one."

"I have waited long enough for it while you have been off playing your mysterious little games. I am tired of watching for scorpions everywhere I step. I want to be rid of them all, the girl, Allisyn, Ravennetus; all of them."

"No more than I, I assure you."

"Tell me then, what do you have in mind?" she asked drawing closer to him in breathless anticipation.

Ravennetus, Fidelis and Randor had traveled many days through the mountains from the south, passing to the west of the Ice Fields of Ninn and down the headwaters of the Mergruen. Now they were but a half day's journey from the City and they approached it with caution. They had heard rumor of Barthol's arrival there, only a few hours before, from the ravens that accompanied them, flying away to reconnoiter, winging back with fragments of news. The three crept anxiously along the rough path, keeping to one side among the trees. On occasion, they saw vultures circling overhead or sliding toward Faenwys on long wings.

In a clearing, they chanced upon a crude encampment, and crept forward until they could hear the voices of those who huddled around the small, smokeless fire. An indigent peasant arrived from the opposite direction.

"What ho, Thruen? What goes on? Were we right that something is afoot in our fair City?"

"Indeed, it seems that the good queen is planning a celebration tonight."

"What sort of gruesome affair does she have in mind this time, roasting a few more of us who can't afford the tax?"

"No, no. None of the routine stuff this time. The Black Devil is back and she is going to make sacrifice to the Golden Pig."

"Who's going to get it?"

"A girl. There is a wild rumor going 'round that it's Princess Allisyn's daughter, but of course that can't be true."

"Poor little thing, whoever she is," sighed one of the women.

"It's a shame," another of the men said. "She's killing us off one by one. And us in no position to squawk about it. Still, I'd do something if I could."

Ravennetus and Fidelis stepped out from behind the tree and strode into the camp. They were at the fire before the peasants realized it. The enormous Randor sat upon Ravennetus' shoulder.

"Hey, who are you?' a big, bedraggled man asked, jumping up and grabbing his staff.

"I am called Ravennetus. And I fear the rumors you have heard may be true. Tandela has indeed found and made captive the girl Daena, my daughter, the daughter of Princess Allisyn, and I intend to free her. Even now I go to the City."

"Right, and I'm Tandela's sewing maid! But what did you say? Are you daft? You can't get in there. No one can."

"Be that as it may, I must try, though I die in the attempt."

"You're serious!"

"I am more than serious, I am determined to set the girl free, no matter what I have to do."

"You have a plan then?"

"No," Ravennetus replied. "I trust in Deus that he will see me through."

"Who's Deus? I hope he has an army!" The peasants all laughed.

"*I* am his army," Ravennetus said.

The big peasant laughed again and winked at the others.

"Where's you gear, then? You know, armies usually have weapons, swords, pikes, and that ilk."

"I have no weapons of that sort. I am armed only with the Truth."

"You're crazier than I thought, man. Forget it. You're going to get yourself killed. No sense you and your daughter both dying on the same night. But come, sit with us. Have something to eat. You look half-starved yourself."

"I cannot stop to eat, but thank you. I must go on."

"No, no, come now. You can't go just yet. Listen, we won't have it. Come join us. We're all outlaws here. Had to

423

run and hide because we couldn't pay the bloody tax. We've all lost our dear ones to that witch, Tandela. But we know better than to go putting our necks in a noose. Come man, sit down!"

Ravennetus threw back his hood so that the mark of banishment was in clear view. The light shone from his brow like beacon on a dark shore.

"It's him. It *is* him!" remarked the woman. "I remember now. I saw them put that brand on him, I did! Saw him stand up to Tandela and the Back Devil himself!" she continued.

"So you did," said Ravennetus. "Now I am going back."

"They'll kill you for sure, once they see that brand," cried a boy who was with them.

"Who among you will come with me? Who among you will stand against this evil. Who among you are tired of living like animals in the hills while the wicked recline on their soft couches and drink their wine and murder the innocent for their pleasure?"

"Me for one!" a lone voice cried.

"Me too!" cried another.

"I'm in," cried a third. "The soldiers killed my son, for nothing, *for nothing,* I tell you! I can't live with it anymore. I've got to do something about it. You can count on me!"

"Good, good!" said Ravennetus, smiling for the first time in days. "Are there others of you? Yes? Good! Send someone to tell them to gather at the altar of Thol-nys tonight before the sacrifice. The rest of you, come with me!" A few of the men went off to spread the word and rally the other roving bands of outcasts while the rest followed Ravennetus; all save one, a pale, vulture-like man with hooked nose, a long craning neck, and stooping shoulders. He stole away in the direction of the City.

The afternoon, well advanced, found Ravennetus, Fidelis, Randor and their band of wretches lying in a glade awaiting nightfall, planning how they might rescue the girl. Every now and then the leader of the band would dispatch one of them with a message or others would creep in to join them. All the while Ravennetus could not help thinking of Allisyn. This was the night he had seen in the World Dream of Deus and he must go to her! He had to see her, to hold her in his arms once more. He could do this, *and* save his daughter. He knew that he could. It was not the will of Deus that they should perish, it could not be!

Fidelis Sampras saw the faraway look in Ravennetus' eye. "What is it, Master?" he asked.

"Allisyn, Fidelis. I must go to her."

"What about the girl? What should we do, wait here and join the others, or go with you?"

"Wait for nightfall, then go with the others, my true friend. Perhaps you must save Daena. I, too... but first... first I must go to her. I will meet you at the altar."

Fidelis had misgivings. He felt an urge to go with his master, to keep him from going on alone. He put his hand out and caught Ravennetus by the arm as if to say, 'don't leave me'. Ravennetus squeezed Fidelis' hand and gently removed it.

"I must go on alone, Fidelis. You can't come with me this time. Not yet."

Fidelis was distracted by Randor who sailed out of the tree and landed at his son's feet.

"Ravennetus," the raven said, "your thoughts are clouded. It is too late! You cannot rescue her! Go to your daughter and save her young life. Remember the Twelfth Pearl, Ravennetus. You have not discovered its meaning! Without it you cannot change things. You cannot save her, I tell you!"

As they spoke another man joined the group, the vulture-like creature that had run to the City earlier. He listened intently as the others spoke.

"Listen to him, Ravennetus!" cried Fidelis. "Do not go. I fear for you!"

Ravennetus looked into the eyes of his friend, then to the eyes of his father. "I cannot do otherwise," Ravennetus said quietly. He reached into his pocket and removed a note he had written. *"My love, meet me at the crossroads of Ostwyn at the rising of the moon,"* it read. *"I have a plan to save Daena."* He handed it to one of the outlaws who lay in the glade with him.

"Take this note into the city and deliver it to the Lady Allisyn. Do not fail me... her life depends upon it."

"I will find a way," the messenger said. When he left, Ravennetus spoke once again to Randor.

"I must go now, although I am unsure of the way," he said. "But my mind is clear. Stay here, Randor, with Fidelis, and make sure that all are assembled at the altar." Randor started to speak, but stopped short before he had uttered his protest. He knew there was no changing Ravennetus' mind. He fluttered up into a nearby tree and shook his head sadly.

"I can show you the way," the vulture-like man spoke up, directing his comment to Ravennetus. Ravennetus, who had not noticed the man before, now looked at him with a vague sense of recognition. A spasm of fear shook the Master as he gazed upon the man, upon hope and death.

"Lead on then," he said and they vanished into the trees.

Allisyn paced her room. She had heard nothing from Bors for days and now the rumor had come that Barthol had returned to the City. What were he and Tandela doing? What were they thinking and plotting? Was Daena here? Was she still alive? Deus, preserve her! What about Bronwyn? Had she come? Had Bors seen her and talked to her? She walked, fretting and fighting back the tears. From time to time she would gaze out over the gorge to watch the ever-changing mists. *"Mother, where are you? Come to me mother. I have never needed you so."* But ever her thoughts returned to Daena, and her heart ached for her daughter.

Presently she heard a knocking at her chamber door. She rushed toward it expectantly, recoiling when she recognized the face and form of Barthol.

"Eager to see me? Did you miss me? There there, now, ...you could not help yourself, could you?"

"Say what you have come to say and leave me," Allisyn snapped.

"My, but we can be haughty at times, can we not?" Barthol said reprovingly. Then suddenly his mood became sinister. "I'll tell you something and leave quickly enough, if that's what you want. Tandela is planning a homecoming celebration for me tonight. Your daughter, Daena is to be sacrificed to Thol-nys. Tandela will be performing the ceremony herself. I've come to invite you to be my guest. We can watch together while Tandela plunges the knife into her heart!"

Allisyn's hand went to her open mouth and she began to quiver. Tears rolled down her cheeks but no sound came from her mouth.

"By the Great Calamity you're beautiful when you're terrified," Barthol quipped as he left the room.

Allisyn fell to the floor, cried all the tears she could cry, and lay there in a stupor.

426

When she finally recovered she sat up, enraged, and pounded the floor with her fist. Then the great sadness, the aching for her little one returned. At the distance of twelve years Allisyn could hardly remember what she looked like. And tonight... tonight she would see her for the last time, never to hold her again, never to talk to her again. She fell back to the floor like a dead thing.

There was a rattling on the wooden planks of the floor. At first Allisyn thought she might be dreaming. She stretched and her hand hit an object lying there. She sat up to see a stone, to which was tied a note. Unfolding it, she read greedily.

My heart,

Meet me tonight on the Bridge of Vapors at the rising of the moon. I have a plan to save Daena.

Your beloved,

Ravennetus

The note shook in her hands as she read it. Deus be praised, this was good news beyond belief! She ran to the window. The sun was setting fast, the horizon already tinged with lavender. Her heart pounded. Somehow, she found the strength to be patient. She waited anxiously for night to fall, watching as the phantoms swirled in the gorge, dampening the dark, cutting wall she had braved as a little girl to escape the vigilance of her elders and come to the hovel of the Old Crone. Then it had been an adventure, a lark. But that was before Ravennetus, before Daena. How she yearned to see them!

Other voices called to her now, voices not from outside her, but from within. Then death had been far away. Now to crawl upon that edge, so high, so narrow, so slick with ancient mosses, seemed a courtship with death itself. She feared to go, but more she feared not to go. Her heart swelled with the love of her dear ones and pushed her dread aside.

She thought of her days of freedom, days of traveling the wide world with Ravennetus, days when nothing might daunt her. She thought of the passage of the Gates of Death. *'Only in unity,'* Randor had said. She must find her husband; they must be together now, in this time of imminent need. She

427

thought of the quest for the Horn when she had given Ravennetus *Coras*, the Pearl of Courage. She must summon it now. If there was a chance to save her daughter and to be reunited with her husband, then she must take it.

It was dark enough. She pulled her cloak about her shoulders, tiptoed to the door of her room, and stood listening for a nervous moment. All was quiet. Turning, she whispered a prayer and dragged herself through the window, out onto the wall high above the roaring cataract.

All that afternoon Barthol's spies, avian and human, had brought rumor of his brother's whereabouts. One of their number had been in a camp of outlaws in the hills and had seen Ravennetus himself. Meanwhile, soldiers had captured the messenger bringing Ravennetus' note to Allisyn and had brought the man to the Dark One. Barthol had read the note with malicious glee. Tearing it up and flinging the bits aside, he wrote another, instructing one of the soldiers to tie the forgery to a stone and fling it through her open window. Now he knew exactly what Ravennetus' plans were. He was attempting to reunite with Allisyn. His love for her would be his downfall, of that Barthol would make certain.

Barthol gathered a group of soldiers and set out to apprehend Ravennetus. His vultures brought him constant report. Toward evening Barthol was informed that Ravennetus was heading toward the crossroads in Ostwyn. Barthol positioned the troop in a narrow defile along his path to capture him.

Night came but the moon had not yet risen. It was dark in the forest and a deep chill had settled in the vales. From the swaying tip of a pine an owl hooted, plaintively searching for its mate, but no answer came back in reply. Barthol and his soldiers waited, their frosty breath adding to the gathering mist in the hollow. It was not long before Ravennetus came walking, led by Barthol's hook-nosed accomplice. When he was well into the ravine, Barthol gave the signal and the soldiers fell upon him. The spy ran. To struggle was useless. Torches were lit and Ravennetus was anchored to a tree with stout ropes. Barthol stood before him.

"So, we are met again, my brother," Barthol said.

Ravennetus was silent. He knew that he had but one last

chance to redeem Barthol and this was the moment.

"There is some unfinished business between us," the Dark One continued. "Now the time has come to settle it. When you left Hethraven I found your journals. It took me a long time to translate what I needed to know from them. I was never quite the man of letters that you were. But in the end I succeeded as, in the end, I always do. I know about the World Dream, Ravennetus. And I know what a pivotal character you play in our little 'theater of the gods'. I know that the knowledge of the Pearls is the key to directing the World Dream. That's why we want them, Mother and I. But you know that already. So, the time has come, brother, for you to give them to me."

"No," Ravennetus said dryly.

"No, just no? No theatrics? Surely you can do better than that!" Barthol roared with laughter. But when he had stopped laughing, Ravennetus hung there implacable as ever.

"How about this then, for a little drama. If you don't give me the Pearls, I will be forced to kill you." He pulled his sword, ringing, from its sheath and pointed it at Ravennetus' chest.

Ravennetus realized he was inside the World Dream now, living it, not on the outside merely observing, as it had always seemed to him before. In his dreams he had watched this scene unfold many times but had denied it. He had thought he could will to make things different but his perspective changed in an instant as his illusions were stripped away. He knew, in that panic-stricken moment, that Randor had been right. He had not discovered the lesson of the Twelfth Pearl. He had once again, finally and fatally, placed his own insignificant will and desires before those of the One God. Perhaps it was too late to save Allisyn now, too late to save Daena ...but not too late to fulfill his obligation to Deus.

He had thought about that too. In that flash of awareness a great peace overcame him. He knew that the Pearls were all that mattered. Seeing Allisyn once again, saving her, were meaningless compared to learning the final lesson. She would agree with that. Before the end, he must know all. And he would, he remembered now. This scene, Barthol, the sword in his hand, were all for him, and he greeted them as one might open the door to a friend. He only regretted that Allisyn would not know why he did not come, that she would think he had deserted and betrayed her. Would he ever be able to make her

429

understand? Yes, now he remembered. He had foreseen that too. But many long, tiresome lives of men it would be, until the Dream unfolded to that moment.

"You say that you know all you need to know about the World Dream, about the Pearls, but you deceive yourself, Barthol, as ever you have," Ravennetus said, purposefully playing into Barthol's hand. The words seemed not to be his own. It was as if some other mind formed them, as though some other mouth uttered them. "There is much that I never wrote against such a day as this. If you kill me that knowledge will pass out of the Now and forever beyond your reach."

"I know more than you think, brother. If the knowledge passes into the Otherworld, then Mother can pluck it from you there. The very reason Deus sent the Pearls into the Now was to send them beyond her reach. If they go back, she will get them and the thing will be done. Give them to me and I will let you go to your precious Allisyn. Oh yes, she is waiting on the bridge for you. I have arranged everything!"

"I am not deceived by you Barthol. I submit willingly to my fate. All proceeds as it has been arranged by Deus."

"Tell me what I want to know and you can go to her. You can greet her with a kiss and you can both run to see if you can save your daughter. I'd like a little game like that tonight. But if I have to kill you, Ravennetus, *I* will go to her. And I will use this same sword on her, and your daughter will die too. So what will it be, brother, the Pearls, or your beloved ones? If you choose not be there for them, I'll be sure to tell them why you did not come."

"If you knew the least about what you are speaking, Barthol, you would know that *I* have seen the end of all things and that sword would be trembling in your hand."

"Don't try to fool me, Ravennetus. Mother and I hold all the cards in this game and you know it. Give me the Pearls." He leaned against the sword and the tip of it punctured the skin of Ravennetus' chest just beneath his breastbone. He winced in pain.

"You are wrong, Barthol. The lives of three are of little consequence in the dance of the cosmos. The Otherworld is waiting and Deus is calling me. It is for this moment of death that I was born. I am comforted, for I know that in my dying, the Wisdom of the Pearls will be born into the Now. Unable to do this in my life by my own feeble efforts, I now accomplish it

430

in my death according to His plan. Thus in death I bring life, in life I transcend death.

Ravennetus closed his eyes and he began to chant a prayer. The sound of it enraged Barthol.

"Be damned then! I hate you, Ravennetus! And listen to me. I hate you most because I have failed to make you hate... you alone! I knew what you were trying to do all along! You failed to create love in me by loving me! Thol-nys conquered you then. She conquered everything then. You failed with an utter and complete failure. I know the defeat that you feel in your miserable heart. So don't try to pretend otherwise. I send you to Deus on your knees, a loathsome failure! Thus he is rewarded for his faith in you!"

Barthol gave his sword a shove with all the weight of his contempt behind it. Ravennetus' eyes rolled upward and his cheek fell against Barthol's.

"Tell me, Ravennetus, tell me with your last breath that you hate me!" Barthol whispered. Then, as if Ravennetus had spoken his last thought into his ear, Barthol heard in his head the words he despised most to hear, "Because you have wronged me, dear brother, I love you most of all. Thank you... thank you for this. For now all is accomplished."

Thus Ravennetus triumphed over Barthol and learned the lesson of the Twelfth Pearl. As his mortal body perished, his spirit was already in the Otherworld, scattering the Pearls according to Deus' plan, into the future of the Now.

The moon peeked above the hills as an ethereal figure stepped furtively onto the bridge, hooded and cloaked. Eager with anticipation borne of long years of separation, Allisyn saw him at once. Spirit-like he seemed in the growing light of Hannys, as he had appeared so many times in her dreams. She saw the well-remembered form, the familiar step. Was it only a phantom, or was it really him? Allisyn ran to her lover and reached out for his hands. They touched. It *was* him, *really him*, Deus be praised; but the hands were icy cold, so cold that the touch of them shocked her momentarily. How long had it been since he had warmed to her touch? Where had he wandered these many years? How many nights had he laid his head on a stone pillow and slept in the cold under the stars?

431

She stood there for a moment with her head bowed and her eyes closed, saying nothing, feeling the heat flow out of her, wanting to warm him, wanting to flow into him, wanting to be everything he needed her to be. She enfolded him in her arms and held him tightly. He returned her embrace, reveling with joy in her trembling arms. She wept as she held him, her knees almost failing her. "Thank you, thank you Deus," she whispered into his ear. "So long, ...so long, it has been so long." His body began to shake. *"He is weeping too,"* she thought.

A sudden fear shot through her that something was terribly wrong. The one she held began to laugh, softly at first, then fully and unrestrained. He threw back his head and his hood fell away.

Allisyn swooned when she saw Barthol. She caught the rail with her hand as her legs gave way, otherwise she would certainly have fallen into the gorge.

"Did you like it?" he said between howling spasms of laughter. "Did you like my little farce?" He laughed again.

"Did you think that he would really come, my poor deluded fool? He has deserted you, ...you, the woman he loved, and your daughter. He loved you little my dear, very little in the end. And now he is dead." He showed her the blood-red shaft of the sword. "I'm afraid I have no love left for you either. You, who have treated me so ill for so long. You never were much use to me, it turns out. I could have done this long ago with little less profit. Thus the darkness comes! And this is my curse, Allisyn. Because you have done your utmost to keep the Pearls from me, may your soul never be united with Ravennetus until I discover their secret!"

Then the unimaginable happened. Raising his arms, Barthol spread his cloak and leaped off the bridge. Allisyn watched as he plummeted, disappearing into the mists. She stood shocked and confused for a moment, not knowing what to do, not knowing what Barthol had done. He was gone. It was unbelievable. Suddenly she remembered Daena. She staggered to her feet, straightened, and began to run on uncertain legs. As she did a black shape, like a monstrous vulture, loomed behind her. A silver flash came out of its belly and struck her in the back. She fell in agony but struggled to her feet again. She had only gone a step or two when the shape wheeled and returned, overtaking her with the speed of hateful thought. Wrapping himself around her, Barthol lifted her up and flung her into the gorge, then flew with haste toward the flickering, golden tower of light that shone from within the circle of the Faenmoet.

At the head of the procession, Tandela wove her way to the statue of Thol-nys, formed of the gold from the caves of Argolas and erected within the circle of the Faenmoet. A crowd had already gathered there. Clouds threatened and a stiff breeze rose as she approached the base of the altar. She placed her foot upon the lowest step and her eyes rose up the stone stairs leading to the altar above. Beyond it, looming upward into the blackness, was the golden image of Thol-nys, the Terrible Mother, whose head was that of a pig but whose body was that of a woman. Fires were lit around her feet and their light reflected off her shining surface. Barthol met Tandela at the bottom of the stair.

"It is done," he whispered in her ear. "Ravennetus is dead and Allisyn with him."

"So soon will their daughter be," Tandela whispered back to Barthol and she kissed him, the whole of her body tingling with perverse delight. Together they walked to the top of the stairs and stood behind the altar.

"People of Aestri," Tandela shouted, above the roar of the waters and the wind howling through the gorge.

"Tonight, we reach the summit we have long sought. You have given of yourselves to build the sacred image of the Great Calamity. And she is pleased. Tonight we will treat her to her first blood. Tonight we will dedicate the altar of her worship. When she tastes that blood, she will know that we are her people, and her blessings will flow to us. To assure that she will continue to bless her children, she will require more blood. And you will gratefully give it to her, the blood of your sons and daughters. For she is our Mother now. Faena is dead. And when the Darkness falls, we, the faithful, will be her dark angels. We, her obedient children, will reign at her side. Bring forth the sacrifice!"

Bors mounted the platform leading Daena behind him, bound with a chain of gold. In his hand, he carried a spear, its tip formed of the same gleaming metal. The wind mounted yet higher. Fearsome noises, moans and screams, rose from the

433

gorge. The torches guttered and fought to burn. The wind pulled at the clothes of all the assembly.

Bors lifted Daena and placed her upon the altar. She looked at him again, with the same undaunted stare that had troubled his dreams since he had first seen her. She did not struggle. Tandela raised the sacrificial knife. Her body tensed, eager to plunge the blade downward, eager to bring to fruition all the plans she had so carefully and deceitfully made.

But in that very instant, the fabric of her gruesome dream began to unravel. The clouds parted and a moonbeam struck the altar with a fierce and desperate intensity. Tandela felt a cold hand grab her wrist and turned to see an apparition, the ghost of Vaalta, restraining the hand that held the knife. Tandela's face convulsed with rage. On the altarstone, the spirit of Allisyn, hideous and misshapen from its passage of the falls, lay across Daena's body.

Barthol saw the spirits too. Momentarily shaken by their appearance, he stepped backward toward the golden statue. Anticipating the signal stroke of the knife, the bewitched Bors did what Tandela had instructed him to do. Raising the spear, he launched it at Barthol's heart. At the same moment, in a reckless attempt to break free of Vaalta's icy grip, Tandela lunged toward the altar, and into the path of the hurtling weapon. Barthol saw it erupt from her back. Without hesitation, he leaped from the platform into the air, transforming himself into a vulture as he fell, and was gone in an instant.

The impaled Tandela stared in shocked disbelief at the freezing shaft, rooted in her chest. The golden knife dropped from her hand and clattered on the polished stone beneath her feet. She wanted to scream but could not, dared not. Her eyes flew to the stunned crowd, suddenly aware that they were were watching her like jackals, slavering with the expectation of her fall. She would never give them that pleasure, never! She staggered. The lights of the torches in the crowd, the luminous eyes of the jackals, dipped and swirled before her. She grasped the haft of the spear with quaking hands and pulled with all her strength, but it would not budge. Her life ebbing, she crumpled to the base of the altar and sat, leaning unnaturally on the tripod formed by her elbows and the tip of the spear protruding from her back. Ringed by ghosts and betrayed by those she had thought to manipulate, Tandela watched her dreams evaporate. With a last burst of hate and a snarling curse on her lips, she attempted to rise, but could not, and fell back panting. From deep within, she heard again the grunting laughter of the Great Pig. As her blood thickened on the cold black stone, her eyelids fluttered, and her body went limp, Tandela, the wicked Queen of Aestri, drew her final breath.

The people, driven to destitution by the excesses of the queen, took her fall as a signal to act. They attacked the soldiers who ringed the altar. Someone pointed toward the fleeing Barthol and a few brave men rushed the platform. Bors, suddenly freed by Tandela's death from her enchantment, jumped into the crowd to join in the insurrection.

Daena sat up, scarcely believing she was still alive, and watched the wind tug at the ghost of Vaalta until it fluttered away, a tattered rag of a specter. Allisyn, once again the image of her beautiful self, took her daughter by the hand.

"Daena, my child. Look upon me, your mother, Allisyn, and know the love with which I have loved you for so long." Then she, too, vanished, borne away on the fretful wind.

High overhead, Barthol circled the Faenmoet, watching the frenzy of death and destruction, laughing in his heart as the people paid tribute to Thol-nys with their lives, and worshiped her by spilling the blood of Deus' creation. This is what he had been born to do, to unleash the ravenous hounds of death and let them plunder, to open the floodgates and let the dark waters swirl, sweeping aside all in their path, drowning every spark of the fire of consciousness, the Fire of Han-Thol.

It had been a good night's work, he thought. Ravennetus was dead, and with him Allisyn. The Pearls were gone for now, perhaps forever. The mindless mob would take care of the rest, destroying themselves and the City. Far below, from within the stone circle, a glimmer of light caught his eye. He gave a passing thought to the girl, Daena. Perhaps he should swoop down and end her as he had her mother. But the glimmer faded. With a rush of midnight-black wings, he wheeled away to the south. *She will die tonight with all the rest,* he thought. But in this, he erred.

435

Epilogue

The battle raged on throughout the night. The common folk of Aestri, wielding only stones, clubs and pitchforks fought the soldiers, better equipped but fewer in number. One by one, then by squadrons and companies, soldiers following the example of Bors, joined the revolt. When the remainder of the army was subdued, the people stormed the castle, looting room after room, finding many articles of value taken from them during the course of Tandela's reign, stores of much needed food, rich cloth and tapestries that would clothe them in the coming winter, and horded gold and silver. Once they had recovered the wealth of the kingdom from the castle, they razed it. For in their frenzy, they sought to remove every memory of the evil woman and dark counselor who had devastated them.

As the castle burned, the fires blazed out of control and the conflagration spread to other nearby buildings. The cisterns of the city were empty, and there was no water to quench the consuming flames. When morning came Faenwys was again in ashes. The people, who had reveled all night in the ecstasy of destruction, greeted the morning with greater sobriety. They milled about the smoking ruins looking for anything of value. Today, the weather would turn colder. Many would be without shelter. In the early light, some ran to their homes and returned with carts. They loaded them as fully as they dared, placing their children atop the piles to hold them together, and began the slow trip home.

When Fidelis had leaped upon the altar and Barthol had fled, he found the girl, Daena, shivering and bewildered. He had offered her his hand and she, seeing the kindness in his eyes, took it. He had helped her down and wrapped her in his cloak.

436

They had run down the stairs and fled across the Highgaet Roed, through the Browse and into the woods finding a thicket in which to hide. There he had explained to Daena that he was a friend of Ravennetus, her father, and she was to stay hidden until he came back. If the fighting went ill and the soldiers were victorious, he would come back to smuggle her out of Aestri. He had vowed with his life to protect her, then run back into the fray. Now that morning had come, he made his way anxiously back to the thicket, and much to his relief, found her sleeping peacefully, although she still shivered. He roused her, smoothed down her golden hair, and walked her back toward Faenwys.

"The people have regained their City, their lives and their dignity," Fidelis explained. "They have taken them back from the hands of their oppressors. It was a work in which your father and mother were long involved. But I fear the price of it has been too high. Look. It is naught but a ruin." As they approached, they surveyed the carnage of the once-proud city.

Soon they came to the altar and statue of Thol-nys, standing among the silent stones of the Faenmoet. A shiver went through Daena, but she bravely climbed the stairs again and gazed upon the altar where she had very nearly died. Tandela's body lay to the side behind the great coal-black stone. Thol-nys had indeed tasted blood, but not that of the intended sacrifice. Tandela looked old and grotesque. When her life force had run out, the evil that had sustained her had fled as well. Now only the corrupted body remained. Tandela was not beautiful in death as she had been in life. Daena turned to face the altar and placed her hand upon it.

"My mother Allisyn was here," she said to Fidelis, to herself. "She died last night. She came here to say good-bye to me. I don't really remember her, you know. The last time I saw her I was an infant, they say. But last night I saw her and I will never forget her face. She told me always to love and to know that she had always loved me. That's what my father told me too, a long time ago. But he left and never came back."

"Your father is a great man," Fidelis replied. "And one with many burdens in this life. He has loved you dearly. I hope we will find him soon." But in his heart he despaired of it. For he knew if death or some other disaster had not prevented it, Ravennetus would have been at Allisyn's side, or here with his daughter. He had not seen him at all that night.

437

Throughout the day, they looked for him, but to no avail. In their searching they found Bronwyn, who had been led to the City by some kind souls. She took her slender charge in her arms and embraced her for a long time. It was hard for Daena to find the words to tell Bronwyn that Allisyn was dead, and it was long until Bronwyn's grief was healed. Fidelis left the two women and walked away, committed to find Ravennetus. He asked everyone he met but none could help him.

Finally, in desperation, he sought the clearing in the wood where they had parted the day before. Searching the ground, he spied the faint trail that led in the direction Ravennetus, led by the peasant, had taken. It was difficult to follow and he took many false turns before he found at last the ravine. There Fidelis discovered the body of his friend, cold as a gravestone, the ground thereabout dark with his blood, still bound to the tree where Barthol had left him. Randor sat in the branches above, his vacant stare frozen on the scene below.

With tears in his eyes and a broken heart, Fidelis untied Ravennetus and lowered him gently to the ground. He knew not what to do, what to say, what to think or feel, so he simply took the precious head and held it in his lap throughout the remainder of that day and all throughout the night that followed. He thought of their friendship as he sat, recalling every word that had passed between them, the occasion of every smile, the thrill of each adventure, and the lesson of every pain and sorrow.

Fidelis Sampras followed Ravennetus into the Otherworld for a time and there they sat, talking about life and death and a time when they would be together once more. Ravennetus instructed his friend to make it known to all that would listen and understand that he had died with love in his heart for his brother Barthol; and in achieving this victory, he knew that some day, if he kept on trying, if he kept on loving, he would bring Barthol out of the darkness.

The light of morning broke once again with Fidelis still sitting in the ravine, still wandering the unearthly landscapes of the Otherworld with his friend. When he returned, grieving, to the Now at last, Fidelis heaved the body over his shoulder. Randor floated down from the branches and perched silently upon it. Fidelis bore them both out of the hills to the outskirts of the City. They found Daena and Bronwyn in the place Fidelis had left them the previous day. He laid Ravennetus' body down before them and together they mourned. Daena kneeled by her

438

father's side, remembering the face, the disfigured brow, the hands that had held her long years ago.

Few in Aestri had known Ravennetus, and few were gathered when Fidelis placed his body atop the pyre of broken timbers and fallen branches. Now and then a curious passerby would stop and watch for a while as he worked. When he had finished, he stood back from the pyre and closed his eyes for a moment. Then he spoke.

"Deus, Father of all, receive the body of your servant Ravennetus. It matters little what we do with his remains, for his spirit is already with you. May the smoke of his burning aspire to you, may it be fragrant to you, and may you know that he served you well while he was among us."

Then Fidelis took his firemaking tools and caused a spark to catch in the dry tinder. He blew it until a flame sprouted, until it grew into a crackling blaze, and leaped from tinder to branch and branch to timber. A great smoke climbed high into the heavens as the flames consumed the body. Randor leaped up from the ground and rose high into the skies on careworn wings. He circled the pyre twelve times, spiraling down from that great height, then came to rest atop his son. The flames engulfed him, and he too passed from the Now.

As the fires died Daena reached to her neck and removed the medallion, the blackened raven, that hung there. She was about to toss it onto the pyre when Bronwyn stopped her.

"Why should I wear it?" Daena asked. "He said it would protect me but it did not. It did not keep them from capturing me, taking me away from you, and bringing me here to find all this sadness."

"You should keep it close to your heart, Daena," Bronwyn said. "For it is all you have that belonged to him. It was his gift to you, so it must be of inestimable valuable."

"He made it with his own hands," Fidelis recalled.

"And though you may think that it did not keep you from being taken from your home and from all this sorrow," Bronwyn continued, "look at the peril you have been through, and yet still you are here, safe and whole. It may have greater powers that you imagine."

"Why did he have to die, why did mother have to die?"

Fidelis spoke.

"Ravennetus used to say to us, 'Something always has to die, so that something better may be born. So when you sense

439

that something has passed and will be no more, look for the new thing, the better thing, that will come from its passing.' He used to say, 'This is Deus' greatest gift and promise to us, it is that which keeps our hope and faith alive'."

When the people had got their individual lives back in order, they gathered together and asked, "Who now should rule?" A few suggested that a ruler was not needed, that every man was his own sovereign, and that their rulers had only brought them misery. But the majority looked beyond the dark years that lay just behind them to the prosperity that had been their lot for time out of memory. And they asked that Daena, the daughter of Allisyn, daughter of Aefalas and Vaalta should be their queen.

So Daena was placed upon the throne of Aestri; and Bronwyn, whose insight could always discern the truth, and Fidelis Sampras, whose faith gave him great wisdom, abode with her and were her counselors, until they too departed the Now and made the journey to the Otherworld.

Daena's first act as queen was to have the image of Thol-nys melted down. Coins were minted of it and given to the people. Some said that the castle and the City should be rebuilt, but Daena thought the time and money that would take could be put to better use. So Faenwys was never rebuilt and the years worked their will with it. Some of it fell into the river as the waters gnawed away the gorge, and some of it, as the mountains were ground down by the wind and rain, came to be covered with layer upon layer of fine soil, and grasses grew there, and wild nature reclaimed what had been hers, that which she had never consented to yield up.

Daena moved the seat of rule to a less pretentious house in the Droemenvael, the bit of Aestri her mother had loved so well, and she lived there in comfort and ruled her people with love. But the long decline of Aestri had begun. Never again was it the powerful kingdom it had been at the height of its greatness under Aefalas, before he came under the spell of the Great Darkness.

Daena passed an edict that the Mergruen should be renamed the Allisyn in tribute her mother who had fallen there, but it was still the River of Long Memory, and the phantom mists of its gorge never ceased their weeping for the tragedies that had been played out along its shores. Over many lives of men, the people

440

settled further and further from its banks and spread into the plains to the east. The Chent of Aestri became a place of wild beauty once again. But the Bridge of Vapors never fell, and it was said that the phantoms of the gorge suffered it to stay so that they might tell their sad tales to the travelers that braved its span.

Barthol made his way back to Hethraven and remained there for a time. He retrieved the journals of Ravennetus from the stone seat in the cave near the Lympha Placida and eventually passed into the east, crossing over the fence of the Utlai and settling in barren lands known as Maasen. There he studied the writings of Ravennetus and listened to the counsel of Thol-nys. There he brooded upon the last words of his brother, coming to despise him yet more for having spoken them. And there he grew old studying and seeking for the hidden knowledge, the secret of controlling the World Dream of Deus, the key to which was the knowledge of the Twelve Pearls.

He read his own fate in the writings of his brother, that his mortal body should not die until the principal of the Twelve, the Great Pearl, the One Pearl, cast into the future by Ravennetus before he died, should be found. And Barthol waited through the centuries for that day with both anticipation and dread. His life dragged wearily on, until he was withered and parched like the discarded skin of a snake, and he walked as one dead among the living, unable to die, yet forbidden to pass into the Otherworld.

Fidelis spread the teachings of Deus and many were His followers in that time. The people turned from the worship of the goddess, embracing the new religion, the worship of Deus the Father-god, and Aestri thrived for a time upon its ideals. But Fidelis Sampras was only a man, and when he died years hence, the people strayed and Deus became a god that once was, a god, they surmised, who had withdrawn his blessing from his people. His name was still sung, but his ideals, the Wisdom of the Pearls, were forgotten for a very long time.

The End

441